Laurence Read is a former playwright, television journalist and businessman who grew up on a diet of Tom Sharpe, Joseph Heller, Saki and Evelyn Waugh. He lives in Hampshire but also spends much of his time in Hungary (where most of *Danube Legion* takes place).

To MER and MPR for their support of all kinds and questioning if a tomato existed within the borders of second-century Rome.

To John Mark Nunn for getting me here through forced marches of all sorts.

Laurence Read

DANUBE LEGION

AUSTIN MACAULEY PUBLISHERS™

LONDON * CAMBRIDGE * NEW YORK * SHARJAH

A CIP catalogue record for this title is available from the British Library.

ISBN 9781035860364 (Paperback)
ISBN 9781035860371 (Hardback)
ISBN 9781035860395 (ePub e-book)
ISBN 9781035860388 (Audiobook)

www.austinmacauley.com

First Published 2024
Austin Macauley Publishers Ltd®
1 Canada Square
Canary Wharf
London
E14 5AA

To the curators of Aquincum, you have created a fantastic resource, especially to researching, would-be authors with children – plenty of distractions and the kids left wanting a second day. To the curators and people of Szőny – Komárom, both a thanks for your guardianship of the Brigetio Fort area and an apology – I'm sorry for interfering with your geography but I needed the hills 20 km to the East of you.

To Academia.edu for all your papers.

Part One
Cold Spring

Chapter One

Dawn of an Early Spring, 104 AD
Legio VIIIth Armoury briefing room, Argentoratum Fort on the Rhine Frontier
Germania Inferior Province of Rome

"Good morning, does everyone have a hot drink? Armourer Cadet Bullo has provided this morning's offering."

"The pastries look like co…"

"Do they taste like them, Lulla? I wouldn't know myself."

"Ruben can find out what mine tastes like if I don't get that copper by midday."

"I am working on it without further incentive, esteemed workshop lead, Lulla."

"Alright, settle down." The speaker then turned to a nervous boy of fourteen with very big forearms. "Armourer Cadet Bullo, the drinks are hot, the pastries do look like cocks but don't taste like them and more importantly there's no gherkin, so well done, lad."

The cadets worked very, very hard at not fucking up the morning meeting's breakfast. This briefing's pastries had honey and walnuts with nutmeg – no gherkin – each carefully crafted into a knot shape that had probably looked great before the pre-dawn fires were lit. Within the legion's ovens the edibles had swollen, to now look like little fat penises covered with 'red dot'.

Chief Armourer Galba watched his team heads gather themselves in the whitewashed room. No table, just stools and trestles facing the massive Numidian head armourer and behind him his second. Ruben was standing with a charcoal stick ready to markup the room's long wall, upon which was a riot of figures, drawings, boxes, dates and patchworks of fresher whitewash applied when projects ended and more space was needed. The chief reads through his morning notes quickly, wax tablets in one massive three-fingered hand while the other held a wooden mug, 'Bulla' carved into it, and a little honey-pastry dong with one of the balls nibbled off.

Chief Armourer Galba looked up when he had finished reviewing his notes and eyed the hulking figure of Acinius Medius 'Workshop' Lulla holding a pastry over his leather breeches, squeaking in a falsetto, "Mweh famiwy is wery wery auld, wuffian, and you are a dirty plebian…"

"Right, fucking eat that, Lulla. We covered off the Honoured Tribune officer's visit last week, DON'T TOAST! You lot. It's not funny anymore. I'll have no arse-licking or insubordination in this workshop. To business, I'm meeting with the Camp Praefectus at noon, by then I want to know that we are doing enough to keep sets coming through while ensuring to stay ahead of ourselves for the campaigning season." A hand raised. "Yes, Fittings Menicitrix?"

"Boss, do we know what this will look like, the season, I mean, of course?"

"Yes, Menicitrix, the newish Emperor has personally given me a full set of campaign notes which is why later today, I will meet with the CP and apprise him of Legion operations for the spring and summer."

"Pah! Come on, Boss, is it a war? Everyone is saying your Emperor…"

"Our Emperor, you Gaul c…" Lulla rumbled.

"Shut up, Lulla. He who desires peace doesn't work in a legio armoury, Menicitrix, but let's put it this way. I think we currently have an Emperor who would very much to paint his face red, or at least have the chariot slave do it for him, so let's be ready. Ruben, repeat what you said to me last night, if you please."

Ruben held up the charcoal stick to the group and gave the military artisans a grin. They all amusingly groaned as the armoury second prepared to play up to his love of a diagrammatic explanation.

"Gentlemen…" started the dapper Second Armourer with his ridiculously posh hostage-Latin, before giving a detailed roundup of the previous winter months' skirmishing strategy and then future possible moves east across the Rhine involving their VIIIth Legion. The charcoaled wall diagram, quickly sketched, saw the VIIIth Legio Augusta on one side represented as leering, slovenly legionary 'Lucio' and the Germans as pigtailed, huge breasted 'Helga' opposite.

"Thank you, Ruben…and as ever, Helga." They all touched their cocks for luck and for Helga. "But potential cross-border action does not mean we go hell for leather repairing the broken sets that come back from scraps. We need to finish the repairs on the workshops and all the other prep delayed because of the fire."

"Fucking saboteurs!"

"Lulla, shut up. It doesn't matter if it was saboteurs or, and I'm not having this argument again, a badly-supervised drunken cadet. We are behind. So, if you've got something useful to say, Workshop, let's hear it."

Lulla gave a shrug. "Well, the armoury is clean now. The primary bellows is optimal, the secondary still has a draught somewhere so we are winding it down and stripping the whole thing later today. All tools accounted for, no problems on that count now the cleaners have gone, thieving monkeys that they are. I do need pliers, though, Boss and 'Guns', old mate, I know you're knee-deep but any chance of a hand getting the heavy press working again?" Lulla was leaning back addressing a short, untidy looking, dark-skinned man with a bristling moustache at the back of the room – 'Guns' – who gave a thumbs up.

Workshop Lulla continued, "Right, we are getting through the backlog on carts, pots and pans et cetera. Cutty stabby stuff's fine, Cadet Briscos has a bit of a talent for the whetstone."

"His breakfast's shit!" muttered someone at the back.

"Sure, but he can sharpen stuff so we've just had him on that all week, think he's going a bit…" an in-out whistle, "…to be honest but Cadet Briscos is a one-man sharpening army, that boy, and he does them properly."

"You haven't talked about sets, Lulla." was the suspicious statement from Chief Armourer Galba.

"Sets are fine, Boss."

"How many complete from scratch? Just twenty? Right, is this Old Sibius' team? No, he's not fine, I'll come by this afternoon and he'd better not be handcrafting a Greek fucking urn. Move on." Galba took a bite and a sip before continuing.

"Fittings Menicitrix! Workshop says cart supplies are coming out good, how's the fitting?"

"Of course, you ask us to fit them..." – shrug of the shoulders – "...we fit them. It is simple."

"It is simple but can we not have a repeat of 'but you asked us to fit the carts, not the bridles'? I want everything that rolls, pushes and pulls to be checked with every chain, bit, harness and pin gone over."

Aggrieved, "Boss, my team has done that. My team has... been... over... everything." Cross-legged, Menicitrix chopped his hand to emphasise the totality of thoroughness that had been enacted, except...

"We have done what we can but...pah! The wood! Splintered axles, loose pegs, how can I fit on to this? Why should I fit on to this?"

Ruben interjected to save time on one of the Chief Armourer's legendary exchanges with the Gaul. "Perhaps I could speak to the carpenters for you, Menicitrix? I'm having something done myself by the carpentry Immunes and will pop over there later this morning."

The Gaul gave a seated half bow. "That would be acceptable."

Galba recommenced. "Lists, gentlemen. Menicitrix, provide Ruben with a list of all that's fitted and what needs replacing by the carpenters or stores. Have one of your little artists red mark everything bad with a paint brush before tomorrow morning. Workshop, same for you and we shall be doing inventories for the summer at the end of the week. Everyone! 'Eat' your forward stores, now is the time to get in as much as possible. If we don't use it, Command will lower the resupply."

Lulla raised a hand. "What about basic metals?"

Ruben turned from where he had been using a straight length to draw up the weekly overview grid. "The Chief Armourer and myself are seeing to the metal."

"All metal, even copper?"

Galba addressed the question seriously. "All metal, just bear with us. Get your orders in and cannibalise existing stores of unworked metal. You all know I've been looking at sources and want to do more with all departments working up our own gear. The sets Lulla's team forged over the winter show we can do it but ore reliability and quality remains the problem..."

Workshop helpfully pointed out, "That was Old Sibius and his team who did the forging."

Galba ignored that endorsement of Armourer Sibius and continued, "We don't want to rely solely on ore crates shipped from the Fabrica, the VIIIth should be able to manufacture complete sets if need be and certainly provide full spares

14

from scratch. The problem is, I think we can all agree, that non-ferrous provision is currently not up to scratch and while decent ferrous ore is out there," he pointed to the wall facing the border. "Not at any scale we have so far identified. If we are going to do this, buying scraps from the villages won't get us anywhere. Where the Germans' ferrous comes from, at this time, still remains a mystery. As for nonferrous..."

A grumbling murmur from the team heads: "Shithouse cottage copper!", "Be better using my mum's fucking cheese.", "Not quite the thing" – that was Ruben.

"Guns, how are you?"

A nod and a tilt of the head. Nothing from under the bushy moustache.

'How did he continue to get away with that moustache?' thought Chief Armourer Galba as he regarded the little, dark, scruffy man. He knew the answer of course – ability. Galba was good with metal; his dad had been great.

Galba could spot 'great' though, even if he wasn't himself, that's what made him Chief Armourer. Guns was great.

Last week Ruben and Galba had taken a ride up with the artillery retrieval team. Over a temporary Infil pontoon across the Rhine to the 'noncompliant' Chatti fort that the Legion had overrun. Two Ballista support weapons had previously gone up by donkey with the VIIIth S&D force.

The chief and Ruben took an after-action tour of the fort: two Chatti braves spitted all the way through, the bolt having already passed through a half-cut plank palisade. A woman with no head sat under a shaft half a length deep in the headman's lodge door. A massive, splintered hole where the gate had been, its post shattered by a heavy projectile to then collapse under the door's weight. Finally, a bloody mess of limbs and guts in the longhouse.

One of the Infil team was still there amongst the smouldering ruins and keen to chat. "...they're all screaming and running about, the bolts are just going bam-bam-bam, blows the fence gate to bits so the Chatti all huddle in the lodge and the Tribune's just like, 'I ain't wasting a single man on any of this shit!' So, they just swing the big bows round on the trucks as they are, and the donkeys just drag 'em up to the gate line. The stupid Chatti bastards inside the lodge just watching them unhook, swing round again, stabilisers down, then – bam-bam-bam. How you get them to go so fast? I ain't never seen faster. Just bam-bam-bam. Inside the chief's house we can see bits of people just coming apart."

So, the Artillery Armourer, 'Guns', was 'Great', as in Alexander or that Greek prick in Sicily with the galley 'upturners'. A master artificer. What Guns did with his various machines of war in that quiet methodical manner of his, always making a series of seemingly disconnected small adjustments, translated into the VIIIth Augusta's artillery outgunning anything, anything the Chief Armourer had ever seen in any Roman Legion or other side of the battlefield.

Back in the morning meeting Galba asked, "How's the new Cadet then, Guns?" The small Spaniard leant back and chuckled.

"He's there to tidy and keep you alive, Lead Artillery Armourer." Guns thought about this and made a gesture suggesting boredom.

Ruben, finishing the tasks and objective list, turned around to speak, "My dear Guns, there is indeed a high responsibility to propagate a continuity of expertise within the noble Immunes serving the VIIIth and Emperor. There is also the other type of armourer who serves the legion in a more mundane and no less important way. Legionnaire Fubo, your new assistant, excels in this latter category. He is a seasoned man, VIIIth Augusta to the core, cannot even look at a wrinkled cot without taking action, thus safeguarding you from any further unpleasantness regarding the obsessions of the Camp Praefectus or his ilk. For instance, the rotting half-eaten fruit or tooth-stick incidents."

An affectionate chuckle went around the room. Guns' toothbrush was now a legend in the VIIIth.

"SATURNALIA, YOU HORRIBLE LITTLE FUCKING MAN!" everyone now chorused in unison. The Spaniard just grinned.

Galba recommenced; "So – nothing we can do for you, Guns?" Guns shook his head contentedly.

"Just remember: reliability always over performance, Guns."

And so far, it always had been. However, Galba had a nightmare of over-engineering that still persisted in his sleep at least once a fortnight. The bad dream was a fire line of high-performance onagers not doing anything in the middle of a savage battle because no one could find the yellow dogs (real, actual woofing dogs that somehow were essential to the firing of complicated catapults). It always ended with Galba running around screaming, "Will this work?" waving an orange cat at Guns, who just stared back quizzically as some hodge-podge of axe-wielding barbarians poured over the embrasures from the depths of the Chief Armourer's sleeping fears.

Back in the real world, "Are we done, Sir?" Ruben asked. Galba leant back in his chair, leather-backed, intricately-carved sandalwood – a proper mark of rank. The Chief Armourer reviewed the new grid of black on the square of white wash behind him, made some amendments, set deadlines, reminded everyone of SOP's – he liked to do this at the end rather than the beginning of the meeting so the reminder was fresh – then asked for any further questions, of which there were none.

"Right, meeting's over, all stand. Attention."

Each man up to this point could have been a contractor or builder anywhere in the Empire but now with a snap their bearing changed; no quips, 'side' or bollocks. "The Emperor Trajan and the VIIIth August Augusta, MARS and JUPITER, we salute thee!" Chief Armourer Galba declaimed,

"THE EMPEROR TRAJAN AND THE VIIIth AUGUST..." The armourers shouted back, two of them slightly crooking their fingers towards the dawn sun outside. Others pretended not to see the small gestures and all the department heads then filed out of the room leaving Armourer Cadet Bullo to clean up.

"Learn anything, boy?" The Chief Armourer asked him, not unkindly, on the way out.

"Think so, Boss."

"Go on."

"Are sets worth the trouble, Boss?"

The Senior Armourer smiled and left the room without answering.

Chapter Two

Same day, morning or just about, 104 AD
Salona 'by-the-sea', a long way south of the Rhine
Roman administrative capital for Dalmatia Province

Just a thin cylinder of light found a way through the shutters. Lady Lassalia peered at it through one half-open eye. She demanded all the shutters in all her houses were absolutely flush. There were no gaps to let the sun through. Horus was to be invited in only as an expected and well-mannered guest. The source of the light came from a diagonally drilled hole made in one single shutter that, again, was a design repeated across all her bedrooms allowing a lone beam to hit the huge mess of a bed at midmorning precisely.

It was still bloody bright, she thought, but resisted the urge to bury her head back into the pillow. Sobe was a dehydrated lump of pain, the worst of it in her head but the stomach was none too good either. Her nostrils snorted away fumes, somewhere in the room was an opened amphora of half-drunk wine further nauseating various poisoned bits of fleshy plumbing.

Sobe Lassalia considered how she was going to get up, briefly thought about interfering with herself thus promoting a rush of sexual energy to haul her carcass out of bed, but discounted the idea. The 'death' would probably banish the headache allowing Sobe to just fall back to sleep again.

The mental tally of how much she'd drunk was a better ritual, because if you got to the point you couldn't remember then it stopped being business and started being something else. Although the Lady Lassalia worried that her memory was too accurate as she totted up the quantities of Falernian, sweet sticky local wine, and the bonkers firewater the near-islanders distilled from Dionysus knows what. Which despite repeated, past experience, she always insisted everyone drink gone midnight.

The small glass cups she had had made up, so you could see the clearness of this Prometheus piss, had been a hit though. Everyone said so, especially the new Imperial-whatever-he-was who had definitely had too much fun.

And she was up. Without even thinking about it, suddenly Lady Lassalia was up and moving, half-tripped over a boot in the near pitch-dark, then threw open the shutters. The sun poured – no – flooded in. Dizzy, Sobe steadied herself against this morning's spectacular manifestation of Horus, forcing her eyes to look at the vista. Lassalia's southern-facing bedroom looked down on the main port and warehouse district of Salona. Sailors, stevedores, pulley men and carters thronged the Mediterranean port. Not that the mistress of the house could really see any of this, still being completely and utterly blinded by the blazing orb above.

"Horus, you are a bit bloody bright this morning, thanks for bothering to rise and all that but you could tone it down a bit, girl's a tad unwell this morning."

A cold sea breeze, it still being a spring morning, followed the sun, swirling around the room driving out the fumes of wine and stale incense. Sobe Lassalia's liver loved the coolness. Salona wasn't as far north as some of the firm's houses but its temperature was why she'd never go home again. Egypt, with that still, heavy motionless air. At best everything slow, warm and sticky, not just the weather but the temperament. Her father's trading house had been an operational metaphor for the country: sweaty, traditional and unhurried.

"Eleazar!" Her eyes split further open in pain and Sobe scratched under her left breast beneath the sleeping clothes, which ached and itched from having slept on it unmoving all night.

As an Alexandrian-Egyptian with Roman citizenship, Lassalia then mentally selected a few gods of the day from across the wide range of options available and dragged herself to the shrine table. *'A-praying and a-swaying'* Sobe lit incense and carried out obeisances to the strange bedfellows of Osiris, Mercury and Flora. With the soul now cleansed, it was time for a more secular wash.

The breeze did the lungs some good and she coughed them into action, sucking in a few deep sacksful of air. Both the painted double doors of her bedroom opened with a sharp squeak.

"Urgg…"

"Apologies, Domina. A bit loud?"

"I thought they'd fixed that bloody door. How many times is that?"

19

"I will send for the carpenters again and see if we can solve the problem once and for all."

It was just the tiniest of squeaks, the eunuch considered without resentment, one that most people could ignore or would never even notice. Yet his lady is incapable of letting a single item of imperfection slip. *'Is this why fortune favours our house? After all, the gods like an obsessive,'* First Secretary Eleazar mused as he picked his way over a broken carafe.

"I can hear you thinking, Eleazar. It's too early for philosophy, sunshine. Anyone would think you were Greek rather than a Jew."

"Do you think we need a clear up in here, Domina?"

She turned and surveyed the wreckage, spilt liquid, half-eaten bread and a mass of twisted bedding. All overlaid on an immaculately mosaic'd explosion of cornucopias spilling wine, oil, wheat and fruit in amongst various Neptunes shepherding laden biremes and licentious nereids. The floor was set in pink and white marble tiles from Sicily, exquisite and wipe-away clean.

"Maybe so, slave. I think I might also have left some wine open in here, I hope it wasn't the good stuff."

Eleazar demurred. "It wasn't, my lady, it was the wine from Spain."

She started at him. "Really? I didn't demand the good Falernian at past midnight?"

Eleazar greeted this question with studied silence. Technically, to lie was a death offence, to have deceived his mistress last night was a death offence. Obviously, neither would occur but the wine game was the first spar of the day. The Egyptian and her slave had a complicated relationship where the boundaries needed to be constantly probed and reassessed.

Example: Lady Lassalia instructs, at the beginning of the evening, not to allow her to open the good Italian Falernian past midnight when blasted unless she is with a certain rank or above, which is unlikely as a certain rank or above, in the political sense, tends to go home. Beyond midnight the Domina then demands the Italian Falernian for her new greatest friends, who are usually a fresh young official straight out of the Army, or second son keen to make contacts in 'their' new region, invariably the city magistrate and his wife, a couple of ship's captains, a flock of Legionary officers and the Factua head who dotes on Sobe and loves being treated like a browbeaten husband each evening.

At midnight-plus, Eleazar always agrees to open the good Falernian and brings the 'good stuff' amphora filled with the distinctly medium stuff that came from Spain and, through a process known only to the eunuch, has had the mint flavour strained from it.

They stare at each other a moment. "I need a wash."

The corridor outside Sobe's room is unfrescoed, a plain yellowy cream but freshly applied.

The floor is greying pine, sanded and wax smoothed.

Head of House Sadiki walks down three entire floors. After her husband went travelling she preferred to buy and renovate this old Salona mansion upwards, near the centre of things, rather than keep the Roman-style family sprawl out in the 'burbs. Arriving at ground level, Sobe Lassalia moves through the back rooms still in her sleeping clothes, all baggy pantaloons and a tunic.

"Morning, morning, hard at it, you lazy bastards?" she shouts and laughs. The boys washing the flagstones grin, the girls carrying wood smile, embarrassed as they are every morning by their crazy mistress. Older women force honey infused drinks into the lady's hand and a large plate of cut fruit – peaches, grapes, apricots and pears – followed the Domina out to the high-walled courtyard. The Lady Lassalia now took a swig of honey and cardamom, spat it into the sluice, declared she is being poisoned by her slaves, then strips and stuffs a slice of peach in her mouth. Two female slaves and a freeman's girl go to the great oaken tub – cost more than the entire upstairs floor – and pull buckets of fresh water.

The first bucket elicits an invective-strewn scream, the new girl with the bucket pauses in fright but is told to keep going by her dripping mistress. So, she does and, once the edge of fear goes, finds throwing cold water over her mistress to be the most enjoyable part of the day, much more enjoyable than the hours spent under Horus' eye filling the huge butt up again. After twenty buckets, "That's a – bloody – enough!" is declared and a stool is brought for the Domina, a colourful, tasselled Persian stole draped over her.

"Eleazar!" Eleazar appeared now his mistress was clothed because while that Roman General took his sexual organs, neither of them – not that he has a choice – particularly want the weird dancing-around-naked dynamic of some such relationships. Unhealthy, impolite and dangerous. Mistresses parading around disrobed in front of male slaves who cannot physically consummate 'the act' bred resentment.

Too honest replies such as, "You have put a pound on your thighs and your belly hangs like a tunny's lip!" tend to occur, leading to rapid resale or even more hysterical activities such as immediate scourging and death. "Do you have any idea how much he cost?" was how divorces began.

The Lady of the house has her long, lightly hennaed black hair combed with an ivory-toothed instrument set with lapis lazuli. The Persian stole is also a startling blue embroidered with gold and green peacocks. She eats some fruit and takes wax tablets from Eleazar.

"Want a fig?" He declined; it is a ritual of respect that she offered. He never took it, though. Much of what is said about eunuchs is nonsense, Eleazer has found, but the transference of appetites was a constant burning truth, and he was not going to become a fat eunuch.

Sobe munched a cut pear, flicking through the day's notes, a combination of yesterday's summary and the applications and messages coming into the house since dawn. The notes are divided into 'work' and 'people'. She held up the 'people' tablet pointing at an etched mark.

"Who is this Mako? Stupid bloody name."

"The young gentlemen that was a little sick on himself last night, just after declaring his undying devotion to you as a widow."

"I'm not a widow."

"He would not take that as an answer and his people removed him when he offered to make you one in a fit of enthusiasm."

She chortled. "Good luck with that, if he can find Hubs. So why am I meeting him again today? I met him last night, sounds like I was a hit. Leave it a week and then let's go get some contracts, keep him panting for more, eh, First Secretary? Keep 'em keen, keep 'em…"

"His lictor came this morning, first thing, requesting a further audience."

"Sorry… Lictor? What's he doing with a bloody lictor? I thought he was one of Suleneous' contracting staff."

"He is, in a sense. In rank, however, this Mako is technically Suleneous' boss's new boss. His presence, though, is not permanent, just a temporary assignment while in Salona – but not 'honorary' – 'actual'. Where shall we put his lictors?"

"There's more than one? Four! What the hell is he? What's four? I can never remember how many is what."

"There are two answers to that. First answer is that his official title following appointment by the Senate…"

"And no doubt important daddy-dearest…"

"Wait for it, Lady…appointed by the Senate with special duties and roving responsibilities for a task or tasks in far off Lower Pannonia, yet unspecified. The second very official unofficial answer for seeing young Mako promptly is him being the new Emperor's nephew."

"Better get dressed, then."

"I would have thought so, Domina."

She returns up the waxed, pine-planked stairs to the third floor, fruit platter all the time following. Dressed, painted and pinned, the Lady Lassalia then moved back down to the second floor of the trading house. In the rooms below her bed chamber are the three working offices of the Sadiki merchant house. Iron latticed windowpanes set with newfangled glass panes are open when she enters the senior executive's suite. A fresh cup of honeyed fennel, more fruit, and the Head of the House (while her husband is away of course) surveys the seaboard traffic to the west. Six ships beating slowly in from the northwest, four outbound on fast reaches racing away from the rising sun. She knew what was in the outbound vessels and makes a shrewd guess about the inbound carriers.

Eleazar concurs with her guess and a boy is sent downstairs to fetch runners. One messenger will instruct a set of Sadiki representatives at the association houses with what to officially offload onto the market in the next hour. The other runner will tell, more discreet, agents to be on standby with buying ranges. The morning game is to visibly dump six tons of iron and flax through the open market, collapsing the commodities value (only to later surreptitiously buy back all Sadiki could through the shadow accounts). With iron and flax cratered, Sobe Lassalia's people would be waiting dockside as the inbound ships arrive, hopefully with the merchant captains too weary and panicked to check average prices over the week or month.

Through pure greed the original buyers would, again hopefully, break the long contracts on the cargoes, usually set at a smaller discount to the average regional price, and try to wheedle down terms on the conveyors' arrival. At this point the House of Sadiki will step, or shoulder, in and magnanimously offer to honour the long contracts at the original, agreed prices as a 'show of good faith'. Thus offering some hope of a profit to the stressed captains. Unguents of 'hope' and 'made luck' glazed House Sadiki, glossing the well-structured machine of cunning and experience.

"The clever bit, if we pull it off, will be we won't even unload. Just re-contract the ships, load up all that lead we're sitting on and send everything off around the corner to Athens as a combined product for a premium."

Eleazar nodded in assent and rang a small hand bell. Three green-peach-liveried men came in: the primary runner to the Association, the secondary to the 'shadow house' representatives and the backup holding both messages who would leave a thousand heartbeats after the first two. The last man being a contingency against competitive interception, morning drunkenness, incompetence or internal fraud.

Each green-tunic stepped forward to be briefed in a whisper by the First Secretary. The backup being the oldest and most trusted of the three men, four years with the Lady and fifteen within the House of Sadiki. A freedman with a family, the daughter of which who had been throwing buckets over the mistress just an hour before Pa's feet hit the warmed slabs of the street heading down to the commercial district.

With that done, the office works in absolute silence. The glazed windows are shut for warmth and Sobe Lassalia reads at a white marble desk with her back to the eastern wall, occasionally glancing up in thought to look out west over the Adriatic sea. Around her are two secretaries, in the middle of the room a circular table with the administrators. Opposite the Domina, back to the western window (a view of the office's eastern wall as befitted his station) Eleazar sits at his desk, flanked also by two secretaries. By the office door is a guard, there are five guards in the house although guests only ever see the four liveried doormen and Ugo the ex-gladiator prancing around downstairs. The office guard is the most dangerous of all Sadiki's security staff and looks like a junior clerk – the fancy uniforms and gilded staves are all downstairs for show. This upstairs man is small with a dark grey shadowed beard, the only thing stopping him being completely nondescript.

His tongue was taken a long time ago so he had run and found employment with the caravans, fought well, and developed a talent for killing that boosted one of the Sadiki office profit lines by a whole two points for five years. Discreet by nature and rough surgery, he was taken off the eastern road trains by the Lady for service at her head office.

The guard just watched the gentle flow of messengers from outside and papyrus coming up from the clearing house downstairs. All of it is either for the administrators or Eleazar, no one approaches the Lady Lassalia until after noon.

She is dealing with trade correspondence and an issue with the taxation levies of a locality, the Illyrian Governor or one of his juniors trying to lazily assert double duty on shipments within the province.

The only sound from Sobe comes as the warehouse and transportation dockets begin to be churned through. "Check this one!", "Why's that for three hundred and the payment for two hundred, do we just really like the town of...? I don't even know how to pronounce this...but somebody must because we are giving them a present of one hundred extra small pots."

Eleazar just took the clay tokens from the girl whose only job is to move between their desks. He is trying to work on a new writ which can be copied into template form by the scribes downstairs. His objective is to incorporate a new level of legalese, to essentially have it as a prima facie civil litigation submission with enough florid insertions to allow the reader to surmise that this is an aggressive, deeply personal vendetta being screamed out to a scribe by her Ladyship.

'Look mate, she's off her fucking head and I know it was windy but do you think she has any idea? A woman?' was one of House Sadiki's greases. Eleazar enjoyed replicating into script his Domina's 'doing a bit of cheeky Aventine one-of-the-boys' playacting, within the soon-to-be subpoena template.

As he tries to write the writ, Eleazar deals with the three sendbacks dispatched with accompanying snorts from the other side of the room. One was a mistake from downstairs, caught – fair enough; one was his fault as he'd missed the docket numbers off, but the three cargo release orders were essentially good. The hundred extra pots were meant for a stage drop before the final destination at – what was that place with all the 'Y's? – with the loading instruction being a gross amount.

With communications thumping up the stairs from the outside world, Eleazar loaded up a wax tablet with key items that needed to be dealt with during the vital working session before lunch. These later morning's issues were primarily in relation to the large caravans due to go out from the northern Sadiki offices once tracks drained and hardened at spring's end. Lady Lassalia and her First Secretary were having a long running debate over the advisability of mobilising an overground transfer between two rivers. The pros and cons were endless but encompassed double handling, time – always time –, security of land versus water, cost and 'repeatability'.' *Never try to do anything once'* was one of the watch phrases of the new House of Sadiki now three years in, since Master went away.

On this bright morning, neither the Lady or Eleazar had made a decision on what to do with the caravan, no fixed positions from either were held anymore on what to do and they oscillated constantly on solutions depending on the day. Last week they had both agreed on the same thing on the same day, but it spooked them that they'd missed something and the decision was deferred. By the next morning, both woke up with opposing stances again.

Eleazar put his head down and scraped out the 'key tasks' list into the wax. Mistakes rectified, misunderstandings checked, all ready for reapplication in the (generally-recognised more congenial environment of the post-client lunch) afternoon. In addition to the northern caravans, the discussion list was so far as follows:

Internal Salona. SPQR out of Baia 'Drusilia' 20 cubits available, west, deviation if filled. Fill two days
Int Sal. Thebes, Conveyance 'Daughter of Osiris' vessel downgrade to likely – un-seaworthy.
External Theb. Uncle Sham introduces son/captain to hon house Sadiki – allocate 'Daughter of Osiris'?
Int Sal. Wine & sundries above non-approval limit.
Int Sal. Further wine & sundries above non-approval limit.
Ext Numidian Carrier 'Prince'. Live cargo {Tall} – 'Yes?' forty cubits special. No fill charge. Reply four days.
Int Sal. Civil court case creditor no.32 – funds received. Release 1s, 1d?

Finished with that, the last stream of work for Eleazar was to review a tablet to the right marked 'Clients'.

Clients could be customers, could be suppliers or political contacts or amusing timewasters. It might be the Army or Navy of Rome needing a favour or a favour needed repaying, or somebody else's army or navy. Civil servants, other merchants, lawyers, dock representatives, builders, judges, hangers-on or, worst of all, relatives like Uncle Sham's son looking for work.

The problem was that today's client meetings entailed a four-lictor-carrying relative of the Emperor Trajan. Entertaining royalty and the overpromoted was something the House of Sadiki excelled at. Two problems, however, presented themselves:

One. Everything First Secretary Eleazar had heard about the Emperor Trajan was that he 'did things', was an 'up-and-at-em' projects person. Nephew, then, was unlikely to be a totally useless wastrel (despite last night's evidence) or a po-faced, recently demobbed officer methodically wading through a regional posting like it was a rainy-day parade drill before being kicked upstairs back to Rome (or killed in a Salona brothel fight by a deserter he didn't have the good sense not to recognise).

Two. The lictors. Why did the Emperor's Nephew have lictors and what was four lictors anyway? Literally, the lictors were large musclebound ex-soldiers carrying the bunched rods and axe to denote a senior government rank. Different amounts of lictors were allowed based on different Roman ranks 'as every fule nose'. For the life of him Eleazar hadn't a clue what four lictors was and had sent a hurriedly written note to his 'good friend' – as the individual in question always insisted he and the Jewish slave, Eleazar were – at the Dalmatian Governor's palace. His 'friend', Aulus Scipio Pallo – yes, those Scipii – was a permanently amused, top drawer aristocrat who replied;

'Not quite a general? Both Curule Aediles going on holiday together? An ambitious lumberjack? Where are you going to put them all at lunch, they are quite big – the lictors I mean? Much love. PS Let me know how's it goes. Kisses.'

While on the face of it these answers were flippant if not totally unamusing, the Scipio had given a clear message. *'The nephew has been given an odd number of lictors because he's here on big boy business, outside of senate structure, so don't just lend him the nice corner office overlooking the park and take him to lunch every day. It is all very irregular and we have to find a way of making something happen because the Emperor seems to actually want something proper and grown up to happen. PS This has nothing to do with my office of cultural affairs but I am…interested. Kisses.'*

Eleazar decided not to send any cancellations or postponements to the usual clients.

He'd let all come at midday thus encouraging a lively antechamber and allowing the town of Salona to see that Sadiki entertained one of the Imperial family. Even if none of the other clients were actually seen by Lady Lassalia today, it was a *'When I was talking to the Emperor's nephew the other day…'* gift to them all and the locals would be grateful. First Secretary Eleazar would have the breakfast fruit platter rearranged and taken downstairs for the clients once she'd finished picking the good bits out of it.

Chapter Three

Roman Infiltration team
Sunup over the east hills, four stadia north of the Danube
Macromanni Kingdom

Point lay absolutely still, eyes half closed, rag-wrapped body pushed down into the sparse foliage of an early spring hillside. The forward scout smells the horse, hears the breaking twig noise under the clatter of bone scales as the rider halts the mount to turn back, no doubt peering hard into the forest. The brown-white mare readjusted stance at its rider's command and a hoof thumped a few handspans from Point's ash-painted face.

Complete quiet. Lead Scout can feel the rider listening. Across the forest path, set back in a clump of old leaves, Point met Six's eyes staring back. The team had not made enough progress during the night. With an arm-injured Three the Infil Immunes party was forced to backtrack up and down the higher ridges through the darkness, many leg-burning times. They were now seven days into the insertion and the eight-man Infiltration team had picked up the patrol on the third evening, just after killing that mercenary having a piss. For the next two days the Romans hadn't laid sight on their pursuers, just the hoof tracks, occasional noise, flight of birds or deer or startled boar crashes from the undergrowth. But they knew they were being tracked and tried every trick in the ledger to shake off pursuit. The pursuing patrol was very good, though. Gradually the hostile riders had circled in closer and closer.

A night had been spent half floating in a brook. One day the team had all run up the sheer, scree side of a small mountain, legs screaming with pack and weapon weight trying to drag you down – this is where Three had broken his arm. The scramble gave the team half a day's space but the horse patrol managed to pick them up again two hours before sunset. These riders were always at the advantage, knowing where their quarry's eventual destination must be: crossing back south over the Danube into Roman territory.

A low bird call sounded ahead, then vibrations passed through the earth to Point's resting elbow as the horse and its rider moved off. Point continued to stay stock still as he lay crouched in the hill scrub and, sure enough, the rider suddenly wheeled the painted horse back again to a stop just a few paces further along the path. The scout breathed steadily through the nose and out the mouth, the horsewoman's eyes scanned and she seemed to look straight at him as her gaze passed by.

'...*grasses and shadow, just winter grass, spring shoots on a hill...*' Eyes unfocussed, lids half closed, Point silently incanted his grandpapee's spell of stealth.

The riders were not Macromanni or any type of local German, they were women for a start. Roxolani tribe virgins, brought down from the far, far northern plains of the Sarmatian lands. Hunched up in the snow, Point had seen them once before at a mid-distance, trotting along a tributary bank during last winter's turn. Celerinus, their local guide, pointing the women out excitedly from the dank hollow – the fabled Roxolani girls and widows. Right shoulders visibly hunched up with muscle, each Roxolani woman having been bound at birth to make those big spear arms. Then, according to Celerinus, only able to marry on the taking of three scalps during the numerous horse vendettas that dragged on in such places. It had sounded like bullshit to Point but now, up close, he wasn't so sure. These women looked well up for delivering a scalping.

Lured by Dacian gold, sex and a constant need to prove their cavalry, the Roxolani queen had done a deal, sending troops into Macromanni territory for a bit of a proxy trouble. The Sarmatians ignoring the feeble old Macromanni king's protestations as the pull from Emperor Decebalus'' mines proved too strong. The hot-headed son, the Macromanni Prince, was probably in on it as well. That's what the Skipper reckoned anyway with Two adding, "Horse people like wearing a bit of gold, don't know why, must be the weather."

None of the Skipper's geopolitical musings were currently passing through Point's mind as these extraordinary irregulars stood right in amongst his team with weapons drawn. All of the scout's focus was on staying still and thinking about being a very small shrub.

Heels shifted to calm the horse as the Roxolani looked directly about the path around her mount's feet. Thorough. She was an impressive sight, not just because of her sex; blue tinted dragon's teeth armour made from split hooves, a tasselled lance held by that enormously-muscled right arm and two small spears grasped with the normal-sized left hand, all the shafts tipped with sharpened bone dipped, by the looks of it, in shit. On her head was a short felt-coned hat, stiffened with green leather and a plume of blackbird feathers that snaked down a long night-haired back braid. Point could see her eyes were also green under the warpaint, she was that close.

The slightest of movements flickered to the left of Point's eye, behind the rider's back. He prayed that murderous Two just stayed where he was, there was no doubt his colleague was repositioning to slit the woman but even if he did so noiselessly, the horse patrol would miss their comrade instantly – then the Infil would be dead. More bird calls warbled continuously now, up and down the sweeping line from the forest just ahead.

'Just a stone in a bush, a shadow in the briar, old winter leaves, don't be a fool, Two.'

Abruptly the black-feathered rider cantered forward down the track, lance lowered, stabbing at foliage. The noise of the hooves was a clattering relief and Point allowed himself a full breath.

No one moved, everyone was to the north of Point, on the other side of the track, downhill.

The team had been making its way up this ridge for two hours now.

Before dawn, they'd made a mad, forced dash on exhausted legs across the flood plain, tripping and falling into marsh water and black mud. From the cover of the Yellow Hat hills, the eight men had made for the forest-covered ridges that rose then fell back down to the great green-blue river. The rising sun chasing the team every step of the way and they hadn't been quite quick enough. Half a mile to the river forest a Sarmatian horn sounded. The Infiltrators didn't stop running, knowing that the horse patrol had lazily, and quite sensibly, pulled out of the night-time cat-and-mouse chase, instead choosing to have a pleasant breakfast. Over rye bread and boiled eggs, the Roxolani cavalry had waited at the edge of the exposed grassland leading back to the river. Then like a sparrow hawk spotting a field mouse, they mounted and flew to the chase. The Romans made the river hills with the thunder of hooves a third of an hour behind at their heels. In the forest rising towards the Danube's northern ridges., that's when the real fun began.

Back in the scrub, Point could see Six still staring back at him. He also knew Four and Five were supporting the injured Three somewhere to the left down-slope. Comms was no doubt further back, but the Skipper could be anywhere. Point looked for their leader, turning his head with the very smallest of movements then – there! Gods, Skipper'd been even closer to her than Two, by the tree right where the rider had made her wheel. Skipper had in turn made his scout, leaning out from the trunk and lifting a forage flat cap so they could make eye contact, Point rose ever so slightly to do the same.

Hand signals from the team leader; *'Move?'* It was Point's decision, without hesitation he chopped negative and gestured behind with a moving back of the palm then finger to the mouth. The Skipper affirmed and sent the command, one by one it hand signalled along the staggered, hidden stick of men.

Sixty beats passed and almost silently another follow sweep of Roxolani appeared, confirming Point's hunch, this time on foot. Two pairs leading reined horses, mounts and riders shod in soft moccasin slips. The nearest couple were close, one grey-haired, wary-looking woman with a buckler of hide and a steel sword – a rarity- wearing a green and white slouch cap. A twig snapped and she scowled at the younger woman following. The admonished virgin held a short bow in the 'withered' left arm; it was made of rods bound together with dyed blue gut-tie, ends ox-bone-tipped and reinforced with twine. The horsewomen were moving along the cross slope path, just as the previous rider had, right through the team's position. The walking Roxolani trod so close that Point could see the grey dapple on the ox-bone bow tips, the coloured tassels on the very long arrows, three shafts held in the initiate's hand with one in the string.

Those arrow lengths shouldn't work on such a short bow but Point was sure, as fifteen years seniority allowed, that the weapons system was a 'goer'. A careful moccasin footed directly in front of Point and he worked hard to control his breathing, heart pumping harder ready to…then somehow the women just kept going without seeing him. The scout made a prayer to the Prey-lord of his home's deep-forest. Further down the slope the other Roxolani pair must have walked right between the wounded Three and the specialists.

Point's virgin and widow continued to creep along the path, crossing by the Skipper's tree, but this time there was no 'crazy girl' abrupt stop. A walking sweep was much slower, unmounted and quiet as it was, so had to keep moving in order not to lose contact with the main search line ahead. Then the women all disappeared into the foliage ahead. In about a quarter of an hour, the forward horse patrol would stop, allow the sweep to catch up and reverse. The Roxolani had the Infil team pinned to well within a fifth of a mile now and the Romans wouldn't survive another overrun like that. Point popped his head up and looked for the Skipper at the tree. Instead, a hiss sounded just next to him and he started to see their leader beside him in a fern. *'How did he do that?'*

A whisper with a wax bag proffered through the leaves, "Have a dried apricot, Point."

"Thanks, Skip."

"I'm not sure we've got another one of those in us. Lead Scout, any ideas? Straight up?"

Point chewed looking up to the top of the ridge, it was tantalisingly close.

"Summit, then run it in over one of the 'T' ridges all the way to the shore?" Point shook his head.

"Thought you'd say that." The Skipper put a half-smile on under his reddish beard. His officer must be utterly exhausted, Point thought. Carrying Three's pack for a day, letting them all sleep an hour here or there while he took watch. The drain of just managing to always be 'there'. A rare thing, a good officer. Lucky to have him.

The team scout looked about, they'd been coming up the slope before dispersing to cover when the patrol came laterally across it, over the top of the hiding Romans. There was something up to the far right, Point saw, the top of a rock just visible. If that knoll was the reverse of what Point thought it might be, previously clocked from one of the south bank recce's, then a possible alternate for escape might be presented, one with advantages. He gestured *'Stay here'* and stood up slowly out of the grasses, snake quiet. His ghillie suit of rags, sacking and grass made him look like a foul-smelling dryad.

On a previous mission years ago, Point persuaded an overly inquisitive local boy that he was a wood spirit, gave him a honey sweet and swore him to a secret oath held by strong magic. The boy had goggled, agreeing open-mouthed, and ran off. Two had cursed the scout for a fool but, as it turned out, not killing the lad had been a good decision: No one came back. The boy was as good as his word, given to the 'children of the forest' tales as he was – no new handle notch for Two. Two tried to kill anyone the Infil came across and the trail of dead herd girls or charcoal burners had eventually led to the Skipper encouraging 'alternative' contact solutions.

Now Point ran along the forest track in the opposite direction to the Roxolani sweep, thighs on fire from the dawn run then the laborious upslope crawls. *'But it don't matter'* because the Immunes Infiltrati counted running like wolves amongst their many skills. The weight of Point's laden pack and weapons sapped him. *'But it don't matter'* because the sun was up and they were in striking distance of the extraction area. It was simply going to be a *'piece of piss'* getting out of this, Point pointed out to his body. *'Front it out, fuck it!'* Lead Scout internally shouted at the bit of him urging a bit of lie-down.

The scout then changed mental tack and muttered a prayer to the woods, to the wild places. The goddess he couldn't pray to, so asked for forgiveness instead.

First weaving track bend he ran round – no. Second bend – no. It was a case of third time a charm. The team scout rose out of a dip and there it was, a rock escarpment leading up to the reverse side of the outcrop known as the Fingers. Point didn't stop but skidded pivoting, his rig hauling at him for a moment, knees wrenching, then back along the track he went. Speed of return was key, there was a very small window to make the escarpment before the women riders were within aural range. If they detected the team making up the rocks, it would all be over in a few minutes of galloping hooves.

 Point allowed his feet to make some noise running back to the team as the horse patrol should still be advancing eastward along the slope face, with about a sixth of an hour before they turned. The scout hit the final return bend into the clearing they'd been hiding in. Now just an empty expanse of forest again even to his well-trained eyes, Point thought with a little pride. The pathfinder gestured up with his palms and the forest floor spat forth seven figures, all immediately moved onto the path at speed, Three slung between Four and Five, specialists before them, with Two and Skipper bringing up the rear. With no slapping footfalls or heavy heel plants, the Point reversed his direction again and off they went towards the rocky fingers that might pluck them out of this shitshow.

The stick ran as fast as they still could along the track. Bend one. Bend two. Skipper saw the cliff immediately and took over. Rock-nails came out, a rope bowlined around the waist of Five who scampered up the rock face like the egg-stealing little Pict he was, pinioning with a canvas swathed mallet as he went.

The climber practically ran up the side of the lichen-clad grey rock, despite a few slips here and there, with the ascent rope trailing down.

A brief conversation was initiated by the Skipper at the escarpment's base while Five tied off around a sturdy elm at the top of the climb, "Well done, Point. The Fingers, right? Good. Reckon we have visibility for Comms further up, agreed? Right, good. Comms, You're up, fella."

Comms flew up the rock face only a little slower that the Pict, the signalman previously having pursued a career as an urban burglar before being offered the magistrate's choice. On making the top he didn't stop but continued past the now anchored Five, taking only a moment to call his colleague a 'monkey wanker', before leaning in, straight on up towards the 'T' hill.

Comms ran up the north-south 'I' slope rising up to meet the crosscutting ridge of the 'T'. Behind that 'T' ridge was a short, sharp descent down to the river. For line of sight, the top of the 'T' would work for the signalman and if this was the rocky Fingers then they were well, well within the 'cone' for spotters, spotters hopefully still waiting on the far bank in the Green Zone of Roman territory.

Comms forced himself up to the ridge line, making his way along a path below the brow on the western side of the rising 'I', reducing any chance of being silhouetted to the riders below. The signalman's knee began hurting again after half a mile but he finally made it and found the perfect spot, a raised clearing with a panorama looking down on to the great river valley. The shallow, winding, dark blue of the Danube stretching out below. Spring sun sparkled off the river flowing between the evergreen and bare-branched forest hills either side of it.

Crawling under a stubby hawthorn right at the apex of the ridge Comms took shortening breaths while assembling the relay kit. The signaller could see for miles, the cold rising sun, the mighty Danube, the endless rising and falling waves of trees following the roll of the earth beneath their roots. Carefully Comms unhooked a padded leather pouch from his rig, taking the code stick to formulate a send. Once he had checked and rechecked the new message, only then did he unwrap the silvered glass.

The communications specialist gave the silver-glass a good polish first, before meticulously constructing a five-sided leather box from his kit, dropping the reflective square face up in the bottom.

'One last wipe, take a breath, look south assessing the pickup cone's possible location.' Taking out a small wooden sundial Comms settled on three signal positions: SSE (due to the curve of the river), S, SW. He set SSE position first, angled for the sun, opened two sides of the box and... *'Send.'*

Back down the slope, moving the broken-armed Three up the escarpment was tough but they did it. Three was several days wounded, the injury was not just the arm, in all likelihood the collarbone had broken too, but no good was going to come of pointing that out so *'Bit of a bruise, you soft twat'* it was.

The casualty was going proper feverish but the man was a mule. Two wanted to go up next, looking for trouble, but the Skipper refused, keeping the killer next to him, and off they sent Point who, once at rope top, made straight past the anchor with a quick salutation of *'Pictish limpet cunt!'.* Tracking Comms' route, Point marked the path uphill with little white painted sticks, pulled out from a belt pouch to be pushed into the mud. It was an easy task to follow the signalman with Comms having moved quickly, leaving tracks, and Point's long familiarity as to where a signalman man would likely push to.

With Three slung in a cradle, the team were quickly on the move following the whitesticks up the 'I' and before long collapsed into the upper clearing of the 'T' top. They lay sprawled about, exhausted. It was all not very Roman but no one was looking and the team were all fucked. A fifth-hour break was called before the final push – one way or another – down to the river bank, a rest and to give Comms, in his prickly nest above the clearing, more time to send repeats. Skipper didn't even bother asking Comms if any responses had come from the far bank. There would be none, not even a quick flash confirmation they'd been spotted.

Even with the Infil team blown and a horse patrol all over them, knowing their likely direction of travel to the bank, some enthusiastic young legionary manically broadcasting back inaccurate return signals to the north bank would only give the enemy encouragement. South Bank's young Exfil officer would know that, hopefully. The Skipper sat up after a short time then crouched, while everyone else lay strewn around in large clumps of rag-tied netting, pulling out a cloth bag from his rig's side-pack. "Now! Who'd like one of my sweets? Point?"

"No thanks, Sir."

"Let us try that again, they're really good this batch." The Skipper made them himself.

"Have a sweet, Point."

"Thank you, Sir." Point put the honey sweet in his mouth and sucked. His stomach growled in protest as the syrupy, salted, nutty fat trail ran down his gullet.

There was always a 'Surprise flavour'. This trip had been the worst. *'What sort of cunt put lavender in a sweet?'*

Five was now being threatened. "Do I have to, Sir? The aniseed ones were the best."

The Skipper pushed the bag under Five's nose and exclaimed in mock hurt, "Yes, you've all made it very clear over the last seven days you don't like the lavender. Next time I'll put aniseed in them. Or…a new surprise flavour."

"That's what you said last time, Skip. Last time when it was asparagus surprise flavour," accused Four, crumpled back on a log, but with eyes scanning the slopes and ridges.

Four then brought up a continual source of whispered debate on this trip, "Skipper: are you sure lavender ain't poisonous, because my Ma…'"

"Only if you're a Skorpion, Four, with greatest respect to your Ma." retorted the team lead. "But couldn't you just ask us when you make 'em, Sir?" Five tried with no enthusiasm. It was a comforting ritual not a real question.

"Then it wouldn't be 'Surprise Flavour' if we knew, would it, Skip?" sotto whispered Six, who was off to one side crouching a shit into a too-full waxed bag.

"That's right, Six, got to keep morale up with surprise flavour. By the way, Six, once you've finished having a dump, here's yours." The Skipper thoughtfully placed the homemade confectionery on a smooth rock then threw another sweet up to Four saying, "Pass one up to Comms." Four crawled through the hawthorn spikes up to the signal area and popped it straight into Comms' mouth, who took the rancid, warm 'treat' without a word as he lay prone, shuttering out a new sequence to the south.

The Skipper walked on crab feet to Three and lay next to him. The man was pissing out sweat and turning the wrong colour; "How are you doing, Audie?"

"I don't want one of your fucking sweets, Sir."

"I'll let that insubordination pass, Three. So – we are going to have one last little push, a fast one all the way down to the river where the Exfil team will, no doubt, be there ready to take us off the bank and away with no problems asked?"

"Bollocks they will."

"Sir."

"Bollocks they will, Sir."

"Fair point but I'll tell the Werewulf you said that. Now, do you think you can make it? One last push, Three? Do it for me because you've got fuck all anyone else who loves you waiting back home."

This made Three dry-chortle. "Yes, Skip, I'll be right."

"Sure you don't want to selflessly demand you stay here with a sword and a flask of piss to give us a better chance?"

"I taught you better than that, Sir."

"Quite right, Audie, fuck that. Are you certain you don't want a sweet? This one looks like it's got a bit of a bee in it."

"Fuck off, Sir."

A noise sounded below the team from the path they'd moved up through, then movement. The men drew a selection of blades, two short bows and the long Marshling blow pipe. Comms had heard the sound to but stayed where he was signalling all the while, focussing completely on working the angle of the sun and box doors.

A pair of clicks, like a cricket. Skipper clucked his tongue, making two back. They relaxed as Two came out of the bush by the trail head. He was the tail end Claudio left behind at the top of the escarpment to spot the patrol on the return flush, but that's not how it had turned out.

"Nothing, Sir, I've been down there for long enough. Can't hear nowt, they're quiet bitches but not that quiet. I reckon the girls have reset again, Sir."

The Skipper thought on this for a moment then canvassed the team starting with Two, "Here it is: if the patrol reset, I reckon it's down at the beach waiting for us to pop up. The good ladies of the Roxolani seem to like a drop back ambush rather than waste energy and I can hardly blame them."

All the team agreed this was the most likely strategy, but the Skipper wanted to hear it from the men.

"Right, so – we could turn back on ourselves but I reckon we just go for it."

The men crouching around him assented, Three lying in the centre of the circle nodding grimly.

Every piece of equipment that could be was dropped and covered in ground litter; beloved ghillie suits, any food not eaten, ropes, pinions, grapples, small pans and lines. This clearing would be the retreat point – if all went completely to shit each man would make it back up the ridge to here, retrieve anything he wanted then it was individual 'evade and escape'. None of the team fancied their chances of even making it this far before being ridden down but you always had to have a backup plan.

The Skipper checked Two and Seven had all the caltrops transferred to them, that Four had the tinderbox and dye sack full of bone-dry pine cones and tied damp grass. Finally, the officer took an evil black bag package from Six for himself.

"As soon as Comms finishes we go, quick as each of you can. I'll ship Three. I want us right down that valley, not on the path. Point will find the shit-brown slope west of the Fingers. Follow him, just get over and down it. Noise off now, boys."

Comms blinked off the last flash, the third round to SW and hand signalled 'End' to the Skipper below. In a few movements, the signalman folded the silver glass and box back into his rig then slid out from the spiky tree into the team circle where Skipper explained the plan once more. Comms listened while stripping off his rag suit, dropping excess kit like the rest of them had done but also took a knife and whittled all the marks off the cipher sticks before throwing them deep into a bush.

The Skipper then nodded to his scout and Point got running south, gathering speed over the early spring forest floor, jumping vines, weaving around young sprays of poplars. Point was fast and his job now was to either make it to the shore and find an extraction position or run straight into the enemy patrol and make a lot of fucking noise as he did so. The scout ran, seven days of constant physical activity fell off him, the ghillie suit gone, most of the pack weight gone, but more so the fact that just down there…that little ridge – one little push – was the river and home. Point hit that rhythm, arms swaying, left hand holding a dagger out, breaths driving the engine. That little bit of honey and salt giving him a boost although he'd never admit it to Skip.

A branch break behind him signalled the others had started out.

Point ran harder so the slight incline didn't slow him, ignoring the draining fatigue. Arriving at the top edge of the ridge he could see they were right on top of the sharp, dark-earth slope Skipper wanted. The scout slowed, broke and tied

39

an elder branch as a marker before running straight off the edge of the ridge without giving him time to think too hard about the drop. *'A straight fall?'*

The slope disappeared almost immediately from under the scout's feet, the whole river valley filling his vision before a falling terror, then almost plunging straight down Point forced all his body weight forward and screamed to himself *'fast feet, fast feet.'* His soles barely touched the almost vertical floor, for one moment he was in free fall before his left foot gained a scuff of contact. Good ankles and eyes, with lungs like flour sacks, that's what made an Immunes Infiltratus.

Then the slope pushed back a little on the soft soles and Point felt a slight rise, saw the huge bramble bush rushing up fast below and pushed.

Bramble bushes are big and full of thorns – facts providing the right combination of strength and give to stop a falling body, even one in leather armour carrying a few weapons. Point tucked his eyes into his elbow at the last moment before crackling into the huge horned beast. The pain of a thousand cuts as brambles ripping through skin, helpfully slowing his descent, would come later. Now it was the jarring thud that really hurt, hitting the dark underneath of this 'forest fence'. Immediately Point was sprung back up, then bounced down for another lesser, impact on to his head before the tangles rippled calmly, the scout left just gently bouncing.

The knife was gone and his scabbarded gladius had also flown away. Through semi-concussed, sparkling eyes lead scout saw the short sword suspended just tantalisingly out of reach in the thorns. With some skin tearing Point got his leg up and pulled the little punch dagger from his remaining shoe. Sharp as a dragon's tooth it cut quickly through the thick, purple senior strands of the older brambles. Point muttered a little prayer to the bush as he did it, just like his grandfather had taught him. Ignoring the growing, stinging burns, he then flopped forward twisting to make an inelegant back roll out of the massive plant.

Before the cuts really began to scream, Point pushed his hand straight back into the bramble, grabbed the gladius and pulled it out. The belt work was destroyed so given the mission's stage he discarded the harness entirely. Blacked gladius in the right hand, punch dagger in the left, Point planted the short sword for a moment and twisted a cedar sapling into a fractured knot, white wood visible, sparkling with sap.

Then forward, direct south, no zig zagging but just getting the team to where they should be, a viable point within the extraction 'cone'.

Moving carefully through the shore copse he got to the river track that ran along the northern bank. The path here was too narrow for a cart used, as it was, for local herding or by those who couldn't afford a river ticket in better times. On his stomach, the scout crawled across the mud track into the grass on the other side like a hunting adder. Now out of the trees and open to the river valley's echo, hooves could clearly be heard by the slithering Roman. Stopping for a moment to leave a thick clump of knotted grass. Point inched towards the water's edge, where he took a chance and lapped up fresh cold water. The spring sun was high now and the air warming.

The Danube itself dazzled in the light, its strong current passing from right to left as the scout surveyed the southern bank. Forest-covered, reflected ridges of the north bank cut like an almond cake by the river's passage. He couldn't see anything on the opposite bank, no sign of life or movement other than the odd bird. So, still low in the river grasses, he moved downstream. After a sixth the scout stopped again, peering through yellow grass stalks at something shiny and bright just ahead. Fortuna was with them – it was the White Stones. Point crawled to the edge of a wide limestone plinth and pressed his cheek to the warming rock in thanks. They were right on one of the pre-designated 'A' spots for recovery. A series of white slabs curving down to the water allowing the space and depth needed for a clean pick up.

Hooves suddenly echoed loudly and the scout knew he must find where the horsewomen were so moved parallel to the river further downstream, just within the grass's edge. Slowly he worked his way around a few tall plants, careful not to cause any vibrations that could alert a keen watcher. The bank scrub began to shorten now, winter's only just done, but some debris helps his task – rotten logs from thaw melt brought up onto the bank. Good cover, decaying dark wood and shadow to keep keen, prying eyes out. Point crawled up to a drenched trunk then adjusted himself to blend with the wet wood. The horse hooves sound close but he realises they in the wrong direction to his cover. From behind Point, hammering down the path, four riders thunder. He is completely visible, exposed in the short stalks if they'd just looked down, but the quad of women are distracted by the bird noises signalling ahead.

Slowly Point regained his breath as they pass by and uses the punch dagger to cut a hole in the rotten bark of the hiding log, affording him a full view downriver.

The passing squadron had pulled to a stop ten paces in front of the scout's woodlouse-infested hide. A dappled grey horse with a long wood-green blanket stands nearest to him, the woman atop it casually holding a huge, heavy boar spear, barbed and feathered with jay's wings. *'Unlucky, Jays.'* Point thought to himself involuntarily. Following her, the Roman scout recognised the blackbird-wreathed warrior from earlier in the day, the Roxolani with green eyes who had been within a flight feather of discovering her quarry. Jayfeather also has livid green eyes and looking from one rider to the next Point deduced they were twins.

The scout spat silently for such evil and touched his grimy cock for luck *'Sod whatever the Romans believe; twins are wrong as wrong can be.'*. Cursed as such creatures are the sisters don't seem to be getting on, probably why the two women missed the lurking man completely as they bicker in some garbled language. The jay twin's dragon tooth armour is a dull reddy-pink, the hooves it was made from stained in the manufacture. The two women are so close Point can now really make out the malformed muscled hunches in the right shoulder and bicep. The twins are pushing each other with their 'withered' arms, all the while Blackbird's fist holding a huge bow and a bone-ringed javelin of dyed, red ruffed feathers.

The older women behind growled something at the younger two.

Sibling-fight over, the cursed pair start to trot down the track, 'widows' following behind. Continuing down the river path until a larger number of riders emerge from the trees, some dismounted holding several bridles apiece.

'Where are those other riders?' Point wondered looking at the new group's led ponies. Taking two fingers he pushed his corneas back into his head and squinted, looking hard – and then he made them. At least five women are in the bulrushes further downsteam, covered in black river mud, half-submerged, probing the water ferns with lances. He counted heads and realised that the patrol has made its first real mistake, well over ten of them, more like fifteen, have bunched themselves leaving a gap.

Point knew well the excitement of the hunt, all the women's patient discipline and search lines have suddenly been ignored. It represented just a small chance though, maybe a few minutes if they can bottle the horsewomen in one direction. The scout watched as a new argument seems to be in progress, horses wheeling and much pointing by the twins. One of the women, knee-deep in the rushes, shouts believing she has something. A bit of confusion as an otter family fight back.

Point slowly wriggled backwards from the log, through the grass – oh, so careful, one shuddered tall stem would mean disaster – retracing his crawl towards the footpath. He holds a few feet back from the track crossing, looking into the foliage across the path he sees Two, with fingers moving to eyes. Two confirming the team also saw the riders. The killer pulls back into the undergrowth's shadow. Skipper replaces him in the shaded gap and a plan is formed via hand signals with the scout. The limestone plinth, that's where they will have to trust hard in the system.

Chapter Four

Argentoratum Fort, Rhine border
Nearly lunchtime, VIIIth Augusta garrison
Germania Inferior Province of Rome.

The stone-pillared colonnade was throwing down short shadows, showing the sun had now risen well above the Rhine Fort's gatehouse. The Rhine border, as the joke went, was in a state of 'Established Fluidity'. The big joke was actually that 'Established Fluidity' was the real, official designation by Army Group West for the Rhine border. Argentoratum so-called *'Town'* was where the VIIIth Legio had been based for five years and the conurbation stood at the more 'peacefully turgid' end of the fluidity scale. What Chief Armourer Galba particularly liked about Argentoratum Fort was that: on the lower Rhine it was the only place from which you couldn't see any trees. The straight-lined buildings and walls that housed the regional government complex meant that if you stayed in the base and squinted it was possible to pretend you weren't in Germania.

The province was vaguely Gaul anyway, which wasn't much better, but had the benefit of decent cheese. Galba helped build the permanent base and personally made sure a wide radius of foliage had been cleared from around the construction area. The original shit-hole Germanian/Gaulish 'town' was still there a stave throw away from the fort but bit by bit it was being upgraded, even if the locals still took a dump in the public bathhouse once in a while. The Roman Chief Armourer never dream of going to the public bathhouse in any case so, as far as Galba was concerned, if the locals wanted to swim in their own filth, let them. It was all about being sensitive to local cultures, as they were constantly told by the wonks from civil administration.

The CA finished his own morning shit, properly located in a latrine, then with arse sponged made his way towards workshop II to find Senior Armourer Ruben.

"Feel it was a useful meeting, Boss?"

"I was having a shit."

"Ah yes, before your morning relief, esteemed Chief Armourer, with Lulla and the other department heads? Do we have accurate spares lists handed in yet, as I've not seen any?"

"That we shall see, Ruben, but let's face it, full lists will probably only appear when we start running out of stuff at the beginning of Autumn."

"We can but try, Chief Armourer."

"Worries for the end of summer, but I want to feel caught up by the end of this week, Ruben. Could you also make a point of sitting in on the field test for primary artillery pieces today?"

"Check they have enough 'yellow dogs' on hand?" said Ruben, making a cheeky reference to his chief's recurring nightmare of over-engineering malfunctions.

Ruben and Galba had worked together for many years. The pursuit of running the key technical areas of the legion's weaponry, transport and infrastructure threw down many barriers of rank and replaced them with the need for shared personal shorthand. A long way of saying Galba was perfectly happy getting pissed up and sharing his deep-seated fears with a subordinate, even if they were in dream form, because nothing could be worse than a not-working war machine. Well, there was, but it came pretty hard on the heels of catastrophic equipment failure.

"He's brilliant – Guns – but you have to keep an eye on these things," responded Galba. "Right, Ruben, let's start with ferrous and work our way down."

On a massive workshop table, whitewashed and spotless, a precise charcoal grid had been drawn. Within each box sat a piece of material necessary for the good running of the armoury and, consequently, the VIIIth Legio. Each commodity or part was accompanied by a numeric sequence written out within its black lined box, in coloured paint.

The Chief Armourer used a massive, three fingered hand to pick up a small hard lump of grey and read out the number. Ruben responded; "Ferrous, Lower Rhine on the Gaulish border, basic pig iron."

"Basic good pig iron or basic full of filth and falls apart pig iron?"

"Decimus has been with the smelter and they like it. He needs a bigger sample, though, but it's up to anything a standard fabrica will have."

Pre-empting his senior's next comment, Ruben went on, "Not of course the standard of either Hispanic equipment fabrica."

The Chief Armourer of the Legion grunted then carefully placed the ore back into its square.

"And that, Ruben, is what I want: Hispania grade. What about this here?"

"Oh, that is absolutely full of filth pig iron from somewhere upriver," Ruben gleefully replied.

Slowly the two men worked their way through all the iron samples secured over the winter months, each piece on the grid representing a larger sample that had been tested by Smelter Armourer Decimus, 'The Nose', supervising the local furnace, whose owner happily stole half of each test bag. Galba turned a blind eye to the Chatti smelter thief – it was the way things worked here – as the man had also been a great help in sourcing all the copper and tin ore now secured in abundance following a series of off-season winter trips. These 'jollies' involved rattling through the snow to attend three-day-long drinking binges in turf lean-tos while the local supplier gathered all that was needed by the silver-paying Roman Army. It was not unusual to find a few wooden skillets tied into the ore bags to cheat the scales, but copper was copper and Germania was Germania.

Pragmatism made an armoury run.

The iron for Galba's pet project was always going to be a challenge because he wanted his sets, the legion's homegrown equipment, to be graded 'Hispanic' – that good. To do that, though, the Chief Armourer needed the best metal. Out there in that big German forest somewhere was quality iron, because they'd all seen the swords and axe heads that came in over the river from contact patrols.

Ruben watched his chief think. "Mulling over the sword again, Boss? I could always get it out the chest."

The Chief Armourer half smiled. 'The Sword' was a magnificent sample piece, captured two years ago. Decimus, Workshop, Menicitrix, Guns, Ruben and every armourer cadet had pored over it, cut slivers off it to drop into solutions, smelled it, licked it, bent it, melted parts of it. Even Old Sibius agreed it was a *'fucking good sword'* but the point was: *'it was a fucking good sword'* because it was made from fucking good steel. Yes, the ornate hunting scene on the handle was exquisite, the jewels perfectly polished, the gold coil work brilliant, but it was the length of gleaming, razor-sharp, strong but flexible, man-cutting blade that had planted the *'Hispanic quality'* seed into the Chief Armourer's mind.

46

Galba declined the offer to open the 'Piece Chest' so Senior Armourer Ruben started to go through the less exciting squares: two sets of rivets. "Two – four – three – one, fabrica supplied short rivets. Three – two – three – one: short rivets from Memexma." The two armourers must pick one of the options today for a full resupply docket to be made out. It is a political decision.

The index structure beginning 'Two' immediately tells the armourers that the first material is from a government supply source, but one the Chief Armourer doesn't have to accept if:

'...the requirements of the Legion and good running and efficiency of said Legion are judged by appropriate senior officers or warrant officers, to be better served via the provisioning from alternate sources, the said officers (Senior NCO etc) accepting full responsibility and liability for such actions with supporting reasons for adopting non-commissary products made out ready for presentation if a request might be made by appropriate authorities.'

The second number in the index sequence, 'four' in this case, gives the province of origin, each province has an Army number, except for Egypt which has a symbol because everything's a bit 'special' in Egypt. Home of old weird gods and the phrase *'Well, we've always done things a bit differently here.'*

In this case 'Four' is Belgica, from the Army fabrica based there. The Army manufacturing centre for northern Gaul and both Germanias conveniently located some several hundred miles away and famously under the control of the second biggest thief in the senate. The biggest thief in the senate supplies the Belgica fabrica with metal and is building a sodding great big house in southern Britannia with Imperial funds, under the guise of gifting it to a local king who, frankly, would be happy to receive something to wipe his arse with.

This is the VIIIth's Camp Praefectus' view anyway.

The last two numbers in the four sequence were just invoice codes.

"So...the second lot of rivets from the private supplier is what you want? I..." Ruben shuffled out a papyrus from a stack. "...Have taken the liberty of drafting a 'Your belief that the legion would be better served...' slip." Galba opened his mouth.

"And, allow me to cut you off, Chief Armourer, as we have little time before you meet with the CP, by advising that I am not going to write the reason for selecting a non-Imperial supply source as: 'by not giving that fat thieving 'C word' the, square brackets, senator for aggressive civil libel claims, a wedge of government denarii for, square bracketed expletive, rivets that will split as soon as it rains.' Instead, might I suggest the following…" Ruben read directly from the scroll he'd prepared. "That the alternative private contractor is selected on a cost, delivery timescale basis and ongoing guarantee of supply to ensure His, capital Huh for emphasis of who we are talking about, VIIIth Augusta Legio's readiness and good standing with regard to the three grades of metal-affixing products as laid down in etcetera, etcetera." The Senior Armourer didn't wait for further comment, he'd always enjoyed the theatre and knew how the 'master-slave' scene should end.

"Please sign, Chief Armourer."

Galba signed and Ruben placed the papyrus in his leather document bag along with all the other papers to be submitted to the General Staff office later that afternoon. This was Ruben's favourite part of the day where he took some wine and hung around the GS area gossiping with people who could spell.

On they went; bronze screws II-IV-1-II, bronze screws III-III-II-II, various greases from III-III-IV-V to III-III-V-II (all locally made).

"I like three, three, four, nine from the Cherusci, it's a good consistency for running grease, but are we entirely sure that where it says in the notes 'rendered special cow' it's not actually 'Boii children'?"

The sands and woods they passed on quickly as *defer to department specialist'* then a further hour passed on rings and finished metals, the last note being 'bosses'.

"This is fresh up from the armoury creche!" Ruben gestured with his stylus to shield boss 'eight – five – six – two' (a white painted 'VIII' meaning Legio VIII homegrown, 'V' – weapons system/inferior).

"Oh…that's what that is. Because I wondered if one of the cadets just wanted a flogging."

The Chief Armourer pinned the shield boss in one huge hand and picked up ingot 'five – five – seven – three'. The noise was incredible. Ruben watched Galba smash the ingot again and again, pinpoint to the same place on one side of the curved apex, into the dome that buckled then collapsed like cheap tin.

The Chief Armourer had barely broken a sweat, he threw the crumpled boss on the floor and went to carefully place the iron ingot back into its grid square. Just before returning the metal to its ordered place in the world Galba turned the ore over in his hand and grimaced appreciatively at the unblemished lump, "Let's give 'fifty five, seventy three' another little production run, eh, Ruben?"

It would have been a good exit but because it was the Roman Army even a throwaway line needed a form so the two men filled out and signed a further purchase order for 'five – five – seven – three' and a 'Returned damaged subject to field test' for the boss, which Ruben would pick up and bag later for workshop return accompanied with some quiet words of advice to Lulla.

The sample room's thick wooden door opened, around it the massive square head of the CP, Camp Praefectus Craxus to be precise, appeared. A wave of the finger told the armourers they weren't doing saluting.

"Come on, Galba, we're having lunch."

Galba blinked, it wasn't quite lunchtime and he needed to pick up all the lists and reports for the…CP. "Yes, CP, I'll be along as soon as I've picked up your reports."

"Don't worry about that, come over as soon as you are done here. I thought we'd eat up on the Mess roof? Right, see you in a fifth. A quarter at the most."

The door closed and then reopened.

"Oh, and Ruben, send someone else over to the GS with the submissions today. This isn't an afternoon to hang about chatting like it's a tart's boudoir, in fact give it a couple of hours and come and join us, we have much to talk about." The door shut properly now.

"That's…unusual, Boss," observed Ruben with a raised eyebrow.

Galba thought, '*No daily submissions and precluded from the GS area?*' The two armourers looked at each other and thought, '*Mobilisation to defend and protect the senate and people of etcetera, etcetera?*'. They smiled. Action.

Despite the CP's injunction Chief Armourer Galba did, however, quickly stick his head around the workshop door on the way to the Centurions Mess, but Workshop Lulla wasn't in. Just old Senior Armourer Sibius laboriously handcrafting a set while his team of three bored armourer cadets looked on, ready to hand over a segment or rivet once asked. Old Sibius looked up and glowered at the lead armourer, but Galba wasn't in the mood.

Once a mobilisation order was announced he'd stamp this inefficiency out for the last time. The Chief Armourer then left the armoury complex, walking across the square towards the Cmess, which as Legio CA he was part of. Two military Tribunes walked the other way towards him, the armourer saluted "Sir." But they kept on walking without answer. No salute but one with a scowl, the other a weak smile. That was also odd.

A thought occurred to Galba – *'Had the Emperor died?'* His stomach sank and he made a mental note of all Legions' dispositions at present, something even the lowest of city legionaries could do at a blink within a season of accuracy.

The Centurion Armourer hoped this wasn't going to be *'Mobilisation to defend and protect the True Emperor, senate and loyal people of Rome etcetera, etcetera against the false Emperor, Senate etcetera, etcetera.'*

Everyone except one bloke and the right Praetorian Guard lost in a civil war but, as an armourer, getting parts was a nightmare. His old mentor Chief Armourer Ursus told a story about sneaking around a field in the middle of the night to swap parts with the armourer of the treasonous XVIth. The young Galba had asked what would have happened if he'd been caught, Ursus had laughed and called him a child.

"Of course both sets of staff officers knew what we were up to: if we hadn't made the exchange and worked all the next day there wouldn't have been a battle, or at least it might have been a bloody shambles below the dignity of Rome. You've got a lot to learn, boy."

The Chief Armourer smiled at the memory as he made his way past the Mess guard, then up two flights of stairs towards the roof. *'They'd probably given each other receipts as well,'* muttered Galba to himself as he thought about the old CA in some wheat field asking if the traitorous followers of the false emperor had any size three pliers.

Galba walked to the top of the Mess stairs then opened the door onto the… *'What???'*

A roar of laughter…"Look at your face Lucinius Vidii Galba!" The huge CP bellowed sitting under a red cloth awning thrown up over the roof. A Mess roof where broken stuff like crockery, drunken Centurions and Optios were usually thrown after a particularly heavy night, that had now been transformed. All the shit had been moved out, floor scrubbed and rugged, a white clothed trestle table, both the CP's batmen were in full uniform, including polished armour, holding decanted wines. The table itself was set with the best Legio silverware including the snack bowls magnificently engraved with the siege of Alesia. Common knowledge stated Old Sibius had made the bowls as a young man having been with Julius at the battle himself some hundred odd years ago.

"Camp Prefaectus?"

"Now I bet when I left you a moment ago, you thought, 'Well; plain as plain the CP is going to have me up as we are at the beginning of campaign season and he'll tell me that, once again, the glorious VIIIth Augusta will be mobilising to protect the da dee da dee da da…'. Right?", Galba just about managed "Right?"

"Except – here I am, up here, with all the best Mess silver out, the best wines…better fucking be the best wines, Curo!"

"They are, Honoured CP," the batman answered, deadpan, staring stock forward over the parapet.

"Good man…all the best wines, you heard him, Galba, and there you are standing like a drying fig and it's all been worth it because – your face! Brilliant. Curo, Bako, look at the Chief Armourer." They did as ordered so by the most powerful non-commissioned officer in the renowned Legion of the VIIIth Augusta.

"Look at him, because I want you to remember that face, boys, and when we're knee-deep in shit or bored out of our minds say to me 'Camp Prefaectus, do you remember the look on Chief Armourer Galba's face when you threw him his surprise lunch?'"

The CP belly-laughed some more and picked up two glasses of chilled white wine from a tray Legionary Bako was holding.

Craxus passed one glass to Galba and then loomed over his colleague expectantly, his physical presence if not menacing, then at least demanding. CPs got to their position having mastered a gamut of important skills: technical, diplomatic, logistical, but being a highly competent killer of the enemies of Rome was always going to be the first rung in the ladder. Even Galba was a little nervous this close up to his childhood gutter-runner-mate and with a furrowed brow began to think hard. They were obviously not having the first toast yet, Craxus obviously wanted Galba to work out the first toast: why they were here, what this full-dress lunch was all about.

The CP couldn't resist giving a clue, enjoying every moment of his game. "New orders came in this morning, Chief Armourer, hence the little celebratory lunch up here so we can survey this magnificent vista of…er…fucking German shit-housery. Don't take it the wrong way, but cutting all those trees down was one of the best things you ever did and you did a lot of good work here. I hate fucking trees."

Still Galba drew a blank, *'New orders had come in…think.'*

"Are we going to war, Camp Prefaectus?"

The CP signed in frustration, "That's your only direct question, no, WE are not going to war. Come on, keep trying."

"I passed two Tribunes on the square earlier. They didn't return my salute and looked at me as though I'd left the edges on their coccyx plates. The General Staff area is security cordoned, you aren't taking armourer reports…"

The CP almost shook in excitement and stuffed a few beetroot crisps in his mouth from the array of tempting 'VIIIth' silver-worked bowls placed on the fine linen tablecloth.

"Very good, Chief Armourer. Here we go – the command area is only off limits…to you and your department today. It's not official but the General's been raging since the courier came in at dawn. Took myself and the other fine gentlemen over there to stop him marching into the armoury planning room and chocking you to death with those fantastic pastries the cadets make. Now, I'm not taking YOUR armourers' reports. I can see your face, don't worry, you are not being court martialled or proscribed. It's much worse than that, old friend. WE aren't going to war. The VIIIth are staying put – but you, chummy, me old mucker…" Realisation dawned on Galba.

"This is your promotion lunch." Craxus raised a silver embossed cup. "To you, Lucinius Vidii Galba, Chief Armourer of the VIIIth, served eighteen years faithfully under the eagle, under this twice-august ancient legion. Fought valiantly, an honourable man made more honourable by his deeds, awarded three times for valour and two for service, faithful son and brother. Loyal to the Emperor, loyal to the Senate and people of Rome. I salute you, Galba. You're a good man and I'll be sorry to lose you – P&T, old friend. Up the Reds."

"Up the Reds." And the junior man staggered to his feet in some shock.

'Promotion and Transfer order'. Galba felt the wine go down his throat and it hit him. Eighteen years boy and man, through the bastard Polis training course with Craxus then…everything he'd ever done all under the VIIIth's banner, great Legion of Caesar. So old a legion they'd fought their first battle with bronze or so the story went – like most legion myths it was bollocks, of course. A legio with enough Mess silverware to buy the whole of Britain.

"Have a crisp, Chief Armourer. We are going to get properly fucked up and you are going to need a good base. You leave in two days, message marked *'Urgent and Mobilise'* – it's the whole department. Everything the General and the rest of us have been twittering on about over winter has proved wrong, the Emperor's not going to push over the Rhine. He's having a second crack back over the Danube and that's where you are going. You and the whole armoury including the artillery."

"North from the Pannonias into Dacia? So, who are we joining, the IInd, IVth or XIth? Who's lost their whole armoury department if the entire team's going? Camp raid or plague? The border up there's pretty lively, I hear, even following the last peace."

The CP cut Galba off and bade him sit. The sun was out and the breeze light but still it was cold and the two ex-Aventine urchins pulled over the thick wolf coats arrayed on the chairs; like proper soldiers they knew never to get cold if you had a choice.

"None of the above, hence the promotion, it's not just a transfer. This is the best bit: you've been 'asked for', sonny, and Galba, effective as soon as the General has calmed down enough to present you with a staff this afternoon, so shall you become a Centurion. Long overdue but that's the VIIIth Augusta for you, everything takes a while, and it's your own fault for being too useful."

Eighteen years with a premier old – the oldest – line Legion had its pros and cons; the preferential intergenerational treatment regarding promotion being a definite downside. The Numidian-Aventine Armourer had told himself none of it mattered, that 'promotion was bullshit and it was all about the work'. Galba's whole body tingled away that lie now he'd been promoted to the Centurionate.

Galba had only joined the Army because his mate Craxus persuaded him to go with. So, they both joined and got the VIIIth because the CP's dad had *'made an early withdrawal of funds'* from the legion. Meaning Dad had karked it on some field somewhere when Craxus was three, his mum getting a pot of cash from the orphans and widows funds with a promise that, should the little boy ever fancy it, there was a place for him in the Augustas.

Unsurprisingly, Mum wasn't keen and screamed at the terrified legionaries to fuck off out of it, keeping the money – obviously. Years later, however, she told the boy of the Legio promise as Dad's memory grew fainter and the family coffers lighter. Galba had kept his dad and wouldn't have changed that for the world but in the Legio Craxus's career had flown, he was a very good soldier but even so. Making armoury chief was also a real accomplishment. Difference was, no vine staff came automatically with it, and Galba would always be an 'adoption' not a 'child' of the VIIIth.

Craxus gave a wry half-smile.

"Not bad for two bits of Aventine Street scum, look at us Centurion Armourer Galba, kings of all we survey."

The Camp Praefectus waved at a midden where some long-pigtailed children were breaking the ice with staves; both men laughed. Then Craxus handed the Chief Armourer a slip of papyrus over the table.

Galba read it in surprise then looked up over the fort's wall, watching two small boys manhandle a block of jagged iced shit into a bucket to be carried up to the fields. "A new legion, well, well. It's now early spring and according to this I've got to get to Vindabona in two weeks. Fuck me! When's it supposed to be in the field, this legion? By the way, do you know what it's going to be called?"

The other man was being topped up with white and telling the attendant, Bako to also fill the red glass and then put some rehydrating beer on the table. "Probably early summer, you know the Army. The Pannonia Legions are still licking their wounds and at a fraction of full strength. Seriously though, we took a kicking in the last Dacian 'victory' and apparently the Emperor does actually now listen to the Army Council. If he wants to have another go pushing north, then it's got to be done properly. My guess is you have the campaign season then this time next year something exciting might happen. The usual 'border incursion' reports will, no doubt, be served up to the senate by Army intelligence as a pretext. Build up a head of steam for a fit of righteous affront to the peace and sanctity of a legal truce."

"Even if it's a small girl with a sharp stick and a goose on the end of a string?"

"Exactly, the bastards. Now, what's it called, this new Legion? Currently there is one proper legion in the field and twenty-eight bands of wankers, so the new legion – drum roll, please…"

"Will be called the Thirtieth Legion."

"You know the Army well."

"Is that it, for the moment? Do we get a name?"

"The Wankers? Galba's Wankers? The Tadpoles because it's near the Danube, see? Not named as yet. I'm sure your new general, fresh from his Etruscan estate, will come up with something appropriate as he surveys this band

54

of pubescents, debtors, paederasts and dodgy first-generation 'citizens' with the woad barely scraped off.'"

"The Screaming Death Eagles?"

"Yes, that's the sort of thing. Here's to the Screaming Death Eagles."

"The mighty Thirtieth, the Screaming Death Eagles. Who is the CO?"

"No one knows, it'll be a wanker. Where's the beer, Bako? Are you trying to get me pissed?"

The batman placed two big silver and enamel mugs of beer onto the table, the VIIIth's battle honours etched into the silver with rather well-done friezes of enemy being slaughtered.

"Now, you haven't asked me 'Why you?', Senior Armourer Galba."

Galba had been wondering this, but the Army and its workings were an unknowable beast devoid of any consistent pattern that could be made out. *'You'd have more success trying to panel beat salami than understand the workings of Army administration',* old Ursus used to observe. Craxus had said something, though: *'...asked for...?'.* Bullshit.

"Not fussed, CP."

"I'm glad you asked me that, so do you remember that Tribune with the funny hat who was here last year? You remember, funny green hat, asked lots of questions, liked a laugh, bit odd but not a complete PT, just your acceptable average clueless Joe. You must remember, he...there was something else about him...what was it now. Legionary Bako First Class, do you remember who I'm talking about?"

Bako was bringing up some hot, wet towels from the kitchen below but had caught the tail end of the conversation and knew what was required of him; "Yes, Camp Praefectus, Cornelius Ulpia Mako is, I believe, the individual you refer to."

"That's him, he had a green hat and there was something else about him...do you remember, what was it?"

Galba has drunk all three of his drinks in quick succession and was driving a scalding wet towel into his face knowing what was coming next.

"Perhaps you are referring to the fact he is the Emperor Trajan's nephew, Camp Praefectus?"

The CP exclaimed in mock realisation and reached over to swipe the steaming towel off Galba's face, under which the enormous armourer was attempting to hide. "Yes, that's it, funny green hat and he's – the Emperor's

55

Nephew. Knew there was something. So apparently, Bako, Chief Armourer Galba, soon to be Centurion Chief Armourer Galba of the XXXth Legio, has been appointed through his...royal connections!"

Craxus exploded in joy and waved for Galba to be fully refilled because, yes, they were going to get properly smashed.

Chapter Five

Salona Port, connecting the Balkans to civilisation
Sun's over the low-rigged Sadiki yard arm
Dalmatian Province of Rome

Fresh flowers were always on show in the trade offices of House Sadiki. If accounts ledgers came in from some far-flung two-room hovel over a Numidian caravan-stop-brothel that didn't show expenditure for flowers, then sharp notes were sent. That the nearest soil able to grow a flower was many hundreds of miles away wasn't the point. The House of Sadiki was a place where *'people should want to come and do business!'*

A typical note ran: *'Suggestion – pile up some coloured rocks inside a weird, massive local pot painted every colour of the dawn. Make an effort as there are enough shitty little rooms with loose plaster and wobbly tables in the world.'*

The House of Sadiki should be aspirational, its mistress felt, not just a merchant house that traded a wide range of goods that, seemingly, had little in common. Seemingly so, except to the Head of the House and First Secretary Eleazar who crunched the numbers on everything and operated the business, since her husband's long trip away, on a strict formula of margin, distance and weight punched into a political risk, weather and piracy/banditry model.

Commodities dipped in and out of the internal Sadiki index, seemingly at random to the outside world. House Sadiki would mysteriously leave and enter new markets, and the profits soared. In recent years reliability of supply had made a name for the House of Sadiki, which consequently brought in more premium long-term contracts, securing huge profits above the index's calculated track points. Everything had a value and the huge shifting set of indexed modulations were safely stored in Lassalia's and Eleazar's minds, perfectly synced with each other as they ground through options, possibilities and risks every early afternoon.

The House of Sadiki, Port City of Salona Office, where the Head of the House – in her husband's absence – was currently in residence, contained a riot of flowers, strange local vases and frescoes painted with the less oppressive cultural expressions of Egypt in addition to the usual muscular heroes of Greek antiquity. All interspersed by on-the-line naughty walls in certain areas. Lady Lassalia and First Secretary Eleazar had finished the morning office work and now reclined in the formal rooms of the ground floor, which were pretty spectacular even for the rich mercantile city.

She'd got a good price for this tall building near the port, telling the selling agent it was probably going to be used for warehouse space. Eleazar had simultaneously, and surreptitiously, bought up a series of small plots around the old house. An overgrown herb plot, a privy area, some waste ground covered in rubbish and an area of old laundry bins were collected together and the shell company applied for permission, through an agent, for a new tannery. News got out about the tannery and the big house's price rapidly went down, the purchase for the new House of Sadiki headquarters being completed at a significantly revised sum. The fictional tannery application was then turned down with the 'disappointed leather maker' disappointingly selling all the plots to the adjoining newcomer on the street.

After six months of screaming and more visible signs of Egyptian oppression, the builders had expanded the ground's public areas four times over with the kitchen moved, the courtyard wet area created, and a series of large hosting and client rooms configured. The Lady Lassalia sold the dreary old Sadiki sprawl, located up with the other houses in the suburbs, to a tannery which horrified her competitors' wives.

The civic bribe to push through the tannery re-zoning had been large but Eleazar felt the idea had also been irresistibly amusing to a certain member of the civil administration. Aulus Scipio Pallo treating the 'new money' and trade to, literally, the smell of the entire town's urine brought up the hill in evil barrels. When the suburban tannery opened 'the Scipio' made a point of going up there and ordering various leather goods he had no need of. Exclaiming to the local populace, holding handkerchiefs to their noses, about the quality to be found there, the finest leather in the region. "How lucky you must be to live so close to such a fine establishment! The convenience!" All the merchants could do, no matter how wealthy, was mumble assent to the patrician nobleman of one of Rome's oldest first-estate families.

First Secretary Eleazar and the Lady Lassalia lay in the smaller of the downstairs day rooms talking business.

"Alright, you are right, bump the route to an eight, but that leaves FX to a four and flax to a three."

"Flax is not a Three, it is Four."

"Flax is always a Three."

"Flax is a Four and you know this to be right."

A grumble "Yes I bloody do…"

"It was your suggestion last week, my Lady, and I agreed, if you remember…"

"I know, bloody hell, but price is at a One. Surely there must be…"

"The total advisability of the endeavour still spits out a Six."

The Sadiki Margin Index ran a rigidly adhered-to 'acceptability' range of between two and a half and five and a half. Above five and a half was overly risky or uncommercial due to all the bad, historically known usual inputs. Lower than two and a half was too much profit, a bubble, something missed: *'Why isn't everyone else doing it?'* Lies, a mistake, bullshit numbers. Three to four and a half was where the bulk of Sadiki profits came from.

But the Lady Lassalia still wanted to sell flax through the Ocxysx sea route to Brindisi and said so.

"You are the Domina, Domina." remarked Eleazar neutrally. By deferring to her rank, he'd underlined a point – she growled. They wouldn't be doing flax to Brindisi.

"Right, next my Lady: empty jars back to Thrace."

"A solid five, always been a nice empty-leg filler," The Domina signed the chit in front of her and handed it to a waiting runner before continuing.

"Double-packed wheat stops from Thessaly is now a six, I see, following receipt of new information relating to road quality, so instead what about wheat from…let's see, we have a tonnage versus speed issue between…which one of you buggers is going to make me the most money?" She was surveying a wax tablet with two supply orders outlined, held up in a large hand tipped with long oxide-coloured talons.

Lassalia suddenly stopped reading and looked up with a smile of real joy. "You know what, trusty and worthy colleague, we are having a bloody good year, aren't we?"

Eleazar smiled, "Yes, Domina, the House of Sadiki is well above the winter projections."

She waved a hand. "Cut out that 'House of Sadiki' shit, Eleazar. No...it's 'We', 'Us'. Now, I'm going to ask you the question again: do you want to be free?"

Eleazar shifted uncomfortably. "Not at this moment, Lady Lassalia, but I'm most appreciative of..."

"Well, what do you want, then? I think being free would be good for you. It's not a pair of balls, but let's face it, they're not coming back, but be your own...eunuch. Carry on working here and..."

"Perhaps just a consideration into my fund, for when I am eventually ready to take on your illustrious name and the honour of Roman citizenship?"

For years, since her husband had left for the Silk Routes, the Lady Lassalia had lived in anxiety over her First Secretary's repeated refusal of freedom from slavery until the patrician 'the Scipio' had sat Sobe down late one night, smooth bastard, and explained how senior slaves worked, especially clerical ones. Eleazar was protecting his legal position and the considerable finances he'd amassed, even if they were all claimable by his master (or mistress), by remaining directly outside of the civil courts as an individual. That was an explanation she could buy and was 'very Eleazar'. Now she periodically asked the First Secretary if he wanted manumission as a barometer of the long-term stability of the House of Sadiki; 'No' meant work still to be done, 'Yes' and she could retire and let him run it.

A cough, "Domina..." One of Sobe Lassalia's splendid-looking doormen entered the receiving room, dressed in the greens, peach and gold of Sadiki (a long, visual allusion to Egyptian trading heritage).

"What is it, worthy doorman?" the Lady asked without looking around.

The doorman announced that, "Imperial Quaestor Cornelius Ulpia Mako has arrived with his ranks of honour and all are now waiting in the atrium with the other clients."

"What the fuck is an Imperial Quaestor? Do we know yet?" Lassalia asked her First Secretary.

Eleazar gave the only fact he had on this previously unknown rank. "It's got four lictors. Shall we have a look?"

The doorman returned to the atrium, back through the tall, dark blue lacquered, bronze-studded doors. Cost a fortune.

Both the Sadiki managers banished the waiting attendants from the room then walked to a lascivious faun frescoed to the right of the portal. Eleazar used his fingernails to grasp two, nearly invisible, pieces of silk and pulled out a cut square of plaster a half thumb length high. They took turns peering through the cheeky pipe player's nether regions. The other side of the peephole was located beneath the shadow of a strategically placed wall vase, all but invisible from the atrium side, even if you knew where to look.

"The fidgety one with too many freckles and huge eyebrows? That him? He was here last night?"

"Yes."

"Did he enjoy himself?"

"Greatly, Domina. He challenged you to a drinking game."

"Really? Is that what the huge bruise running down his face is?"

"I imagine his night-time journey home was challenging even with civic bodyguards."

"Big bastards, aren't they? The Emperor obviously wants his nephew back from whatever jaunt he's been sent on."

The four lictors were massive, even by lictor standards. The bundles of axe-strapped rods were like twigs in their hands. In the middle of them fidgeted the short, wiry soul with dark unruly hair, hair struggling successfully to pop from under the oils poured on it.

"What's his name again?"

"Cornelius Ulpia Mako, Domina. Don't mess the Ulpia bit up." She turned and grinned at the eunuch.

The First Secretary added, "Apparently, *'Everyone calls me Hedgehog, even my mother.'* I doubt it is a sexual pun."

"Of course it isn't, look at him. He looks like a bloody hedgehog. The Patrician class, eh? Jupiter and Horus help us all! Right, let's go."

At a signal the heavy, bronze-studded double doors opened in sync and the waiting room full of clients stopped eating fruit or trying to edge towards the Imperial member. At the last minute, Sobe decided to go informal and smothering. "My little, little Hedgehog! I feel like death this morning, how could you make me drink like that? I trust I didn't do anything embarrassing?"

She chose right, that was part of her magic, as the young patrician's face lit up with a braying laugh; "Ahahah, no, my dear Lady Lassalia, you were…ahaha…magnificent…I perhaps did not conduct myself to quite the level that, er…ahahaha…some might perhaps wish me to…"

She grinned back, "Like the Emperor, perhaps?"

Mako, slightly sheepishly, smiled back, "Ahaha…no, I mean yes…definitely he would not…Is that a double negative, I can never tell?"

Lassalia moved across the atrium, ignoring everyone else, to the opposite side where two off-white ivory clad double doors opened as if on cue.

"I won't tell. Now I thought we'd go in here; the colours are a bit darker and I think we could all do with some calming visual ambience. Help me, though, Cornelius Ulpia Mako, I'm just a simple merchant's wife. Would your lictors like to come with you, or I have some refreshments laid out especially next door? I just don't know, what do you do with lictors? Why don't I have lictors, they are so nice looking! I've just got a bloody eunuch."

Everyone in the room laughed, no one harder than First Secretary Eleazar.

"Erm, well, I think they go everywhere with me, but, er…"

"We have wine, meats and snacks all ready for them next door served by my maid servants – but only if that's appropriate?"

"Er…"

A rumble emitted from a massive slab of man whose hair had managed to grow a month out from a haircut worn scrupulously for twelve years before being given this 'honoured duty'.

"I think you will be perfectly safe here, Lord. Any problems and we shall come running."

'Good' thought Eleazar. He had seen tattooed dots on at least one of the lictors' arms and believed these civic body guards weren't that civic in their forging. The meeting would go much better with them next door, fewer ears. In any case, if the lictors felt the need to 'come running' everyone in the house would be dead within a third-hour, of this the First Secretary was certain.

The dark client room was frescoed in deep blues with explosions of exotic plants and song birds. Four thin wooden columns painted in faux marble marked the corners of the triclinium, the floor was mosaic in shadowy geometric patterns picked out with white tiles.

The white edges had been retrofitted when there had been a few too many stumbling incidents late at night on the midnight-shaded floor.

"Lady Lassalia, your house is astonishing! If I, er, promise not to get quite so excited again, perhaps I might impinge upon your hospitality in the short time here for…for…oh, well, just here for…chilling?"

She bade the aristocrat and First Secretary sit on the couches. "Of course, come and just hang out, darl, I'll tell the doormen to let you in. Eleazar will join us today, if that is all right. He is my right-hand man while my husband is away."

The three sat upright on the cushions, the imperial relative refused wine and took some fresh, clear water served to him into glass, from glass.

"I would love that of all things, maybe not all, but definitely…I mean: Yes! Thank you. And by the way, Eleazar, it was very good of you last night, I mean – one of my men, well they're not my men, I suppose, one of my symbolic officers of…office, I suppose, well, anyway – he said…"

Eleazar gave an exactly appropriate sitting half bow that intimated it was both his pleasure and that he had no recollection at all of what it had been his pleasure to do. It had however involved sick and a fresh toga, the laundered garment would be discreetly given to one of the lictors by a maid.

The Lady Lassalia took a gulp of wine. "So, to what do I owe this double pleasure? You just couldn't keep away, could you? Careful, my husband might be travelling but he is a jealous man!"

The aristo gabbled that it was nothing at all like that and he would "…treat her as if she were his honoured mother…"

Eleazar locked his face as the Lady Lassalia gave a sideways glance to him. To move the conversation on the First Secretary enquired, "Did you come straight from Rome, may we ask, my Lord?"

'The Nephew' Mako nodded, "But I was only there in the winter. Last year I spent time up on the Rhine looking around, bit of a tour. My uncle wanted me to just, you know, have an informal look around. Identify good people, steady chaps, that sort of thing."

'Really? Why?' Both the Sadiki principals thought simultaneously, the communication passing between them like Telemachus and his Pa.

"So, then, back on the way home…nearly got killed by pirates… ahahaaaha… but they took me for some sort of, er, holy man…don't know why…"

'We do, you strange boy.'

"Threw me back on shore like – er, I don't know, a fish fishermen don't want – or do they want all the fish? Fishermen? I'm not sure. So anyway, back home I reported in and…ahhahhaha…bizarrely my uncle who's, you know…"

'Yes, we do.'

"…anyway, he was actually pleased. Bulls of Jupiter! Sorry, my Lady, forgive me. Mother says I'm a clever idiot. Father just thinks I'm an idiot but, as our matriarch always says, 'your father's not the Emperor for many reasons.' So, there we go!" Silence.

"Oh, right, yes, so then the next bit is I get sent here for the next…bit. As it turned out, I went to the Rhine for a reason, I mean an actual real one. I thought maybe it was just to give me something to do, or you know…ahahahah…to make sure I didn't come back, but Mother says I'm not really any threat to anyone but maybe myself. Hey, cripes! She's a sharp one. It's my other cousin, he's really good at things, a real, you know…thinks about stuff, and I was supposed to meet him in Germania but got the dates wrong and he'd gone back to Rome. But it was alright because he left me his notes. I saw my cousin when I got back to Rome and he said, 'Hedgie, you fucking idiot!' and we got quite pissed." Silence.

Cornelius Ulpia Mako mustered his train of thought and decided some wine might be a good idea after all.

"Could I perhaps change my mind about the…oh yes, thank you. You have an excellent cellar, Lady. So…there we were the next day after getting legless with my clever cousin, and I got called into the bloody palace. I was hanging. So, as it turned out, all the things I'd seen and done in the summer – using my cousin's notes, haha! – were, er, really well received, can you believe it?"

'Hmm.'

"Apart from losing all my cash on the first day playing dice with a legionary of the VIIIth…ahahaha…he was made to give it back. Felt quite bad about that, actually, so I did slip him a bit of gold and I think it was all right as a month later he stopped me from drowning when I fell off a bridge. Did you know they could all swim, legionaries? All of them. I mean I can barely, you know, sit in the bath. So, the Emperor said, *'Actually, well done, Hedgehog, your mother's right, you are a clever idiot, and that's useful to me.'* So, he then said *'I'm going to ask you*

64

a question' and I said; *'Right. It's not a maths one, is it, or something in Greek because I'm, er, really shit at those?'* and he said *'Shut up, Hedgehog,'* so I did because he's, you know, the Emperor of Rome and the known world and all…ahaha…so he asks me the question and I must have sort of, um, got it right because…here I am."

Both the principals of the House of Sadiki considered the Emperor's Nephew, their faces light, full of friendly amusement as the cogs whirred seriously beneath.

The Lady Lassalia adjusted her top to remove all cleavage; the young man obviously had a focus issue and all distractions must be nullified. "Well, you must have answered it really well because here you are, an Imperial Quaestor. Help me, though. Out here in the provinces we are a little secluded…"

'Which is why we expend huge amounts of money on a vast information network,' thought Eleazar. "What is an Imperial Quaestor?" she continued.

The young man frantically nodded his head trying not to snort wine out of his nose. "Yes, yes, quite. No one knows! I can tell you this much: it comes with four lictors." *'Right.'*

"My clever cousin says I'm the first and…ahaha…will probably be the last. He says the Emperor's done it on purpose so no one's quite sure what I'm doing. I mean, I don't, so why should anyone else…ahahaha…not even the Senate committee who gave it to me. It gives me enough Imperium to do stuff but not hang myself, Mother says."

'Interesting.'

Eleazar tried a light push. "So, what are you going to do, if I might ask? What was the question the Emperor asked you, mi'lord?"

Cornelius Ulpia Mako took a fig thoughtfully, chewed, then decided otherwise halfway through a nibble and put it back in the tray. Eleazar tried to radiate an infectious calm upon his mistress, but she had her flash points regardless of rank. Sobe was eyeing the half-eaten object like a volcano noticing an impertinent town had sprung up on its foot.

"*'How would you form a new legion, second nephew?'* that was the question. I thought He was joking at first. The thing is, though, He wasn't and I'm a bit out of my depth. But then yesterday I was told I should pop by here and I'm so glad I did, because I think you could really help – well, you know – get me out of the shit, really…"

The Lady Lassalia slowly leant forward, teeth bared, emanating crocodile, "Well, well, and may I ask, who shall I thank for this introduction?". Mako told her.

The Lady Lassalia stormed up the office steps and the house slaves prepared her bathing things. The House of Sadiki was going for a very angry swim.

Chapter Six

The Danube at high noon
Southern 'Green Zone' bank
Grey area within either Pannonia Superior or Inferior Provinces of Rome,
depending who you ask.

All peered north as the relay spoke.

"Smoke, smoke, smoke…" the legionary spotter repeated in a measured rhythm, arm held out straight, eyes unwavering from the coloured haze rising from the far northern bank.

The Tribune in charge of this specialist unit of Immunes was young but had made this position his own over the past six months, with some success. This would be the officer's fifth full-extraction mission.

"FCL, check please, if you would be so kind."

The veteran First Class Legionary moved up the branch-covered bank, behind the relay's shoulders, following the spotter's eyes and arm to a north eastern point downstream. "Tell me what you see, Relay," ordered the Tribune calmly, working through the set Exfiltration deployment process.

"I see coloured smoke, dyed purple, northeast and five stadia downstream on the limestone rocks."

"FCL?" their officer prompted.

"I confirm purple smoke within the extraction cone, Sir."

"Is it right and proper?"

"I confirm purple dye smoke within the cone…" and even though the FCL knew the answer to the day code, they all did, he formally checked the wax tablet taken from a belt pouch. "I confirm the day code, purple dye is a correct day code."

The young Tribune nodded, flash signals from the hill an hour ago and now smoke - this was it. Only then did he walk up under the low hanging branches to take a look himself: a thick lilac smudge drifted up over the river. Satisfied, the officer waved to the FCL to follow and walked downstream, under the rag-roped old fishing nets that concealed his forty men and the three, large river catamarans tied up to the banks. The boats were adapted parts of the XIth Claudian Legion's pontoon kit, all heavily refitted including with wicker palisades. Of the three-river craft the Gunboat had two Skorpion crossbows mounted in the central line, the Xboat – the exfiltration craft – held one similar piece at the back. The last carried large dangerous men with spears.

"Get the men ready, FCL, then go to your Triari. Relay! Keep doing what you are doing."

The Tribune arrived at a small yew tree at the far end of the Exfiltration team's line. On reaching a knoll he looked up, searching for the two unarmoured legionary scouts in the branches.

"What do you see, Werewulf?"

One scout remained focussed on the north bank while the other, older, wiry man twisted back and leant down. "They'll be back in the foliage. Sure enough, there's a horse patrol's been waiting for them. The riders are moving down river and haven't spotted the signal yet. You've checked it's the signal proper, haven't you, Sir?"

"Yes, I have, Werewulf, but thanks for the reminder. We are 'G' for Go." the Tribune now jogged back to the embarkation point which was teeming full of assembling Immuni troops. "Let's go, Exfil! And it will be hot, hot, hot. Launch order is: Gunboat first, Triboat, Xboat."

The FCL veteran already had his embarkation troops stood to in three lines and gave landing and cover orders in a few words. The Skorpion gunners and slingers boarded first with the Gunboat pilots untying slip lines. FCL's veteran spearmen, heavily armoured Triari, clumped up a plank, grumbling, on to their boat, with the Xboat team of retrieval squad and medics with stretchers boarding the third craft. Last on the Xboat was the fresh-faced Tribune leading this enterprise.

The FCL looked across the protective wicker panels to his officer; the Tribune was making a circling finger gesture to all pilots. "Here we go again" he growled. Legionary pilots returned the instruction with a thumbs up, the Gunboat captain doing so with a broad grin as he was now in charge, as senior pilot, and had a nice buzz on following dawn-light's breakfast with 'roots n' herbs'.

"'G' for Go children, hold on to your hats!" the Lead Pilot shouted across the deck, the message also picked up and passed along all three boats. Every boat-borne passenger crouched or lay down, gripping strong hemp ropes lashed to the decks.

The pilots themselves stayed standing with a rope in one hand and a paddle pole lifted upright out of the water in the other.

The Gunboat's Lead Pilot, bandana and sunhat shoved down hard in place, turned to the senior Immuni engineer standing behind three pieces of large, menacing-looking hydraulic apparatus, each contraption located flush to a boat's stern at the bank edge. Legio XI had been a long time on the Danube and developed the *'River Goat'* mobile dynamic launch system a decade before.

The Lead Pilot gave two parallel chops of his hands. At the signal pulleyed lines whipped up the camo nets into the trees. Shadows gone, spring noon-sun poured over the now exposed craft and their prone men.

The engineer checked everything was clear of the catamarans, no ankles in looped ropes which could really spoil someone's day and, satisfied, shouted, "RG Gunboat prep and ready!"

"Prepped and ready!" confirmed the Immuni engineer hunkered down by the downstream 'Goat' with his mate holding a ratchet handle.

"RG Guns, go!" shouted the lead engineer.

The two-man engineer crew repeated the order and pulled the ratchet down. A heavy looking series of ballasts hanging in frames started to move, an angry gurgling sound came from two iron-bound barrels that lay sideways on the bank, which began to flex ominously. The double rams rattled for a second within their stern mounts at the centre of the catamarans' central beam. Then with a hissing roar the hydraulics fired, punching the Gunboat forwards off the bank in a spray of water, bow skidding across the river's surface at right angles to the stream. Men held on for dear life, the Skorpion crews bracing themselves against the crossbow secure lines to give extra security to each artillery piece. The catamaran's bow skipped like a flat stone then dropped and the high, buoyant hulls sped forward reaching the river's midpoint in thirty heartbeats.

"Turn, baby, turn!" the Gunboat captain screamed ecstatically and his four-man crew fixed oars to raised static oarlocks and, standing, dug, sculled and rowed in frantic unison. The Gunboat's front now slewed downstream towards the far shore. For a moment, the boat's momentum fought the stream current and eddies sucked the port bow dangerously low into the water. Lead Pilot shouted in delight as the pilots knew their work well, locking then turning oars to 'pop-plane' the front back up again with a spray of foam, using boat speed to free the hull through its own force.

Lead Pilot shouted, "That's it, bambino!" then, "Set course and run." The pilots had brought the Gunboat within half an arm's throw of the opposite bank in under a sixth hour. Now the crew adjusted the track straight down the river, purple dye smoke rushing up to them on the port bow from the fast-approaching limestone rocks. Satisfied, the Lead Pilot transferred command to the fire team. "Up and ready. Over to you, Caller my man!"

The Fire Caller sprang up, ordering "Fire teams, make ready!" The two Skorpion crews untied the launch lines then ratcheted, arms rotating in a furious rending of torsion weight and spinning handles. A Crew chief broke open the leather canisters, pulling out bundles of long metal-headed bolts, passing them to the loaders. Each loader took a single shaft and dropped it into the stock grooves with a shout of "Set!"

Around the crossbows some of the best slingers in Claudius the God's finest legion busied themselves with laced thongs, Greek and Jewish citizens soldiers mostly – no auxiliaries allowed on the Exfil teams, that was a standing order. Stripped down to leather kilts the slingers fitted polished stones or darts into hide cupolas and held the 'bag' with their off hands 'ready and rocking' with the movement of the rushing boat.

The Lead Pilot glanced back to the home bank. Exfil's Triboat was somehow right behind them despite the launch gap and running fast. Senior Pilots of each boat looked at each other – understanding passed in the glance perfectly and adjustments were made. Without slowing the Triboat, heavily armoured old grumblers still crouched down glaring out from under their helmets, curved back up into the current and made for an overlapping course. The cat lost track speed as it did so, avoiding a crash into the Gunboat, now positioned ready to weave back in and deploy on the bank.

The Xboat was much further behind despite a clean launch and was just beginning its turn downriver. Lead Pilot saw a head bobbing in the water behind the command craft – new kid or unlucky, it didn't matter, they were all armoured in retrieval so the poor sod was done. He hoped it wasn't the Tribune, he was 'alllll-right' for a young officer, turning a blind eye to the late-night weird parties within the River Pilots' tents, as he did.

Gunboat Pilot now turns forward again, adjusting course more from feel than sight, setting straight downriver towards the growing violet haze. It took massive focus and a slew of micro adjustments to hold the bearing as, even with the worst of the meltwater gone, the Danube was sprinting today. An Eastward breeze brought the first tendrils of dye-sweet smoke over the boat. The Fire Caller shouted a warning from the bow that was impossible to hear properly, but through the purple cloud movement could be seen.

"Roxi! Roxi in the trees!" Lead Pilot screamed, then muttered "Raging hormones and bitter widows. Man, is that fucked up!"

"Priority is clear the Xpad!" shouted the Fire Caller to his gunners.

Nearly every man allowed his head to turn left as they rushed past the smoking signal smouldering on the limestone plinth. "There!" Just for a moment the Lead Pilot's eyes locked to another man's in the foliage, still as a fox and staring back; white red-rimmed eyes bulging out from a face full of dirt and exhaustion. The figure gave him a salute with two fingers crooked towards the sun and the pilot knew the man, recognised him from the Dark Cave. Lead Pilot's right arm made the private, bent-finger sign back before shooting up in a more public, elbow-bent half square for *'mark position'*, then up in a fist for *'personal confirm'*. A co-pilot leant back, looking for a return signal from the command Xboat.

After a moment the co-pilot bellowed, "Signal got!" – *Position is a-knownar-e-ar!'* thought the pilot with satisfaction. At that very moment, the Triboat, to direct starboard, dug oars hard into port, water sloshing up and slewing hard, careening towards the bank, just cutting under the Gunboat's stern by a thumb length. The Lead Pilot managed to pull his oar up in time to save the steering, and likely himself, from being shattered. In a few heartbeats the Triari catamaran passed behind them at right angles and the Lead dropped the oar back into the water to gain control. *'What a trip!'*

A thud of boat and bank shook the Lead's teeth in a way that can only happen to boat people. "Tri – Launched!" the Co-pilot shouted and the Fire Caller half waved in acknowledgement, his gaze, however, fixed on at least fifteen horsewomen racing towards them upstream along the path, only ten heartbeats from passing at most. The Skorpion controller slung a yellow bag, with a perfect arm, onto the bank ahead of the Roxolani and it exploded in a burst of fine yellow dust.

"That's your mark!"

The Skorpions adjusted accordingly. But a rending shout suddenly sounded from one of the boat slingers, the half naked man falling back on to the deck screaming, with a long, long white-feathered arrow sticking out of his guts. More arrows, each the length of a full ballista bolt but much lighter, smacked the deck or overshot into the river.

The Lead Pilot had spent a lot of time in the Fire Caller's company, because *'shit like this only worked if there was a relationship, you feel me?'* One of them should be explicitly in command right now, but that didn't actually work as well as just feel. For what was coming next needed a combination of speed, soldiers and ballistics.

"Sycamore! Right break ready – Break!" The Gunboat pilots slammed in two oars, spun the catamaran a quarter turn and then pulled against the heavy current. A flight of arrows splashed into the bit of river they'd just been in. Each Skorpion had readjusted, anticipating the rotating deck, and the slingers leapt out from in front of the artillery's maws. For a moment, the catamaran gently spun in the purple wisps and bright yellow dust cloud; the Lead Pilot marvelled at the experience. More yellow dirt was beaten up from the bank's path under fast, heavy hooves. The next command was simple. "Fire!" the Fire Caller screamed.

At this point, the Gunboat was barely fifteen paces from the northern bank, the thick reverberations from the Skorpion torsion bars thwacked, and instantly the yellow cloud exploded in a screaming bloody soundscape of horses and keening. The Gunboat slowed to a drift for the slingers, who couldn't see much even at this close distance, so released cracking missile after missile into the confusion of sulphur powder.

A screaming woman came out of the great jaundiced plume holding a sinew-hanging forearm up, jutting bone visible, tears streaming down a war-painted face and half a magpie headdress ripped off. Two iron slinger darts hit her immediately, the first with a hip shattering crack, deflected vertically up, the second a thick wet thud lodging into the skull above her ear. She dropped like a sack of turnips. In return two arrows flew out from the dust cloud, one glanced off the forward Skorpion, the loader yelping as the bone head snapped hitting him in the face.

The Lead Pilot shouted, "Bumbumbum!" and half rotated the catamaran again, the bow slewing round to face upstream. All oarsmen then pulled hard to lose as little station as possible in the current and provide effective fire support for the other craft. The Gunboat gradually slipped downstream, though, the river pulling the cat directly adjacent to the yellow cloud where the enemy patrol seem to have stopped. None had yet to gallop out on to the upstream path. That changed quickly as before another volley could be fired, mimicked birdsong warbled and the first Roxolani emerged from the sulphur clouds like demons, slung low to their mounts' sides, pushing on to get past the murderous boat.

The marker cloud began to settle, other riders could now be viewed wheeling their horses about, trying to make back downstream, but the path was congested with thrashing bodies and animal legs. Slingshot fire came thick and fast chasing the escapees, the Gunboat letting off a hail of metal darts, iron shot and shaved stones. The Roxolani within the dissipating cloud tried to shelter under bucklers but it was the horses themselves that were the main target of the slingers. A shot hit a horse in the fetlock, smashing the bone and the piebald messily collapsed, crunching the rider before tumbling off the bank into the river with a huge splash. The beast in the water was crazed and thrashed dangerously near the Gunboat's bow, a gunner took up an artillery lance, reversed it, and drove the placer tip through the creature's neck once, twice, three times before it stopped moving.

"Set!" both gunners shouted almost at once.

The Fire Caller screamed back, "Opportunity!" letting the crossbows off the leash.

Both gunners swivelled the Skorpions on the rotating floor disks the XIth engineers had created for the vessels, aiming at the upstream path towards the riders making a dash for the exfiltration zone.

WHOOSH! Suddenly everything was on fire, slingers and one of the Skorpion crew screamed as a burning net bag of oil-soaked leaves crashed into the deck. The hit Skorpion fired wild up into the air, the other gunner ignored the cinders falling on him, allowed for a last movement of the boat and wrenched the ratchet.

A single, heavy bolt with a sixth of an ingot's worth of fluted lead at one end, flew. There was more distance than the last shot, the aimer could see the arc was higher than he wanted. He'd been sighting for one, possibly two, horses, to slow the riders down and hold back the pursuit. Instead, this shot went up hitting the shouting head of a young Roxolani Initiate, exploding it into pink mist, the bolt carrying on into the trees. The girl's torso just sat rigidly upright, blood streamed down her body and legs, over the white horse she sat atop which just cantered to a lazy stop, to chew some grass. Both the woman's hands remained where they were, one holding a lance, the other a buckler shield. Just headless.

"Time to split!" shouted the Gunboat pilot. One of the oar team had gone down on fire, the slingers had stopped whipping their cords and were kicking clumps of fire into the river or dragging incapacitated, charred comrades to the far bow, pulling buckets and dousing the burnt or burning, screaming soldiers.

A slinger went to stamp down into the centre of the netted mess. "No!" screamed the Lead Pilot seeing a leather bulb pushing out from the netting.

Liquid fire erupted across the deck and engulfed the stamping slinger who ran about, roaring, like a torch, laying into his mates until the Fire Caller stepped forward and kicked him sole first into the river. Everyone still on their feet grabbed oars or beat down flames. The pilot tried an old bargeman trick of his dad's, lashed his steering oar, then planted it in the shallows near the bank making the catamaran spin stream-ward. The blazing Gunboat span around madly towards the middle of the river and away from the bank. The sharp turn then cut a deep slice of water with the outer deck plane and as the port bow came up again river poured across the deck in a great steaming cloud, hissing like a bucket of asps.

A last few arrows followed the Gunboat but the Roxolani patrol now focussed on the real hunt. The first horsewomen who had survived the yellow marker were riding hard upstream towards the purple smoke. Not relying on the Exfiltration team actually turning up, Infil Two had positioned himself downstream of the plinth behind a quickly set up 'Whites Delight' – a neck-high trip raised as a rider passed and named after the infamous racing team. Two pulled hard, the cord flicked taught breaking the neck of the first, pigeon-adorned women, but the second rider brought her lance down with conviction onto the trip.

She'd seen Two in the bushes and pushed past her companion's whining horse into the scrub ready to stab down, dagger handle, into the now running man's back. Two had left a nest of inch long caltrops in his ambush position which cut short his imminent sticking. At the moment of her thrust, the second rider's mount went berserk, screaming as the iron thorns pushed up into unshod hooves. Rearing to spin away from the pain, the chestnut mare's back legs also trod on the spikes and the creature thrashed itself, bucking the rider forward into a tree trunk to crash flat down on to her back.

The rider exhaled, completely winded, and tried to move. The last thing she saw was her prey of the last seven days, eyes opened in horror as a filth-smeared demon leant in. Two clamped her mouth shut, more out of habit than necessity in the open battle, stabbing his dagger at the point her chin met the wind pipe, up into the base of the skull. He gave the knife a twist, a crack sounded within, a rush of dark blood from the wound followed, claret pissing out from the nose, mouth and ears.

Satisfied, Two ran full pelt through the woodland upstream, until the cover narrowed, forcing him on to the river path.

He didn't need to turn, Two could hear the next riders right behind him shouting into the gallop. Ahead was a line of welcome steel and shields, however, and he might just do it.

Two gave it his all, not thinking of anything but *'Run through it.'*

The heavy legionary spearmen, veterans to a man, observed the dirty, disgracefully-bearded running individual with some interest. Not much, though.

"Two denarii if he makes it."

"If he touches, if he makes a shield touch, right here," the other vet said, tapping on his huge shield with the long spear.

The other man frowned. "No. Proper makes it."

"Fuck off, you won't let him through then I'm two denarii down."

The FCL's voice sounded behind them; "Shut up, no one's betting on him, no one's not letting him through. He's gonna make it, that cunt owes me five denarii for a start. RUN, SERGIO, FUCKING RUN!"

"Jupiter, is that Sergio? Looks like one of those marsh creepers."

"OPEN!"

Two ran full tilt at the shield wall, not slowing, which opened at the last – very last – step then he was straight through the formation's rear, and just kept going, not turning, to where he could see the Xboat approaching the bank right on the pickup point, wreathed in the purple smoke signal.

"Ungrateful bastard," said one of the gambling veterans.

The shields closed instantly with a clatter, the enemy riders pulled up in front of the veteran spearmen in time but suddenly four legionaries rushed out with a speed that defied their age, surprising the women who had expected a static line. One heavy spear went into the chest of the leftmost horse, another through the stomach of the wheeling right. Both mounts reared and twisted but the grizzled old veterans, all heavy spears and armour, pushed into the crashing beasts. The other two spearmen stabbed into the necks and flanks of the creatures, ignoring the riders trying to turn and stab down with the feathered cavalry lances.

A horse is a big animal and they take a while to kill but the Triari were expert anti-cavalry troops, using their spears to pin and cut into vital organs. In less than a minute, the mounts were down, blocking the path, twisting and kicking but losing strength. One scarfaced legionary bounded over a dying brown cob. A sickle knife flashed up at him but the horse warrior below was held fast by the weight of her dying beast. A red-feathered band around her head and copper colour war paint down both cheeks, she was a young one. Suddenly the horse warrior could see there was no escape and yelped in terror.

The old legionary gripped her wrist and crushed it until the sickle dropped, then knelt on her shoulder and methodically ran his fingers under the horse hoof cuirass. Pulling one of the dragons teeth up, he exposed the overlap where the chitinous plate was sown to the jacket then slipped his wide-bladed pugio knife up through the fabric, a twist of the blade and a wet hiss – he retrieved the weapon and moved to the next rider who had been thrown.

This one was older, one of the 'bitter widows'. Legs, ribs and one arm smashed, she was trying to crawl back down the track. An armoured shin plate crushed into the rider's back, a be-ringed hand hooked under her chinstrap and the dagger crunched through the back of the neck and out the throat. The veteran then grabbed her weapons belt and heaved the newly dying body up between the two dead horses, a colleague doing the same with the younger women pulled up atop the cob.

The four legionaries fell back behind the blood-soaked barricade of bodies and with five marched steps the whole Triari line came forward to join them.

Down the path the remaining horsewomen thundered up two-abreast towards the veterans.

"Turn and set a thicket!" ordered the FCL.

The Triari turned side on, spear butts dug into the dirt backed by the trailing boot, heavy shafts lowered to the right of each shield.

"I think we are ready, you old bastards!" the Triari leader shouted to his men, then turned back to check on progress behind. The Xboat had made the bank and was holding, kedged with two pilots positioned downstream, oars jammed into the mud. The Exfiltration's retrieval team was hitting the bank, pilots driving pinions into the earth with 'ready wrap' hold lines attached for a 'touch and go'.

Then the leader of the veteran cavalry-killers heard the faintest of hoofbeats and, even given the valley echo, his well-attuned ear told him they were coming from the wrong direction.

"Bollocks!"

Exfil Tribune had already been alerted to the new threat. Two boatmen always kept a lookout back to the observation team on the home bank and forward to the Gunboat in order to triangulate a greater field of tactical awareness. Just before the Xfil boat hit the bank flashes came from Werewulf's obs' post up the tree in the Green Zone, followed by a single tasselled, whistling arrow fired by the old scout upstream, behind the command vessel. The arrow wasn't meant to hit anything, just note a direction. "Sir, Obs post report possible contact upstream." The Xboat relay held his arm directly toward the area where the marker arrow was aimed.

"Come on, let's go! We have a west contact." shouted the Tribune. The pilots onshore continued to drive pinions into the bank with heavy hammers then leapt back onboard with the preset lines, leaning back to brace against the spring current. The fully armoured Retrieval Lead ran forward onto the limestone ledge kicking the small, smoking fire out of the way. "Get that out he roared!" to his second who smothered the signal with a wet blanket.

"Gemini! I repeat, Gemini!" shouted a voice from the bushes.

"Lucky Twins, Lucky Twins. You are clear to move…"

"Gemini coming out!" shouted the Skipper from the treeline. "Don't fucking stick us!"

"NEW CONTACT – RIDERS!"

"Fucking move! Gunner, take them out!" screamed the Tribune from back on the catamaran deck, sighting the cavalry charging full pelt towards them from the west now.

"Yes, Sir!" The Skorpion gunner on the Xboat fired almost immediately and the bolt shot out towards the newly-sighted squadron thirty paces away upstream. The missile didn't make a clean hit, the tip clipped the bank and spun into the lead rider, whose horse stumbled for a moment before picking up rhythm again. The Roxolani horsewomen gave a war shout, "Ayayayayay!" driving their mounts to new speed.

Out of the treeline and onto the limestone shot Six, Four and Five carrying Three, followed by Point and Comms, then finally came the Skipper having done a last check. "Where's fucking Two…?" he shouted and took one step forward onto the bank's track.

77

Running full pelt on the same path, Two almost immediately crashed into the Skipper as the Infil's boss stepped out from the bushes and they both hit the ground in a heap. "Stupid wankers!" the armoured Retrieval Lead cursed and the huge unit head picked up both filthy men by their rigs and carried the pair bodily onto the escape boat.

"Go, go, go!" screamed the Tribune. The Infiltration team were thrown unceremoniously on to the catamaran and the pilots released the slip lines then made straight for the oars.

Without shore ties, side on to the current, the boat quickly backed and wheeled round a preset kedge anchor. In a few heartbeats, the craft was whirling out into the stream, running past the moored, Triboat still lashed to the bank.

"Typical," muttered the veteran FCL watching the others pull away.

"Go, go, go!" shouted the Tribune to the Triari on the shore who were fighting the downstream horsewomen over so much dead-piled flesh.

Upstream the new mounted warriors screamed in rage at the Infiltration/Exfiltration Teams' escape but, seeing the veterans with all backs turned and fully engaged, let up a great shout and picked up the gallop…into more screaming carnage. The lead rider's horse flew up, jumping crazily.

On the Xboat Two, watching the agonised horses, sprawled back on a sandbag and grinned.

"Must have dropped my spare thorns, youse bitches."

"You really are quite unpleasant, Two," panted the Skipper. "Aye, that I am, Sir."

The rearing horse crashed into the bushes, two riders behind dismounted and walked forward kicking the caltrops off the path and into the river.

At the Triari line, neither the legionaries nor the mounted riders could find an effective reach over the dead-piled bodies. The FCL knew it was time. "Pull back and recover! Alternates, release now by the numbers."

Every other veteran took a step back, hefted the long spears up into the reverse grip and flung a volley at the riders. A few hit and the rest caused a moment of retreat. Using a step and scrape motion, the Triari line pulled away up the path. The FCL directed the line backwards, his spear held down lengthways into his troop's backs, then artfully curved the withdrawing formation around towards their catamaran, each soldier turning and leaping onboard at the last moment. Except for the front rank. By the time the forward spearmen had made it to the embarkation point, the upstream riders were upon them and four of the downstream women had dismounted, clambered over the dead bodies and ran at the retreating force with long-curved knives drawn.

The FCL leapt to the front of the veteran rearguard sword out, smashed a boss into a fighter dressed as some sort of giant angry kestrel and slashed out at a fetlock. A veteran next to him took the full force of a horse-driven lance into the neck while his chest was smashed backwards by following large animal, flinging the legionary off the bank, over the starboard bow and into the river never to be seen again.

"Push, Eleventh Claudian! Eleventh Claudian, push!" screamed the FCL and the remaining veterans drove forward with shields up, spears slashing legs and horses in a desperate rushing scream. A flicker of black shapes. Everything suddenly exploded in spraying blood, dust, screams and splinters.

Something heavy crashed into the FCL knocking him face forward on to the path. His breath knocked from him, head swimming, he tried to push himself up but a wave of dizziness sunk the man back to the beaten earth. Everything was strangely still and quiet, a Roxolani warrior staggered in front of him blearily. She was unmarked, weaponless and gazed unfocusedly around like a drunk – she looked just like the FCL felt, the old legionary thought. Someone then chopped her head off, which seemed a bit unfair.

The FCL began floating upwards, somehow. He was looking straight up and moving. The blue spring sky was nice, all golden cold sunlight with small puffy clouds. It was nice, pretty nice and quiet. Just floating.

"Is he dead?" a faintly familiar voice sounded. "Two denarii if he doesn't make it back."

"Back through the gate."

"No, not through the gate, just if he doesn't make it…"

Chapter Seven

Night party, small overflowing roof, Argentorate Garrison
Probably the Rhine border
Lower Germania Province of Rome.

It was far into the night and Chief Armourer Galba's lunch had grown, the small roof of the Centurions Mess was crammed full of well-wishers and both invited and uninvited guests, particularly one guest who was taking up a lot of room.

Galba sat on a chair next to Camp Praefectus Craxus enjoying his two new gifts. The first was a silver cup emblazoned with the symbol of the VIIIth Augusta, set within the usual exquisite work of legionaries killing Gauls from past glory days, with wine topped up to its brim. The second gift was even more satisfying…a vine staff with brass ends, the base engraved with his name, the top carrying iron studs for legally hitting Roman citizens with, if the mood took him.

"I mean, it is symbolic, but your vine staff's got a good weight to it. It's functional and you will be surprised at how useful that is sometimes, but only when you need to. Restraint, you see, Galba? Remember old Centurion…balls, what was his name?"

"Pallas, CP."

"Right, yes, him. Jupiter! He got up and hit his barber, then hit the Mess orderlies at breakfast, hit his Optio, hit his…I mean it just used to be a day of hitting."

"He hit both of us quite a lot. Do you remember losing our tent?"

"Oh, he gave me a right good hitting for that, Galba."

"Didn't he break his vinestaff on your arse?"

"That's a bit of a myth, but one I don't discourage. Thing is, do you remember why he stopped being so fucking hitty?"

Galba nodded. They both thought back to the hot, midday sun many years ago at a rest break when Legionary Mecs, Legionary Mecs exiled Prince of Something-or-Other and a massive German bastard, had been overcome in the heat and wandered a bit too far away from the civilised norms of Roman society. Young Galba had been eating an apple at the time, watching the latest explosion of rage from Pallas, then been be quite surprised when big Mecs had simply picked up the fully armoured Centurion and thrown him off the escarpment to disappear for good in the river a long way below them.

Obviously, there had to be a big show of discipline, but no one's heart was really in it, everyone knew the angry little bastard deserved it and life subsequently got better for everyone, even the officers. Except of course Mecs, who's life ended after a long-drawn-out and painful period but – rules are rules, and you can't go around throwing Centurions down ravines when you feel like it, especially when they are sadistic crazed dickheads.

The guest taking up a lot of space had started shouting again, "Let's all sing a song…again…let's sing *'March to dawn goes the boys…'*! Yes. Come on now!"

Everyone started singing *'March to dawn goes the boys…'* for at least the fifteenth time because it was tradition and also because the very drunken initiator's *'Let's…'* could be construed as an order.

"General's completely wasted, Camp Praefectus Craxus," Galba whispered in the chorus.

"Yes, yes he is, newly minted Centurion and Chief Armourer Galba. Now fucking sing!"

It lasted just one more verse as the General didn't quite have the mental focus to get any further and conversation continued.

Galba beckoned Ruben over. Neat, assured and sober, the armoury second approached greeting the pair formally. "Chief Praefectus Craxus. Centurion Galba, may I congratulate you properly on your joining the Centurianate."

Craxus spoke first. "You may. Now sit down with us, Ruben." The CP turned around glaring at the huddle of junior officers next to them sat in a corner, this was the Centurions Mess after all. One officer was obviously destined to go far as he took the hint and vacated his seat for the enlisted man.

"How long have I known you, Ruben?"

Ruben sat on the folding canvas seat and crossed his leg to keep the cold out. Without looking, Craxus reached behind him again and pulled one of the Mess wolfskin cloaks straight off the shoulders of the second young officer, nearly launching him from the parapet, and threw it at Ruben. The man made to protest but instead decided to shut his mouth. Years later, he would tell the story with pride at a senatorial dinner about "Salt of the earth, old Craxus! When I was a young Tribune up on the barbarian border…"

Ruben took the fur. "Thank you, Camp Praefectus. To answer your question, though, I think it must be…at least ten years, Centurion, since our paths first crossed. Two years in you helped me into my current position at the armoury and most grateful I am too. My thanks."

Craxus and Galba raised their cups in salute. "I must have seen something in you, young Ruben, to have sent you to our renowned armoury and, if I may say within the natural boundaries of rank, to friend and comrade Galba."

"Centurion and Chief Armourer Galba, actually." The new vine staff waved in correction. "Get that thing out of my face or I'll shove it up your arse, Galba. Where was I? Ah, yes. You have done well, Senior Armourer Ruben, you obviously lived up to that spark of talent I saw, fanned as it were in the bellows of the furnace."

"You always get poetical after your fifteenth drink, Craxus."

Ruben knew not to join in with Galba and Craxus's 'banter', instead nodding his further thanks with a reminiscence. "I remember the very day you transferred me to the armoury, Vulcan smiled upon me, and your words have been my guide throughout the years, Camp Praefectus."

Craxus leant back on the chair, furrowing his brow; "Really? Good. What did I say?"

Ruben took a sip of wine. "That every man must know his merits and let those merits be employed in their place for the glory of the VIIIth Augusta, the Emperor, Senate and people of Rome."

The Camp Praefectus furrowed his brow further. "Did I actually say that? Seems unlikely. Good words, though, I like that…All dignified and shit."

Ruben nodded in confirmation. It was an exchange between men who worked closely together for time measured in decades but kept in strict relationship to each other.

Galba practised pointing his vine staff. "That is odd, Ruben, because I remember Centurion Craxus bringing you over at rapid march and saying *'Legionary Ruben, you are a fucking shit soldier, you sound like a poof, you think being funny isn't going to get you and everyone around you killed – by the way,*

I know that dirty, filthy but well-drawn graffiti was YOU – so I'm giving YOU to Chief Armourer Galba who will find a use for YOU or make sure YOU have some sort of horrible accident involving a winch!'"

Craxus nodded in appreciation. "That does sound more likely, I have to say. Although you were Second Armourer Galba then because Ursus was Chief. I know this stuff; I can give you the fucking month of all your promotions. Go on, ask me one." He pointed over to Workshop Lulla scoffing his face at the side buffet. "Acinius, workshop lead twenty-two months seniority, Menicitrix next to him fifteen months seniority as fitter. I can do it in years if you want? Or I can rank everyone here by their commission date…Ask me one."

Ruben did. "Old Sibius?"

The Camp Praefectus shouted in protest. "Oh, fucking hell! That's cheating! I mean he's – what? a hundred years old? I mean, he was a hundred years old when we joined. If I had to guess, he was last promoted by Caesar. The first one, our one, big Caesar…although not as big or as important as the current one. Obviously," Craxus added, just in case anyone was listening.

Galba beckoned over batman Curo for more wine as this had veered into politics, and while a CP was a CP, just better not to. It was also an alchemical fact that Craxus would alter subject if you refilled his glass. It worked. "Still, young Ruben, you aren't the worst soldier I've ever sent to Galba. Donkeys' balls, I'll miss your team except for that little Hispanic anti-Legionary. Hope you're going to take his bedmaker with him as they might not be as soft as me in the XXXth."

Both armourers looked at Craxus with some incredulity as this last statement was uttered without any irony.

"The only reason I've stopped harassing the Hispanic for filthy habits is because of what the little sod's done with all the pieces. He's another one I sent to you, Galba. You see I have a gift for talent and you just thought I was sending over every shit useless bedroll-creasing twat I could eject from the line. Point is though, talent should be rewarded and Centurion Galba and I have been having a chat. He would like you to be his Optio, Ruben, in addition to Second Armourer. Technical Optio."

Galba reached forwarded and clasped Ruben's arm, the junior man's savoir faire dropped for a moment. "Thank you, Camp Praefectus, Centurion Chief Armourer. I would be honoured." The three smiled and would have enjoyed the moment a little longer but a tripod of burning coals was knocked over by a hulking figure.

"Careful there, Sir!" Craxus said, immediately sobering. He was halfway out of his chair to 'lend aid and assistance' but was waved down. Everyone froze, ready to help, but the head of the Legion steadied himself, grabbed hold of Bako's shoulder and then had a long noisy piss off the side of the roof. The General felt better for this, turned and walked a few steps to where he push-pulled the chair out from the last still sitting junior officer, who he politely told to fuck off, and crashed down next to Ruben, who in turn sprang up to attention.

"Who the fuck are you? SIT DOWN!" Ruben sat back down.

"This is Optio Armourer Ruben, Sir," Craxus intervened.

The General squinted at Ruben then clinked a toast with the armourer. "Very good. Been with us long, Optio?"

"Ten years, Sir."

The General processed this information. "Ten years? Good. And have you enjoyed being with the VIIIth Augusta? We are so august we are twice-august, august augstatatar. Did you know that, little Optio?"

"Yes, Sir."

"Answer the bloody question! What has been the…best bit?"

Ruben paused. "The marching, Sir."

Galba and Craxus took a quick breath each as they measured Ruben's answer, it was certainly edgy. But then the General burst out laughing. "'The marching, Sir!' Oh, goodness me! Ah yes, a soldier's answer, the honest joker! Lucio the Legionary, eh? The Roman Legionary, the perfect being. And an Optio, it's the best rank in the whole army, an Optio, did you know that…Optio? I wish I could be just an Optio. Get things done, not like these…fucking these…fucking Centurions. With their fucking…" he waved at Galba and Craxus who were expressionless and knew their General of old in the rare evenings when he really decided to tie one on.

"…fucking all this…bits of fucking stick."

The head of the Legion's gaze worked to focus on Galba and the General leant forward, "They even got you in the end, eh Galba? You were a good man, good armourer. But in the end here you are, with your baton. I'm glad I gave it to you; do you know why I didn't all these years?"

"No, Sir."

84

"Because I wanted you to do some fucking work rather than rushing around being a Centurion. All the shouting here and there and endless problems. We all know the Optios and armourers do all the real work." The General clasped Ruben around the shoulders and demanded a refill from Curo who was hovering ready to make a full bodyweight catch. "But, Centurion Galba, now you're leaving the VIIIth, THE EIGHTH! One of Caesar's Legions – the first one, not this fucking one…"

Everyone on the roof pretended to be looking at the midnight black nightscape of the local Rhine area. "The actual Caesar – and now you are leaving to go off and be part of some new legion, created by our newwww Caesar. I've given you the promotion because it's time you had a holiday. Fuck off to Dacia. I've got men here, like young Optio Rudi…here…who are going to work hard and bring new glory to the old VIIIth."

Craxus's eyes bored into Ruben telling him this was not a time when his attention to detail would aid the good of the Roman Army by reminding the General that the entire armoury had been transferred.

The General stopped, looked down, beckoned, and noisily threw up into a golden scrolled VIIIth Legio spittoon, deftly produced by Bako. A laugh sounded and Craxus whipped round in his chair, the trio of officerlings blanched with fear and went back to looking at the fascinating lamplight coming from the village brothel.

The General then randomly threw his wine cup off the roof asking for a beer instead, sitting for a while sobering himself. "I really thought we were up for a campaign season," he eventually muttered somewhat mournfully.

Craxus nodded sadly in assent. "I know, Sir."

"I am obviously…disappointed, Centurion Galba. All the work you and the teams have done, I'm not blind to it. We have, we had…I believe…the best artillery in the whole of the Empire. You did that. Now you are going to have a crack at the Deccis, that's a secret by the way as they've got a treaty, but that's where the action will be. No second front across the Rhine, you shall be fighting on a different river. As of tomorrow, you are not of the VIIIth, but I want you to know, Galba – you will always be of the VIIIth. Carry that honour with you into this…XXXth Legio. Fight hard, win honour. Don't disgrace us. You will be a little sister Legion to the Bulls, make sure they really know that, Galba. Your legion."

Galba straightened fully and stared back at the General, "I will, Sir. Thank you, Sir."

"Now, I really should go to bed. Camp Praefectus Craxus, thank you for your invitation and hospitality."

"It was our honour, Sir."

The General stood in a fluid move as did everyone else, the informality dropped in a moment, ingrained in everyone present.

"Good night, gentlemen."

"Good night, Sir," everyone present returned.

"Best of luck, Centurion Chief Armourer Galba. You too, freshly appointed Optio Ruben, those pictures you used to do on the latrine walls, me fucking a pig with Helga plaits, god that was funny. Make sure you take enough of those charcoal sticks from stores before you leave. Christ knows if they've even worked out how to do charcoal in Pannonia. I'm glad we found a use for you. You are a prodigious finder of talent, Chief Praefectus."

With that, the General turned and walked straight as a die across the floor and down the steps as though he was fresh from his bed, leaving a slightly stunned Ruben.

"He's a class act, gods love him," stated Craxus not without a little emotion.

"To the VIIIth August Augusta – the Bulls! – and the General," he added to the floor.

The toast was returned with gusto.

"Now he's gone we can really start drinking." Craxus turned first for refills, "And we are going to properly fuck these up behind us…" then to the three fresh-faced officers, "Young gentlemen, it would be an honour if you would come, sit and share a libation with us, two humble Centurions with our newly appointed Optio."

What happened three hours later was never told at a future senator's dinner as there was just not enough nostalgia in the world to tint that memory.

Chapter Eight

Danube, midstream
Daytime
The Pannonias.

Three double-hulled boats drifted with the Danube current. No noise other than the rush of water and wounded grunts as the medics worked across the vessels. The Skorpion gunners still standing scanned the north bank but the horsewomen had turned back into the forest some miles ago, unable to do much and exposed to the deck-mounted crossbows flinging bolts of discouragement.

At the rear of the convoy on the Xboat, the successfully retrieved Infiltration team lay about dozing or drinking and eating under the crisp sunshine. Worn down by a sleepless week of evasion, only the Skipper still sat upright with murmured exchanges passed between himself and the younger Exfiltration Tribune. The Infiltration team leader clutched the packet to him, a bulging, oiled black leather bag, toggled shut at the opening. Five ate an apple, Point was fully asleep bent backwards over a sandbag, Three was properly bandaged up and attended to by a medic cooling the fever with a river-cold cloth pack. Two leant into Four back-to-back, both heads slouched down, while Six swapped raid souvenirs with a pilot for 'something exciting' in a flask. Comms diligently finished his notes, passing them to the Skipper, and hunched himself back against the wicker gunwales, staring downriver.

While the Exfil officer talked with the Skipper he maintained a watchful eye on the forward boats, swapping communications using the bow man as a forward relay, a leather cone held up bellowing updates along the squadron. The fire was long out on the Gunboat, the worst hit of the three vessels – a Skorpion knocked out, listing slightly and the catamaran visibly blackened.

The Gunboat had taken a large number of burn casualties and when safely out of range of the contact area the Exfil officer had ordered a close up of the squadron, allowing medics on to the other boats. The medics and the pilots did all the work now, during the passage downstream. Bandages and salves were applied, wounds were bathed, cloth picked out of flesh where possible – make do and run for home.

Casualties were, however, lighter than the Exfil Tribune could have hoped for. This whole area was so hot now he had not really expected to see the Infiltration team again, the 'Green Zone' was a fiction. Arriving by wagon at their pre-selected station the Exfiltration team had set up and sat in silence, no fires, waiting on the southern shore for a week. In that time they'd seen Roxolani scouts, Macromanni levies and mercenary foot patrols at least once a day. On the third day, hulled down under the camo nets, Werewulf spotted coracles with armed men crossing south above them, doing the mirror image of what the Infil team were tasked to do: information and alarm.

Two coracles paddling with a line that allowed a ferry of horsewomen over the river. There was nothing to be done, that was not the Exfil's mission, and they could not risk revealing the extraction cone's position. Three days of arduous journey by road to then set up the pontoon boats, artillery, camo nets and assemble the dynamic launch apparatus could not be wasted.

For those five days waiting the Exfiltration team just prayed the enemy were raiding further into the Green Zone hills and not slipping in behind their positions. If attacked it was a fight the Legionaries could win but any result would completely compromise the primary objective. The Special Operations Group, to which they were all now tasked – 'The Remnants' as the Immuni specialists designated themselves – had made it very clear that enemy patrols were the sole responsibility of the local Legions. The river troops had seen one foot patrol of the IInd, it had passed on the upper pathway just a half throw from the Exfil camp. The sector legionaries hadn't seen them, just walked straight on, tramping Westward.

Werewulf had also warned the Exfil officer not to make the IInd aware of their presence, so the officer hadn't. This was the officer's fifth extraction mission and he'd quickly learnt to listen to the team of river specialists handed to him.

The Tribune now looked across the water to the Triboat worrying, they had taken wounded and lost men in that last dash to get away. The FCL leader went down leading the aggressive shove forward that had got most of his men off, just as the Skorpion volley fire hit. The veteran leader seemed to be sitting up now,

88

but leaning heavily on three tripod stacked spears. The FCL's helmet was also off which was a bad sign, the veterans usually wore their helmets to bed, as far as the young Tribune could tell.

Seeing the Gunboat was now listing even further the young Exfil commander ordered the Xboat to take over the lead. It was slow progress, they and the Triboat constantly putting in oar brakes to allow the burnt craft to catch up, preventing the small convoy from splitting. All this navigation was carried out by able pilots, however, and the three boats managed to hobble along in the middle current. Washerwomen looked up from the north bank and ran, the gunners opened up sending bolts after them and into the undergrowth. Anything that moved on the north shore was fair game today and the artillery pieces fired periodically at any life, or even suspicious clumps of bush or wind movement amongst the trees. It kept them sharp and the north shore's head down, the Exfil officer knew, so let the gunners get on with it. Following the occasional clank, twang and whistle of their outgoing fire.

Turning back to look over the stern, the River Officer eyed the Lead Pilot over on the Gunboat and waved, receiving a wave back from the grinning maniac in return – all was good, or he was completely wasted.

Inboard the murmured exchanges with his brother Tribune were uncharacteristically bleak. The Skipper was usually irrepressibly upbeat, it's what made him so suited to wandering around hostile territory hiding in ditches. This new black, evasive humour from the Infil Lead unsettled the young Boat Tribune, especially as they were now heading home.

But then that was the problem, home wasn't really home anymore, now it was just another base following the Immuni's abandonment.

The base area in question eventually made itself visible as the final river bend in the squadron's journey revealed the bare, mangled north shore. 'Before', at every opportunity, XIth Legionaries would cross the river to burn and chop away the foliage facing the southern fort. This had been going on for all the years of the XIth Legion's deployment at the fort but now the dead zone was sorely neglected, even coming out of a hard winter. The forest break wasn't as stark as it should be. Early spring growth was already springing up, scrub, ferns, grasses and small trees.

A few months and the great scar in the wild, that allowed the parapet guards full vision of the main hostile approach over the Danube, would be taken back by nature. The crossing point was still quiet for the time being, long Macromanni race memories held the collective stories of what happened to anyone making the river in force. Only ambitious young men with too much drink tried it, to be mown down by the heavy ballista fire of the rampart overwatch teams. So far it didn't seem that the hostile's spotters, of which there were always some – in all seasons and weathers – had ascertained that the fort wasn't what it had been, known once upon a time locally as the *'the Pike'* on the bend. Or the enemy were just waiting for the right moment.

As the catamarans eclipsed the last turn Exfil Tribune had the flagman signalling. Brigetio fort was a riverside permanent legionary base, heavy wooden stockade, artillery locked into place with all banners flying. Today it all seemed to look normal but the boat signaller checked his day codes and sent a series of flags, one in each hand; blue cloth/pink cloth.

The eastern tower of the fort had a flat roof with a wicker palisaded Comms nest atop it, always manned. From the birch woven parapet a signaller could be seen making shapes back – blue cloth/yellow cloth. The receipt signal was checked against the day's codes by the Xboat's Flagsman and, with a nod to the Tribune, was acknowledged *'good'*. It was now decision time as to whether to leave the safety of the midstream and the Exfil officer took a moment to survey the fort scene; men with a cart, legionaries on palisades, an old git with hunting dogs and a boy with a pig.

A single fishing vessel was tied up illegally on the military quay, its owner waving at nets, no doubt full of fish to sell, while an angry Roman soldier of the shore crew shouted soundlessly back. Exfil decided all was good, gave a downwards signal with his hand for his Xboat's lead pilot then made for the quarter pilot to pass the message back through the convoy that the landing stage was 'G' to go and make in.

The Xboat quarter pilot flashed hands back to the two, trailing helms, then set to work. Oars turned in perfect synchronisation and the three catamarans fell off, angling southward cross current, slipping a quarter-ship at speed to the quay. The Shore Master had obviously got the approach message from the signals tower, and had his men bargepole the fishing boat off the mooring, cutting its nets lines and pushing the screaming owner into the river. The fisherman and his family would go hungry but a life had been saved by this piece of arrogant Roman imperialism as the Xboat flew towards the landing stage.

At five feet Co-pilots threw out drogues then, still moving at pace into the quay slot, the command boat hit an arrester line held by dragging shoremen, before coming to a jarring halt, pinpoint to mark nestled into the third landing stage. Shore crew threw out more wicker fenders and the Xboat was softly squeezed into its slot against the duckboards. The Gunboat was coming in damaged, but the Lead Pilot was a master, stopping the boat dead at the arrester despite the wallowing left hull. More shore teams jumped into the water following the dead-stop, lashing pigs' bladder floats to the boat in case it sank, a platform trolley already on standby for recovery and repair. With the Triboat whispering into the second berth Exfil Tribune looked around, giving a double thumbs up to the pilots and Shore Master for disembarkation.

Waiting by the Brigetio fort jetty a medico evac cart quickly loaded up the wounded onto stretchers. Fitters and shore crew helped the able team members down, making sure they didn't stamp on the 'no step' yellow-painted hatchings of the catamarans' soft parts.

Less welcome visitors were the three grey tunic'd SOG leads. The trio waited to one side while the area cleared. Boat pilots made safe, tidying up to hand over to the Shore Master before going on a hard bender. The Triboat veterans tramped away in full lockstep towards the fort, ignoring the protests of the crews to be careful of the canvas. The last of the injured, especially from the Gunboat, were 'stretchered and stacked' on the medico carts which then raced straight up, thundering through the gate, to the infirmary. Apothecaries and medics running or riding with them all the way. The Infil team were awoken and, carrying their stinking kit, swaggered down on to the landing stage, all except wounded Three in the evac wagon.

Six Infiltrati team members stared at the SOG leads as they walked past, the three grim-faced intelligence officers ignored these men, instead clamping their own gaze on the Skipper, the last to disembark, holding the oiled, black packet. Point to Comms clambered aboard a waiting, covered, cart flanked by night-robed contractors, which moved off at speed to the 'House'. The old administrative centre of the XIth and now the special quarters and debriefing area of the SOG.

The Skipper's long-limbed walk brought him up in front of the grey robed intelligence 'persons' and he raised the oilskin package. With nods, all four walked together at a brisk pace through the fortification's gates.

SOG's interview rooms had been a happier place for the Skipper once upon a time, when he had first joined the XIth Claudian, an actual Legion. This one had been a recreation room with a nice view, with nice chairs out of the sun where officers could come and relax. There had been a barbecue out on a patio. Now the view had been bricked up and all six planes of the space whitewashed; even the wooden table was whitewashed. The Legion had taken all the furniture when it had left last summer, what was left was stools. The Skipper had been on the lam for over a week and really wanted a chair with a back.

So, here he was- stranded. The old Legion had taken 'everything worthwhile…', as the FCL always joked, '…not including us'. The river Immuni were now all legionless legionaries, 'unattached', cursed to wander the earth in the grey half light of 'Intelligence'.

No one had even told them what was to happen. Just like that the teams were expunged from the rolls of the XIth while 'out' on a job. Fifteen days away on that last summer's mission. The cats had pulled round the bend, expecting approach signals but there were none, no nothing. Exfil Tribune had ordered the three boats to draw up short. All of the small force then spent two days observing the fort for any signs of life before gingerly making their way inside, weapons drawn.

Everything was gone, supernatural soldier explanations began to form until a note to the Skipper was found nailed to the admin door. This was when the entire River Immuni had been assigned, even if they did not yet know it, directly to Army headquarters at Aquincum in Pannonia Inferior, under something 'new' called the Special Operations Group – they were no longer part of the Legio XIth Claudio.

That's when the fort wasn't home anymore, some of the XIth banners had been left up on the palisade walls to cover the redeployment but the Immuni's home had been quickly taken over, whitewashed. After three days of waiting in the fort having to hunt for food on mission-exhausted legs or buying from the town to the south at exorbitant prices, a ragtag of politicos, strange rankers, mapmakers and mercenaries started appearing.

It was alright for the Legionary pilots; they had always been apart from the rest and life in the hashish tent went on practically unchanged. For the other Immuni – the Infiltration, Exfiltration, Shore Teams and Triari - especially the veteran spearmen – they felt bereft, discarded as their line cohorts went off goodness knows where.

When the SOG organisation arrived in full, they deemed it correct to replace Brigetio Fort's long-gone legionaries with various weirdos. Couriers, strange cargoes and spies constantly moved in and out of the gates. The whole admin block, now known by the SOG as 'The House' – where the Skipper now crouched – was completely off limits without invitation and full of unsmiling civilians that could occasionally be seen bustling about on the upper balconies. The House was cordoned by guards, not Army but Assyrian mercenaries, black-clad with long, curved cutting blades, and answerable only to SOGI.

This was the man that now came into room 'RIV'. SOGI, probably equestrian class but could be from anywhere. Thinning sandy hair, maybe forty, lean and always unarmed in a grey tunic. He looked like nothing.

SOGII and 'The Scribe' followed their leader in through the sole door. The Skipper stood, exhausted but one last surge of 'fuck you' hauled him up for a debrief. The Scribe, a miserable looking Etruscan, placed a tray of dates and watered wine down before the Infil team leader. Sugar and alcohol were not a kind consideration at such a debriefing interview, nor was it optional to eat as sustenance had a purpose, so the interviewee gulped down an entire beaker in one and tore through two brown fruits. Skipper fought down the sudden exhilaration in his blood. He resolved himself. The more clear and thorough his report was, the sooner he could go wash and sleep.

Collectively the SOG didn't even bother to welcome Skipper back, just waited at the walls staring at their subject. The officer was glad of that at least, fuck courtesy, fuck feigned politeness. Years of service to the XIth Claudian, including that desperate retreat from the swarming Dacians, all now nothing. At the end of last summer his Legion had just pissed off while they were 'out'. He'd lied to the men about the nailed note waiting for them, made it seem like there was a plan Skipper was in on, that the XIth needed the River Immuni to do something meaningful but still loved them. In fact, the note had just read *'Stay put'*, signed by a junior Tribune with a blue wax seal stamped using their general's borrowed signet.

The SOG continued to watch the bedraggled officer clutching a bag, leaning on the crisp walls, trying not to blink. Certainly, they were not eating or drinking. *'Was it poisoned, the dates and the wine?'* Skipper wondered. It would make no sense but then it didn't have to, not with spooks. SOG was apparently created as, famously, the local legion's own military intelligence hadn't seen the great Dacian king and his war host pouring across the Danube years before. *'Confined cattle raids as leverage for long-term discussions'* was the last legio brief the Skipper had seen, three days before everything went to shit and fire.

'Focus,' thought the Skipper and he started to open the oily black bag. The Scribe recorded everything.

"Item I: Package reveals forearm cut to the elbow. Pertinence: Legio tattoo mark, number expunged by scarification, thunderbolts and eagle still visible. Locale fifty starta north of drop at enemy training camp. Observed one hundred Macromanni combatants training in formation throughout one day. Trainers appear to be Legio deserters. Infil team retrieved Item I from night-time insertion into training camp." The Etruscan intel scribe etched an addendum to the verbatim note onto his wax tablet; *'[SOG senior team note, rate Priority I with doubt. Verify from own sources, second proof needed.].'*

The Infil Skipper continued pulling findings out of the stinking oilskin.

"Item II: Package reveals gold bracelet with horseman. Infil assertion is Roxolani-Sarmatian, confirmed eyes on and by Exfil team – Sarmatian female Initiates operating within the area as previously advised." *'[SOG senior team rate Priority I to II. Confirms active military alliance on northern borders? Verify from own sources, second proof needed]'*

The exhausted Skipper brought out more stuff from the package, methodically arraying Infil team's collection on the whitewashed table where SOGII would then place a numbered tile marker next to each item. With every piece of intel retrieved from the fetid greasy bag, the Skipper made a description. An arrowhead lifted from a train of laden carts complete with the vehicle's direction, speed and the fact the wagons were covered in straw.

Receipts for silver bits given out by the Infil to charcoal burners, wandering children, tinkers and even a band of highly surprised bandits who gladly exchanged all they had seen for precious metal, having awoken to daggers at their throats in the middle of the night. With the receipts signed, the Infil had then killed the bandits anyway. Yes, the team divi'd the silver, but bandits were bandits and couldn't be left to roam around. If left to do so, before next noonday, the thieves would be happily selling on the fact a Roman Infiltration team was wandering around what was obviously fast becoming a major mobilisation zone.

Long stalk hay wrapped in wax paper was carefully retrieved from the bag, taken from a big store behind the far hills. Southern Macromanni farmers didn't store with the full stalk so this harvest-type was of particular interest to the SOG. The sample would go off to the agriculture analysts in the House to ascertain the crop's origin. Supplies outside of the kingdom were coming from somewhere, most likely this was from Dacia, but evidence was needed.

Broken pottery from a large pile of the stuff. On site, Four had thought it just rubbish at first. Then Comms had meticulously picked through the broken shards and found makers' origin stamps stating the stores were from Sarmizegetusa Regia, the royal capital of King Decebalus of the Dacians. An earthenware shard was now picked up by SOGI, who turned it in his hand while listening.

Finally, a human head bound in sticks came out of the dark sweaty bag. Bearded and earring'ed the Skipper beckoned the SOG leads to smell it, which they did without hesitation. The hair was oiled and perfumed – sandalwood from the east – with an old cut down the lips. The earring itself was special and Skipper prised it off with a knife and held it up for inspection; it was a Roman equestrian ring fashioned into a lobe adornment. Obviously cut off a dead Roman officer in some disaster in the last twenty years.

Exotic perfume could mean a noble, ruling class whether it be Germanian or Dacian, but the scar and the fight he'd put up in the wood said successful mercenary to the Skipper. The Infil Lead hid his distaste that the SOG interrogators just inspected the inscribed gold ring then placed it on the table with a numbered clay tile without comment. If this was a Legio debrief there would have been respect and a solemn undertaking to return the family seal ring to its rightful family. Not with the SOG, though, this was all very different.

The questions started then; the 'whys?'

'How do you know that?', 'Did you actually see that?' Pick, pick, pick. The Skipper knew each of his team were going through the same thing somewhere else in the House and prayed Two didn't kick off again.

More wine, figs and honey cakes were brought in and the officer was ordered to *'get comfortable'* as *'the process'* would take a while. Finally though, the two SOG leaders stopped questioning and stared at their filthy stray for some minutes.

"I think that is enough for the moment." SOGI stated, standing up and with two knocks the secured wooden door was unlocked and he left. SOGII also rose. "Time for you to go, Tribune. We might need to talk to you again so be available, won't you?"

'In a fort, in a forest, on a hostile border, under military discipline, I should be unavailable?' the Skipper fought down the urge to respond to this last bit of bullshit. Three knocks and a black-robed Assyrian guard came in, making a follow gesture to the Skipper. Holding empty, soiled kitbag with his rig slung over a shoulder, the exhausted Roman officer did so, down a dark corridor lined

with doors. He noted each old Legion door was now fitted with an external lock. Scuffling and splashing sounds came from behind one portal but the Skipper shut it out of his mind, followed the contractor downstairs where an external door was opened by a second black-robed desert killer.

Outside it was just still light. A fresh evening and the Skipper breathed in two sacks of clear spring air. The Assyrian guide escorted him all the way to the House perimeter, the boundary staked with 'no pass' markers painted in red, white and green paint and constantly patrolled by the mercenaries. At the boundary edge, the Assyrian looked at his charge and nodded a farewell, palm to chest "Farewell, Tribune". The Skipper looked back surprised, the contractors never normally gave a thing away, so the Tribune returned the salutation before walking across the old parade ground he had grown up upon.

His feet walked themselves all the way up to the new Infil quarters in the old General's apartment. The SOG team didn't seem to care about precedence or tradition, all the spooks just holed up in the House, windows shuttered and bolted up. On arrival, in the dead of night of course, a week after the Legio XIth had buggered off the horses and carts of the SOG leads had arrived. They'd woken the Infil team immediately turning the scouts out of their old bunks, in a small dorm by the admin block, and told the Skipper to put up in the Legate's rooms. This didn't sit right at all with the Immuni scouts and they had gingerly picked their way through the hallowed quarters of their old general's rooms.

Pretty quickly the Infil team got used to the change of surroundings, though. The Legio XIth were never coming back, the general wouldn't suddenly walk in to find them in their skivvies. The only uniqueness was that they were now in the only rooms not whitewashed. As the Skipper entered the rooms he wished they were freshly blanco'd though. The old frescoes picked out over years by the best artificers in the XIth Claudian set against the mess of bedding, cook pots, soldiers' weapons and clothes sprawled everywhere depressed him. Four and Six had also spent a drunken night drawing moustaches and cocks on most of the nymphs. The team's weapons were always clean but other than that they'd let military discipline slide a long way. No one gave a shit and everyone just focussed on what kept them alive.

"Skipper on deck," drawled Six at the officer's entrance through the door. Across the adjacent rooms men slept or just nodded an acknowledgement. The Infil Tribune was offered a bowl of hot soup from a pan bubbling in the ragged firehole left behind, ornate bronzework stove ripped out and carted off with the rest of their life. Skipper sipped the broth and asked after the injured Three. Three was at the medicae and sleeping, apparently. Skipper made to leave and go down to the apothecary's, his limbs protesting with the effort, but Six rose quickly, hands up.

"They gave him a draught, Sir, he's out. Eat and sleep, Skip, see him tomorrow." Still the Tribune hesitated.

"You're covered in dirt, Sir, you can't see him like that," added Four sitting on a rush mat.

Five now wrenched himself up from the rush mat floor and took the stinking black bag from his Top, chucking it to Four who threw it out on to the back balcony. The Skipper was led to his bed in the corner of the adjacent room, the soup bowl taken from his hand. His rig, tunic and leather cuirass were then efficiently stripped off by the crew who sat their Skipper gently down onto a raised cot. Moccasins pulled off, a quick but thorough clean of the feet was made by Four, inside the toes and around the heels with a stained rag. The soldiers then gave the officer's face and hands a wipe before efficiently stowing the team lead into his bed. Blankets were brought and tucked hard over him into the cot's base. Once done, Four and Six saw the Skipper was already asleep. They took the Skipper's equipment and started cleaning it wordlessly. Sometimes you forgot the habit of full sleep so they'd just have to wait for it to come.

Chapter Nine

Salona municipal bath complex, not the 'members only' section
Late afternoon
Dalmatian Province of Rome

Salona's bath complex sucked in trade money like a running sluice. A multi-pooled leisure complex with outside pools, inside pools and every scrubbing, scraping and other – informal – service available. The lockers were mostly secure and the water even got changed with a small village's worth of night slaves scrubbing and mopping for the entirety of their lives, unless they nicked something, then it was a short walk down to the galleys.

Lady Sobe Lassalia and First Secretary Eleazar changed into bathing gowns and got lost straight away. Usually they both frequented the segregated female areas or a spectacular, invitation only, section full of mosaics and overly prosperous floating elites. Their quarry this afternoon, however, was perverse and never frequented the mosaic, free wine and nibbles vaults but instead liked to 'slum it'. Mistress and slave took another turning down a long brick lined corridor, leading to a massive outdoor pool for afterwork plebs. They crossed it and were completely unable to find the red door that was supposed to be there.

Instead, a green door presented itself whereupon they descended a long staircase into a labyrinth of hanging white drapes, discreet-cubed masseuses plying their trade, and what sounded like a particularly noisy blowjob.

In frustration, the Lady Lassalia hit a fat male backside the other side of the 'slurping' sheet, producing a yelp, and loudly advised the women in there that, "You're not charging enough for all the effort, love, whatever it is he's paying you."

An angry male face popped out of the drapes and quickly retreated back in. Too late, Lassalia had seen him. "Where are my bloody tiles, Muvo?" she screamed at the cubicle.

"Wednesday, mi'lady, I promise!"

98

"Yea, you're 'on it' aren't you, Muvo? Eleazar here is going to give the girl a denarii to use her teeth, you lazy little shitbag."

Eleazar didn't, but instead gave a coin to the bath bull who had appeared, scowling at the sound of trouble. The ex-wrestler grunted, took the payment and gestured for them to jog on. So, around these old baths they went, corridors, mermaid pools, endless stairs, green hot baths, a plaza, into a gym of sweating men.

"Sorry, we can't stay, boys. Are you for sale? I don't care what your civic status is, love, think about it." Cackle. "This is fun, Eleazar. What do you think, girls, do I fit in?"

"You are Aphrodite, Domina!" the benched prostitutes called back.

"Aw shucks, gives them some money, Eleazar. You're all so sweet. Didn't I sell you? I thought so, glad things are going well."

More aimless wandering until the House of Sadiki grew bored, grabbed an attendant and had Eleazar pay him one now, then one on arrival to their destination of choice. Off the old bath slave went, bowlegged down a long dark set of steps, through a lower-class changing room and a foot bath so rancid she invited a new bull to carry her over it, which he did with a certain amount of mutual amusement and a light grope.

Then they were there, Bowlegs got the second coin and scuttled away. It was a dark domed hot pit with cloisters where things went on in, on and over the stone benches in the recesses. A single oval opening at the top of the brick dome letting in light as bathers bathed in very hot water.

"Sobe, what a surprise! Dear Lady, come in and enjoy the heat," exclaimed Aulus Scipio Pallo, flashing an amused smile to Eleazar, who returned it.

"What an absolute shit-hole!" the Lady Lassalia sneered, walking down the steps as the Scipio politely asked a nice young man, in his best Greek, if it would be at all possible to kindly make way for the merchant scion. The Greek fluttered his long black eyelashes and said it would be his pleasure. Sadiki submerged herself to the neck for a few moments, Eleazar sat on the bath steps, legs together with calves in the water.

"It's bloody hot, I'll give you that mi'lord."

The aristo laughed. "I am a connoisseur of life and this is the very hottest pool in the fair city of Salona, one of my many futile discoveries." Elbow resting on a step edge, rock hard white body jutting straight out into the scalding spring water, the civil servant continued; "So, to what do I owe this unexpected pleasure, 'milady?'"

She snorted, knowing that Eleazar had exchanged a string of pithy little notes all afternoon to ensure this encounter occurred. Educated boys, I ask you.

'Never answer anything directly' was the first rule of trade. "Do you like my earrings, Scipio?"

The Patrician did; they were gold loops with gaudy sapphires.

"I thought I'd come incognito as a prostitute. They rather work, don't they? One of those maids of mine, who was a professional, did my make up. I think I blend right in rather well down here."

Amusing the Scipio was key to getting anything out of him.

"It is all excellent, but no amount of artifice could mask your aura of virtuousness. It's practically sweating out of your pores, the virtue that is. Also, those earrings are really gold all the way through. I will make you a present. Lavinia, my sweet, would you come here?"

From a stone bench down came a girl, anywhere between sixteen and thirty depending on the light, or lack thereof, to glide through the green water, smiling.

"May I have your loops, Lavinia? I have been admiring them on your little circuits of the pool and wish to make them a present for this esteemed lady friend of mine."

Lavinia wordlessly took a circle out of each ear and presented the pair to the Lady Lassalia with a low bow, showing her tits off to best effect – you never knew.

The Scipio liked to be a connoisseur of everything, even a whore's earwear. "These seem to be the real deal; genuine foiled copper. I always imagine the girls have to buy a new pair each week because they must just dissolve away in the waters."

"You are sweet. Please, darl, take these…" Lavinia's eyes widened as she was handed the Lady Lassalia's Midas loops. "…And put your lovely adornments in my lobes." Lavinia dipped the copper earrings in the hot water, gave them a wipe, then stood and carefully inserted her old pair into the Sadiki earlobes.

"Great tits, by the way."

"Thank you, Domina. Hold them in the coldest water you can bear each day."

The Lady Lassalia arched her eyebrow at Eleazar to make a mental note of this tit bit.

"Now, do I look like a proper whore?"

"Not at all, Domina."

"Only as a candle to the sun, Sobe," the Patrician smarmed with a half smirk.

'Got him.'

A single finger movement from the Patrician banished the prostitute back to her grotto, gold in hand.

"Now, Sobe, you have a new fan."

"That's the basic premise of hookers, Scipio."

"Not her, another fan. One who only this morning exclaimed 'She is sent by both Mercury and Isis!'"

The 'She' in question knew she'd have to endure this repartee but it still kindled her ire – there was so much to do back in the office. The aristocrat prided himself on only speaking the truth, but only the bits that amused him to do so. This last statement confirmed the worst, that the proposal made by the nephew earlier in the afternoon was serious.

"Is this Army contract being offered around, Scipio? The Veneii? Clachos? The Greeks?"

The Scipio pulled a face. "No, no. Whatever gave you that idea? No. There is not a government tender process here. Or at least not at my low level..." Lassalia just about managed not to roll her eyes.

"There's no bid or scope of works being issued hence I am here floating about not working hard. This contract comes from the very top. The Emperor orders his nephew to get the job in question done and quickly, without all the normal rigmarole of equal bidding by the local Governor's office. Remember; this has got nothing to do with Dalmatia province, even if there was a tender. We are just a grateful host and temporary scenery for the mighty endeavour before you."

Sobe slapped the water with her palm. "I have not accepted anything."

"As I was saying, this is from on high. If its ballses up, those involved won't be answering to a senate committee in a year's time or filing cross and questioning letters into the *'don't give a fuck'* box. Eleazar told me about that box, most amusing, I must build one but then I'd just put everything into it."

"Fine, so you don't care because it's nothing to do with your province!"

"To be fair, only if it goes well am I truly apathetic. If it doesn't, we are all in the soup. So, this project…what are we calling it, by the way?"

Sobe scowled, "Project Bankruptcy? Project Misguided Nepotism?"

"Project Invictus is the official designation," put in Eleazar, Scipio chuckled. "Dear me, the thing is – Project 'Invidious' has to go well. So, Sobe, go and do whatever it is you need to do for Rome then after six months we can all relax again. I mean we've all seen our Governor's own lictors, right? Yes, the Governor has more of the rod carriers than the gilded nephew, but you've met those four. Did you see the dots on their hands?" Eleazar nodded. "Now that's a set of lictors that really says 'Imperium' regardless of the number. It is a very clear message to those in the know – and I do know about these things."

The Lady Lassalia dunked her head under and screamed before coming up again. Scipio frowned in concern at her submersion in the dubious water but the Head of House Sadiki was famously robust. "Alright, I don't know. 'The Dots', you were talking about them earlier, Eleazar. Let me into the little boys' secret club."

Eleazar leant forward a little just to be on the safe side. "They are a special type of legionary tattoo, Domina."

The Patrician piped up, wanting in on this act as the straight man. "Except that it is perfectly normal for ex-soldiers to serve as lictors. Soldiers, builders, loyal trusty sons of toil from back at the family estate."

Eleazar half-conceded the point, like they were doing excerpts of Plato. He then continued, "Except 'The Dots' these four civic guardians have inked, mark them out as 'not just legionaries'. They are Praetorian Guard."

Saying it out loud, not even the first-estate-born administrator fancied cracking a joke.

"Actual, real Praetorian Guard? What? They've served their term? Can you be an ex-Praetorian Guard?"

Both men shook their head. You could be an ex-Praetorian Guard but then you usually took the form of smouldering ashes in an Imperial palace courtyard.

The Lady Lassalia sank under the water again and stayed there for some time thinking, then emerged and pulled out her new earrings. "They're bloody itching. Oi, girl, you can have them back," and the merchant threw the pair carelessly into the shadows where Lavinia was on the water clock with a fat factor.

Sobe looked up at the light well, squinted, then down again at the men. "Well, we don't do direct Army contracts, I told him that. The bloody hedgepig."

Scipio flashed a questioning glance to Eleazar who confirmed this utterance. The aristocrat blinked once in contemplation then waved a hand. From the recesses his gentleman appeared, fully attired in Scipii livery, and sweating hard, offering three small pewter beakers with a leather flask.

"So, here we are. Three old friends at the bathhouse. Let us use our logic to walk through where we are, like reasoning Roman citizens and honoured other."

The First Secretary kept his face blank at this. The conceit was preposterous, a first-estate, a woman and a slave eunuch at a bathhouse. It sounded like the start of joke liable to censorship.

"Eleazar, have a drink and you start."

The eunuch took a pewter cup from the sweltering valet and reflected on the relative joys of freeman-ship, before doing as he had been courteously ordered.

"The Emperor has unfinished business with Dacia which is too tempting. This time he's coming in force, peace treaty or no, but has learnt some lessons and is going to take his time building a sizeable force. Wholesale redeployment is not an option. Some of the Rhine Legions may be shuffled over time but your Empire's borders are always busy. Project Invictus…"

"Pleeeease call it Project Invidious!"

"Shut up, Scipio, I can't afford the legal fees for slave treason."

Eleazar went on, "…thus, Project Invictus is created, except now the emperor Trajan has learnt that pushing fresh meat on to the recaptured border, let alone pushing across it, is going to lead to bloody slaughter. Or at least the wrong type of bloody slaughter, the type that will keep the grave masons busy for some while."

"You don't really get commemorated if you die losing, annual marble artisan expenditure actually goes down in those circumstances."

"Thank you for that statistic, my lord, I shall remember it. So, the Emperor sends family and close aides out for a year identifying useful units and men to lift, to salt into a new legion."

Scipio drank and interrupted politely. "So, entrance to the stage Cornelius Ulpia – don't forget the Ulpia bit, Sobe – Mako. Our spiny little friend. He does such a good job in actually staying alive wandering around Germania, that he makes it back to Rome with a shortlist of units for transfer. Back in Rome Mako proudly presents the list of capable units to Uncle Tra-Tra. Except that he does too good a job and is now possibly ruing the, er, assistance another family member gave him on his Rhine work."

Lassalia took her turn to drink. "The clever cousin."

"The clever cousin, and he is really rather clever. Hedgehog missed the cousin on his visit to the Rhineland, but no doubt this was anticipated by the more astute Ulpia who probably wanted to stay one step removed from the adventure…just in case…but left some of his own meditations to assist. So, Hedgehog goes off and follows the notes to a T. Uncle Tra-Tra…"

Lady Lassalia had to ask. "Really? Uncle Tra-Tra?"

"Really. Uncle Tra-Tra. Uncle Tra-Tra thinks '*Boy has hidden depths and I need the clever cousin here in Rome. Send the surprising Hedgehog off to form my new legion ready for the great campaign.*'"

Eleazar wished to ask a question and raised a finger, the Scipio encouraged it, as answering questions at length was one of his three favourite things. "Uncle…the Emperor Trajan must have some inkling, however, that possibly his nephew might not, let us say, present a consistent level of performance?"

"Indeed."

"Why take the risk with him?" Lassalia added.

The Scipio rose up quickly and stepped down into the scalding emerald waters, head now just visible, arms working. "That is a slightly different question but let me answer it first, if that is acceptable to Eleazar."

The slave eunuch Eleazar acknowledged it was, out of form. Still, it was nice be asked.

"The Emperor is a man – still a man, and that's the key – in a hurry. He needs this campaign to 'ascend'. What can he do? Send a senator? No, everything would take forever and become extremely expensive. Send a current General? No, for a variety of reasons, but the most fundamental one is that Imperial families and the First Estate, they…"

"'We', you mean."

"If you will, my Lady. 'We' like to keep things in the family, we trust our families. Maybe not to actually be competent but at least not to become enthusiastic. Hedgehog at best might raise one Legion as instructed, but is not going to raise three in a fit of unsanctioned enthusiasm and begin a campaign for the best needs and requirements of the – etcetera, etcetera. Because this one, this thing that is going on, hopefully both successfully and well away from me, is going to be the Emperor's 'thing'. No one else's. Neither is Hedgehog going to start raising Legions and take them…"

"West. Because he can't find west even if it's sunset."

"Good girl."

"I'm ten years older than you, Mi lord."

"But your skin is so well, Sobe." The Scipio emerged up the steps, retook the pewter cup from the gasping servant and resumed a horizontal lounge, feet crossed. He continued, indicating to Eleazar, "Now we come to patient Eleazar's question which is slightly different from yours, Sobe. 'Consistent level of Performance'."

The Lady Lassalia kicked the pool's under water step to restrain a rising tide of impatience

"'Consistent level of performance!', I say again. My friends, do you remember a shipment of blue glass from last year?"

That took both Eleazar and the Lady Lassalia by surprise. Eleazar thought hard before recalling the contract, a profitable but complicated 'one off'.

"Luxury aqua glasses, twelve crates. The order was split into 'pick up' and 'destination'. Four crates caravanned then shipped to Greece, overland for the Aegean then sailed before being recrated and land hauled. The other cargo was a ship to ship to north Africa, Leptis Magma, and up to a villa in the hills for a Patrician family. A new villa for one cargo, and valued eastern clients got the rest of the glass. Paid well."

Suddenly Lassalia got it.

"There was a bonus! No breakages and on time. We had to do all the logistics, remember? All the argument about why they couldn't just send transport to the warehouses, but the money was good and the routes themselves safe, just long and complicated. It was a 'five' but worth it and payment made almost immediately on completion, including the bonuses which we met. The client was…you made the bloody introduction, Scipio! It was a test, this wasn't about glass, was it?"

Flour-pale hands wide spread.

"Oh, for Binki it very much was about his precious sodding glass collection. He was most impressed with your service, everything he'd heard about the House of Sadiki in terms of efficiency and organisational logistics was proved true."

"Heard from yourself, perhaps, honoured Scipio?" Eleazar commented. The Scipio ignored this and focussed on his hand gently caressing the water. "Binki is an old school friend…"

"Is he not also your brother, mi'lord?"

"Very good, Eleazar. Well done, you. Binki is my half-brother and, of course, a very influential senator."

"Of course," Sobe repeated drily before her First Secretary added, "And sits on the advisory committee for Army Group We…"

"He sits on several, I believe, hard to keep track. I am not an ambitious man, as you know, so I don't really follow these things."

The Lady Lassalia couldn't keep the sneer down. "Everyone needs a clever cousin or older brother. Except – you're the clever one, aren't you, Scipio minor. Is Binki just the ambitious one?"

The patrician grinned. "Actually, I'm major and hence a dreadful disappointment to my father."

"I'm sure, privately, your father is not that disappointed."

It was at this moment when a mask slipped with a brief flash of annoyance from the noble towards Eleazar. The patrician chumminess was wiped clean in a moment.

Sobe stored that for later. The man was too cool for school, and he and Eleazar were friendly in the way metropolitan elites could be with others, regardless of station, stuck out in the far provinces. Her First Secretary had obviously worked something out and decided now was the time to put it into play for a reason. A slave didn't just throw out an opinion like that, a slave certainly didn't go around making assertions about a first-rank patrician and ex-Pro-Consul papa without a reason. The Scipio revelled in his louche *'I'm friends with anyone'* mien and worked hard to laugh everything off, but this had got under his skin. Time, however, to get to the point and sort this problem out.

"So, I'm so glad the reputation of the House of Sadiki has stretched so far, even to the hallowed hard marble benches of the Roman Senate advisory conclaves. The problem is – I can do glass. We can do all sorts of things – but we don't do direct Roman Army contracts. Lots of people do main Army contracts, they fight over them and pass them down across the generations. Lellentus Cargo is practically grandfathered by the Legio III."

"Four generations of corruption and incompetence," the Scipio acknowledged with a nod, wry grin restored.

"Whatever. House Sadiki is not set up to do main Army contracts, so it's nice to be asked, and I'm so glad to know that this Hedgehog didn't just snuffle into my house last night of his own accord, before deciding to vomit turbot and best Falernian all over himself and a good sofa. Instead, he came on the high recommendation of you and your half-brother, but – here's the thing once again – we don't do Army for money. Just manageable favours for them."

Before the Scipio could give his smiling answer, Eleazar needed to interject.

"That's the point, my Lady. We have been selected because we aren't venal army contract suppliers, in the same way the fresh-faced nephew has been sent out to create a new legion. 'Project' Invictus has to happen."

"It's a bloody nine point five!"

The Scipio was delighted at this. "Ah, the famous Sadiki contract model. Without giving me any of the detail, Eleazar has been kind enough to walk me through the premises of it. What you have done while your husband has been 'travelling' is truly amazing, Sobe. Goodness! I could never be a merchant." His gold ring of status glittered in the green water. Literally, he couldn't.

"Now, it is a 'five and a half' or something you need, right? Higher is bad and very low is bad? I have never quite got my head around the 'very low, too profitable bit' but then I'm a civil servant posho who can barely manage his tailor's bill. So, my Lady – you 'calculate' this Invidious endeavour to be a nine and a half risk?"

Eleazar agreed. The Lady Lassalia added that it was somewhere between nine and a half and a thousand, in terms of potential loss.

"Please…" said the Patrician. "If I may? If I understand correctly, you will be 'inputting' the inevitable late payment of the Imperial Treasury, massive amount of diverse goods needing time at delivery, changing and continuous needs then transport into hostile areas – because Project Invictus is not going to be sitting in Iberia getting drunk and molesting the local daughters on a Friday night. What else, difficulties of dealing with military organisations and individuals, what have I missed?"

The Lady Lassalia punctuated each of her responses with a twitch of her cup.

"Currency type, no return leg profits with carts, arbitrary confiscations, source to destination, scale, storage and warehousing liability, taxes – as in the reality of having two thousand pounds of perishables with a greedy local port official who doesn't care what you say about military exemption. Scipio, do you want to flesh out the other twenty-odd reasons for not doing this for our snuffling friend ?" Eleazer made a small confirming nod to the Lord.

The Scipio laughed loudly and beckoned them to take a little walk around the hot pool. Various groups of proles made way except for three local young toughs wanting to make a point. The patrician merely smiled at them and circumnavigated the group as he spoke. "It is such an impressive model you have: I will say it again. You aren't keen on doing this are you? I'm getting that. Lady Lassalia, did you communicate these sentiments to the nephew when he visited you this afternoon?"

"I made it clear we were very honoured but Army was not the House of Sadiki's specialisation."

"That was a very clear and polite way of putting it, my Lady. Now, as we have established in this wonderful fuck tub…" Lavinia had found another client with her new earrings and gave them a little wave with her free hand as she undulated mechanically. "…the usual suppliers will not do, and the Senate and people of Rome hold the House of Sadiki in their highest esteem. May I appeal to your sense of patriotism, Lady Lassalia?"

She grimaced. "Knock yourself out, darl."

The Scipio smiled at this. "Quite. So, I know little about the workings of merchants but I do know something about the workings of government. Under law it is difficult to enforce the signing of a supply contract, it goes against our very Roman nature of commerce and freedom, but you both know this." They both did.

"It would be difficult. Commercial interests in the Senate would talk about dangerous precedents, breach of a citizen's rights, the cities wouldn't like it, and the landed class would tend to agree because while they – sorry, 'we' – don't give two shits about merchants we do rather care about their supernatural ability to make money and any infractions on liberty that pertain to money. As for the courts, well, bringing such a complex case would be presented as petulance and heavy-handedness by the authorities, such a course creates the kind of disruption and graffiti unhelpful given the Imperial strategy of the moment. With some sad inevitability this leads to an under-resourced Army and the consequent loss of personnel – gravestones or not to be decided upon, as Mars wills it. So then, we are at a seeming impasse. Except there is one last process that can be undertaken by the head of government in such circumstances. Eleazar, do you know of this?"

Eleazar said he did not know of any such process that could impel a citizen to provide services to the government outside of martial law.

"Aha!" The Patrician was triumphant, "In that, you are correct. What can happen, however, is a special letter of observation. It is usually drafted by one of the Palace's third special secretaries, observed by the Emperor but neither signed nor sealed by his office, but instead using a special light-green-coloured, very creamy wax, it is sealed with the stamp of the Third Secretarial Office. The document is then given to a palace courier who walks through the administration complex of Rome to the senior government lawyer, but then keeps going. The messenger then comes to the Consul administration office of submissions, but then keeps going. In fact, this messenger, who – let us imagine – is eating a pastry, just keeps going, without worrying any office, bureau or representative of our great social enterprise. It is instead just handed to a messenger.

"Now released into the world, the letter makes its way to a Governor, in this case our own 'Big Ovix' two floors down from me, who breaks the odd little green seal. He would probably check the seal first against the code master and, noting certain small marks around the Owls' ruff, takes a stiff drink before chucking everyone out of his room. Scipio made a face thinking of his superior, then continued.

"The letter of observation is exactly that. Itemising a series of – hmm – semi-official observations, no more, about something or somebody, but behind these vagaries there is a…sentiment. Being a Big Ovix the Governor would think about the contents of the letter, panicking for half an hour, before calling everyone back into his office and asking, "What the bloody hell does this mean?" The letter would be passed around the senior, professional civic staff such as myself, who having conferred, would attempt to explain what the letter is and also what the letter IS. Our Governor would still probably not understand and ask what to do. The staff would explain and then leave to go and enact…sentiment."

'Here it comes…'

"The process is, at this point, quite simple; you and all of House Sadiki are either slaughtered, sold and sodomised. Or a mixture of those sanctions. Your House ransacked, and a series of very short secret trials, both criminal and civil, are concluded. You defied the Emperor so the Emperor destroys you and takes all that you have. In the dying moments before being put to death for, say, killing your husband? I know you did not and it is a slander but, please, think how these things work – it is you who will have, wait for it…observed…Imperial displeasure. So, with that singular input into the model, do you see how not doing this contract is probably a risk above a six point five for the long-term commerciality of the House of Sadiki? Or have I missed something?"

The Lady Lassalia and Eleazar ensured they were visibly unfazed as the situation was explained to them. The pair were expert in the nuance of threats and in fairness to the Scipio this was not a threat but an actuality that needed practical attention. The trio ceased their promenade and walked up the steps out of the water.

Sobe turned, returning the pewter to the Scipio's tray bearer. "I imagine this is the moment where you point out all the potentially lucrative opportunities a new campaign and territory could bring to us?"

"I would not insult your intelligence, Sobe. One last thing you should be aware of, though."

Eleazar made an educated guess. "Cornelius Ulpia Mako already has the letter with him, just in case."

"Very good, Eleazar. When are you going to make him a freeman, Sobe?" he said with a wink. "Will I see you both later? A soiree?"

She nodded and took her leave, a special evening party needed arranging with a conciliatory invitation to Imperial Nephew. They found their way back to the lockers with ease, dressed and met the Sadiki office guard at the bath entrance. Outside the three young toughs were standing in the street naked looking less tough as a bath bull whipped them with a wicked switch away from the establishment and their clothes. The Scipio's man was drying out in the sun supervising the activity.

"First – bloody – estate, Eleazar. Right, we have a Legion to build for the glory of Rome."

"The glory of Rome, Domina."

"In-sodding-deed."

Part Two
Warmth

Chapter Ten

Late Spring/early summer, Brigetio Fort, night in the Immunes Exfil digs,
Farts and snores rattle the old general's quarters.
The Pannonias.

It was just the faintest of glows from an open-shuttered north facing window that had awakened Point in the deep night, but then that's why he was 'Point'. His fingers reached for the cot-knife while he listened to the smallest of sounds from outside. Silently the scout rolled off the drawstring bed on to his knees, took a cloak and left the old general's office by the back way, the second-floor balcony to the rear of the building. The cookstove embers of the fire still glowed in the main room's grate and no part of the scout's training allowed him to leave, back lit, by the main door. Instead, he checked the perimeter at the rear, which was moonlit dark, a lone veteran sentry silhouetted, walking the rear parapet as he should be.

It was still many hours from dawn but a faint orange glow was visible, coming from the main buildings of the river fort, from the 'House'. The point-man stuck a foot on to the balcony rail and hauled himself slowly up to the tiled roof of their dwelling, spreading his weight across the fired clay squares, stalking upwards towards the apartment building's apex. Near the top Point lay absolutely flat, slithering a last few handsbreadths, then broke up his shape raising a hood over his shaven head. The scout very slowly raised his eyes over the roof's ridge.

He watched for several minutes until there was no doubt about it. The House was packing up and leaving. Point ribbet'd with his lips, waited, then ribbet'd, waited, then ribbet'd a third time before a ribbet came from below. He didn't move but in moments could feel soundless black shapes moving behind him, confirmed by two light taps on his ankle. In silence cloaked figures emerged to his right and left, all hooded, and with long practice two new sets of eyes slowly rose above the building's coping tiles.

Below them in the parade ground carts were being loaded, the activity lit with torches held by Assyrian guards, swathed in their usual black and with curved swords unsheathed. Files, equipment and small stores were being stacked on to cart after cart which, once one was filled, were tarpaulined shut then coupled up from a line of waiting mules. SOGI could be seen on a horse, watching the operation from the shadows of the main gate. A lower door of the House opened and a string of chained men and women were led, and in one case stretchered, out of the interrogation area. Each was hooded and had to be guided up the steps of a cage cart. The captives filled two such vehicles which were then also covered and coupled to move off, forming up into the train being assembled in the old parade ground. The Immunes support troops, the Triari veterans, still manned the gate and walls, Point noted. They were in on it, whatever 'it' was.

SOGI suddenly looked up towards the Infil quarters before turning to receive an inventory from the Etruscan scribe. That was enough for the Skipper, who tapped Point twice on the hip. Point passed the gesture on to the now-recovered Three lying next to him then slowly they all melted back down the roof to the balcony.

No one had come to get the Infil yet, no one had told them anything. None of this was good. A big decision.

Skipper made hand signals and within minutes, full rigs were on and the Infil team dropped and shimmied down a rope from the back balcony. Then, in twos, they crossed to the south east palisade and ascended the stair. On the wall Skipper watched the walking triari sentry, thinking hard. After a moment, the Tribune made a decision and straightened, walking towards his 'brother' making a small, deliberate scuff on the palisade floor planks. The veteran heard it and turned, looking straight at the Skipper for a moment. The guard raised a crooked fingered hand up the shaft of his spear. The Skipper crooked his index finger in salute and the sentry hesitated, then turned and took a step forward into the open wooden tower, looking steadfastly out into the dark black of the hills. Exhaling, the Tribune made a prayer to the Lightbringer before signalling behind him.

A rope was secured and over the wall Infil team members went. Skipper waited, however, he was sure he'd seen a shadow pass the guard from behind, so he held up a finger and wagged it towards the darkness. Sure enough, on the other side of the turret Two sheathed his punch knife and moved away from the veteran sentry, swinging over the wall to drop into a bush with the smallest of thumps. Infil team moved quickly over the night lit ground to reassemble at the prearranged assembly point for this area, a yew, then skirted the foliage towards the gate before silently working up the eastern ridge. The team stopped at the well-used observation point that took in the river, road and fort from the east. There they waited in silence and before long could see torchlight and movement coming from the general's old quarters.

"Well, that's not us, we're all here," muttered Two helpfully.

"Perhaps SOG came to say goodbye," whispered Coms.

"Perhaps," replied the Skipper.

The Infil Tribune can now make out SOGI on the balcony with an Assyrian backlighting him with a torch. The intelligence officer was staring angrily back out into the forest, scanning one way then the other.

"'E's not happy," snorted Two in disapproval. "Great way to get shot, standing in front of a torch at night. Anyone got a bow?"

"Was he going to slot us, Skip?"

The Skipper shrugged. "Or bring us with him. Neither option particularly appealed, Point."

"Where's Exfil team in all this?" Three asked from low in a shrub.

The Skipper considered the question and turned his attention to a compund area where the boatmen were stationed, all looked dark and quiet. Point, however, spotted something on the Exfil roof. "Looks like someone's got the same idea as us." Up by a dark chimney shadow a figure crouched, also watching the parade ground activity.

"Werewulf?" asked Six.

"Must be," confirmed Point.

Comms moved up to the team lead. "Shall I try contact, Sir?"

The Skipper signalled negative and turned back in, gathering the other seven men together. "Right, this is how I see it. The House is moving out. Exfil have seen what's happening, or at least Werewulf has, who will then wake them up. Whatever SOG is up to, there are many more Exfil than us. While the Triari have obviously been pre-briefed on whatever-the-fuck this is, they are nominally Exfil support. I don't see the FCL slitting Honoured Boat Tribune's throat unless he really has to, or letting the Assyrians do it. Exfil Tribune's dad is something in finance so Pa will miss him, it's probably not worth the bother."

"What about us, Skipper?"

"No one will miss us, Four, not even your Ma." A quiet chuckle.

"That's why we wait here and watch, then take a view at dawn. Thoughts?"

"Are we deserting? I don't particularly mind but it'd be nice to know."

"Great attitude, Two. No, I don't think we are. You see, we have never really been given actual orders, just a set of strong suggestions. All wholly deniable of course, because we have been pissing about in Macromanni territory, which is technically 'friendly' with bits of papyrus to prove it. Trust me, I think this is best."

"Really, Skip?" Comms muttered nervously.

"Trust me, he says." Three chuckled but went on, "Don't worry, Comms, we're just getting a bit lost. A great Army tradition."

"Thoughts?" their officer asked. Two's outline shrugged. "Fuck it."

"Good, Skip," from Point.

Three: "Aye, aye."

In reply, the rest of the team just moved out to good observation points or cordoned the areas behind them.

Down below the rank of carts stood in the courtyard, three by five, flanked by the Assyrian torchbearers and with the SOG Staff mounted to one side. SOGII gave a signal, light flared from inside the old administration building and black-swathed guards moved quickly across the first-floor balcony, rapidly making down the stairs to join other contractors pouring out from ground level. Their robed commander counted each man out and nodded to SOGI. SOGII gave a second signal and the Triari opened the gates, one cart file after another proceeding through the arch and turning right, downstream, on to the river path. Orange light grew in strength from behind the old admin buildings shutters and the Infil team realised the House had been fired. The glow increased as flames caught floorboards, timbers and in all likelihood a great pile of scrolls, maps and other items that needed not to exist.

As the last carts left the fort, senior SOG team, satisfied their office was ablaze, turned horses and followed. Assyrian guards on foot, flanking the caravan, extinguished torches in a bucket as soon as they reached the gate and within a tenth of an hour the Special Operations Group were gone, dissolved into the night. Behind them a giant beacon was emerging as the flames licked through the roof of the old admin building. By this time, Werewulf had come off the north east building and reported, in full, the disappearance of the caravan, and the Exfil team came out of their dormitories to watch the flames licking up the fort's centre. Point could see the Exfil Tribune moving forward and begin to call for buckets but, as he did so, the senior veteran Legionary, the FCL, came off the gatehouse and waved the boatmen away. A heated conversation ensued but the First Class was having none of it and a cordon of fully armoured veterans was established across the parade ground.

"What the fuck is going on, Skipper? You must be able to see the fire for ten miles north," whispered Six from a bush upslope. "Do we shadow the convoy, Sir?" he asked.

"No, Six. Pass it around – we stay put. The convoy will be heading to the bend then south to headquarters at Aquincum is my guess. There's no point bumbling about in the dark after them, those contractors know their business and SOG Leadership will not have liked that they don't know where we are."

"Sir. Passing it along."

"Movement on the north bank, Skipper," signed Point an hour later. He had moved further down the slope to the bank, out of the treeline to an obs position without obstructions, relaying back the signal through Comms who was flattened against a thick log.

The whole of the wide river valley was now illuminated by the blaze so Point, who had very good eyes, picked them out with ease. The Skipper moved around the trees to look over the Danube. He found the watchers eventually, high up, just below some ridgeline scrub. The cover shouldn't be available at all but with their – or to be more accurate – the XIth Legion's cutting parties gone, it was easy to hide over the water. Three riders at least were watching, white hoof plate torsos and lances glittering from the fire.

"Your girlfriends are back, Two."

Two didn't answer but gave a low two-tone whistle. All eight of the Infil team pressed into cover and stayed perfectly still despite the huge distance and a great big river between them and the Roxolani. Barely visible hand signals then started to flash around the Skipper, something was moving up the slope towards them. It was completely silent and proceeded in small, slow bursts, merging in with the ferns. For a moment the Skipper thought it was their collective imagination running wild as what he saw didn't move like a person and his eyes kept losing it. Five, lying next to his boss, was also frantically scanning the forest in front. Then at just ten paces ahead something suddenly stood bolt upright. The Skipper could feel the collective start across the team. "I know you bastards are there somewhere. Well done though, good try."

Werewulf.

The Skipper didn't move and neither did the team.

117

Werewulf sighed. "The other young officer says come down and have a cup of something hot, what with the big fire and all. No one knows what the bollocks is going on, the Triari say they've just been told to make sure The House burns down, then they are at a loose end themselves."

The Skipper stood up from the scrub. "Alright, Werewulf, let's have a cuppa. Team!"

Four appeared right next to Werewulf who moved back a little in surprise. "Well done, lad. Make a scout of you yet."

Four grinned – that was praise indeed – then they made their way off the ridge.

"That's the way, boys!" Werewulf said in his thick Vedi accent, "Let's go and get warm while our betters decide which bit of Army property to destroy next."

This comment would normally be crossing a line for any Tribune, but the Skipper pretended not to hear. These were dyed-in-the-wool legionaries, Immunes with honours to a man who had been abandoned by their Legion, treated like slaves by spooks, then had just watched a Roman Army border fort being set on fire. Their fort. It wasn't just that it all felt intrinsically wrong but that they were, no doubt, tonight's big news in the sector for every scout, shepherd and planner in the north.

The first light of dawn was appearing downstream, a dawn-blue with just the faintest of auroras from behind the eastern hills.

Returning to Brigetio the Infil team came via the gate this time and the usual unit rivalry dropped away as the veterans just nodded them in, wordlessly acknowledging their mutual disgust at current proceeding. As they made inside, the Skipper could see pilots were on board two vessels making ready to slip from the quay. A good precaution, the Gunboat quickly cast off and rowed to the middle of the river where it made station with kedges, Skorpion gunners primed their heavy crossbows, scanning the north bank for movement. These pilots knew their business, the Skipper thought, although whatever they'd been doing prior to the scramble someone should probably tell them to lose the grass skirts at some point. The Infiltrators walked onto the parade ground and the two other unit leaders greeted Skip.

"Cuppa for my brother Tribune." The Exfil officer passed the Skipper a wooden mug pre-empting the obvious question. "Don't ask, I don't have a clue, neither does the FCL."

"Report, Legionary." The Skipper wanted to hear what 'nothing' sounded like from the veteran Triari himself.

"Yes, Sir. We were briefed after the evening meal to cover the decampment and make sure the main building was burnt. It was an order, Sir," and the FCL took a meaningful glance at the Exfil Tribune. Military order and discipline were frayed to the very edges and disagreements with an officer regarding the prevention of said officer stopping the destruction of a Roman Army building was new and wholly unwelcome territory for the twenty-two-year veteran. Not for the first time, the FCL cursed roundly but strictly inwardly, at how he and his men had been left in this situation: detached, legionless. Good long-serving men discarded from a life in the XIth Claudian while out on action. Left with this ragbag of specialist teams and then taking orders from some sort of Army intelligence cult for months on end. The only plus point in recent proceedings had been seeing an Assyrian die from frostbite and winning the sweepstake.

The Skipper sipped the drink and also took a bowl of hot oats proffered to him by a vet.

"That you were ordered, I have no doubt, but, FCL, do you not think that by now anything in the block that needed burning has been thoroughly burnt? More importantly that the risk of this fire spreading is significant?"

Exfil Tribune nodded in agreement. The First-Class Legionary looked at the fire, now shooting way up into the sky from windows, doors and a collapsed roof. "Agreed, Sir, fuck it. BUCKET CHAIN! Cordon, disperse!"

As the cordon stowed their weapons into tripods, other men raced to the fire stations for pails. Stored carefully behind the Exfil dormitory was all the river equipment and the River Tribune ordered the hydraulic rams to be detached and brought around to the gate. Here they were quickly reconfigured with leather hoses running from the river to the River Goat's intakes. Soon water was pouring on to the blaze, but it would be a very long haul.

"What would you do in their situation, FCL?" the Skipper asked the veteran leader, pointing with a spoon at the far bank.

Exfil Tribune interrupted. An important clarification was needed first. "I've had the gate bolted shut and the Gunboats put out to monitor and suppress close enquiry. We have, since you have joined us, sixty men under arms. Given the circumstances, Skipper, I think we need a clear chain of command. We are both Tribunes but you have – er – significant years of seniority…"

119

The Skipper chewed porridge. "Command's yours young man, you can have the seniority, sod dates. I need to manage my team; those are my orders. You also have more men under your command. It's all good, command of the fort and units is the Exfil's. The question still stands, though, what would 'you', as in – if it were 'you' up there in those hills disliking Romans a lot – be doing right now?"

The Exfil Tribune didn't answer while uncomfortably digesting his exciting new promotion. He had been expecting – and hoping – to cede command to the older man.

"What would you do, Commander?" the Skipper repeated, neutrally.

Exfil looked around. "Well, there's only about sixty of us in the entire legionary fort. We are on fire and a large contingent of our force left in the middle of the night. I'd roll over us."

The FCL winced a little.

"Legionary First Class?" Skipper prompted.

"That's probably right but…"

"Speak freely FCL, no hesitation," the Exfil officer ordered with the force of a man who'd had his life saved on at least three occasions by his own men.

The FCL looked around the fort and gestured. "It's just all a bit too fucking weird, isn't it, Sirs? Those watchers up on the hill must have been asking each other a lot of questions since midnight. They see a night-time move with prisoners, the deliberate arson of the enemy's own fort by the enemy and, if they had forward scouts lurking on this side…"

"Which they do," put in the Skipper, making a meaningful look at the forested slopes behind the fort.

"…seeing another unit – your unit, Skipper – sneakily hopping over the back fence, hiding on the east rise then coming back in again…? The Exfil stationing a Gunboat in the middle just throws in another unknown. Are two full Legions about to rock up and cross? Is this a diversion for something else along the border? Is it bloody magic? Magic's important on a border. I would also say hostiles haven't come near this place, up until now, partly because the Assyrians look like the usual 'dark spirits' crap that give the Macromanni the heebie-jeebies."

The Exfil felt this was unlikely. "They're Germanic, not Britons dancing around in loincloths every time a squirrel farts."

The FCL had first served in Britannia, and his early years had been fairly coloured as to what constituted all foreigners. "Point is, young gentlemen, if I was up there on the ridge or in the enemy CP listening to all these messages, I probably wouldn't do anything right away. I'd be thinking '*What the fuck are they doing?*'"

"Agreed, FCL," Skipper said. "I mean, even we don't know. And if they do come over the river in force, or from this side – as somewhere behind us is always lurking something – nothing is stopping them. So, let's come straight to the last point, Commander. What the fuck are we doing?"

The Exfil officer had no idea but tried, "I suggest we put the fire out and have breakfast. I'm sure there is an overarching strategic plan that will no doubt become apparent."

All three of them had a good smile at that, then the Exfil walked off to kick a malfunctioning hydraulic system. The veteran FCL turned to the Skipper and, not for the first time, said, "Do you know, Sir, I think he's alright for a young officer. Wasted on boats."

The Skipper agreed – "Fucking boats" – more out of Army tradition than feeling.

Chapter Eleven

Bright warm morning
Aquincum on the Danube, a warehouse deprived of sleep
Imperial provincial centre of Pannonia Inferior.

Newly-made Optio Ruben had been unexpectedly seconded to his own living, systems-based, Elysium. He had been this happy only once before, when the news came that he wouldn't return to his father's wattle hall at the end of the 'loyalty assessment' period which formed the rudimentary part of being a hostage. Ruben was the Romanised son of a strategically important chief somewhere in the never-never, with many brothers, so his father didn't want him back anyway. On Ruben turning fifteen his 'host', a minor senator, felt it was time to put a natural stop to all the poetry and bathhouse time First Son enjoyed with the 'barbarian'. First Son had cried, the matriarch also protested, sad to lose the *'civilising and cultured'* influence their *'guest'* had brought to the house over the years.

A patriarch was a patriarch, however, and the head of the family happily supported Ruben's Citizenship before packing the teenager off to find new and exciting opportunities within the Roman Army, the VIIIth Legio no less. *'Young Ruben should be thankful, got him a spot in my old Legion!'*

Ruben actually was thankful as he had never fancied First Son that much, just his library, and was still enough of a barbarian to fully appreciate being on the right side of a Roman Legion.

Four weeks now in Aquincum following 'an adventure' down river from Vindabona this new, current paradise was a riverport warehouse, walls decorated with a riot of planning and a staff of fully literate, ladder-bound attendants utilising different coloured paints, chalks and charcoals. Bliss. The logistic walls were packed with painted annotations, spider grams, weights, prices, times, materials and vehicle manifests. In the centre of the converted river warehouse was a massive table, half of which was dominated by a freshly-painted relief of the whole empire overlaid with an explosion of coloured wool lines affixed with pins, female Sadiki staff pushing little painted boats and carts about with long poles. Each model vehicle – representing a convoy or caravan – annotated so its itinerary and full detail could be read up on a wall.

The high beamed room bustled. At the other end of the big map table was a mass of papyrus and wax tablets with Ruben's new personal goddess of organisational detail standing in full evening wear from the night before. She was asking a senior staffer why he would put the request forms in with the approved forms.

"…because how would I know which is which? But I have the stamp, it is my stamp, so why I am reviewing things I have already stamped with my stamp? Or should I just go through each one and read it before seeing if I've already – go on, have a guess – yes, stamped it? Is it because you think I'm not busy? But why would I want to review them all together? Because – no, listen – it isn't all part of the same dispatch until I have approved the requests which then become part of the dispatch, otherwise why would I approve them? I could just stay in bed and we could transport – let's have a look at this one – six thousand arrowheads from Brindisi."

"Noone makes arrowheads, here? What, with four Legions in the area and a fabrica a few hundred miles away? In fact, if I go through them – here we are – I've already approved an order for one thousand arrowheads to be purchased from surplus garrison stores. The garrison stores being – what? – three hundred paces down the road? Did you think I needed more? Because I've approved one thousand arrowheads already and now in this mixed pile I'm shipping another six thousand arrowheads, the weight of which is…"

She looked at the wall to the left of her, finding the information immediately. "…four cargo units. No, it's alright, because I want you to learn, so let's look at the board and see what the supply target is for arrowheads and…there it is, it's one thousand two hundred arrowheads. Take all these away and go through them, remembering to check the boards before returning. Go bother our lovely blue-eyed boy Ruben from Army liaison here and come back when you're ready. Do not cry! First Secretary Eleazar has been working solidly for two days straight and had his balls cut off when he was nine years old, and you don't see him crying."

First Secretary was buried in a wax tablet stack. However, the part of Eleazar's brain that was always on 'Domina receive' produced an "Absolutely not, Domina. Every moment a new challenge."

The senior administrator lumbered off.

"Now, that reminds me…Oh, blue-eyed boy!"

This was a strange and new world Ruben had entered, in a room with a female second-estate civilian merchant's wife, husband apparently away on business, but the Optio was definitely swimming not sinking. He was her blue eyed boy.

"Yes, my Lady?"

"Why one thousand two hundred arrow heads, why isn't it a thousand or one thousand five hundred? It's mathematically perverse and I don't like it."

Optio Ruben shrugged apologetically. "It is the Army way, Madam."

This had become a running joke over the last month since meeting, and Ruben dutifully put a coin in a pot marked 'Stupid Army platitudes' as the woman pointed at it with a lacquered claw.

A peach-green liveried runner, matching her nails, came in. "All assembled and counted, Lady Lassalia. They are now in the pens as instructed."

"Finally! Worse than bloody sheep, aren't you all, Optio Ruben? Right, let's have a check of the board, though. With the sheep outside we have: twenty units of basic stores, two days' personal rations issued, two days' water flasked – quite why I don't know when they are marching next to a river but if I've learnt anything…take it as said…" and she threw a coin at the jar, which bounced off and a very junior assistant scrabbled around and slotted it back in. "…more basic stores; the blankets are here, axes we've gottt…" she was now wandering to a large wall panel, looking at ticks. "Spoons, do we have the bloody spoons?"

Eleazar looked up and removed the stylus from his mouth. "Came in last night with gauze, basic wood and most of the other camp spares."

"Should be crossed off, Eleazar." She waved at a slave on a ladder to do so.

"Apologies, Domina."

"Spoons, spoons, spoons. Optio Ruben, have you checked this?"

Ruben took a last, his fifth of the hour, nervous scan then nodded.

"Right, then let us get the little sheepies on their way!" And the Lady Lassalia marched towards the warehouse loading doors, Office Security following at a discreet distance.

They had been good but hard, sleepless days and nights so at first Ruben giggled a little, until he realised she wasn't joking and was actually going through the door. "Eleazar, is she serious?"

Eleazar gave him a look that conveyed *'Yes, I'd run if I were you.'*

The small warehouse had been chosen well as the Aquincum Town operating base. It was small for storage and Landlord had thought he was pulling a fast one leasing it to Sobe, set back as it was from the river port with a huge field in front of it. Expecting the usual port congestion he'd been kind enough to do a per cubit, per day cost – no upfront payment or ground rent – as 'She was just starting out and didn't want any horrendous overheads.' The Lady Lassalia had almost wept in thanks, then cackled manically when the agreement was sealed and the landlord had left. It took a fortnight before all the local merchants began to realise what they were dealing with in the little warehouse, when goods stopped arriving and routes to Aquincum became *'unavailable'*. Sobe had to have her Landlord thrown down the steps of his own building as, infuriated, he tried to claim the *'swindling bitch'* should pay for storing *'all the writing on the walls and people'*.

The writing had certainly been on the wall when he marched to the Aquincum civil court with a writ. The newly-installed Temporary Magistrate for *'Military Affairs concerning the XXXth Legion Investiture'* listened earnestly to the writ, asking many diverse and seemingly unconnected questions, particularly enjoying the esoteric notion of *'storing information.'*

"I'd pay nothing, nothing to store…ahahahaa!" It was at this point Landlord completely lost his rag and called the Temporary Magistrate something 'really not very nice and I was trying my best!', as it was later reported to First Secretary Eleazar. The case was rejected on the basis of the plaintiff affronting the dignity and grace of the Roman court. The landlord became even more outraged, whereupon two of the new magistrate's lictors dragged the man outside into the alley and beat the shite out of him with rods.

The Temporary Magistrate had no idea about the alleyway beating until afterwards, his civic officers assuring him it was 'absolutely necessary' for the interests and security of his person and that of Rome, in no way at all being because the lictors were bored and liked hurting people. "Oh, well, very good then."

Now also standing on the outside steps of the small warehouse, aforesaid Temporary Magistrate was waiting to greet the Sadiki merchant as she emerged from the planning room. "Lady Lassalia, it is all going very, very well. Thank you, thank you!"

Cornelius Ulpia Mako, hands clasped, was fidgeting about in the way that he did, hair fully escaped upwards in joy. Sobe smiled appreciatively, not so much because of the sanction of her ability but because Imperial Nephew had waited for her outside, and not gone into the small warehouse. It had, after a few days following arrival at Aquincum, been decided that his dignified presence was not essential within the logistics hall and, heartily relieved at not having to sit in the 'mind boggling' room of 'things', Imperial Nephew took up the suggestion of being a Temporary Magistrate. Sitting on any cases relating to Project Invictus. There had initially been a surprising number of cases submitted to his court and Mako had been afraid that, once again, he'd found himself doing something he was not really that 'up for' in terms of capability.

Civil writ – reparation for use of contracted vehicles.

Civil writ – reparation for monopoly of oxen.

Civil writ – damages for gross slander and false accusation.

Civil writ – communal track damage.

Civil writ – damages to crops.

Civil writ – reparations for prevention of passage by vehicles.

Civil writ – reparations for forcibly secured port berths and overbidding on long-term river transportation.

Contractors and merchants flooded the court as the Mediterranean-wide new multinational entrant to Aquincum flexed its, or her, significant commercial muscles. Almost overnight local trade dried up as long established, lazy and convenient agreements were swept away by a storm of purpose and money.

The four-lictor, special 'whatever he was' and Temporary Magistrate did not lack in enthusiasm, however. Diligently listening to each case at great length, ensuring to ask many pertinent and probing questions in order to 'really get to the bottom of this', a phrase used frequently when a certain level of impatience arose from the gallery. Frustration, Mako began to observe as the cases mounted up against the XXX's contracting merchant, seemed to be a consistent factor within the Roman legal system. When it came to sentencing, Nephew was guided by the law and the Emperor's words. Indeed, the Imperial personification of justice had summarised the legal position quite clearly: "Get it fucking done, Hedgehog, don't screw up!"

With this in mind, Mako felt it only right to provide a full summing up of his feelings to each jury at the end of a hearing. Often the summing ups were somewhat obscure or conflicting, in which case one of the lictors would bend forward to the foreman desperately trying to discern the Imperial will and whisper, "Dismiss it, you cunt." Which the jury always did.

Particular demographics of the town were left very unhappy at the new legal situation and one afternoon in the public forum venerable old Senior Magistrate (incumbent) took particular issue with how this 'young man from Rome' was conducting himself. This public admonishment set in train a conclave between both sets of legal representatives with the question of jurisdiction quickly settled, the elder man issuing a full public apology back in the forum only half an hour after his initial declaration, followed by throwing the Nephew a rather nice private repast at the house. News of the savage fight behind the forum building – well, not really a fight – that had left one of the old magistrate's lictors a gibbering vegetable had spread fast. If not indeed ever into the Emperor's Nephew's hearing, who carried on with life blissfully unaware of the smaller cogs of Roman judicial life. After that, the writs against the House of Sadiki seemed to dry up and Mako spent his days milling about asking, "Is everything going well?" and trying to look helpful.

This early morning on the warehouse steps, though, all their hard work seemed to be, very visibly, paying off.

Lassalia beamed back at Mako from the top of the rough hewn stair. "Good morning, young Imperial Hedgehog. Well, what do you think of them, your boys?"

"Magnificent, my Lady. You are the most splendid of women – of people – persons."

"I think I bloody am, actually," as Sobe regarded her handiwork.

Seven thousand and some men, shaved raw, tunic'd and standing in roped-off counting pens wandered about aimlessly in the morning light. A wolf whistle sounded and the Head of House Sadiki gave a friendly wink which got a little cheer. A Training Centurion marched into a pen and punched the joker full in the face. Still, the assembled men had grown to like 'the Lady' fast. Most of them had been living outside for months on end before marching into the Aquincum assembly field. She was the one who had loudly insisted that 'as she'd gone to all the bother of providing tents, they may as well use them', she'd made sure there was a bit of wine as well as water, the cheese was definitely her.

So, the legionaries made her their patron and goddess, the level of deeply disgusting scrawled pornography at the rear of the warehouse was always affectionate, on some level, and anyone describing her as the 'W' word was soundly beaten. She was definitely posh, first class, filthy totty who'd gladly give them all hand jobs if they were wounded out of the kindness of her heart because she loved them. In fact, the rumour that if they came back wounded to the garrison aid station, she had guaranteed a topless hand job to any man of any rank, no matter how lowly, was one of the very first Legio legends of the XXXth. Celebrated through a special toast four hundred years hence at the disbandment feast – in a much more sanitised form.

"Morning, boys!"

A hearty "Morning!" back and a single "Show us your tits!" which had another Training Centurion wading back into the throng.

"They love you!" remarked the Hedgehog admiringly.

"Well, I'm pretty, but we must now say goodbye. Right, where is my friend with all those beautiful feathers in his hat. There he his. Yoo hoo, my lovely chickadee! Are you going to make me come down there and get all sweaty in this heat?"

Not so muffled laughter erupted. She had a voice that carried like any First Spear.

The Senior Centurion, the man with the feathers in his hat, fought down bubbling purple rage and turned from his position at the edge of the formation.

"Steady, SC," one of his Optios muttered, somewhat worried.

The SC marched to the bottom of the warehouse steps and took a breath, "Ma'am."

She beamed and held out her arms to the port road. "Well, I will miss you and all your lovely boys. Got them here safely, didn't we?"

"Ma'am."

"Did you find those pens helpful in the end? Stop them wandering off? What do you call it – 'deserting'? Did I get that right?"

"Ma'am."

"So, off you go. You are all packed, present and correct."

"I beg your pardon?"

128

At this point, Ruben came running out. "Lady Lassalia, I think there is something we need to look at inside, one last thing…"

Annoyed, she brushed the Liaison Optio away. "We need to get this lot off my field as I've got supplies arriving in a few hours. Now my lovely be-feathered friend – fly!" and she waved theatrically towards the town's north gate.

Ruben just froze.

The Senior Centurion stood very still; eyes wide open. "Optio Ruben. As liaison, can you liaise something for me? Is this…Lady…actually ordering one of the Emperor's Legions to…march?"

Optio Ruben had seldom disobeyed an order but had…nothing.

The Lady Lassalia waved her hands, nails more obvious this time. "What's the matter, why are you being cross? You are ready to march off and fight valiantly for the glory of Rome. I've provided the sandals to do it. I know that, you've even…" she said in stage whisper, "…got spoons! Now off you go. Have fun!"

The SC raised his vine staff alarmingly. "Have fun? A Legion marches at its commander's orders, not at the whim of some…"

Lassalia crossed her arms, pointedly revealing the ring of social rank tapping up and down on her finger and glared back. "Well then: where are your commanding officers, SC, at the time of departure?"

He did not respond.

"Hedgehog, do you know the whereabouts of the Military Tribunes this morning? You're all sharing that debauched posho boys' rat pit in town?"

The Hedgehog shuffled. "Um, they were still 'pre-breakfast' when I left. I had eggs and bacon, if that's of any use?"

Both the SC and the Lady Lassalia gave him a look. "Enormously mi'lord. Alright, Centurion, here's the thing…" She stepped down to the bottom of the flight and stood in front of the fully armoured veteran. "You aren't actually a Legion yet. You won't be, if I am right in thinking, until you are formalised and recognised. Am I correct, Temporary Magistrate?"

"Um, yes. Yes? Yes. Probably."

"Am I right, Optio Ruben?"

Optio Ruben decided to remain inanimate.

"Jupiter! I am right, Senior Centurion. So right now, you are escorting a convoy and these…" She pointed to the seven-thousand-odd human beings. "…are still 'cargo' under my transportation orders from Army Group West. I have a large amount of food arriving soon, for you – all the season stores – and need the space. Now, you're very cross with me, I can see that…"

Sobe liked to believe she was sensitive to the feelings of others. "…I know I can come across as somewhat brash, so why not get away from me and I'll ensure all the food for you to eat this, busy summer, follows? It's a win-win, plus you get to enjoy your officers' having to catch up because they've been in bed fucking whores all night while we've – and you've been up as long as I have, I know that – have been working. You can blame the whole thing on me. Deal?"

Within a third-hour, the not-yet-Legio XXXth marched. An hour later four Tribunes fell out of the brothel door to find their first command had disappeared, all seven thousand legionaries with marching support train. A mad scramble on to horses was enjoyed by the town prostitutes who cheered, and the officers left behind many essential kit items in their haste, which were sold off by lunch never to be seen again. When they caught up with the column marching north, one look from the Senior Centurion sent the four scurrying back to hide behind the spoon cart.

All this was observed from Aquincum's central administration building. The Governor of Pannonia Inferior smiled as the un-Legion marched out, Aquincum's merchants all standing in a semi-circle behind him. Now it was time to act.

Chapter Twelve

Vindabona port-city, upper Danube
Same hard-working morning
Pannonia Superior province of Rome

Way up river Centurion Chief Armourer Galba, late of the VIIIth, had just been *'reassured'*, which left him with a suspicious taste in his mouth. He ruminated on the intelligence officer's earlier words watching the derricks load five heavy river barges with all the armoury supplies. As he did so, metal-infused, charcoal-stained fingers turned over and over the weeks-old message from Optio Ruben, now downstream in Aquincum with the supply agents.

The armoury equipment had, amazingly, all arrived on time and complete to the provincial capital. Housed in boxes marked with the palm and eye of Osiris signifying the Conveyer. The Chief Armourer had never heard of the House of Sadiki until sitting in a cold, Vindabona Town billet two months previously when a massive package of forms was brought to him by one of the company's local representatives. Galba had been in one Legion his whole life and logistics on this scale were, up to this point, managed through the quartermasters under the Chief Praefectus' office. Ruben and the Sadiki local rep had gone through the sheafs, huddled around the filthy anteroom table with a small brazier burning in one slightly less damp corner of the room.

On arriving at Vindabona with the armoury, both the Army men had quickly realised that their new 'detached' status was both a curse and a curse. No longer with the glorious old VIIIth Augusta the armourers were grudgingly assigned the worst billets possible. Having checked in with the Upper Pannonian administration building at the port city, it was also made clear they would be allowed no access or stipend for personal stores. Firewood, victuals and drink were to be paid for out of their own pockets and even though Ruben kept receipts noting all expenditure, reclaiming funds from the Army had a special canon of longstanding jokes all of their own.

Bent over the billet-hovel table it became also apparent that the House of Sadiki had a form for everything, it was worse than the Army, which did have enormous bumf but very few actually read it. Galba knew that essentially the VIIIth Augusta had run on endless wrangles with the Belgae Fabrica backed up by giving sums of money to Konis the Greek who would steal half the request and deliver a quarter of what was actually needed, usually a season late.

The immense detail of everything to be delivered all in one go was also overwhelming. This wasn't a Legion with constant trickledown supply; they were starting from nothing. The new Legion's base was to be somewhere called Brigetio Fort roughly halfway downstream between Galba's current location at Vindabona and Aquincum in Pannonia Inferior. Brigetio Fort itself, the wharf bar-frequenting armourers were reliably told by merchants and fisherman, had been stripped by the outgoing XIth Claudian, with a hodge-podge river patrol and some sort of military prison left behind.

From a working assumption of 'Nihil' the trio had fought through the docket work for days on end, bringing in each department head up the rickety apartment staircase to list equipment from stools to special ratchets. Lulla had asked that Old Sibius come up and check the supply requests and the Chief Armourer, grudgingly, agreed, then sat having to contain his rage for two hours, listening to:

"You haven't got any AB spacers, are we going to be using catapults, then? No big pliers. No crankshafts – you've got the cranks but no shafts. Won't work without a shaft because then it's not really a crank, is it? An old Greek said he could move the world if he had a lever long enough, but we don't seem to have any. Well, that's the modern Roman Army for you right there, isn't it? Shift plates! Goodness me, where are the shift plates?"

Optio Ruben had suggested the Centurion sit outside for a bit, which he didn't. Galba would take his medicine although it didn't help that the Sadiki man gushed about the 'invaluable' help the subordinate, ancient, armourer gave at every new mistake picked up.

At the end of the listing process, Galba sat over some good wine – supplied by the rep – and asked about the Sadiki man's employer. The Centurion Armourer almost choked when he found out the trade house was currently being run by some merchant's wife while her husband was away, unlikely to be expected any time soon. Bloody Army had stitched them up with an untried supplier run by an – actual – woman. He could just picture it, some fat bribes to a civilian wonk. This shitty little green Legion with no long list of benefactors, famous and important Senators who'd vowed to always 'look after their boys', having served twenty years ago for half an hour. Galba decided they'd both go to Salona, he and Ruben, to 'sort things out properly'. The weather was better further south for a start. The Sadiki rep pulled a face.

"Well, you could but…she runs the House as if it were a…matron running her home." Whatever the fuck that meant. They'd go to Dalmatia to keep the silly bint from flogging them copper swords.

After a week, though, messages came back. It was quickly ascertained that the Sadiki head was, herself, moving from Salona to Aquincum, the matron planning to oversee operations directly. Galba had made to pack his things and go immediately if the muster point was to be the other Pannonian garrison, but a strongly worded note 'instructed' him to stay put.

"The Lady Lassalia kindly requests you remain in the upper Danube. Your armoury equipment supplies are moving straight here, to Vindabona. Being technical in nature, they more easily come through the Alna trade route and our proposition is that you and your men remain to take receipt. As per your army movement orders."

Galba had demanded to see the note, and after much protesting had eventually just grabbed the rep and prised it out of his clenched fist. The message read:

'What are you doing? Handle the client. Tell the blacksmith to stay put. I'm not shipping designate/heavy cargo to muster to then ship back upstream, final destination. We've got a big river travelling downstream – use big river travelling downstream. Firmly impress this or will take all clients' hammers away. STOP.

HOS Lady Sobe Lassalia Sadiki, writ. 10th April in transit Sal-Aquincum. Kisses.'

After Galba shouted 'Blacksmith!' for some time, more wine was poured with Ruben massaging the news towards the original plan of the Armoury staying put, paying heavy emphasis on the Army move order, not, of course, whatever 'She!' was saying. "In a sense, my Lady is being subservient to you and the Army and not the other way round, surely?" tried the rep.

"Bollocks."

"Well, it might look like…"

Compromise – by morning Ruben had been dispatched downriver to Aquincum on his own. To mollify matters the rep suggested, 'for the good of communications', that Centurion Chief Armourer Galba take rooms within the House of Sadiki, Vindabona Office, itself. Galba stewed in his damp rat-hole for a week then, curious, called in at the House of Sadiki Vindabona to do some 'chasing up of lists'. Having seen how the other thousandth lived Galba quickly agreed that it was 'in the best interests of Project Invictus' to move in immediately. He had never slept in a room with flowers or a huge frescoed dolphin along one wall. These he could leave, but the big fire and food were a step, or an entire staircase, up. It wasn't bad for a 'blacksmith' he thought, which had been his father's profession.

Galba's armoury team were themselves billeted above the Vindabona fish market. The only advantage of this was that the armourers were only too keen to get outside in the fresh air and guard the mounting supplies as they came in. By barge and carts every day for a month, all the metal work and high specification wood materials for the new Legion poured into Vindabona. All stacked and packed at the main Sadiki warehouse in town, the merchant guards reinforced by legionary armourers day and night. In the first week of arrivals, two youths and a gang of professional thieves had been carted off to the Magistrates but the buildup of goods only led to more interest in the building.

One night the Sadiki rep had urgently sent a runner for reinforcements and the men turned out, swords drawn, to beat off a serious incursion on the supplies. No Magistrates were needed this time, but two of the armed gang were put in the ground for good. The Chief Armourer had looked over the bodies but saw no markings. The rep believed it was a rival trading house that had been 'blocked' from routes, but if it was that, or a more tactical incursion against the Army stores, the quicker the armoury moved off this quay the better.

Today was that day. One last check of the crates had been done, thoroughly, with Old Sibius grudgingly admitting everything 'seemed' to be there. Menicitrix had gone through all the fine tool inventories, Workshop his department, and Guns the huge boxes of disassembled field pieces. In addition, the little Iberian artillery man had brought with them two crates of his 'specials' which CP Craxus had looked the other way on when they had departed from the VIIIth's garrison.

With all the barges contracted and assembled loading had begun at dawn, once complete the convoy just awaited an additional guard to arrive that was coming from inland.

"Not that you will need them, Centurion," the Intelligence Tribune drawled, up at local headquarters that morning. "The border is stable other than some cattle raiding, just the usual banditry. The truce with the Macromanni kingdom holds, that's the policy, you see?"

'*No, no not really, Sir*' but Galba just saluted and returned to his men at the quay.

On the river dock armourers and department heads swarmed about the wherry men. A new batch of carpenters had also turned up the previous day, completely unexpected, from the XXth. 'Lively' Sicilians who Galba stashed overnight on some trout crates.

Armourer Cadet Bullo appeared, covered in sweat, and, like all of them, smelling of fish.

"The forge is on, we got it done, Centurion Armourer."

Galba gave the lad a pat on the shoulder, it had been a serious undertaking getting the forge onboard. It was a big beast, completed to Workshop's specifications. Who knew what the XIth had taken from Brigetio so best to be sure. After all, 'if the army was willing to pay for it...' which it seemed they actually did, for once. That was one of the unexpected boons of Project Invictus; money for armoury supplies was no object. No quibbles, no push back, all dockets processed. This fact unsettled Galba at night when not dreaming of losing an important four-legged piece of technical kit.

The Centurion Armourer gave the boy some coins and told him to get breakfast for himself and the forge-handling team. Bullo thanked his Boss and raced off excitedly to one of the wharfside eateries doing a brisk trade at this busy time of the day. Another half hour passed of last-gasp stowing and lashing before all the armoury team and carpenters were assembled with the civilian pilots and the Sadiki rep.

"Right, everyone, that was a real effort and you are to be commended, breakfasts on me for a change – Cadet Bullo's made a start already as you can see. But let us just go through it once more. Workshop?"

Lulla knew the roster backward by now. "It's all on, Boss. I say again, though, what's in the crates exactly we won't know until the other end but the sample checks hold up."

The rep interjected, "If anything is missing, I have contingency of most of the lower to medium technical items. Essentially the containers' contents have been checked against the dockets of the fabrica which crated them."

"That is understood, House Sadiki. Good arse covering. Thank you. Menicitrix?"

"What?"

'Fucking Gauls. Breathe.'

"Are all the fitters' tools and spares loaded?"

"Of course. You asked me to load them so we have loaded them. Why would I not do this thing you…?"

"That's a Yes, then. Guns?"

Guns was eating an onion. Wearing sailcloth trousers tied with a piece of string and a fisherman's jumper, he gave a wave of the onion to signal assent.

"Good. So, we are just waiting for our bloody armed escort to turn up when they feel like it. Now, on that, I went up to HQ first thing and I've had the intelligence briefing: the river is completely secure and no hostilities expected."

Workshop spat. "Was this from Immunes scouts, Boss?"

Galba made a thumbs down. "Military Tribune, Intelligence no less, fresh from the horse's arse."

The assembled party groaned.

"What does the House of Sadiki think?"

The House of Sadiki apparently didn't deal in conjecture but – "We have arranged it such that a serious armoured escort will be travelling with you, and we're having to pay the bargemen double the normal rate. Put it that way."

"So, we all know what that means, everyone gear up. It's time to be legionaries again. Sets on quick and let's get something to eat."

Galba turned to the rep as the men fell out. "The escort, any idea when they are arriving?"

"A messenger informed me last night that the escort are on the road ten miles away from here, coming from the north west. They should have been here by now, though."

The 'serious' description of the armed escort by the rep had set off a warning sign in Galba's mind.

"Know how to fight then, these boys? Or are we going to be fishing them out of the water?"

"I'm not an Army man, Centurion Armourer, but I would say so."

Everyone was strapped into their set of segmented plate with one notable exception who continued to eat his onion. As the sun rose the armourers and carpenters strung out along the Vindabona wharf trying to find shade from the end of spring sun and a comfortable place to sit. Quayside prostitutes were shooed away by Galba as he wasn't in the mood, he'd already dragged Armourer Cadet Bullo out of an alleyway, then gone back into the alleyway to retrieve the boy's dagger, unknowingly stolen by the tom.

"Put that away, and put that away," the Centurion said, handing the idiot his dagger and pointing at his prick. "Go and sit over there by Old Sibius." That would take the edge off anyone's libido. Sibius himself stood hunched, dressed in his own handcrafted scale armour, each piece methodically beaten by three hammer sizes, "When apprenticeships were apprenticeship in the Army!" admonishing the young cadets on the wharf. Bullo did as he was told and enjoyed another hour listening to life in the golden era of the Legion armouries under Chief Armourer Ursus, "Who I trained myself!"

As the day pushed on even the rep began to grow flustered.

"Where are your bloody mercenaries, Sadiki?" Galba growled over his fifth hot drink of the day.

"They are not mercenaries, Centurion Armourer, they are more of your lot."

Galba frowned. The muster was nominally occurring in Aquincum way down river. However, odds and sods from across the Empire would be joining the Legion any way they could. It all tended to work out in the end, the Army, thought Galba. Except when it didn't, and everyone started dying.

Shouts rang out from the main road leading from the city gate to the port. An odd thing happened as two legionaries from the Vindabona city garrison, a slovenly lot, ran at full pelt straight past the armourers with faces of rich terror, then bolted straight down an alley.

Galba stood up from the tavern stool he was sitting on, adjusting his belt, and walked across the cobbles with the rep to see what was going on, just as what was obviously their escort emerged around a corner. They didn't march, they didn't swing their arms, they didn't swagger, because these men had long ago left behind any need to.

"Oh, fucking shit!" gasped Galba. "These are your legionary escort, I believe?" The rep asked squinting.

"Those aren't fucking legionaries. GET UP, EVERYONE, FUCKING GET UP AND PARADE, NOW!"

The armourers started at their commander's sudden eruption and, before moving – because armourers and carpenters move to a different drumbeat, wearing armour or no – they all took a moment to ascertain the source of their boss's excitement individually…then it hit them and they sprang up like shock coils/heavy ref. 'MMCCVII'.

That was when the escort's leader saw the waiting armoury and a wide smile broke across his face. Behind him were the entire complement of the new XXXth Legion's Centurionate. Fifty-plus representatives of the Centurion class with Optios, the lowest of whom would be a highly-decorated and respected leader, all of them brought together from old, established serving Legions to be here.

"Salve, Centurion Armourer!" the leader shouted happily. Twenty years service at least but moving like a lad, greying chestnut hair and built like a brick. What was obviously the new First Spear by his marks, greeted Galba. Behind Galba rang a continuous clatter of weapons being dropped and plate-banging as his men attempted file discipline.

"Salve, First Spear." Galba saluted nervously.

"Don't worry, don't worry! We're still on holiday, aren't we, boys?" Behind him the Centurions laughed with hands on pommels or taking sips of water. "Good to meet you, Centurion. First Spear Felix, recently of the Vth Macedonian, 'Eagles of the Mountain' or 'Hill Pigeons' – but we can say that, you can't." and he clasped the armourer's hand good naturedly. The hand was greasy and the armourer looked down to see blood a few hours old.

"We are late, Centurion Armourer," the First Spear stated. "But, Centurion…let me get this right…" Pointing to a happy-looking, dark curly-haired man covered in red splatters.

"Alba…? Yes, Alba has a good excuse. We had a bit of hiccup this morning. Explain our tardiness to the good Centurion Armourer." Centurion Alba, a very Senior Centurion of the Xth by the looks of it, was delighted to. "Bandits, Armourer Centurion, can you believe our luck?"

"And theirs!" said someone from the back, which got a big laugh.

Felix grinned some more, "So there we are, Centurion Armourer…"

"Galba, FS. Recently of the VIIIth Augusta, long service armourer Immunes, just promoted Centurion." In front of his new 'brothers', he wanted to get that out straight away.

"August Augusta's fucking twice-august Legion, very good. No harm in a new Centurion, I am a freshly minted First Spear and look forward to all our work together within the XXXth. You are our brother and we shall be the fathers to this new Legion, eh, boys?"

The Centurions and trailing Optios gave a happy shout of "Ooh ooh ooh," like they were young legionaries.

The First Spear's eyes looked along the armourers' parade line. Galba's arse clenched but Felix put him at ease. "Don't worry, don't worry, Centurion Chief Armourer Galba. I've been around a bit, you know. Immunes are Immunes, especially armoury Immunes," he said with a wink at the legionaries. "Did the XXXth get the whole of the VIIIth's armoury team?"

"Yes, FS."

The smile again. "Your General must have been mightily pleased. I'm glad it is the case, though." He raised his voice to the Legionary armourers. "Your reputation precedes you, armourers formerly of the VIIIth Augusta. Just more of the same, lads, and I can't wait to see your fabled artillery in action. What do you say to that?"

"Ooh ooh ooh!"

"Very good, now as you were." The armourers, with the entire complement of Legion Centurions on the quay, just stood at ease having enough self-preservation not to go back to lounging about the place 'as they were' previously.

"Is that man wearing trousers tied up with a piece of string, Galba?" asked Felix mildly.

'*Bollocks.*' "Yes, he probably is, FS. Thats our 'Guns'."

"Ah. Is he one of those savant, can't-make-a-bed types?"

"Yes, FS."

"Well done, Galba, I see you know your job because – I take it? – that murderous creature next to him doesn't leave his side and cleans occasionally, am I correct?"

"You are, First Spear."

"Good. Word to the wise, though. Our SC – who is not here, he's with the muster coming upriver – I know of him a bit. Lose the trousers at some point on our little cruise."

"Will do, FS."

Off to one side stood the rep, hovering.

"You look like a man who needs something signed," observed the First Spear indulgently.

"Vindabona representative of the House of Sadiki. Could I respectfully ask you to review this docket?"

It was reviewed carefully, line by line, with ease by the First Spear. "Now let's see. First of all, I have no idea who the House of Sadiki is but I commend you on your efficient handling of the Centurionate. I must admit that when I saw the town-by-town rendezvous days I thought it was an elaborate joke, but if it was one, the punchline eludes me because everything worked perfectly. Accommodation and victuals would have been correct, but now reading this I can understand why it fell a little short."

The rep's face fell. "I…I…Apologies but we arranged transport and victuals for fifty-five men at the Centurion rate expense laid out…"

The smile. "But not the Optios. We each bring our own Optios, man of Sadiki, they are the men with the big sticks at the back. No matter, we made do and frankly when these movement orders happen we mostly end up sleeping outside. Sharing a thing blanket under an early snowfall, through some cockup or deliberate graft. By comparison you have excelled, House of Sadiki. Egyptian? Good, convey my thanks to your master. Amend it and I shall sign it. Luckily, we have a lot of cash with us so could cover the shortfalls, with receipts obviously. Funny thing that, having full treasury coffers for once. Meanwhile, Centurion Armourer, have you already briefed your men for the cruise, and if so, what did you say?"

Galba relayed the intelligence opinion and his instructions.

"Fucking hell," said the First Spear, grimly amused. "Well, you said the right thing."

The Centurion Armourer also passed on the note from Ruben, which he had held back from his men. "This is from my Liaison Optio at Aquincum. He travelled the river a month ago and has been overland about the region."

The First Spear read it quietly out loud. "'*River unsecured, eight miles from border - orange to red assessment. Highly porous. Encountered enemy on trip. Passed fort of destination – highly unsecure.*' So and so and…so…local military intelligence says green, everything else disagrees. I imagine your Optio travelled on a nondescript commercial boat? Right, so now we are going to head down

140

river in this massive barge convoy full of advanced war gear which has been watched building up by every two-denarii rat in the place? Do I have the gist of it, Centurion Armourer?"

Galba confirmed that the First Spear did. The FS casually turned. "Centurion Alba, can you get everyone around for a chat, including the armourers. No parade square, I just want everyone in."

Most of the men had heard anyway, listening in as soldiers do, and Centurion Alba led the rest away from the food stands to the quayside forming a rough semicircle beside one of their great black barges loaded with crates. The First Spear made his way to the middle and took a single step up onto an embarking truckle.

"Centurion Chief Armourer Galba, could you come and join me please?" Galba took his place below the First Spear, facing the men. The fact that he was the most junior Centurion by date, if not rank, itched slightly but it was time to do a job.

"Here's the thing, everyone. Centurion Chief Armour Galba has made an assessment of the situation which I fully concur with. We are revising this morning's Army intelligence that the border route is 'safe' to being 'completely unsafe'. Yes, alright, settle down, it is what it is and always will be. We will be attacked and, I believe, in force. The convoy is a high value target, known about. Intel will have been moving out of this port quick as a sunbeam since loading began this morning."

"Our delay, the delay of the Centurionate, has not helped, being all but unavoidable. On the plus side, we have just got here and haven't been milling about. Whatever is waiting for us downriver has made an assessment on intel at least four hours old. We push off immediately. That is, however, the last order I am going to make. I am maintaining that command of the convoy is with Centurion Chief Armourer Galba. I repeat: the Chief Armourer has command. This is his equipment and we are here to escort it. Does everyone understand?"

Assent, rather too loudly from Bullo which got a laugh.

"Well, I'm glad you approve, Armourer Cadet," First Spear said kindly. "Centurion Galba, you good?"

Leading the convoy was not going to be a lot of fun for the Chief Armourer with centurions in tow but he was going to command this morning so he made his mind up to think nothing had changed. "I am, FS."

"Can I suggest I sit in the lead barge with the bulk of the Centurions, Optios in the middle ones and Centurion Scirix at the rear?"

"Yes, First Spear." Galba hoped this wasn't going to be 'I make all the decisions but you're nominally in command if it all goes to shit' but decided to give the FS the benefit of the doubt and took charge.

"Armourers, you will be deployed across every boat. Guns has already broken the special stores out. Every third man is to be issued with a maniballista and as many bolts as you can carry. Group in twos. Department heads, you will be fire control. Have ignition sources in each group but ensure buckets are on standby."

First Spear liked this news. "We get to see our artillery for the first time? This is turning out to be a good day. Centurion Armourer, anything else?"

"For the Emperor, the Senate and people of Rome."

The phrase was returned, spoken clearly by each man.

"We board now. Department heads count your men on and in a tenth of an hour we push off. Cadet Bullo, bring the bargemen to me." instructed Galba.

Felix jumped down off the box and patted Galba on the back. "Good, you handled that well…Boss. Let's do this, Galba. The key thing is…"

"Don't fuck it up."

Felix grinned, "You and I are going to be fine."

Chapter Thirteen

Aquincum, afternoon
A task complete
Pannonia Inferior Province of Rome asserts its superiority

The Lady Lassalia, First Secretary Eleazar and Optio Ruben saw off the last of a number – two hundred and twenty-six to be precise, which they were – of supply carts, with a contented sigh. As soon as the troops had departed the parade square, the huge caravan that was blocking all traffic for ten miles along the western road rolled into town over a period of two days. The XXXth's whole season of food supplies were then all checked and docketed by the Sadiki staff.

To her immense satisfaction the Lady Lassalia loudly proclaimed, "Everything is there!" over a drink in town, allowed this rumour to circulate about Aquincum, then bought up the difference in reality at the subsequently-crashed prices, artificially held high by the locals for weeks before. Three days later the Legion's season supplies were re-hitched and ready to caravan out for the last leg up to Brigetio Fort, trailing the marching Legion. The stores were flanked by some Auxilia cavalry borrowed from the XXXth's Senior Centurion, who at the time of asking seemed to be unusually glad to release them for the job.

Finally, off the train now trundled in a blare of switched oxen. The Sadiki merchant and slave, with their army liaison, then repaired for a drink on the little balcony at the top of the small warehouse. As she made her way through the temporary operations centre the Lady Lassalia instructed everyone to "Go get some sleep, shag or get smashed. Back here tomorrow morning. Party at dusk if you want to come, then we are a-going home to Salona-by-the-sea-o!"

Watered wine was poured by the Sadiki balcony-slave and Sobe slouched on a lounger while the two men leant on the rail. The frenetic pace and ability demonstrated by Sadiki over previous weeks erased any qualms Optio Ruben might have had about drinking in the company of a slave. Instead, he clinked earthenware with First Secretary Eleazar as a colleague and they drank, surveying the port for a whole, peaceful, moment.

"Why are we drinking out of earthenware?" shouted the matron suddenly, opening her eyes, having heard the noise of fired clay.

Ruben had not yet got used to all the strange eddies of House Sadiki and tried to protest it was 'perfectly fine'. Eleazar knew better and just kept drinking while he could.

Sobe got up and shouted inside, bringing the offending slave out and began a long, questioning monologue regarding the presence of clay cups on the directors' balcony, "When She – Me – had quite clearly outlined that it must always be precious metal or glass up here?"

The Domina continued to ask if the slave was too busy and if indeed, She, Herself, should come and help him, thus diverting Her from the work downstairs to make sure all the catering was in good order. The level, verbal assault continued and Ruben took his cue from Eleazar and began ignoring what was going on behind him. The Optio looked out west over the churned-up field, at a fat barge sailing in. "What's that?"

Without really looking Eleazar answered; "Oil barge, Decimax class. Just a river runaround. That drum being set up on the quay is one of the offloading vats. It has got probably four taps for the amphora pour. There should be three more vats set up to do it properly with the whole process running for three hours. It'll take them ages with a single four-tap."

"Does the House of Sadiki 'do' oil?" Ruben asked.

"Lots. Good business but only combinations of certain quantities, qualities and routes. Wheat and oil, backbones of the Empire, but 'oils not oil' and wheat is as sure as shit's not wheat. As it turns out, wheat is sometimes straw, or a bag of stones in the middle of a bushel being weighed."

"Would you do that contract, I mean, that boat there?" and Ruben pointed to the oil barge.

The First Secretary looked up and down the quay thoughtfully. "Possibly, depends where it is from but possibly. Decimax is a little small, especially given the size of the river. I'd spend a bit of capital to go up a class. But, then again, maybe it's a high-quality product from a premium supplier. Tell you what, this is what I would do: behind the oil tanker what do you see?"

Ruben looked out at a string of different barges and river boats at anchor in the shadow of an upstream island. "Which one? Which one of the boats are you talking about?"

"All of them, but not what's in them, what are they doing?" asked the eunuch.

The Optio loved these puzzles with Eleazar and looked hard at each boat, trying to think like these merchants did. The boatmen were milling around, playing dice, coiling rope, lying in hammocks. They were barges just anchored or roped, bobbing about. A scene of total inactivity, doing nothing. Then Ruben had it; "They are waiting!"

Eleazar smiled. "Very good, Optio, very good. They are waiting because this quayside is way too small and inefficient. Do they, though, look particularly concerned?" One sailor looked like he was masturbating over the side. "No, they do not."

"Why?"

"Because…they are not paying for the time?"

"Again, I commend you, Optio Ruben. You should be a merchant. How much do you earn, if it is not an indelicate question?"

"Less than you, Eleazar, and you're a slave, but please, go on."

"These boats have made port in the correct time and if the goods are not unloaded or indeed – see the high-floating barge at the end – loaded on time a charge to the contractor will be levied."

Ruben thought. "So – you'd build more port?"

"Eventually I might, but it is a pain running port real estate. No, I'd buy the waiting time, demurrage options."

"I still really get lost on your options."

Eleazar spread his hands in a gesture of *'everything being actually quite simple'*. "A fee is paid by the merchant on all his cargoes to me, or indeed to the House of Sadiki may it thrive as the gods will, and I pay any of the demurrage – waiting – costs occurring. The combined fee I charge is of course lower, quite a bit lower that the average transfer delays the merchant is used to paying, so the merchant thinks: *'Hey, great, what a sucker these newcomers are!'* What he doesn't realise is that I'm going to start making things efficient so there are next to no transfer costs – thus turning a profit."

Ruben had no doubt this was within the First Secretary's abilities but saw a flaw. "So, once you've alleviated all the delays, what stops the merchant cancelling your contract at the end of the term and he goes back to business with things now improved?"

"Nothing. In fact, he probably will."

"Hmm, what do you do then?"

"I wait for him to come back begging to reinstate the demurrage option and charge twenty percent on top of what he was previously paying?"

"Why would the merchant do that?"

"Because of the Fire."

"The Fire?"

"The Fire's only the start of it. That he could have handled, but combined with the wherrymen strikes, pirates, new unmarked wreckage and the theft epidemic it becomes all too much."

Ruben ruminated. "Do you think you might actually do that here?"

"We started two days ago. Watch the dredger."

The municipal dredger was making its way downstream, having finished its last scrape, and Ruben spent the next half hour watching it pull alongside the moored boats. After a soundless exchange of words over bits of parchment with a Sadiki man, who had popped up out of nowhere from a hold, goods began to be loaded on to the huge vessel. Once done, the boat ambled over to its assigned, inviolable spot – always clear, and if it wasn't the huge dredger didn't stop. At the spot a big oxen team stood waiting to haul the scraper up for the next shift's pull.

As the dredger prepared to be heaved upriver by the sweating beasts, suddenly a fleet of carts, a young peach-liveried Sadiki representative in the lead up on a running board, raced out of town towards the municipal pad. As they pulled to a dusty halt, Ruben could see the adolescent rep throw a pouch to the dredger captain and pass out bottles and bread to the dredger crew. Then the cart teams worked at full pelt unloading. More wherrymen with trolleys, seeing the excitement, poured out of the town to help.

"Won't the authorities mind you using the town dredger for your own commercial use?"

Eleazar shrugged. "They may or may not. Maybe we make some unofficial form of civic contribution – who knows? – but using the dredger as an offload is one of the oldest tricks in the book. There are plenty more where that came from."

At that moment Ruben and Eleazar got crashed into, had their cups removed, both clay mugs lobbed off the balcony smashing below. Pewter goblets with enamelled sirens were then shoved into still open fingers. The balcony-slave appeared sheepishly from behind his Domina, filled the metal vessels and apologised profusely.

"Good, better. Because next time it might be someone important not these two bloody wasters."

She cackled with laughter as the server scurried off, and then flung her long arms around both men.

"Boys, boys, boys! Well, well. That was an experience. I suggest we get some sleep, up at sunset for the party then go sample the finest hospitality Aquincum Town can offer. Which, admittedly, is probably a group of men watching two dogs screw in the forum, but we should absorb provincial culture before returning to somewhere with some."

Eleazar wasn't listening however. Instead he was now looking back towards the balcony door at a small arrival. "Domina, you have a messenger."

A boy, a new local fresh to the Sadiki, adorned with a single House Ribbon.

"What now?" the Lady Lassalia muttered.

All the messengers received training, in fact everyone within Sadiki received training on an almost daily basis. This included the boy who, all credit to him, when he looked up and saw his beloved mistress didn't shout "You must come now!" or "There is a problem!" Instead, the lad took three breaths, as prescribed, and said, "Half an hour ago the great food convoy of House Sadiki going north with the XXXth supplies has been stopped and not going on. It is the merchant Holgur, who is a rapist, and a long soldier-man with many feathers who are doing it."

The Lady Lassalia took the information in but also gave a downturned smirk and tilt of her head. "That wasn't a bad go. Getting better. I liked the additional information but First Secretary Eleazar will have a word to you about something called 'defamation'. Well done, though, boy." and she threw the orphan a coin.

"Ruben, you are our bit of Army, get on a horse and let's liaise with whichever 'feather hat' is causing a problem. Eleazar, find the bloody Hedgehog. Boy, get my chariot harnessed."

"Do you have to take that thing, Domina?" Eleazar asked, leaving the balcony.

"It's an Egyptian thing, it's cultural, you wouldn't understand, slave."

"Because as a Jew we can only drive chariots properly, Domina?"

A short distance outside Aquincum gate Legionaries of the IInd Adiutrix had pounced at their General's direct instruction and started to secure the food convoy with Army teamsters. At the front of the great winding, wheeled beast the Sadiki caravan leaders, a highly-experienced man and wife team, were being pushed around by soldiers. The local 'magnet', there was always one in every town, named merchant Holgur had the woman's arm and wasn't letting go. Husband was bent double, having been backhanded by a tall, crookedly unpleasant-looking officer infused with malice. The thesis was simple: supplies had been stolen from the IInd Legio, much-needed supplies for the Aquincum Garrison Legion, and now they were taking them back.

"We are taking the whole fucking caravan for starters. The mules, the carts, your cunt and arse." And Holgur squeezed. It had little effect on the tough-as-nails caravan wife but she knew how to play the game and pretend squealed while watching and assessing. The woman could smell trouble from a mile off and sent the messenger boy running as soon as the road block appeared a handful of miles from the city gate. Wife had also sent one of the liveried Sadiki messengers at the same time. Sure enough, he had attracted the right type of attention, been run down by two legionaries, dragged back and given a kicking by Merchant Holgur's thugs.

The boy got away unseen.

The carrion stork of a Tribune sneered as he pronounced. "You two will be confined by the Legion of the IInd Adiutrix at the Garrison, the stores are being confiscated by this…" He held up a stamped, sealed papyrus. "…court order from an actual, real magistrate."

Heavy hooves and a clatter. One of the IInd Legionaries who'd served in Britannia for four miserable years grasped his gladius reflexively. "Chariot approaching, Sir!" a Centurion called out.

Running along the verged bank at an alarming tilt, bypassing the convoy blocking the road, came the Head of the House of Sadiki in a whirring of spokes. The two-horse team were pure white, her bespoke cradle a hybrid of a racer and war rig, adorned in the family palm and eye of Osiris. Sobe drove it herself and the charioteer, a once notable 'White' champion hung out hard, slope-side keeping the weight balanced. The chariot took the escarpment high, then swung round and down behind the startled soldiers before Sobe skidded the rig sideways to a stop.

The Lady Lassalia flicked her wrist and walked the team directly up to where the lanky Tribune stood, who tried not to flinch as the horses' nostrils flared wet, grassy breath into his face. There was nothing he wanted to do more than smack the beasts away but the pair looked like pure racers and to lay a hand on one invited the type of trouble his ornate cuirass would have no chance against.

"Fuck off, you thieving bitch!" screamed Holgur, the alleged rapist, at Lassalia, forcing the caravan wife to the ground. The woman carefully looked up at her employer and touched the folds of her tunic. Lassalia's finger made a small swing gesture in the negative.

"My goodness, Tribune, this informality in the provinces. Should I be offended, Sir?" Sobe stretched out her palm towards Holgur, be-ringed rank showing.

This observation did wipe the sneer off the Tribune's face. The fact that this woman seemed to have some sort of undefined legal status as a merchant was an ungodly state of affairs, a view compounded over the past weeks by the IInd's lead supplier- Holgur. The disgusting little merchant continually railed against the Lady Lassalia as being entirely responsible for all the recent supply shortages since the 'Egyptian mummer show' arrived in town (and also for any problems in the preceding five years, which even the Governor put down to enthusiasm). All this was now totally overridden by her assertion relating to social hierarchy, which hit every one of the Roman officer's main, ingrained prejudices.

"Holgur, apologise for your outburst."

"But…"

"Many thanks to you, Tribune, it is not necessary, but if he could release my employee, or face immediate litigation, it would be appreciated."

The Tribune turned back from admonishing Holgur, looking up at the merchant woman. "These people, your people, are in the custody of the IInd Legio, as so you might be very soon."

Lady Lassalia bowed respectfully. "And myself and my employees willingly submit to such detention if so ordered. Please note that I, in no way, have any objection to your Legion's punishment of my people, now lying on the floor. You must have had just cause and these soldiers administered the correct course. He…" pointing to Holgur, "…is not allowed to harm my property, he is a…non-person. Please, Tribune, if you feel this woman of mine needs further

149

chastisement at the hands of the legionaries you will have my full support. Unless, of course, this man Holgur, who I had believed to be a local merchant, holds some sort of equivalent military rank with you, Sir."

Sobe could lay it on thick when she had to.

The very suggestion shocked the Tribune who sneered at Holgur. "Release the woman now. Legionaries, take this creature into custody with her husband." Three soldiers stepped forward dragging the couple out of Holgur's reach before manacling them.

"Am I under arrest also?" asked the Lady Lassalia, looking down calmly from the hybrid chariot.

The Tribune walked around the horses and rig. "These supplies are going to the IInd and Provincial Army Command. That rabble who went up the road the other week can wait. We have pressing need of consumables for the border and operational requirements for the sector take precedence. I am reliably informed…" the officer said, pointing to Holgur. "…that these goods were ours in the first place and some sort of merchant shenanigans your sort engage in, have prevented their proper deployment. Any objections?"

The Head of the House of Sadiki considered these words. "Yes, many. Slap on the manacles because I choose arrest." And Sobe stepped off the rig. She was tall and still almost the same height as the officer, who didn't like the fact, or that she was standing just a little bit too close, eyes locked.

"Manacles won't be necessary, but you will come with me. Not on that contraption, however." The Tribune replied, pointing at the chariot.

Chapter Fourteen

Summer morning, Brigetio fort, or what's left of it
South bank of the Danube,
Pannonian Imperial province grey area.

Five days later the House was still smouldering. The Skipper and the Exfil Tribune had three boat-oxen chained and this morning began dragging the heavy, sodden, black timbers out of the Houses' wreckage. Most of the building had collapsed in on itself, what remained was being pushed down by legionaries with poles and mallets. One bad concussion and it wasn't even noon yet.

"Sir, better come and see this," the FCL called out, standing with a work team in the middle of the ashes. Both officers picked their way through the bricks, half-burnt timbers and pools of water to the grimy men. The legionaries were dressed in duty fatigues, leaning on spades and hooks looking grimly down to one spot.

A short-blackened brick column stood at the centre of the group.

"What is it, FCL?" asked the Exfil Tribune.

"Best just come and see for yourself, Sir."

Two legionaries stepped back, letting the officers through.

"Love of the gods!" the young Exfil commander muttered as he saw it.

Around the brick pillar five charred skeletons sat, all the flesh gone, with the chains that bound them hanging limp around wrist and ankle bones.

"Were they…?"

"No fingernails, Sir, and this one looked liked he – or she'd – ripped one foot off to get out the shackles, see where it's all broken?" The FCL pointed with an entrenching tool to the shattered ankle.

"Bastards." The FCL spat to one side. "That's no way to die, burning."

The Exfil turned to the Skipper. "Who were they, do you think?"

"They were not valuable or important enough, that's what they were. You've sent the Assyrians over on snatch raids and we've taken prisoners at least twice for the House. The SOG were collecting people for interrogation all winter. You ever seen anyone leave here who was carted in?"

The Exfil Tribune shook his head.

"They'll be farmers, country people, shepherds, and foresters. Knew bugger all so here they now lie. FCL…"

"Sir?"

"…say a prayer."

The legionaries and officers bowed their heads and the veteran said an old prayer for peace and restful shades. This was their fort after all, and no one wanted ghosts. The Exfil instructed that the bodies be taken to the Legion cemetery outside the walls. As the day rolled on more chained corpses were found in the rubble. All of them were buried in a pit marked with a cairn.

A shout from the gatehouse and both officers left these first charred bodies, walking across the parade ground and up a ladder to the gate parapet. Atop it Comms stood signalling with a flag. More hostile riders had appeared on the opposite ridge and even some foot soldiers. The Skipper peered over the river, after an assessment saying, "They're some of the Macro levies being trained by our old colleagues, I swear to it," and Comms made a quick look back with a nod of confirmation as he continued to make the message.

"Where is he signalling to?" asked the Exfil lead, following Comm's gaze straight forward across the bank.

"Certainly not there, Tribune, Comms's just looking straight out to confuse the watchers. See? The enemy are sending a sweep down the hill looking for the source. Don't look, but we have your Werewulf over the other side, upstream five hundred paces. He's flash signalling back, and my Four is right above us in the roof with a sack over his head receiving the message." The Exfil officer looked up into the covered rafters of the gate parapet and, sure enough, an Infil specialist was jammed into the roof beams looking towards the area Skipper had described, cutting a wax tablet.

"What's happening, do you think?" asked the Exfil Tribune and CO to his nominal second. "The enemy are gaining certainty about our situation, that's for sure."

"Flash stop, Sir." said Four from above.

The Skipper caught the tablet tossed down to him, opened it and read out loud, 'PatHxII, WH IID'

"Shit, incoming river traffic." The Exfil swore. "Try and work the Gunboat upstream?"

The Gunboat was currently stationary, holding position between the fort's river port and the opposite bank. The Skipper grimaced. "I say leave it, concentrate all fire arcs around the base."

"Give them no free passage over, you mean? Agreed. Must be more troops downstream as well, I reckon. The sand bar is wading distance from the far shore down there, best place to cross in small boats. Skipper, I'm not going to muster until something really happens, though. Don't want to provoke them. Play it like it's any other day. Like the veteran said, maybe we buy some more time."

The Skipper smiled. "How long have you been here now, Tribune? You're getting the hang of this officering."

"You mean: Listen and do everything the senior men in the ranks tell you? Hades, Yes."

Stood up on the gatehouse, the two officers continued to scan the far bank before the Exfil Tribune turned to his colleague again. "If they come in force...?"

"We'll be absolutely fine," the Skipper said loudly, glancing upwards to remind the Tribune that Four was still above them.

"Oh, yes, right. So...Book VII of Heroditus, is it?"

From the parapet ceiling above came: *"For knowing the death which was about to come upon them by reason of those who were going round the mountain, they displayed upon the barbarians all the strength which they had, to its greatest extent, disregarding danger and acting as if possessed by a spirit of recklessness..."*

The Skipper scowled and looked up. "You're too bloody clever by half, Four. Who said you could have an education? I certainly didn't."

"Sorry, Skip."

At that moment, the opposite ridge erupted with figures. Hundreds of armed men poured down out of the treeline running down towards the north shore. A mish mash of levies with hide shields and more effective looking spearmen all in bronze. The noise of their shouts carried across the river in a muffled roar.

"Here they come, Tribunes!" Comms exclaimed from the signalling step.

"Not sure playing it cool and bluffing it out's going to work anymore, Commander."

Exfil nodded. "Infil Comms, sound General Alarm!"

The Romans didn't even have a proper Cornicifer so three short horn blasts from Comms it was. The hunting horn rang out. Down in the parade ground Immunes legionaries jogged to their stacked armour in twos, buckling and checking. Gunners raced up ladders; ratchets sounded from the winding gate ballista. The Tribunes both stepped back as the two gun crews prepped the covered fire area over the gate. On the opposite bank more bands of infantry were now flowing over the high ridge, ignoring the tracks and just scrabbling and sliding down the side of the hill.

Amongst the foot soldiers Roxolani horsewomen were visible but they stayed back from the shore, in the scrub. Probably remembering the recent encounter with the Gunboat, bobbing menacingly about midriver as it was.

"Incoming signal," Four spoke calmly from the gatehouse roof.

Out of the corner of his eye the Skipper could see the odd flash from Werewulf's silver mirror. Four didn't bother passing down a slate this time. "Boats, not ours, incoming upriver, Sir."

The first thwacks sounded as the Gunboat's two Skorpions fired from its station midstream, in line with the gatehouse. The far bank was too overgrown for a proper line of sight and the bolts disappeared into the shrubs. Shouts sounded though, so whether the bolts hit or not the first enemy warriors reaching the shore were at least having a good think.

"FCL, your men on the gate!" the young Exfil Tribune and CO shouted down, and received acknowledgements. The veterans were already forming up, the Triari rigged in heavy sets of plate. The rest of the Exfil team were assigned the walls, which they now ran to.

"Where do you want us, Skipper?" Two shouted up from the bottom of the parapet ladder.

"Use your initiative, Two. By the way, you look good in that," the Skipper responded, noting his men were actually in metal armour for a change. With that, Two took the team of four to a bit of unmanned wall likely to involve imminent killing.

"I can see boats upstream, far side," Four communicated down from the gatehouse rafters.

A small armada of river boats appeared to the west, flanked on the northern shore path by the running shore troops Werewulf had also spotted. Foot soldiers with an array of hooks, helmets and brightly painted shields ran obliviously right over the old scout's position, low down as it was in a bed of reeds. Three hostile boats laden with men sculled out to the middle stream, at least fifty souls apiece onboard, and then a mass of transport craft followed, hugging the far shore.

"Pilots!" the Exfil shouted down to his team on the dock. "Get the boats out of there, now!"

The enemy assault craft were still a way off but the current was racing, especially in the river's fat. The Xboat and Triboat were released from the ramps with splashes, the shore crews lending weight to the sterns in order to get the craft moving off the pontoons. "Clean launches!" shouted the Shore Master and as the two craft made their escape the Lead Pilot on the Gunboat could be seen shouting instructions to his crew covering the evacuation. Both the Gunboat Skorpion teams turned their pieces to the fast-running enemy craft approaching. Lead Pilot was waving happily at the enemy fleet.

"They're a mad bunch, your lot," observed the Skipper. Exfil didn't reply, watching the closing fleet in-between shouting a series of orders regarding buckets and a backroom store of pilums that had been recently discovered.

The enemy assault boats sculled madly and picked up more and more momentum, all three craft diving with glee upon their prey: the Gunboat and her fleeing sisters. On the far shore a mounted young man with an impressive silver hat was, however, frantically trying to get the assault crafts' attention, clearly reminding them they were meant to secure the landing zone. It was just too exciting, though. All three enemy craft were at a cracking speed, the best armoured warriors the Romans had seen so far were in the vessels, beating shields as they prepared to smash into and board the first catamaran, the Gunboat itself.

Lead Pilot timed it perfectly. Twenty paces away the anchors were slipped and oars churned. Still the forward assault boat bore down on them but just as they were a few lengths away the Gunboat frustratingly edged towards a matched speed. Twenty beats later just a few steps separated the moving boats, the armoured warriors screaming in frustration at the Roman stern and spitting at the Lead Pilot who gave them the universal sign for 'wankers'. One fighter even jumped forwards in rage and went straight in the drink, mown down immediately by his own boat. The military pilot smiled and saluted backwards before ducking down. Only one warrior realised what was about to happen but it was too late.

"Fire!" shouted the Fire Caller and two heavy bolts exploded parallel, blood spraying, splintered paths down the entire length of the enemy assault craft. The nearside bolt ended its journey in the chest of the rudderman, punching him off the back. The screaming barge then began to yaw and whirl out of control, blood streaming from the gunwales like a pre-dawn abattoir before market day. The enemy assault barge behind it had been too close and rammed the leader, breaching the forward boat's side. The second crafts crew ran forward manically to pole the hulled boat off its bow.

Oars thrashing behind, the third assault craft managed to pull up and, turning dramatically at the last moment, threw anchors towards the shore and swung in making for the pontoon dock. A fresh Skorpion volley from the Gunboat tried to reach second boat. Instead both missiles slapped into the broached assault craft. Each bolt sped low through the hull and the lead barge heeled and was almost instantly thrown over by the current, sowing a harvest of armoured, broken men to the river bed for the catfish to nibble at.

An enraged shout went up from the second assault boat at the boiling wake before it. A warrior rushed to the back of the boat and, after a brief exchange, pushed their rudderman off the stern, took command himself and steered the bow straight down river to seek vengeance on the little Roman catamaran.

"The man in the silver hat seems quite put out, Sir," remarked Four.

Sure enough, the mounted enemy commander on the far bank looked like he was about to erupt in snakes as the man watched the second boat, with its warriors, disappear off downriver after the nippy little catamaran.

The third enemy assault craft, however, was on target and moments away from the pontoons. On the river quay a desperate-looking last stand of Exfil shore crew stood ready, ten men against the fifty-odd about to disembark in thirty heartbeats. Oval Roman shields badly closed up, wedged into the middle berth landing. The assault boat made straight for the Immunes technicians. "Did you do a test after reassembly?" asked the Skipper watching the trap put in place days before for such an eventuality.

The Exfil shook his head. "No time. I think the lead engineer should be pretty motivated, though."

The legionaries on the quay crouched ready to take the full assault of the armoured warriors, who themselves screamed, extremely ready to leap down and slaughter the small Roman force as soon as their bow crashed into the quay.

A lever was pulled.

A massive hiss, a huge churn of water and three enormous bangs as the River Goats blasted out, each of the hydraulic pumps working perfectly, one stationed in each of the three main berths.

Not designed or reinforced to take such an impact the middle River Goat ram, dynamically, went straight through the assault boat's bow just as the vessel closed the quay, shattering the entire front below the waterline and propelling the whole craft backwards with enormous force. Every warrior was sent flying, many into the water, even the oarsman went down, and their boat captain was thrown forward straight onto a 'friendly' spear. The assault boat drifted slowly backwards and, missing its entire front panelling, sank almost immediately.

"Triari! Ten men, go!" the Exfil Tribune shouted down to the parade square. Out jogged the veterans with their long spears to join the Exfil shore crew, who themselves were retrieving stacked pilums or trusty boat hooks from the equipment shed.

The water was not that deep on the pontoons, enough for a barge to land or a man to stand in to neck height. Absolute bitch to fight in, however.

With the assault boat hitting the bottom, enemy warriors tried to recover and wade out of the water. The only place they could go was towards the pontoons, where the Roman Army stood about and poked down. Some warriors screamed with rage, some tried to walk or swim away and disappeared almost immediately, some begged or tried to surrender. The legionaries just kept stabbing or pushing downwards at the enemy trapped in the shallows, like one of those macabre fish festivals where the prey is driven to the shallows and the old women come out with clubs beating the water. Indeed, the Shore Master thought wistfully of his old mum and nonna as he pushed down hard on a struggling mercenary until all the puff went. When all fifty-plus enemy were drowned or skewered, the engineers detached the River Goats and sank them into the shallows. Either they'd be retrieved later or be lost to the enemy.

"Well done, back in!" shouted Exfil from the gatehouse and both his Shore Team and the ten Triari veterans quick timed back inside the gates, which were then bolted shut. The young Command Tribune leant over the back balcony and gave a thumbs up to the Shore Master, who was white as a sheet but humming *'A-beating the wet we go, lil' fisheys.'*

More figures swarmed over the opposite ridge and down the slope. On the far bank a score of the new landing craft arriving from upriver were being loaded. In all the excitement, Exfil only just now clocked that a large raft had come down the Danube in the shadow of the assault craft. "They've got a ferry, Skipper. See that fishing boat behind the other boats, that's got the shackles and line."

"How many can it take, Tribune? Because there's close on five hundred men and women over there, and counting."

"At least one hundred combatants."

"Any ideas?"

"Hope a particularly large fish eats it, because there is nothing we can do other than fire a couple of Ballista from here, and you can see the sides are being palisaded right now."

"Many of them then were driven into the sea and perished, and many more still were trodden down while yet alive by one another, and there was no reckoning of the number that perished."

"Stop that, Four! I'm not in the mood."

"Sir."

A runner came from the east wall and up the panting up the gate parapet ladder. "Sir, message from spotter on the hill." The Skipper looked up at the hill to their right. "What has Point got for us, runner?"

"Message reads 'Hold on.'"

Both Tribunes looked at each other. "And what else?" demanded the Exfil.

The messenger gawped. "Just that, Sir. I'm pretty sure. Confirmation end and everything."

"Well, signal back 'Thanks for the tip!'" retorted the Skipper, and the messenger nodded and made to run off. "Boy, belay that. Just keep your eyes on that hill for more signals." The messenger took a moment to process this, but had a mind that could simply replace contradictory orders after a single moment, and ambled back to the eastern tower.

"So – your man Point up on the hill: just doing his bit for morale is he, Skipper?" asked the Exfil Tribune and CO, cheerfully.

"I don't know, but in the meantime, let's just 'hold on', shall we?"

"Let's do that," the Tribune concurred.

The boats on the far shore were loaded with armed men and, in a more co-ordinated manner than the strike force, launched purposefully forward. The little fishing boat was also moving, hanging a ferry guide rope up on a stay from the stern. One of the other bigger vessels was not filled with warriors, just a lot of oarsmen. It was the largest vessel and positioned itself upstream, using its flanks to provide a current breaker for the smaller craft. The oarsmen on this vessel

158

worked furiously and threw boulder kedges, constantly pulling and fighting to hold station. It worked though, and before long a mass of craft was halfway across the river, partly protected from the current with marginal drift downstream.

The Exfil commander took a breath then shouted across the fort, "Alright, men. This is it! For the Emperor, for the Senate and people of Rome."

"Ooh ooh ooh!" every man shouted back, clattering weapons on shields.

Two long horn blasts rang out from the enemy far bank.

"Shit, what's that?" said the Skipper. "Comms, make signal to southern towers: 'R we flanked? Are they at the back of U'?"

Comms ran out on to the parapet and flag signalled to the south western tower.

Four relayed the answer. "Receipt: 'N' for No, nothing."

The Exfil ran about the gatehouse, looking in all directions but forward. "What does that horn blast mean?" he demanded.

A voice from the rafters. "Sir, look there, the boats are turning away."

Unconvinced, both officers continued to look around the forest but gradually their gaze came back to the most obvious enemy. All the boats were now falling off into the current, making downstream and steering for their home bank. The first craft hit the shore with a soft *thunk*, disembarked everyone then cut away the empty barge and poled it into the current. At the enemy muster point, Skipper could now see Silver Hat surrounded by Roxolani light cavalry, obviously a patrol that had just ridden in. Hands were waving and the waiting troops then turned and began marching off upstream, along the path back towards Werewulf's observation position. The rest of the boats repeated the first one's actions: landing on the far shore, disembarking at speed before being just cut loose into the Danube. When all the enemy warriors were back on shore, smoke started to appear from the huge ferry-raft and soon it was ablaze as levies and mercenaries trotted back up the slope.

"What's going on, Skipper?"

"I have no idea, but it's a clever diversion if it is one."

Again the eastern messenger burst up the ladder. "Sir, message from hill spotter. Troops approaching us on south bank road."

"What troops?"

"Didn't say."

The Exfil grabbed the idiot by his neck scarf. Instead of him being bawled out, the Skipper calmly interjected, placing a hand on the young CO's shoulder, "Did Point say how many, boy?"

"Yes, but I think I got it wrong." The neck scarf tightened in Exfil's fist.

"I did check!" the messenger protested. "but it can't…be that many…!

Exfil started to throttle him. "Message flashed 'Thousands.'" The idiot gargled.

A whistle came from Four above.

Skipper scowled, "Are you sure it didn't indicate 'R' for 'Red'?"

The boy said no and the Exfil put him down exasperated. "Get back to your station, you silly sod. Well, Skipper?"

"I would say it's been a strange old day and if they're not ours coming up the road. And that…" he said pointing to the repairing enemy, "…is a cunning grand stratagem, I can't work out what it is, Exfil."

Brigetio's CO whistled to himself, then stoically decided, "Not much we can do about 'thousands' either way. Right. Everyone take in some water, pass along the line."

"Fancy something stronger, Commander?"

"Yes."

The Skipper took a Ballista bolt from the gunner's mate and poked upwards. "Four, throw down that flask of illegal contraband in your harness."

"Sir?"

"Now – Virgil."

The bottle came down on a strap with a mumbled, *"Through pain I've learnt to comfort suffering men."*

"Shut up, Four!" Both officers said and took turns drinking his booze.

Chapter Fifteen

Aquincum Town, Governor's administration building/palace
Day wears on 'assisting' the authorities
Pannonia Inferior province of Rome.

Lady Sobe Lassalia and her caravan couple had eventually been carted back through Aquincum. It had taken an age to turn the great rolling store-train around, back past the town gates to the Governor's palace under legionary guard. The Head of the House Sadiki was not chained to the moving plank floor so had leant forward to check on her teamster leaders, who were themselves firmly bolted down. The couple just shrugged as if being beaten and arrested by soldiers was 'business as usual' for overland caravan teams, which it was. Although both man and wife remarked that such things usually occurred outside the Empire. Sobe also asked if they had been searched. The pair replied that they had been frisked by the soldiers but, yes, still had a full of array of secreted knives, garottes, files, lockpicks and silver and gold bits about themselves. Satisfied, Sobe leant back on the juddering bench.

Reaching Pannonia Inferior provinces' main administration building the cart stopped, with the caravan leads dragged off towards basement cells, and the Lady Lassalia escorted to a crumbling room with solid window bars located on the top floor. It was now a world of dangerous variables and Sobe had to admit relief when the food trays started coming into the flaking room with regularity over the following days. Immurement was generally a private, family matter between a man and wife but...you never knew. At a wobbly table on a shifty chair, the fish and bread was gratefully wolfed down by Lady Lassalia at least twice a day.

Sobe had been to the administration building just once before, to introduce herself to the Governor and Head of the Garrison on arrival in town. Neither luminary had been particularly interested, and Sobe got the brush off from a flunkey having never made it further than a waiting room 'inferior'. Aquincum was a long way from Salona where she could always be guaranteed a formal

161

audience with government if needed, which she rarely did, using the Scipio instead to get things done as tedious a task as that could be.

The Lady Lassalia had obviously got the Pannonia (Inferior) administration's attention now and in her days locked in the bedroom – there was a single raised couch with worn but clean sheets – she brought into mnemonic focus the various court cases Honoured Imperial Nephew had been whirbling about while she had been busy, pondering that:

'The officials weren't honestly asserting that by supplying one Army Legion efficiently, using every means she had to deliver the Imperial will, she had impinged upon other…Army bits…that could not themselves harness the forces of a free market?'

The jagged-limbed stork of a Tribune – quite old, quite cross and obviously not on the rise – who'd vaguely detained her, had accused Sobe of 'stealing'. *'The gall!'* she fumed. Buying up a series of contracts at source, deliberately kept on short leases by the local suppliers to drive costs down, was good business, not stealing. Stealing was what little provincial pigs like Holgur did, made worse by countenancing Army quartermasters who were either on the take or thick as shit. The Governor of the area was obviously also incompetent and Sobe was now paying the price. An unloved goat thrown to the crocodiles by the useless praying for a change in fortune rather than addressing systemic, detailed errors.

Less than a full week later, the room's lock rattled and a civic administrator entered with a trailing legionary. The wonk looked at her lying on the couch with pure hate. He was actually quite lucky, she thought, as Sobe had just been considering her third wank of the day to pass the time.

"Please follow me, my Lady. The Governor of Lower Pannonia will see you now." Flunky announced grandly.

'Lower Pannonia! Wow!'

The first thing Sobe noticed was that the formal receiving room was falling to bits, plaster coming off, a fawn on the wall had lost all the interesting bits.

Inside the 'great' room a group of men in togas and military uniform stood, standing angrily at her. It wasn't the first time this had happened and neither would it be the last. She noted two Assyrians were incongruously also in the

162

room, full black headdresses and knots of the Hatra. She glanced down to their waist ropes to ascertain which of the seven tribes they were from. *'Interesting.'*

"Madam…" This was the Governor, purple-striped and looked like a man who had hoped for Sicily but got the political posting equivalent of the clap instead. Border provinces were unenviable with problems hard to eradicate, also much like most venereal diseases. The Civil Legate for the region seemed to console himself in his predicament by eating and sweating.

"…you have caused great disruption: you have caused what amounts very closely to the undermining of the people of Rome and their safety."

She noted he didn't mention the Emperor. This was going to be difficult, some old patrician senator yearning for the days when the Senate wasn't just a place your wives made you go to. Probably why he ended up here and not Sicily or one of the plum eastern provinces to merrily loot within the boundaries of acceptability and public immunity.

"Surely I have supplied a new Legion at the request of…"

"WHO GIVES A FUCK ABOUT THE NEW LEGION!" shouted a fancy uniform at the top of his lungs. This was the General of the IInd who was very, very angry. Sobe had only seen him from afar up to this point but he was always angry so she tried not to take it personally. The General would rasp away up and down the town quay, ride around with officers in tow screaming and, so her representatives told her, had also sat in on a few of the recent, special, court cases.

At the judicial sessions, the General apparently looked as though he might audition for a new (short) life in the circus at any moment by leaping up and slaying the Emperor's Nephew, there and then, in the middle of a court of law. Not that Cornelius Ulpia Mako noticed at all and blissfully carried on talking about *'…if we could know if oxen could really decide anything themselves…?'* or some such thing.

The Lady Lassalia remained silent for a moment and thought. Then spoke, "All the goods and transportation for the XXXth has been carefully receipted and documented. I hope there is no suggestion of financial wrongdoing levelled at the House of Sadiki?" and she looked at Holgur and four other low-rent river merchants glaring at her from one side of a cracked marble table.

None of them took the bait, they weren't that stupid.

A grey man, a Roman obviously, nondescript with close-cut ash hair leant on a wall as casually as you can flanked by two Hatra killers. He spoke next in a flat, tepid voice. "The House of Sadiki, in supplying the new Legion, has blocked vital trade routes into Pannonia. You took all…"

'Took? Paid for…'

"…all the transport and other cargo space leading into Aquincum two months ago, prioritised your own goods and drove up the prices on all contracts into the region. Your greed is treasonous."

Treason? The public sector, bless them! "Sorry, and your name is…?"

The Governor interjected, "This is the head of a special department for the region, you don't need to know his name."

'Probably a spy.'

"What he does is vitally important, with a deeply troubling security situation developing."

'Spy.'

The spy spoke "Call me Marcus if you must. I admire your enterprise, woman."

'Bad spy. "Woman"?'

"But this enterprise will be at an end. Possibly so shall you be too," SOGI commented in a mild voice.

The Governor did blanch at this threat to a citizen, but the merchants and the IInd's General did not.

'They cannot be serious?' Sobe thought. "Those goods are property of the XXXth Legio, not mine. They have already been released in order to bolster – assuredly – the rapidly deteriorating security situation in question."

The IInd's General snarled. "Good, so then you can fuck off back to wherever you came from, back to your husband-citizen. I served in Egypt and I don't like you or your people."

She liked the General. He at least was forthright. The question then was: were they letting her go or putting her in a bag and killing her? They seemed confused themselves. She asked the question directly. "So can I go then?"

The Governor pulled himself up. "No. Despite my colleague's expressions you are not going anywhere. Your goods are confiscated and you shall work with all these gentlemen to address the overall supply situation."

Now was definitely not the time to point out 'we don't do Army'.

"This mess will be cleared up even if you spend every last denarius from Sadiki coffers on doing so. In addition, we have issued you with a fine, or more accurately a punitive fiscal structure."

Behind the Governor an old civic magistrate moved forward and solemnly presented the Lady Lassalia with a writ.

It was a very large number but she didn't blink, just folding the papyrus and tucking it into her dress…

"Anything else I can do?" she asked breezily.

"Yes, there is," said grey 'Marcus'. "You will now also assist me when needed."

This was definitely turning into a Sadiki index rating of 'twelve'. Working for whatever Marcus was meant death. That's how her father disappeared, running whatever it was into Italy during a period of civil confusion because the 'Office of Cultural Affairs' in Alexandria had made him a suggestion.

Dad never came back and the Roman representatives for dancing and singing disappeared off the face of the earth when her mother tried to find out what had happened to Pa.

"Of course," answered the House of Sadiki.

"And now that your Project Invictus is finished, woman, we – the honest traders of this fair town - shall also be applying to the magistrate, the real magistrate here in this room, for reparations. You created a monopoly!" This was Holgur's contribution.

The Head of House Sadiki stayed perfectly calm and sought clarification. "Monopoly on what? Grain? Wine? Oil? I did none of these things."

"That…" said the old magistrate pompously. "…will be a decision for the law. THE LAW!" finished the judge with a little wobble for emphasis.

The General of the IInd hadn't finished and felt like some purposeful explication. "This province is being raided and incurred on all the way along the border east of Vindabona. Even down here away from the front we can't move about freely because this…" and the Military Legate pulled out a gold coin. "…Is pouring in all over the place. Know what this is?"

She peered. "It is a Dacian sovereign stamped in the last year at the Sarmizegetusa mint. You can tell by the crease on the little sceptre." Sobe Lassalia really knew money.

'Marcus' the probable spy turned to the scribe who was also in the room, and indicated a note should be made of this detail.

"SHUT UP!" shouted the IInd's General. "It's a gold coin, and these gold coins are everywhere causing problems. My men suddenly don't have access to rations and spares. Now, admittedly at first I thought these thieves were just taking the proverbial." The Legate indicated the merchants, who all bowed. "I thought it was just the usual pack of bloody excuses, it seemed ridiculous that some woman who barged her way in here just weeks ago could strangle all my supply routes, but then SOGI here…"

He pointed to 'Marcus'. Sobe became bored at this point, so while pretending to listen instead concentrated back on the Hatra Assyrians, there was something wrong with them, but she couldn't quite place it…

"…confirms it was YOU! So, YOU can get it sorted, we are going to break you but you might escape with life, Roman citizen or not, to scurry off to your husband and tell him what a fucking mess you made getting into men's business. You can tell him all this while you beg in a barrel. Remind me, magistrate, what are the financial qualifications for a second-estate citizen? I don't know these things, having never been one." The magistrate provided the information in a longwinded fashion.

'Why twelve knots on these Assyrians' belts?' Sobe thought, half listening. The Governor was speaking now.

"Thank you, General, and learned magistrate. Now, my Lady, be so good as to go with these men." He indicated the merchants. "Who will find you a secure space to work in. One of 'Marcus' men will accompany to provide secure contact with your main Sadiki office. Our black cloaked friends shall convey the necessary instructions, as per payments, we shall require from you, to your staff. Is all of this clear?"

'Twelve knots, but only seven Hatra tribes?'

The Lady Lassalia nodded contritely, then tried something.

"This is my Damascus!" she wailed in a plaintive voice.

"What the fuck does that mean?" shouted the General. "Damascus? You're not going to bloody Damascus. You're going to a fucking cell…"

"It is not a cell, General. It is a supervised area for a Roman citizen." The Governor sighed; this meeting was being minuted. "As of now, the Lady Sobe Lassalia is under house arrest, just not in her own house."

"I will fully cooperate, my Lords." A deep bow.

"Good, now go and make restitution for your meddling."

Holgur smiled and SOGII crossed the room towards Sobe, making a gesture to the door. Something about the man indicated Sobe could leave by her own volition or be dragged out by her hair. Lady Lassalia smiled weakly – she practised this regularly in front of a mirror- turned and walked behind SOGII and in front of Holgur. She felt the merchant's hand grab her arse and leave it there as they walked. Sobe ignored it as the trio went down the steps to a back door which opened straight on to a waiting, covered cart. Once aboard, she was shoved to the driver's end.

One of the Assyrian guards approached muttering in soft Latin, "Her people are outside but we are dealing with it," to SOGII who then indicated the black swathed contractor should also board the vehicle. The cart pulled off at speed and they all bounced on the suspension. Just for a moment, under his black headdress, she fancied the Hatra Assyrian looked directly at her.

'Have I hooked a little fishy?' Sobe thought and began to remember everything she could about magic bread.

Alerted to the meeting inside that day through the outlay of coin, Ruben and the Hedgehog rushed to the palace gates. There they now stood at a distance, enclosed by the four lictors who were on 'full offensive stance'. Fasces had been disassembled in an obviously well-practised move and the huge officials each held an axe in one hand, a now-revealed short sword in the other with rods scattered around them. A score of IInd Legionaries, with shields planted, spears levelled and stopped, prevented any attempt by the Emperor's Nephew to enter the building. A group of Assyrians with their long-curved cutting swords, had worked around behind the Imperial group and the two rear Praetorians tracked them warily.

A toga'd civic functionary, flanked by some more Hatra contractors, stood behind the row of IInd troops placed in front of the administration gate. He addressed the small group.

"Respectfully, Imperial Quaestor Ulpia Mako, the Governor is very busy today on a serious matter of security. A matter which is not wholly unconnected with yourself, and which I am sure the Emperor, your uncle, will be alarmed to hear about."

The local populace gathered around at a safe distance. This was more fun than watching a good fire. "Don't let them push you about, Hedgehog!" shouted a man in encouragement. Cornelius Ulpia Mako's time as a magistrate had gained a great following in Aquincum. He was seen as sticking it to the merchant bastards who ran the wharfs, his orations and summations were repeated word for word in taverns to all round entertainment and he hadn't hanged anyone yet. Just a goat in a judgement over criminal damage.

A stone hit a shield. Soon a patter of stones and other projectiles began raining down on the legionaries. The assembled mob left the Assyrians alone, however.

A whistle suddenly sounded from the little Sadiki boy who ran around the side of the administrative building towards Optio Ruben. "The Lady Lassalia of the House of Sadiki is in a cart heading west with those Roman spies and the rapist Holgur. There is one of them with them." he shouted, pointing at the Assyrians circling behind.

"Um, what do we do? What do we do now? Shall we rush them!" ventured Mako.

A half-eyed glare from one of the lictors answered that.

"No," said Ruben. "I'm at a loss. It is all very clever."

"Is it?"

"Yes, because as soon as the supplies officially passed to me on leaving the town gate, they are under military command. Arguably that authority could extend to the senior local military leader – the IInd's General. The XXXth don't even have a general yet. Or now any food now as it turns out."

"Right...er. I can't believe they won't even talk to me! I mean, I'm a special sort of Questor, I'm the blooming, you know, well..."

"With respect Sir, what were you sent here to do?"

"Well, you know. You are part of it, I mean. I'm here to help create the new Legion for Uncle, well you know, the Em..."

Ruben nodded. "And as soon as the men reach the fort you will have essentially done that. Both the Governor and sector commander have allowed you to follow the letter of that Imperial command. The poor XXXth won't starve, they'll be drip fed but we'll be some shitty little third-rank Legion doing every type of shitty duty until a Legate with clout is sent and the thing is: the IInd have real clout. They are an old Legion and their General's been fighting here for years, kept on after he should have gone home after the last Dacian war. You, Sir, have however done your job and that's what that lot in there are banking on. In the next few days the Governor will summon you, thank you for all your work and suggest strongly you return to Rome."

The Hedgehogs shoulders dropped. "But, what about the Lady? Is she going to be alright?"

Optio Ruben looked at the noble with a little kindness. "No, Sir, she is not going to be alright. She will lose everything, I expect. Go home, my lord, and I'll go to my 'Legion' although I'd quite like a hearty meal before I leave. Let's go and find Eleazar, wherever he is. The boy will know."

The Hedgehog looked at the floor and fidgeted unhappily. "The thing is, Optio Ruben, it's all a bit more complicated than I've let on."

Ruben started, "Why…?"

"I can't tell you, but it's really really bad."

And at this moment the lead lictor caught the Optio's eye, nodded very slowly and spoke in a soft rumble with a touch of a Baetican accent. "We ain't going nowhere, little Optio of the XXXth."

From the steps a voice shouted, "You there, soldier! Come here."

Ruben turned to see a grey toga'd official looking straight at him, walking forward with blue shielded linesmen. For the first time since being a nine-year-old, Ruben ran full pelt away from an approaching Roman force. He found it was a skill you picked up pretty quickly again.

Chapter Sixteen

Somewhere on the Danube River. Travelling east.

The armoury convoy's first day moving downriver had been conducted in high spirits, no one had fallen in as yet. All the troops were alert and excited by potential action, a welcome break for the armourers after being cooped up in Vindabona for many weeks stinking of fish and lifting crates. On shore, waiting for stores, all the familiar, technical, routines of a legion armoury were absent and left the men with nothing to do. Galba had tried to stop the Immunes going feral. He, Lulla and the other department heads made an effort, especially with the armourer cadets, but with no tools, long hours of boredom- equating to trouble in the Army- had reared its head. Old Sibius had come up with 'simulated blacksmithing' – a hugely unpopular activity.

"A proper armourer, first thing in the morning and last thing at night, should spend an hour with his eyes closed imagining the entire process of a task."

Now they were doing something with purpose and the wide river provided new vistas and activities in the fresh air.

On either bank traders and carts moved peacefully under the watchful eye of nearby civilisation. Fisherman fished from boats, pulling stave-poled nets up to the surface. These little craft tried to approach the barges for an 'on-the-fly sale' but were warned off by the legionary guards who would brook no approach to the cargo and, frankly, had had enough of fish for the time being.

Each of the barge's crew, hired 'commercials', had spent a lifetime on the Danube. The oarsmen shifted each huge craft's course in strange directions to avoid known, invisible, shallows, taking advantage of secret local streams or eddies aiding the swing of the vessels around a particular curve in the river. At the end of the first day, the good-natured harmony aboard the lead barge was broken by an exchange between Leading rudderman and the Centurion Chief Armourer. First Spear Felix sat, crouched in his bow camp, listening but did not speak or intervene in any manner. The rudderman had announced that the convoy was coming up to their overnight mooring as a spray of shacks on the southern 'Green Zone' bank appeared. The only stable-looking constructions in the river-slum were a series of large, thick mooring poles off the bank, linked to the shore by gangways.

Galba wasn't having any of it and made it clear the convoy would push on with all available speed through the night. The convoy's 'captain', backed by his men, shouted incomprehensible local gibberish and broken Latin at Galba, detailing the many ways it was impossible to carry on. As a Chief Armourer used to difficult individuals insisting something was 'impossible', he listened to the bargemen nodding. As a Centurion responsible for getting supplies to his new Legion Galba weighed up the pros and cons and ordered the rudderman to push on, with hand signals for clarity.

This brought about more protesting and shouting, culminating in the captain of the lead barge returning to his platform and steering for the bank anyway. Galba gave another clear hand signal, to his men this time, and gladius swords were made live, the tips under the working armpits of each rower on the barge until the track was encouraged straight down stream again.

The captain screamed some more in his own language. Galba just stood listening until the man blew himself out. As he did so, the leading two barges passed the point where they could easily adjust to drift into the 'overnighter' moorings. Ashore the cousins of the barge crews flocked to the bank – disappointed hawkers, traders, 'sisters' and drink sellers could be heard shouting, thinking that some mistake had occurred as all had fully expected rich, rich pickings in barter, sale, information and even possible theft from this established night-time stop.

Once the whole convoy moved well downstream of the shacks Galba had his men 'swords down'. By this time the rudderman also quietened but glared in seething resentment at the Chief Armourer. Loudly Galba turned to the barge captain and declaimed, in very deliberate Latin, "If we ground tonight, we do not leave the supplies. We shall disembark and burn everything to the water line."

The captain's eyes widened. "This my boat! Not Romans!"

Galba just ignored him: the boats were in fact the bargemen's boss's and he had to be sure of 'motivating' their conveyors to prevent any 'accidents'. As the sun set a few fishermen were signalled to approach, a negotiation commenced led by the second bargeman, a more genial brother of the captain by the look of it. Concluded with a sensible explanation to Galba, the Chief Armourer passed coins down and the fishing skiffs pushed off ahead of the river convoy, a box of long-burn torches in each craft.

Watches were set as night fell, First Spear Felix allowed the Centurions a leg stretch in ones and twos. During the day Felix had the Centurionate mostly hunkered down in the lead barge of the convoy, obscured from any watchers under tarpaulin hides at the bows. Now the NCOs took the night guard, letting the Legionary armourers sleep.

Galba stayed awake well into the night keeping an eye on progress in a dark lit only by the half-moon and the fishing skiffs' torches burning ahead of his lead barge. Shouts sounded out constantly in the flickering shadows when the lighter fishing boats moved too far in front of the forward transporter to provide useful illumination for the convoy. The captain cursing in local at the riverfolk to pull back.

An hour past a starlit midnight the fleet came upon one of the many shallow bends. The lead two barges slewed up near the northern bank and then began a slow turn, carried on the outside current into the right-hand curve before plunging back down to the river's centre. Shouts in the bargemen's language suddenly sounded from the silhouettes of the trailing craft, all now higher up on the port quarter than the lead vessel. Atop his tower of packed crates Galba looked back, trying to make out the sense of what was happening, then gradually realised the increasing alarms were directed at his own, barge.

Sternward the captain shouted shrill instructions to the crew who shipped long oars into the raised oarlocks and began sculling furiously on the starboard side, white foam glinting from the stars, arresting their right turn. To the rear, the Centurion Armourer could see the black shapes of the following vessels moving away from their course, back to the northern river edge ignoring the follow lights of the shallow-draughted fishermen's boats in the middle course.

Anxiety hit Galba like a furnace blowback and the Centurion looked forward towards the torch light of the guide skiffs. The river was wide, very wide here and the inside bank far away, yet the lead-captain was furiously shouting at his crew who fought to move the laden boat up from the middle river. It looked like a fuck-up. It was.

A grinding screech reverberated, followed by a jarring crunch just at the moment the lead barge began to adjust upwards, then a massive juddering shook through the entire vessel ending in a crunching stop. Centurion Armourer Galba flew off his crate-tower into the side of a box with an explosion of splinters and jingles. He then crashed downwards, shoulder landing in clang of metal and heavy flesh, nails tinkling down on him from the crate he'd just ruined with his weight.

"Jupiter!" Galba wheezed struggling for a breath, a tack fell plumb into his open mouth, the Centurion Armourer chocked the sharp metal out, cutting his tongue. The grinding scream continued until all movement left the barge. Stopped moving forward at any rate because the stern felt like it was lifting. The shape of Old Sibius appeared above Galba who, with a sigh, grabbed the boss's shoulder harness and pulled the massive Chief Armourer to his feet like a spoilt child. The Centurion winced at the pain and staggered as the heavily-laden barge yawed up, a roar of water rising as the strong current now spanked the static aft quarter.

"We have run aground…at night, Boss," said Old Sibius, emphasising 'at night' but not 'Boss'. The Centurion sucked in a breath and spat blood. Forcing himself upright he made for the back of the boat like a Lupercal drunk. Moving along the hawsers Galba lurched in-between the starboard bargemen who, having discarded oars, drove long mooring poles into the submerged sandbank the vessel had obviously grounded upon. Port side tipping up now, the bargemen were unable to push into the ground properly without falling over the edge, the water below them churned weirdly as the great barge was held in place at an unnatural angle against the screaming Danube current. Grasping packing ropes, Galba, ribs on fire, made the steering platform. The captain wasn't so chatty now, spark out, crumpled unnaturally as he was on the deck with water spraying over the stern which was rearing higher and higher by the moment.

A snap was followed by a scream and a massive crash. One of the upper crates had broken loose tumbling down, smashing a lower box in a great explosion of metal parts before crushing the oarsman below with a carnage of speartips, cut timbers and ropes. Another bargeman hit the river with a splosh. More tinkling followed; hundreds of bolt heads pouring out onto the shadowed deck.

"Secure that!" screamed Galba and two port side Legionary armourers who, having had an intrinsic protectiveness for stores beaten into them, scampered like monkeys up the sides of the leaning stack. The technicians then slid down to starboard where they grabbed broken lines and whipped up holding knots preventing further slippage through sheer brute force. More men joined them and

Galba turned back. He climbed up on the now alarmingly high port quarter and made the situation.

"Everyone up port, this side, this side!" Men followed the command rushing to balance the boat. It did little considering the weight of the vessel but might buy some desperately needed moments. The injured captain was hauled up by his colleagues who were all screaming a lot in 'whatever'.

Galba ignored this. "Bullo, Bullo! Get on that."

Without hesitation, Cadet Bullo, who had never really been on a boat before yesterday, rushed back along the port hawser, past his Boss to the steering platform. The Cadet was immediately spray drenched, but he gasped a breath, stood up in the torrent and grasped the abandoned tiller oar like a good'un. "Heave it straight, Cadet Bullo!" and the boy heaved, huge metal beating arms wrenching the oar straight, a fraction of the heel came off but with one look at each other, the two men who worked materials every day of their waking lives knew that the rudder couldn't hold for long.

"Have you a little problem, Boss?" came an accented shout from across the dark water.

Galba whipped round; it was Menicitrix calling from the fourth barge, coming up fast on the Centurion's stern. The fitter had 'persuaded' his crew to get closer to the stricken vessel through Gallic charm and a torch being held threateningly at their rudderman's face.

"Lines, Menicitrix! Lines, lines!" The Gaul pushed a protesting river sailor out of the way and as the following barge came up had the fitters throwing ropes to the grounded, lead vessel. Galba's men took the throwing ropes inboard and somehow, in the dark between them, a handful of coils were grasped and secured, most falling short into the water or slipping out of hands before they could be lashed down. Maybe five lines were caught and the outside boat was now rushing past them. Menicitrix's rudderman was going berserk and began to turn the vessel away despite fearing a lit brand up the nostril.

"Hold the lines and feed, hold lines, be ready!" shouted Galba to his men. Some of the barge crew had got it now and were also shouting across to their compatriots on the fourth barge while quickly grabbing ropes from the Army landsmen. The slack rope in the water was rapidly taken in then, one after another, the force hit and spray flicked up between the barges as the hemp whipped up. The first line took the full force of both barges all by itself and snapped instantly, firing back into the chest of an armoured fitter on the fourth barge, smacking him off the side. He was dead.

The soldier from Galba's command who had been holding this first line screamed and cursed, the rope biting the flesh off his hands in a huge ripping burn. The outside barge barely slowed but then two more ropes held, the crewmen timing the tension in unison to save the lines, franticly letting out slack as soon as the double thwack came, before pulling back in. Neither rope tore and instead there came an ominous creaking from the hulls. Menicitrix's barge was now well past the stricken vessel's bow quarter and as the tow was made, it swung unhealthily towards the midstream sandbank. New lines flung back from the Fitter's stern were made fast. River sailors and soldiers quickly spun a web between stranded fly and benevolent spider.

Galba, still high up on the port side, suddenly dropped several feet as the barge was pulled back down flat with, *'may the naiads of the Danube be praised'*, their stern jolted flush to the current. The roaring spray abruptly dissipated with the lowering of the steering platform.

One look at Bullo told Centurion Armourer Galba that the rudder pressure had gone, the steering now knifing into the back current.

He took a breath and made a further prayer of thanks. Another shudder as more stern lines bit, but no more movement than that. Galba looked forward to see the barge in front had arrested its arc towards the sandbank but was still swinging about unhealthily ahead of its tow, neither boat making any progress forward.

It was evident hauling the laden barge off would not work: all the forward boat could do now was swing dangerously around like a pendulum. "Drop the front tow!" Galba shouted. Axes chopped the lines and the Fitter's barge shot forward, their bargemen steering hard to port, off and away from the sandbank.

"Goodbye but, perhaps, not farewell?" the black shape of Head Fitter Menicitrix called back from the disappearing craft.

Galba ignored the Gaulish wit, climbed up to the steering platform next to Cadet Bullo and assessed what he could see; the upper hull was broken where the crates had fallen, smashing through the gunwales, letting in water. Sailcloth was called for, carpenters and armourers racing to plug the leak.

Before the rest of the convoy moved out of sight Bullo was swapped out on the helm, being sent forward with a code-man and a signal lantern. Up on the bow Bullo let off a string of signals opening and shutting the bronze lantern's door communicating Galba's situation.

Meanwhile armourers were sent looking for further damage and their discoveries were triaged and addressed. The Centurion Armourer got the gist of the barge crew's own view on the problem at hand. Hand signals, fear of drowning and common sense proving a much clearer guide than their unconscious boss's pig Latin. Poles could now be safely shoved into the river and showed the depth of the bar – very shallow. The vessel was wedged well into the river mud.

Two crewmen bowline'd themselves and went over the side, the Legionaries above holding the rope ends and torches. In the dark rushing water the pair stood and ducked in the current, gradually pulled forward by the stream to the bow where they were then pulled out. Once back on board, hand waving and happy faces reported no major damage or splintering had been found below the waterline. Getting off the bank to then immediately sink would not be counted as a success.

Further signal light instructions from Bullo brought up one of the fishing boats which slowly reached up past them under a dirty sail. It tacked and, coming along the port side, lashed on tight with vine rope of dubious quality. The Centurion Armourer briefed one of his men to, listened to the message repeated back, shouted at the armourer that he was an idiot and sent an accompanying Centurion to ensure fleet communications were delivered perfectly. Both of the men unhappily aboard the fishing boat, it untied and shoved off with downstream speed into the night.

'Now, how to get out of this mess?' muttered Galba to himself. The current was the biggest hindrance to doing anything, the Centurion decided, and so two unlucky armourer cadets were volunteered.

Thick driver stakes were found and taken out of a bundle from stores while other men roughly sewed sailcloth loops. Stripped naked, up the pair of Cadets went on to the steering platform, maletting a first, thick bridge stave into the sandbank off the starboard stern quarter. A rickety extension platform – or a plank nailed from boat to post as it actually was – was then directed over the river by Old Sibius. "Wobbling about on a bit of four-by-two, naked, at night, in enemy territory, holding a bridge pole so it can be hammered into an invisible, submerged riverbed – now that's proper Army that is, right there!" Old Sibius shouted encouragingly to the Cadets whimpering and hammering in the moonlight.

"Hammer the post in good and deep!" Sibius instructed. "Like a bridge your nans's going to cross." Balancing and hanging on for dear life the Cadets drove more thick staves into the mud. Once the first foot was in, they had something to brace into and both could use mallets, alternating strikes. Driving the first foot of a pole, however, was a nightmare. Plunging a post straight down into the river, one Cadet desperately bracing it against the current while the other smashed the top with all his fury to sink the pole far enough to take the pressure, all the while listening to, "Lose that stave or that mallet and you're jumping in after it, boys. I've not lost a bit of workshop equipment yet and don't plan to start now at my advanced age."

Panting on the second rickety plank nailed between the tops of the thick poles, hanging over jet-black water the Cadets completed the third pile.

"Now! Let's see if you got them in deep enough, boys," Old Sibius remarked as he had the huge canvas passed out from the steering deck, three long tubes now sewn into the sail cloth. The two Cadets hauled the material out from the boat, prised the planks away from the tops and shinned on to the piles, pulling the tubes over the end of the bridge staves.

"Safety lines!" shouted Old Sibius. Two bowlines are thrown out to the Cadets. The boys taking them create a second, bow knotted loop around the staves, the rope holding them to the piles. At Old Sibius' command both Cadets slide down the outer poles pulling the canvas towards the waterline...then submerge. Old Sibius and interested parties survey the river's surface, no sign of the boys can be made out, just twitches of safety line. With a shot the canvas starts to be pulled frantically down in bursts.

"Feed it to them!" and three agile armourer cadets jump up on to the piles, crouching precariously to push the canvas sheaths downwards. More sharp tugs and suddenly the huge sheet shoots all the way down into the water so the canvas tops are just visible above surface. Both safety lines whip forward, the spotters letting out slack then slowing the ropes until two shapes break to the surface at the barge's midships. The boys roar up splashing and choking, bargemen lean down and haul them out. It has worked – the canvas billowing into tight 'C's with the fierce current suddenly reduced across the stuck, starboard side.

Galba came over to inspect the work. "Good stagger, Sibius," he grudgingly admits, watching the river's force redirected away from the vessel.

"Yes. It is, isn't it?" The first two piles were catching the current, the third offset stave further forward allowed the stream to be deflected, prolonging the diversions survivability. The two armourer cadets are coughing up river water, blankets thrown over them by mates and a medic ready to clean up various cuts and bruises. "Nice swim, lads?"

"Yes, Boss."

"Don't fancy joining the naval Legions then?"

"No, Boss."

"That's the spirit. Good work, lads, nicely done."

The Cadets nod their thanks and grin. Now the cold and terror of drowning, of being smashed into poles, river debris or the barge, has gone they realise this might be a not bad step towards becoming full armourers. As the Centurion turns away, the lads begin to joke through chattering teeth.

Sibius cuts them off. "That was alright but let me tell you what you could have done better…"

Galba now has some flat water to work with and has men over the side with planks, not poles, to try to lever the barge off. It is no good. Worth a try but, as the Centurion Armourer expected, the barge is just too heavy to shift. He has the lever crew come out of the water. Just as the last man was hauled up a shout came from Bullo at the front. "Light, Boss!"

On the far north bank was a pinprick of flickering orange light. Galba ordered Bullo to repeat 'two short' flashed at three hundred count. After the second set, the orange small light goes off before flashing twice back, then illuminated steady once again. Slowly the foreign glow grows in the distance, a single lantern, until a black shape is seen crabbing behind it up the shore.

They couldn't see the men yet but the shape was a barge being hauled slowly upstream along the north bank. Gradually a group of men appear from the shadows of the path, walking in unison at a steady pace, lines running back to the carrier. The hauliers come parallel to the stuck vessel and Galba sees a team of Optios, remorselessly pulling one of the huge barges, unladen now riding high as it was, against the upstream current. *'Optios do all the real work…'* "You're going to be popular." Galba ignored Old Sibius at his elbow.

The NCOs didn't stop pulling but continued to haul the craft past the stern of the stuck vessel on and on along the bank. It seemed like an age until Bullo saw new flashes and relayed the message to his Boss.

"Everyone ready with lines!" Galba instructed.

A last set of flashes came from upstream, where the unladen barge had been dragged to, and were acknowledged. Galba brought the crew to readiness. The pinpoint light was higher now and moving in an even motion from left to right. Presumably the lantern was now set in the bow as the unladden barge was swung from the bank back into the current. Suddenly two flares of illumination lit up in the water. Lulla's work, Galba reckoned. Workshop liked playing around with pyrotechnics and two straw wreaths were seen running down the current with bright burning oil fires emitting from both. Floats with pots that followed the current made the barge running behind them just about visible. Galba realised he owed Workshop a drink for the buoyant flares as the illumination allowed his crew to better judge a highly fraught coming alongside. The approaching barge was moving fast towards them, its crewmen backchurning with oars to slow the descent downstream.

The unladen vessel's crew skilfully set the huge craft to run a parallel course to what would just be a spearlength from the static port side of the grounded barge. Running in, all oars braking, the approaching bow crossed the other's stern and the shout of 'Lines!' came up from both boats. Ropes flew, men ran along the decks and a hasty lattice bound the outer barge fast with much creaking. The prone vessel leant slightly to port this time but as the two craft warped into each other an equilibrium was established. With the barges lashed together tightly, Galba stood up on the port side, relief washing over him but still knowing a lot could go wrong. Everything just needed to work now.

"Move all cargo on to the outer vessel, begin!" Immediately Optios leapt over the thwarts onto the lead boat and got stuck in. It was their captain, however, who passing the helm to his second, got up high on to the grounded boat and gave instructions on what was to be moved first, in what order and where it was to go. "Not lose two boat!" he said to all assembled but pointing directly at Galba.

"Jumped-up little sod," came a voice from a tunic'd soldier lifting up a crate. Galba turned and saw it was First Spear Felix, who just grinned in the half dark and hauled up a box of tools as if it were a silk bolster.

All the way through the unloading Galba had hoped his barge might free itself but that wasn't to be. At completion of the transfer he found Felix and their captain. "Cast off now, we'll try and get ourselves unstuck. You go back to the other barges, FS, send one of the fishermen back halfway and let's see if we can set up a relay for signals."

179

The other captain seemed to understand, walking away shouting instructions, and Felix went to work the lantern relay out. Lines were dropped and run in, no push off to prevent the grounded boat being further wedged, so oars braked and sculled the launching boat out, driving it into the port stream. Slowly the newly-laden barge moved off and floated away into the dark.

Galba's ribs were really hurting now, as soon as the other barge left, his side flared up in a wash of pain making it difficult to breathe. He just had to push through it and brought the men together. The first bit of news was that his convoy captain was dead. His brother received a few coins gratefully, Galba made some sympathetic noises before exhausting his reserves of giving a fuck, and got men back in the water. Everything he could think of: basic planks levering in unison – didn't work. Placing the upstream mast in the mud and trying to cantilever with ropes – didn't work. Kedge anchors set and pulled– didn't work. It was the pigs' bladders that made a difference in the end. Brought out of stores after some searching the bladders, twenty of them were inflated. A score of metal rungs were also found then driven into the hull underwater by shivering armourers and carpenters.

Bladders were then pulled under the surface along the hull using these basic winches. When all the floats were down, men poled, oared, kedged, hoisted and leant until the smallest of shifts was felt. "Slit the brake!" Galba shouted and the two previous Cadets jumped out of their rugs back onto the piles of the current brake, stabbed into the canvas with knives then dropped down into the water cutting sailcloth all the way to the bottom. The current roared into the starboard, sandbank side.

"Push!" roared Galba. The slightest of judders and the barge…then just glided off with a long squeal. More lines were thrown out and grateful men bowled over by the current were pulled in, some having to swim hard or be left behind by the barge picking up speed. Old Sibius was not impressed by the Cadet and his chum when they emerged back on deck.

"So, when we put the piles in, we had safety line on, but tell me why it was much safer to jump straight into the river unattached, without the platform, holding a knife?"

They couldn't.

The relief and joy was enormous, everyone gave a cheer including the new captain whose brother had just died. Grief did not seem to overwhelm ambition and the fresh captain seemed much jollier and 'can do' than his deceased sibling.

A further bag of Roman-minted coins also washed away any resentment towards the Romans, or more specifically the Centurion Chief Armourer, for what was just a natural hazard of the job. As they cheered a light signalled from ahead: *'Hurry up!'* reported Bullo.

Galba just grimaced at what was certainly First Spear Felix's message. Soon the barge caught the relay, two damp Centurions balancing in a hide skiff with a rancid old man. The fishing boat approached the side and both NCOs were hauled in much relieved, took some wine and confirmed the news of lead barge's release having been relayed forward.

A tenth of an hour passed and the river curved north slightly. There on the port bank were moored the four other barges. Dawn was rising and Galba could make out a small landing. Two barges moored adjacent to the jetty but the rest were stacked, lashed against each other two and two. Galba's barge glided in, men waved and came down to the bank with lines. Thus concluded the first night's adventure.

On edge, the Centurion Armourer stayed awake. After an hour pulled up, collecting themselves and repacking, the convoy slipped away again. The fishermen finally finding the right distance for their lanterns to provide a proper guide now the sun was coming up. They would still want to be paid a bonus, though.

First Spear Felix sauntered up to Galba and patted his shoulder. "Get some sleep, Boss, you'll need it for tomorrow. I'll take this watch."

"If it's all the same, FS, I'll stay up."

Felix held his armoured shoulder this time. "That's an order, Galba. Anything happens and I'll wake you up."

"I thought I was convoy lead?" muttered Galba, tired, petulant and aching.

"You are, Galba, and so far, you're doing a very good job of it, which is why I'm sending you to bed. Because I'm First Spear and can do what I want."

It was a friendly joke and it wasn't.

"First Spear," Galba grunted, and made his way to a new little platform made by the reloaded crates. Young Bullo was sprawled there already so Galba removed his own armour and belts, stacked them as a pillow, pushing the lad over who was gone for the count. The Chief Armourer lay down and spread a worn, grey blanket over himself and tried to breath. The Centurion looked up, the dawning sky still with a crescent moon. Leaning treetops at the edge of his vision. It was incredibly peaceful and for the first time in a long while Galba felt calmed despite the pain from his fall. Exhaustion floated his mind away from aching ribs, up towards the firmament above him. Then sleep.

The second day on the river Galba woke midmorning, shook Bullo who had a bit of a shock seeing his bunkmate for the night had been the Big Boss, and they armed and relieved the Centurions. Felix ordered the senior NCOs back under the increasingly fetid tarpaulin hide at the bow of the lead barge as during the day, like shades, they were never to wander about in view of the bank. The bucket was emptied at every lunchtime by an unhappy cadet armourer.

New lead-rudderman was fast asleep having piloted since the grounding. The barge crew had not expected to sail through the night or need a shift system, but something had been worked out as river sailors now slept while others took the day watch.

No fires were allowed on the barge. There was a boat stove but it was buried under the weight of the full load packed onto the river craft. Instead, breakfast was barrels of local beer, oats and bread. Being a Centurion, Galba had a bit of sausage which he cut coins off, offering two to a grateful Bullo. The Centurion checked on his command and signalled up and down the convoy for status reports: all was satisfactory. He couldn't see the fishing boats any more, they had done their job and the moment each had been paid, buggered off. Either dropping sail or heading bankwards for the long pull back upriver to their home waters.

First Spear Felix was still up and Galba offered him cheese and sausage in a slice of bread with a cup of watered wine. The NCO accepted it with a happy "Ta."

"All uneventful this morning, Boss. It's nice, more than nice, doing a bit of real soldiering rather than looking for the next problem to fix."

"You miss the good old days of marching all day as a simple Legionary under the fatherlike care of the Centurionate?"

Felix grinned. "Fuck that for a game of soldiers, I prefer to be on this side of the perks. Thank you, Centurion Armourer, I was getting all misty-eyed there for a second. Do you know how far I marched with the Vth Macedonian in my first year? Three thousand four hundred and sixty-two miles. I added them up. Two full campaigns and six months of shadowing a Parthian column. I had calves like iron. Six men in my cohort died of heatstroke. No, you are right Galba; give me a bed in my own room any day of the week and I'll never whinge about the vinestaff again. You must have had fun coming up in the VIIIth, didn't one of your lot throw some bastard C off a cliff, that would've been in your youth?"

Galba chewed and nodded. "Saw it, FS."

"Jupiter! Save us all from the evil mad fuckers."

They both touched their cocks. "Thank you for breakfast, Boss, I'm going to bed." Felix turned and made off to the hide at the bow.

Chapter Seventeen

Merchants compound, Aquincum
Time of day difficult to assess
Pannonia Inferior province of Rome.

Locked in the house of a man whose sobriquet was *'the rapist'* was not *'enviable'*. The Lady Lassalia had no misconceptions that she could prevent such an assault happening if the merchant Holgur wished to enact his moniker. It would take just one or two of his thugs to come in, beat and hold her down. Having spent some time inside the river trader's house, Sobe saw Holgur had a wife: a drawn, destroyed creature, whose weeping could be heard at night – no sisterly help from that quarter was to be expected.

What protected the Lady Lassalia for the moment was: one, the spooks had left a couple of their Assyrian guards on the door: two, she was complying utterly with the Governor's plan to extort and bankrupt Sadiki in an efficient manner.

Holgur had entered the cell on the first morning with a scribe, threatened to kill her and all the Sadiki officials here in Aquincum, and begun dictating instructions to be sent to the small warehouse where the Sadiki administrators and representatives sat. All of it then signed and marked with Sobe's seal.

She said nothing except, "My slave Eleazar is the only man who can process all this."

Holgur grabbed the back of her hair. "Your fucking gelded creatures fucked off, woman, that's the loyalty you command, so what you say better not be true. Try again!"

She whimpered in fear at this, but thinking *'Silly boy'* at the voluntary divulgence of valuable information. Eleazar had gone to ground.

Imploringly, Lassalia looked up. One of the Hatra guards stood behind Holgur's scribe.

'Knots, knots on the belt all wrong. Seven tribes but twelve knots…Let's try it – Gallan.'

"Perhaps, perhaps my man Gallan, a Third Secretary but still quite capable, could do all you wish, he might be able to…"

Holgur got very angry very quickly, all spit and puce.

"Perhaps! Try a-fucking-gain, Gypt' cunt."

'Gotcha' then out loud, "I'm sorry. Yes, yes. The Third Secretary can do it all! All you ask."

"He fucking better." And Holgur shook Lassalia until she begged him to stop, crying for mercy.

She sobbed, "I will write Third Secretary Gallan an instruction, I will write him to do everything…please stop!"

"Better." And Holgur had quill and papyrus slapped down in front of her.

'That easy? Should have stuck to the pre-drafted documents, old son. What we need first is a cipher.'

Lassalia scrawled a plaintive message to Gallan, Holgur had it read and satisfied, let her affix her seal using the lone ring Sobe had been allowed to keep for administrative reasons. All the documents were gathered up out of the room, the personal scribe scuttling after the provincial trader leaving just the Lady Lassalia and one Assyrian guard in the dark, damp cell.

The Lady sobbed, face down on the floor. She had been preparing for the moment, it had to be precisely executed. Beyond having a liver of stone, constitution of an ox, prodigious height, and good thick hair Sobe Lassalia also had a memory as sticky as pitch.

"We beseech thee, Lord, bring us back into the light as you did for your Son." She sotto whispered to the flagstones beneath.

Just a hint of a breath, nothing more, and a shift of weight. Sobe allowed herself a small smile. Important not to overreach oneself, though. Holgur would learn that lesson, so Lassalia didn't 'push' but just crawled to the straw mattress on the floor and curled up against the wall, heaving. *'Come on Eleazar, wherever you are, ask the right question "Why choose Third Secretary Gallan?" and work it out.'*

Chapter Eighteen

Early evening, early summer, a hidden room in Aquincum Town
Analysis and uncomfortable levels of condensation
Pannonia Inferior border province of Rome

The boy-messenger, First Secretary Eleazar, Optio Ruben and the Imperial Hedgehog stood around an oil-lit table considering the documents written, or at least affirmed, by the mistress of the House of Sadiki. The key papyrus was the paper instructing young Third Secretary Gallan, written in Sobe's own handwriting to do everything set out in the other, obviously pre-drafted, documents.

"Perhaps it's – you know – a secret cipher or a…?"

"With respect, Sir, it is unlikely to be a secret message as we don't in fact have a code in place currently, that's the problem. But we desperately need one," replied Eleazar to the Emperor's Nephew.

"Egg white! Hold it over the flame…"

"Unlikely, Sir," countered Optio Ruben.

They stared in silence at the message from Lady Lassalia and the accompanying list of Holgur's demands. The documents themselves had come by way of the small warehouse, currently surrounded by IInd Legionaries, from where the package had been delivered by Holgur's scribe and an Assyrian earlier that day. Third Secretary Gallan, to whom it was all addressed, read the messages, copied them and had the originals folded into small squares to be slingshotted off the directors balcony in a large lead ball.

The boy-runner, newly promoted due to his recent performance and by dint of being one of the only Sadiki staff members not under arrest, had waited every day in a prearranged spot at the rear of the bakery on the far side of the loading field. At Gallan's instruction the Sadiki office guard slung the hollow lead ball precisely on target. Straight into the stacked white, luminous painted pots positioned innocuously by the flour door on the very first day of the House's arrival (for a small fee).

The boy had waited at the pots every night for weeks at the appointed time, before the night bell sounded, until the 'plink' had finally come. Then the wharf rat found the metal ball, and easily skirted legionary patrols running straight to the centre of his town. He slipped past the door bulls to enter the municipal bath's bar, ran up some back steps, then pushed behind a screen where a crawl took him into two, first-storey rooms located directly opposite the Governor's building. The usual door to these rooms down in the bath maintenance area had been boarded up with 'Lime spill!' painted in large threatening green letters.

As always Sadiki pre-arrival operatives had paid for the room's rent via one of the many front companies used for such purposes and prepared the 'backup office'. These particular rooms had been rented from the bath's barman's brother, a local butcher, whose son was also now doing quite well in Vindabona. If Eleazer was betrayed the local Vindabona rep would have the lad drowned, all understood the bargain, apart from the butchers son himself.

Eleazar had first removed the tightly folded documents from the hollow lead ball with a pair of bronze tweezers then read out the contents. Ruben's mind turned. The Optio's thoughts on what he was doing here in this humid hidey-hole were mixed: *'Was he technically a deserter?'* was at the top, however. On the one hand, Ruben knew he wasn't technically subject to local Army command, on the other he was subject to the authority of the XXXth and he wasn't with them either. *'How far does a letter of secondment stretch?'* Probably not very, given that the individuals he had been placed with were all incarcerated or in hiding from Imperial authority.

Best see if there was a plan. "What are you going to do, First Secretary?"

Eleazar looked up at Ruben with a half-smile. "Obey a command from the head of my household and put young secretary Gallan in charge of bankrupting us."

"Even under obvious duress?" Ruben questioned. "Should we try the Special Quaestor avenue again?" He gestured to Mako and looked out at the courthouse facing their slatted window, next to the regional administration complex.

The Hedgehog fidgeted and gestured to the second room where the lictors stood sweating, watching the street.

"Well, I can give it another go, happy to, but I've tried twice and the Governor and the local magistrate, well, they just won't do anything I say. They were very polite about it, though."

"Well, that's good," remarked Ruben, Ulpia Mako looked crestfallen. "I asked the guys if we could – you know – just barge in but…"

Ruben smiled. "They said there is an entire Legion and a large group of contractors to fight?"

"Yes, they did. I wondered if we could sneak in through the sewers or on a cart but…"

Ruben nodded. "…but Roman Legions have special teams patrolling any sewers or waterways that might be in the proximity. In addition to a complicated system of day codes and passes relating to entry to a civic building, then the supplies being checked within a confined room. Not to mention the plainclothes agents any Legion worth its salt has within and without a complex looking for, for instance, four massive men and an aristocrat dressed up as washerwomen?"

"Yes, that was very much the gist of it. Sorry, I'm bloody useless."

First Secretary Eleazar countered. "You are far from bloody useless, mi'lord, in fact you are very valuable. The thing to remember is that 'She' always has a plan, we just don't know what it is yet, so the golden rule is 'do as She says'. The easy bit will be dealing with the clumsy demands for cash – that is where you come in, my Lord. We may be missing something from the general scheme, so best get on with the rest until that stratagem emerges. You, Sir, shall pay the exorbitant fines on our behalf with our funds. If that is agreeable, of course?"

The Hedgehog was perplexed but nodded: he was always agreeable if nothing else. The First Secretary smiled warmly and sat the Imperial Nephew down to 'coach' for his task ahead. At the exercise's conclusion, Mako gathered his lictors and went for a bath. Through the wall crawl royalty went dragging a massive bag of gold and silver and a temple note for extra coin, even more confused but with carefully written instructions pinned to the inside of Mako's cloak (by Eleazar).

Once Nephew had gone Optio Ruben, also bemused, eyed the eunuch. "You are expecting that silver back, I take it?"

"I rather hope I don't," Eleazar commented drolly. "I hope it's 'Hippos'. Ever seen one of those things go at a person, Optio Ruben?"

Ruben was none the wiser so didn't respond immediately. "There is really no secret message from the Lady Lassalia?"

188

Eleazar grimaced an acknowledgement. The personal addendum relating to Gallan was a short, simple note written in her own hand. Ruben stared at the writing from the other side of the wobbly table, he had reading at angles down to a fine art from a life coordinating an amourary. Eleazar summoned the boy to get up from his stool. "Wait in the other room, sonny, and eat all the honeyed almonds you can find there. That is a command." The boy happily moved into the next room and savoured a treat worth half a month's pay.

Eleazar now stood to one side of the bathhouse window looking down on the entrance to the Governor's complex of Pannonia Inferior. Below IInd Legion guards were at attention, messengers moving about under the colonnade, the thick heavy main doors shut with a working day door being opened and closed continuously even at night. The First Secretary considered both friendly, comradely, clever Ruben and the IInd Legionary guards. Eleazar watched for half an hour, the changing of the guard, a Centurion doing his rounds, a marching four. All of the activity reminded Eleazar that Ruben was of the Roman army despite all the hostage-learnt conviviality, an Optio no less, and the eunuch made a decision not to share his realisation after all.

Instead, he brought the now sticky-mouthed boy back in, scribbled a slip with the words *'Proceed'* and told him to go to the small warehouse at dawn. The boy was to deliver the message to Gallan in person, no need for further subterfuge. Once things were seen to be moving greed would work for them, the cordon around the small warehouse should lift so the mechanics of graft could flow. As the boy crouched down by the hole to leave, Eleazar said, "Boy, also, if you can remember it – tell Gallan his work for us over the next week is key, but remind him always to have in his heart, his 'Soul', 'What' is most important, have you got that?" The boy repeated it back.

"Good. Does your mum like fish?"

"She's dead, First Secretary."

"Do you like fish?"

"Live by a river, Sir."

"Well, take this coin and buy yourself a nice fish. In fact, take two, buy one for Gallan as a treat. Tell him it's from me, though, when you deliver the message. Got that?"

"Thank you, First Secretary."

Eleazar looked at the boy with a small concern regarding the temptation of money. "Look, buy yourself whatever you want but get Gallan a nice fish, he likes fish. It is important. Tell him it's a gift from myself and the Domina. Got it?"

The boy grinned *'a gift from the Domina herself and he would deliver it!'*, affirmed, and crawled off through the hole in the plaster to buy some wine and steal a fish.

"You hold great store in the motivating power of a nice bit of fish? Your man Gallan also a Jew?"

Eleazar walked back to the small desk and sat down. "You would be surprised at the motivating power of a nice bit of fish. As for him being a Jew, interesting question, funny thing being a Jew nowadays. Certainly, he wasn't born one."

Ruben went back to looking out the window and reflected on a life where people gave you small, nice presents to do what you were supposed to do.

Eleazar knew that the motivating properties of fish may also be slightly terrifying. There had been no secret message, but there had been a secret Lassalia was playing with regarding Gallan. Eleazar had set it in motion but for the life of him couldn't think why.

Chapter Nineteen

Scipio's bijou office, Governor's building
Summer smells from a baking Aegean dock
Dalmatia province of Rome.

The Military Legate had worn a toga today, there would be plenty of time for stamping about in full uniforms later and he much preferred the great piece of asymmetrical, civilian formal wear. It was a new garment cut from the finest fine-woven wool and with the thick, but not as thick as his last one, purple band of office clearly visible at the running hem.

On entering the small, light-filled room he was greeted warmly: "Scauri! How lovely to see you, I heard you had arrived, come in, come in."

"Good of you to slum it with us plebs, Aulus Scipio Pallo."

Legate Decimus Terentius Scaurianus entered the small office tucked away a few floors above the Dalmatian Governor's formal receiving rooms, from where he had just attended a formal greeting ceremony.

"Come now, you know me – man of the people – and the modern Rome is about action not lineage. Now you, Scauri', have always been 'a man of action'!"

Scaurianus raised an eyebrow as they clasped hands. "Do you actually believe that…Aulus?"

The Scipio grinned at the deliberate informality of 'Aulus'.

"Yes, former Pro-Consul Scaurianus, I might just at that. You don't, obviously, but perhaps it's about time you got that chip off your shoulder."

The aristocrat then bade his guest sit before pouring very good wine, taken from an exquisitely lacquered cabinet, into bad leather cups. "Anyway, 'what is truth?' as some old Greek said once. Speaking of which, as in the opaque nature of veracity – how's 'he who must be obeyed' downstairs? 'Ovix Maximus'."

The Legate looked uncertainly at the leather cup he was presented with, the red contents of which could buy an entire cow. *'Aristocrats, who knew why?'*

"The Dalmatian Governor and I had an informative and useful discussion. He will give me all the aid needed to fulfil my task as soon as possible."

"You mean, leave town as soon as possible?"

"Exactly. No one likes another Legate hanging around, especially not a recent Pro-Consul, especially not a jumped-up little oik like me. I told him where I was going after the meeting. He sends his regards."

"Really?"

"No, no, not really. He grunted. Just grunted and said nothing."

"I was schooled with his son; did you know that?"

"How would I?"

The Scipio continued, "A most entertaining fellow, the son, a maternal trait I imagine."

The Legate was still regarding the badly-stitched leather cup and couldn't resist.

"What are these, Scipio?" he asked, raising the sewn beaker in three fingers.

Aulus Scipio Pallo mock spluttered, "My new cups? What's the matter with them? Some of the finest leatherwork in the city, in the Empire. I buy all my leather goods from this little place in the suburbs, doing my bit for the circular economy. Cups, this desk pad, saddles…"

"Do you own a horse?"

"Several, I believe. I had a few purchased for the saddles. Aprons, they do great aprons."

Scaurianus tried not to think about the aprons. Aulus Scipio Pallo was so convivial you had to work hard to remember what he actually was. "I shall have a set of campaign cups made and sent to you, Scauri."

The Legate shook his head.

"I'm afraid I leave in the morning so will decline that kind offer. I was going to get a dinner off you if free, then go at dawn."

"The dinner would be my pleasure and I was going to offer anyway. However, you are not leaving in the morning."

Having served at length in the highest levels of Roman civil and military society, making his way up from, if not the bottom, then very much the upper end of the bottom, the Legate took this revelation levelly. Scaurianus knew there must be a problem, every day there was a problem, it was what constituted life. The Legate tried to feel pleased when there was a problem. His philosophy was 'When you got to the problem, or 'issues' as they were known in the plural, then at least you weren't waiting for them to appear.' Uneventful days just meant you'd missed something.

"Go on."

Aulus Scipio Pallo passed him a papyrus note. "This came in two days ago from Aquincum."

Scaurianus read it, digested it, reread it. "Oh good."

The civil servant always liked sharing woeful news.

"Yes, it is a rather knotty problem, isn't it?"

The Legate took a sip of wine. "I told Them…"

Both men collectively understood that the 'Them' in question was an amorphous combination of the Imperial Service, Senate Committee, Army Command West and anyone's wife who had an opinion on the matter.

"…not to mobilise before I arrived."

"I think it was less 'Them' than 'Him'. Him is still a man in a hurry not to be. Did you suggest all this to 'Him'?"

Scaurianus didn't even bother to answer that. "Well, at least the supplies actually arrived even if they've been stolen by the IInd, you were right about that, the suppliers. Your Woman seems, though, to have been over-efficient. I wouldn't have thought such a thing possible with regards to Army logistics."

The Scipio pulled his seat round. "Do you know the General of the IInd?"

A shrug. "We've met at parties."

A wistful sigh. "I remember parties, they were fun, weren't they?"

"Parties bore you and you make trouble at them, Scipio. I take it he's been read the orders for the XXXth, the General of the IInd, I mean?"

"I imagine so but, without the XXXth's General in tow…what would you do with a sector in turmoil?"

"I am not the General, just the Legate, remember, but yes, if I were the IInd's General then plundering an unsupervised, unattended child of its cinnamon stick would be tempting."

The Scipio considered this, "Does it get less weird every time you say it, being the Legate but not the General?"

"No, Pallo," Scaurianus replied. "It doesn't. Which leads me to the next question which I have to ask, even though I know the answer: have either the Lower Pannonian Governor or the Military Legate, who is actually also the General – lucky man that he is – of the IInd Adiutrix and sector, been told who the General of the XXXth actually is?" The Scipio just smiled in the negative.

"Jupiter!"

"State secret, Legate."

"Isn't the Emperor's Nephew in tow, organising all this? Wasn't he in the IInd? Surely he could have a quiet word, make a steer?"

"It's the other one. The other nephew."

"What? You don't mean the…?"

"Yes, I do mean that precisely."

Decimus Terentius Scaurianus finished his drink and got up. "Well then, I need to be going right now, I'm afraid, friend Scipio. Riding east to retrieve my supplies and assert the XXXth's reporting chain before both are eaten up by the IInd Legio."

Hands raised in calming request; the Scipio stood. "I just ask for a few days before you do so."

The Legate eyed the civil servant.

"Given the circumstances, what is so important that I must wait 'a few days' before leaving while my – sort of – new Legion starves to death and gets trampled over by Lower Pannonian Command, leading to inevitable disgrace and treason?"

"Me! I'm coming with you."

Scaurianus tried to feel happy that he was encountering all of the bad news for the day at once.

"What? Like actually on a horse, outside in the fresh air?"

"Extraordinary as it may seem, yes."

Things must be bad,' thought Scaurianus but instead said, "I'm not calling you 'the Scipio' in front of people."

"I'd never dream of it, now bugger off while I sort things out and then we shall have a nice dinner before two weeks of eating goats' heads served by people with comical ethnic hats."

Chapter Twenty

Aquincum Courthouse – the big chamber
Early summer's day
Pannonia Inferior province of Rome

The old magistrate was overjoyed: this must be the pinnacle of his career as he sat in his best robes of office attended by Aquincum Courthouses's full complement of Apparitors, codex recallers and contribution calculators who would keep a track of every last denarius wrung out of that vile woman and the House of Sadiki on this fine summer's day, everything witnessed by the great citizens of their burgeoning community who packed the benches.

To the magistrate's left were the merchants, writs in hand, with Holgur holding their attention by retelling, "How he had the cow firmly tethered, ready to be milked!" The magistrate frowned at this terminology.

The Head of the House of Sadiki, no matter how repugnant to the laws of man, was of a significantly higher estate to the so-called merchant, who was just a river trader really. Somebody would have to 'have a word' after the proceedings when they all repaired to the baths opposite to celebrate. The old man scratched out a laborious note to do so.

For the time being the magistrate let the comment pass as his team were busy. The 'new money' of the town could smell blood with further writs for compensation coming up to the dais thick and fast as kidnapped donkeys or five units of delayed cherries were suddenly remembered. He allowed all of it and the scribes busily pinned new applications to the already extensive roll of grievances.

To the magistrate's right the tall, stooped Tribune to whom the IInd's General seemed to allot all unseemly, non-military functions was present with a Centurion, an Optio and the Legion Cornicifer – for the receipt of their money, no doubt. The bent-backed officer was looking smug behind his huge Roman nose and had constantly been referring to the whole Sadiki business as "…his operation, getting things back under Army control."

Which of course it was not! The magistrate knew. The keystone to this business was the apparatus of the Roman court, the writs and fines were the doing of the magistrate and his good friend – *'yes, I think I could say that now'* – the Governor of Pannonia Inferior. *'Important men working together, almost professional…equals.'*

At the back of the court, a couple of those deliberately nondescript 'administrators' with their black-clad guards lounged about. They didn't have any writs but were apparently here to 'observe'. The magistrate had got no more from them when they had entered the court this morning and decided to leave the matter alone. *'All very hush hush,'* he thought.

The judge's own adult sons were here as well, learning the trade, coming along to see their father preside over the great machinery of the Roman state. A good thing, his wife had said so as she kissed him goodbye after breakfast, remarking that he deserved this important day after all the recent 'difficulties' that had left him so unhappy around the house. A few further remarks were made on 'retiring at the top of his career to allow his offspring to take the great judicial responsibility on'. Nonsense of course, today just proved the magistrate was at his prime.

The provincial judge felt it appropriate to say a few words. At a gesture, one of his staff called for quiet and all stood.

"Gentlemen, first we may say a prayer to great Jupiter, Minerva and…"

"Pluts'!" a whit shouted: this got a laugh. The magistrate frowned at the reference to the god of wealth.

"…and Justice, she is both blind yet sees the truth…"

It was a testament to the general, happy feeling that the assembled mostly listened to the rambling opening with good-natured attention, many looking earnest as people do when a dubious venture is about to gift them 'serious' money. The magistrate, with the Governor and Army's full backing, had no such moral qualms. "…and knowing the unnatural ways of Alexandrian businesses are contrary to the good laws of the people of Rome and…Aquincum and the Pannonia Inferior province…"

This got a cheer. He still had some of the old magic from when he had been an advocate.

"…this MINOR Egyptian trading house…"

Boos and hisses. Too much. He settled them down to dignity.

"…this minor Egyptian…so-called…'business' has now submitted to the court's jurisdiction and this day shall pay ALL writs and fines immediately…in cash or metal equivalent." A definite cheer.

"So, for those of you who have not had the Roman currency or silver equivalent calculated by my independent assessor…" he said, pointing to his son. "…please do so now in order that you are sufficiently recompensed for the significant damage that has been caused to so many individuals in our fair town, not least the Roman Army and the mighty Legion of the IInd Adiutrix."

The long-backed Tribune practised for his long-delayed civilian career, subsequent to the Army, and stood taking a solemn bow all round. The magistrate swore he saw one of the 'Observers' snigger at the back.

A last flutter of petitioners ran across the floor to the magistrate's son where the 'independent assessor' essentially agreed weights in silver, not far off the equal weight of a donkey, with little thought to depreciation of an animal that had actually fallen off a hill three years ago.

The magistrate continued, "Now everything is submitted, I will go through the items in a careful order, as I see it, as being in preference of payment. First, we shall deal with the judicial and administrative fines, as suggested by the Governor himself…" he added, just in case anyone wanted to take issue with the pot of money the court system and Governor were taking.

"…Then the Army itself is seeking financial restitution in addition to a clear undertaking of the reinstatement of supplies, at cost, to the military command. However, these latter agreements are a military matter and quite distinct from the court's scope, so it will be only the writ for damages that…shall…be dealt with here…today." He had slightly lost his place, but then found it again, "…and finally, our town's merchants' various writs, including previous submissions, thus reinstated now that the – uh hum – Special 'Imperial' magistrate has discharged his duties to the – now absent – new Legion that passed through here some time ago."

Boos and a "Wanker!"

The magistrate let that pass as he did not in any way regard himself as a hypocrite and the earthy word encapsulated many of his own views towards the Imperial Nephew, especially following the excruciating apology supper he had been impelled to hold.

"So, I think that is all now in order…"

"Make the bitch squeal!" one young cloth merchant jeered.

The magistrate tut-tutted. The mood of the room changed: neither the Tribune nor the Observers, obviously Rome born and bred, liked that at all. "No, no, that is quite wrong. Her husband is a Roman, a Roman citizen of the second estate. No, no, I won't have that."

The cloth merchant tried to sink back into his bench but had got the wrong type of attention from all the wrong type of people. His trader colleagues looked firmly down at the floor and thought about rapid diversification into the cloth business as a new opportunity seemed to be appearing.

"Also, perhaps our less informed friend misunderstands that women should indeed be allowed to participate in these direct proceedings or be recognised in a court of law. I am not sure how things are done elsewhere but I can assure you, good citizens, that a woman is not recognised in this court. I have in fact personally taken great pains to establish the correct legal boundaries for this course to proceed. The true Head of the House of Sadiki, The Husband, is a Roman citizen of good standing but apparently unavailable. Poor man that his affairs have been led so far from what they should be into a court of law and the approbation of both a Governor of Rome and the Roman Army itself." General murmuring of assent.

"On that note, good merchant Holgur at the request of the Governor has taken the deluded Lady Sadiki into his house for care and protection, a duty for which I am sure we are all grateful."

A round of feet stamping and Holgur put on what he thought passed for a solemn patrician face, although it was way too furtive and sweaty.

"House Sadiki's second 'Man' is a eunuch!" Big laugh.

"…A eunuch who has fled at the first sign of trouble under a warrant for arrest. Which I think says much. However, a Citizen Gallan of the House of Sadiki – and I have read all the relevant documents to find that he has the rights and status to act for his employer – concurred with the findings of the court, of which I am a mere servant, and is sending a representative with full proxy rights, a male citizen of Rome apparently, himself subject to law, today, to make full…full restitution." More stamping of feet.

A servant of the court ran in and whispered to a clerk who in turn whispered to another clerk who whispered into the magistrate's ear.

The magistrate, still standing, announced, "And with that, this proxy of the House of Sadiki has arrived, so let us open the court." The judge leant to oversee the writing of the first minute.

Steps came, sound of a stumble, and the court doors swung open. Everyone leant forward like wolves or lounged contemptuously like hyenas; this was going to be fun.

"Hullo, hullo!" Silence.

The magistrate stammered, "No, no. This has been sorted out, with respect...Lord. We do not..."

Cornelius Ulpia Mako did a half skip and a handwringing and waving dance of apology.

"Oh, sorry, no, no, absolutely right. I completely get it, not here to do any lawing."

The magistrate straightened a little. "Ah, then you are here to observe. Well, please do – late as you are – and take a seat to watch proceedings and perhaps, if I might say, learn a little to then report on how Roman law is dispensed, even in a province so far from your, to your...well that is to say, the Emperor!"

The Hedgehog stopped in the middle of the court then shuffled to the left, finding a spot in the sun he'd always liked looking at when he'd been up on the dais.

"No, no. I mean, yes! Yes, I'll make a point of telling Un...The Emperor, if he remembers who I am – hahaha! – all about the splendid work you are doing here. I've actually already written him about that lovely supper you were so, so kind to have me over for, with your wife. Sorry about the vase again. I know! Add it on to these bills – haha!"

"Please sit down, my lord."

"Um, actually, I'm not here to observe – still keen to learn, though!"

The magistrate stiffened, thinking.

"Why are you here then, Sir? I do not see your officers of state?"

Everyone else made a surreptitious survey, mostly over their shoulders, for the infamous lictors but found none.

"Left them at home, yer'honour, hope they don't eat everything. They eat bloody loads, sorry it is court, my apologies, blooming tons, lictors I mean. Should get them to cook and eat the condemned in a big pie if I was, you know, doing more judging. Perhaps I should? Haha! Judging, not getting my lictors to eat murderers and, er, you know rapists and such. Haha! Is rape an offence? I don't know actually, is it? Should probably find out."

Holgur blanched. *'Was that a threat? Surely not, the man was a fool!'* but the image of being stuffed into pastry by those four huge officials that had dogged the town would not quite go away. Holgur's mind turned *'Or perhaps they'd just eat me raw?'*

The crookbacked Military Tribune sent the IInd's Cornicifer down to the clerks and passed on a message.

The magistrate listened to it and nodded. Using a verbal formula he employed with basic river people who appeared before him, the old judge asked, "Are you here as a private citizen, yes or no?"

Ulpia Mako warmed to this, his uncle often used a similar form of communication but this time he wasn't having small pieces of fruit thrown at him. "Yes!"

"Are you here to join the gallery?"

"No."

"Why are you here?"

Mako was hoping for another 'yes or no' question and was slightly thrown, but then he remembered *'The note!'*

"I have this." He held a slip up to the court.

"What is it? No, better still, clerk, please bring the document to the bench, with your permission of course, Sir."

"Oh, please, please do."

The clerk walked over to Cornelius Ulpia Mako and bowed low with a beseeching outstretched hand. The Hedgehog happily handed it over for the court to read, he had had it all explained a few times by Eleazar and knew what it did, the papyrus, probably, but wasn't sure why him.

The clerk brought the small document directly to the magistrate. The magistrate read it and looked straight back at Cornelius Ulpia Mako, who grinned back hopefully. Rereading it the judge then sat down and beckoned the clerks to gather around. The codex bearers started to flick rapidly through the rolls. Heated whispers grew, junior clerks who had worked on the deal were checking tablets and stammering.

The gallery was stirring and grew impatient. The magistrate stood. "The court will adjourn for a short recess while certain points of law are addressed."

The nasty Tribune loped for the magistrate but the old man and his retinue fled to a side door and recessed at speed into a retiring room, bolting the portal shut. Chatter erupted back in the Courtroom and every person took a turn looking at Cornelius Ulpia Mako with expressions of hatred, nervousness or examination – the last being the SOG team assessing if their 'observation' role might need to 'adapt'. Hedgehog just smiled ingratiatingly back and hummed a little tune to himself, reflecting on how he had got used to the reassuring presence of the lictors.

'If only Uncle Tra-Tra could see me now!' Mako thought, *'He'd probably fucking kill me.'* And Ulpia Mako gave a little stammered laugh out loud at the notion. This unnerved the assembly even more and the agitation increased – *'What was going on? This wasn't the plan.'* An Assyrian was sent out of the court by SOGI to check for large violent men, the spy now very much unslouched from the court's back wall.

For a while, the Military Tribune tried banging on the retiring room door but to no avail so sat down again. As soon as he did so, the door swung open and he, with everyone else assembled, sprang back to their feet. The court emerged, slowly and solemnly, the magistrate stopping in front of his chair as a clerk bade sitting. In the judge's hands were the original note proffered by Ulpia Mako and a new, still drying, parchment. The magistrate stood reading them both through one last time before taking up the new document.

"I as magistrate of Rome for the provincial capital of Pannonia Inferior, Aquincum, have taken receipt from the…Citizen of Rome, Cornelius Ulpia Mako, who is a man in good standing, standing before the court this day, a proxy. Cornelius Ulpia Mako has in no way been summoned to this court to appear nor has he…" the magistrate looked up at Hedgehog in a much more friendly way. "…chosen to appear at this court in any other role but as an individual private citizen. Is that right, Sir? Please say 'Yes' if it is."

"Abso…Yes, just yes. Yes!"

"Yes. Good. He appears today, that is Cornelius Ulpia Mako, holding a proxy. The proxy is to represent the House of Sadiki, as a private citizen, in matters brought to the attention of this court by other citizens and parties." This last part *'brought to the attention'* rang some alarm bells.

"Cornelius Ulpia Mako, have you in any way been coerced or cajoled into appearing here today?"

"No, mi'lud."

"Are you sure? No one has put pressure on you? Or led you to believe you had to be here today? Because I will tell you right now you do not, you have no obligation or duty to be here right now acting under this proxy. You have fulfilled your Imperial duty while amongst us…admirably…and can just go home to Rome, if you so wish?"

The magistrate looked imploringly. Someone snorted in derision and the magistrate and the Army Tribune shot daggers at the cloth merchant.

Mako just smiled. The magistrate sighed and continued.

"As an officer of the law I'm concerned that you may have been led to believe that you should be here when in fact you don't. You can just walk away…"

Hedgehog wasn't sure so tried all the answers.

"Yes. No, yes – I mean, no. I mean, I'm happy to be here – well, not happy – all a bit, you know, grrr – but I'm happy to – you know – help. Happy to help out, always. That's what got me here in the first place. Well, not quite, I was told to by the Emperor. But not this time, now, obviously, because he's in Rome. Probably throttle me if he knew I was in court, hahaha! No, I thought I better come and help sort it all out. So, I've got all this money…" and Hedgehog revealed his heavy satchel and placed it on the ground, flap open, visibly full of silver bits and coin.

A Praetor's ransom at least. Something activated in the Hedgehog's brain and he felt a grand gesture might help so he upended the leather bag, pouring the precious metal and coins out in a great tinkling crash onto the floor.

No one moved, except for some who even recoiled from the spinning, rolling metal.

The Magistrate froze. *'How much of an idiot was this boy really? Think…'*

"So, it's all here. Crikey! I hope I didn't lose any. Sorry, I think some ran under your chair."

The clerk in question picked up the high denomination coins spinning beneath him like they were snakes and scuttled across the court, immediately returning them to the Imperial Quaestor, who was today a private citizen – possibly. One of those first-estate 'private citizens' whose uncle happened to be the Emperor of Rome. The clerk made a great show of shaking his clothes and showing empty hands to the entire court.

"Thanks. Right, just tell me who owes what and it's all yours. Perhaps some of the…?" Mako waved at the calculators hiding behind their counting boards on the dais. "…, these chaps could help with all the actual counting. I mean, I

202

trust you, I'll just sign whatever you need signing. I have to get signed receipts, though. Apparently, that's important."

'SIGNED RECEIPTS!' the words screamed in the magistrate's mind. Politely batting the aristocrat away in recent weeks had been a fairly safe course of action, the Governor and General reassured all, but taking money 'with receipts' from a member of the Imperial Family...?

"Sir..." the magistrate asked in an almost quiet voice. "...Could I ask, whose money is this?"

Mako was ready for this question, Eleazar had been coaching him a few nights before: "One; turn up on time. Two, remember the money. Three – this is the really important bit...Yes?"

"Yes?"

"Yes. If they ask you whose money it is, just say 'Well, it is the money.' Yes?"

"Yes."

"Whose money is it?"

"Well, it's yours. You just gave...Ah! No! You tricked me, didn't you? Ahaha! Brilliant! Got you...'It's just money'?"

"But whose money is it?"

"It's money?"

"Is it your money?"

"Oh, no, it's just mone..."

"No!"

"No?"

"It's just money."

"That's what I said."

"No, you replied 'No, it's just money.' Don't deny it's your money, don't affirm. You just say 'It's just money.' Or 'It is the money.'"

"It's just money."

"Very good. Did I give it to you?"

"Yes...Oh no...!"

"Let's try again. Don't worry, we'll get there."

'It was amazing' Hedgehog thought, *'It was almost exactly the same in court as when Eleazar tested him. How did he know?'* Even more amazingly, for the first time in his life Mako felt adequately prepared – *'That's why palaces had so many eunuchs!'*

The magistrate kept asking the question and Mako just kept saying, "It's just money." It went on for ages, finally the old man stopped and asked Hedgehog, "Would you like a drink of something?" and he'd said, "It's just money!" *'Haha! Hilarious, brilliant, what a story!'*

Mako's clever cousin would hold his head in his hands when told over a glass of wine or ten.

'Classic!'

Now the magistrate wished he'd retired last week, rather than being sent to a galley. Then the oldest legal recourse in the book once again rose unbidden, like a cosseting mother to soothe the pain away: points of procedure. The judge coughed.

"Given the civic and dutiful appearance of Cornelius Ulpia Mako, taking on such a heavy burden of responsibility as a fellow magistrate, a colleague, thus a representative of the courts themselves, I find it would not be proper or correct to put the interests of the court itself, being merely an administrator, a conduit of the...local government, senate and people of Rome, ahead of the plaintiffs themselves. As the submitter of the administration fines..." (*Don't mention the Governor by name and he should be grateful*) "...is not here in person, we shall bring forward those others here today seeking remuneration. I therefore turn to the next on the list, the representative of the Legio IInd Adiutrix to outline their submission, now if you would please..."

The Tribune, even more hunched than usual, looked at the magistrate with venom and for a moment the SOG observers thought the officer might rip the silly old sod limb from limb because, as it turned out, he was quite a shrewd old sod. *'May be more useful than we thought?'* sandy haired SOGI whispered to SOGII regarding the judge.

Instead, the officer stiffly unfolded upright. It didn't help that Cornelius Ulpia Mako was trying to helpfully and noisily shove all the silver back into the satchel.

"At this time, I believe the best interests of Rome are not served by pursuing frivolous court cases, indeed it was never anticipated that we, the Roman Army, would in any way bring such an action through these MINOR courts, or indeed any other courts." He knew his General would have his guts for this one but major career suicide, no matter the reason, was preferable over the more literal alternatives. "It was merely an insurance to see that the proper and good running of the..." and he did the full 'etcetera, etcetera' for good measure.

Adding at the end, because you had to cling to some hope, "My personal view is that as Honourable Cornelius Ulpia Mako stands here today dutifully taking up a burden of responsibility for the House of Sadiki and Rome, surly we must lighten this burden for him?"

There was a cautious round of applause from the Optio and the Cornicifer who, as regular distributors and responsible persons of, and with, Imperial funds, with a capital 'I', had a very good appreciation of the evolving situation.

Cornelius Ulpia Mako himself had only registered the last bit of the Tribune's speech.

"So, ah – how much do you want to lighten me by? It's blooming heavy this bag...haha!"

The Tribune waved his hands. "No, Sir, you misunderstand me. I do not want to lighten you of some of your silver."

Hedgehog frowned.

"You want the lot? Well, I'm sure we all want to do our bit for the mighty Legions. If that's alright with everyone else. Take it all. It's just money after all!"

The majority of the court attendees interpreted the line about 'helping the mighty legions' as definitely being an overt threat.

"Look, why don't I just leave it here and you guys divide it up then come and find me with the receipts?"

"NO!" shouted the magistrate, the Tribune and many of the merchants who had now fully cottoned on to something Mako was utterly oblivious about. "NO. YOU MUST STAY...right here Cornelius Ulpia Mako, Sir. With the money. You must not go anywhere, please."

The Hedgehog threw up his hands.

"Oh, right, sorry. No, I'll stay here, stay put, right on this spot. It's a good spot with the light coming down, I like it anyway. No, I'll...yes. Staying the course. So how much does the Army want?"

"Nothing, nothing at all. The IInd withdraws any misunderstanding and seeks no funds. None."

Hedgehog didn't understand. "None?"

The magistrate quickly jumped in with agreement, "None, none at all, Cornelius Ulpia Mako, so let us move on to the civil litigants. First up: for loss of certain dried fruits, I call..."

Each merchant knew exactly where he was in the running order, each one had anticipated the glorious moment their lengthy suit for damages, pre-approved, was read out in full and they walked away with a very nice fat wodge of dosh, even minus the court's cut. Now each merchant awaited his writ as though he was a proscribed man going up in front of one of the more arbitrary former leaders of Rome. Each merchant sprang up like a hound as soon as the magistrate opened his list to call the case. "No, sorry, there has been a misunderstanding. Apologies but this was submitted in error by a very junior member of my…in fact they're a contractor really, who I no longer use, and I am only here today to expunge this ridiculous mistake."

The merchants had been assured by the Governor and the General that the farce of the special court for Project Invictus had been dealt with, that the Emperor's Nephew was a fool and had been circumvented, in actual fact was heading home. The murdering lictors would go with him. *'All back to normal…General's on the warpath for the new Legion's supplies and everyone's going to get what they deserve…smash up the upstart woman's business and make a great big stack of cash in the process.'*

Here, though, the Emperor's Nephew was back, with money from an unspecified source representing Sadiki and anyone taking that money would be recorded. They would have to sign a legal receipt as soon as the cash was handed over. *'And whose cash was it really?'* – that was the question. Who wanted to have their mark, and it wouldn't just be a mark, but a fully made out receipt for legal damages paid for by…possibly the Emperor himself?

However indirectly.

Holgur's excuse itself was the best one.

"I am unaware of any writs today. My apologies if I have come at a busy time, I had not realised. My presence here today was merely to have signed a formal application to the Governor, to be witnessed by the provincial magistrate, that some form of additional taxation actually be levied towards the mustering of the new XXXth Legion. This whole embarrassing situation, I mean – I'm not sure quite what's happening, I'm not a lawyer, but a simple man who pulled himself up by his sandal straps. Anyway, in the meantime I want to make a loyal voluntary contribution to Rome…"

This brought an angry glare only an old judge at the twilight of his career could produce, especially with two grasping sons nodding indulgently behind him.

Holgur went on with his civic mindedness.

"…Anyhow…as it turns out the honoured Imperial Quaestor is here himself today so perhaps I might be permitted to make an immediate contribution from Holgur & Sons itself, to aid his Excellency Cornelius Ulpia Mako with his work with the new Legion. Let us say…"

And the merchant named a very considerable sum. Holgur was not entirely safeguarding himself from the horrific turn of current events, he could scent opportunity. Holgur & Sons could wear the contribution expense, other merchants in the town could not but they would now have to match it.

One by one each Aquincum merchant proclaimed his support for the Emperor's Nephew and announced a voluntary contribution. It was infectious. Hedgehog just thought, *'Bloody hell, how am I going to keep track of it all? Shiiiit!'* At a gesture from the magistrate the calculators rushed forward recording the contributions and picking up theatrically thrown bags of silver.

At the visible sight of the Imperial Nephew having visible, monetary, signs of loyalty written down, by court officials no less, suddenly the Tribune piped up and announced, "To aid my brothers of the XXXth, like older brothers, the IInd would of course match the merchants' contribution." The Cornicifer blanched but reached into the chest at his feet.

Up in the cheap seats SOGI indicated to SOGII, who passed a pouch of gold down, but then they always had money…

The show of patriotic duty continued until finally: "Well, I want my money! Loss of flax in situ, loss of conveyance and twenty rolls cut material spoilt because I couldn't get storage or make the overland route. Oh! and my donkey died due to…well, it died because of what happened with that woman."

The whole court turned to look at the dim cloth merchant incredulously. His bench fellows really did move away, reconsidering the idea of getting into the cloth trade. There may well be a space in the Aquincum fabric market emerging, but questions like "Who's the cloth merchant in these parts?" would be asked by inquisitive outsiders from Rome and men have ended up in mines for less obvious misidentifications.

'Thank Jupiter!' Hedgehog thought. He'd cocked this whole bloody thing up again, he was supposed to be helping Sadiki settle their fines but for some reason it had gone to shit, again. *'Fuuuuuck!'* He'd actually ended up with more bloody money than he'd started with, which he'd probably lose or leave in a tavern.

'*Can't let that happen, though.*' Two thoughts ran parallel in Cornelius Ulpia Mako's brain which emerged as followed:

"Great! you want your money? Right, could one of the clerks please work out how much and pick it off the floor and we'll need a receipt. I think it's got to have both of our names on it."

The cloth merchant was making his way down to the court floor, smiling. Then the second strand of Hedgehog's thought process emerged. He turned to the court door.

"Could someone send for my lictors, please, and could we lock the doors of the court?" He turned to the magistrate. "For security purposes. Against myself mostly, ahaha!" The magistrate nodded to the doormen. '*For security purposes.*'

Mako turned back to the approaching fabric seller and was startled. '*Woo! Why's the cloth merchant staring at me funny? I don't like that...*' The heavy bolts slid shut on the court.

The cloth merchant had finally caught up and was gibbering now, and people were shuffling. Mako didn't know what was happening. '*Maybe the little merchant is really grateful? I mean, he'd lost his donkey!*'

Hedgehog liked donkeys. Anyway, '*Head down and get on with the job.*'

"Now, how's that receipt going?"

At the back, SOGI stared and muttered, "He's a cold bastard, that one."

A half hour later the Court closed, from behind the bath house shutters of the secret office First Secretary Eleazar watched them all leave quickly noting, with a smile, that no one crossed the street to enter the main doors under him for a celebratory bath.

Chapter Twenty-One

Dust approaches Brigetio Fort
Afternoon, a few clouds
Porous Danube border.

Dust, that was the indication that Point's flash message of approaching *'thousands'* was, after all, probably a correct signal from the spotter's hill. It was a huge plume of dirt thrown up to the east of the fort, rising through the far trees along the south bank. The dust came from the same path which, in the opposite direction, the Special Operations Group had snuck out along in their 'moonlight flit' (trad Aventine term for legging it when the rent got to be arrears-y). Except, instead of taking the chairs and the kids before the landlord noticed, the spooks had upped sticks with their black files, truth rendering equipment and individuals not yet wrung of every last drop of involuntary helpfulness.

The dissimilarities were also stark in terms of the manner of their exit. Any good family of the urban poor too far in debt knew Landlord would only come after you for so long. Even if you had left your rat-hole with dog shit all over the floor and middle boy's disgusting drawings on the wall, pursuit would end after a point. Economics just didn't justify wasting time and money on violent men chasing around asking questions of the – for want of better phrase – uncooperative poor who were all, also, usually living a month away from the same decision to flee at any moment.

"What you don't do is burn the fucking building down as you go!"

But then the Special Operations Group weren't the urban poor. "They're more like a landlord who decides he'll live in the house you paid for, beat up all the neighbours, make you live on the balcony and fetch water before – yes that's right – firing the basement before leaving because: he's the landlord and can do what the fuck he wants." This was the veteran Legionary First Class's view anyway, and a metaphor he now shared on his gate station watching the

209

approaching dust cloud, a grumble just to take everyone's mind off what was coming down the track.

Most of the surrounding Legionaries murmured agreement at the FCL's summation, although Infil team member Five had gone straight into a forest dwelling Legion from his uncle's shack outside a Pict clifftop fort – his road to citizenship had been an unlikely and complicated affair – and was dying to ask more basic questions about 'flats?'. He didn't, however, and assumed it was like living in a really big fort, it sounded alright but where did the food come from if there were no fields?

Five had been in towns – he still didn't get it though but was too embarrassed to ask. Perhaps there were eggs on these balconies?

The soldiers of Brigetio Fort stood to as the sun poked out from a few clouds, took water and ate some pottage rustled up as soon as the far-bank enemy had sodded off back up into the hills. Normally they'd enjoy the burning ferry over the river but today it just was not enough of a distraction from whatever was coming up the track.

As the dust rose, however, the tension amongst the scratch Brigetio Garrison began to ebb.

A comforting view was concurrently being formed by the Skipper, the FCL, Werewulf – still hiding half-submerged under a log in the rushes upstream – and anyone else who had been around a bit.

Suffice to say the younger recruits, including the rampart messenger, were still shitting themselves in the stoic manner of the Roman Legionary who knew that any crying would result in a stone-scarf beating from seven tentmates that evening (if they survived). Even the young Exfil Tribune and nominal Fort Commander was shuffling about and drinking a bit too much from Four's flask. The older men noticed the younglings' nervousness and, enjoying this necessary part of growing up in the Army, did absolutely nothing to assuage the furtive imaginings of their less seasoned comrades. The fact of the matter was, though, that it was the right kind of dust. The way it moved, the way it seemed to be layered. That was 'the good dust' the older men all recognised, it was the well-ordered thrown-up ground of Rome.

One person who wasn't watching the dust was an annoyed Four, still up in the rafters of the covered gatehouse, who was watching his homemade 'country wine' disappearing down a jittery officer, but he knew better than to say anything.

The young messenger burst out of the eastern rampart and ran full pelt along the palisade towards the Skipper and Exfil Tribune at the gatehouse tower. Once again, he puffed and hauled himself up the ladder reaching the officers out of breath.

"Report, Legionary," the Exfil Tribune said to the panting man as he took a first step on to the platform.

Skipper took the bottle from his brother officer and passed it to the messenger.

"Have a drink first, chum. Be warned, it's booze."

The messenger took a swig and rasped a half thanks from the bottom of his lungs.

"Signal from eastern hilltop. Approaching force are Roman, I say again 'R' for Red, Legion strength."

Exfil Tribune sighed relief and turned to the Skipper clasping his hand, unable to think what to say. The Skipper smiled and gestured to the men. "Go on then, Commander."

The young Tribune who only a few seasons before had bumped up that river road, all shiny and green as grass but now looking like the lower Subarru on race day – dishevelled and covered in filth –, strode to the railing of the gatehouse tower like a veteran line commander.

"Men, attention! It is a Roman column, one of our columns approaching! The IInd are here from Aquincum!"

A cheer rang out as the news made its way along the ramparts and across the parade ground.

The Skipper turned back to the messenger and took the flask off him, passing it upwards where it was gratefully retrieved by a lowered arm, then asked dubiously, "Is it the IInd from Aquincum?"

The messenger shrugged. "Signal just read 'R' for 'Red' army column, legion strength." The Skipper thought: Point would know if it was the IInd and specify. Furthermore *'legion strength'* didn't sit right. The IInd were spread all over the eastern border trying to fill gaps against the Dacians' interpretation of a truce, that's why their own former Legion, the XIth, had left Brigetio and marched towards the rising sun to help out. Still, everyone seemed happy they weren't about to be slaughtered and the Infil Immunes officer didn't have any better ideas so fell back on one of the two great tenets of soldiering: *'Let's just wait and see,'* the other one being *'Never volunteer for anything!'*. For some reason he'd always ignored the latter rule but it was too late for that now, the Infiltration specialist reflected ruefully.

Another hour brought the head of the mysterious force into sight. It certainly looked like a column on first appearance as, all green shields and horse shit, unknown Auxilia horsemen numbering at least thirty galloped towards the gate. Gauls, by the look of it. Twenty of them passed right by without even a glance to the fort. Ten riders remained looking at the dead bodies bobbing about in-between the dock's pontoons, giving an occasional lance thrust just to make sure.

"Typical fucking Gauls, Skipper, they'll claim that poking as a victory."

"I thought your father was a Gaul, Four?"

"I know the bastards, Sir."

The Exfil Tribune started down the gate ladder. "You have the fort, Skipper. You, you and you – with me." The fort gates were unbarred with the CO walking out to the cavalrymen with the FCL and two other veterans. The Skipper watched the exchange which was conducted without the Auxilia dismounting but visibly laughing a lot. The Exfil officer came back up to the rampart almost as quickly as he left, suddenly looking quite young again.

"Who are they?" the Skipper asked as the CO screwed his face up.

"First, the Gaul said 'That is the answer we are all searching for, no?' when I asked."

"Fucking Gauls!" shouted Four in his own Alpine-region dialect, which got some confused looks up from the loitering cavalry.

Both officers ignored that. The Exfil continued, "The leader then said we need to talk to 'the boss', apparently there's a Centurion who's in charge making his way up the road."

"A Legion – with no officers?"

"I asked him that. There's no Legate, just four Tribunes. I think 'the Centurion who's in command' was a joke, Skipper."

It was the best type of Army joke, being not really a joke, probably true and insulting most of the people listening to it.

"So where are they going, do we know that? We could use supplies…"

The Exfil Tribune looked at his colleague warily and just pointed down twice with his finger.

The Skipper frowned. "Here? To stop?"

The Exfil shrugged. "Definitely here. Let's just wait and see, eh?"

The Skipper couldn't argue with that logic so while they waited, orders were made to receive friendly forces. The three Immunes components of Brigetio Fort: the Infil, Exfil and Veteran river teams had somehow conspired to exist without having a single Centurion amongst them. This was highly unusual as even latrines had a Centurion attached to them but at least understandable. None of the odd Immunes duties even came close to being as attractive to one of the vaunted, professional elite of the Army as ensuring camp hygiene.

Small specialist units, strange engineering teams and, most of all, boats made the river scouts about as desirable a posting as '...*being third in line on a prostitute with three days' stubble, crying through the makeup as she drunkenly fails to keep her dick between two meaty thighs.*' Another metaphor of the veteran FCL's regarding their work, who often shuddered at the bad days of the Iron Gates campaign and the infamous 'morale wagon' that made its way up and down the mountains bringing terror to each Legion outpost.

No Centurions in Brigetio and they all looked it as both Tribunes knew, surveying their men from the gatehouse rampart. Word was passed and the FCL took it upon himself to cobble together some form of visual consistency.

More outriders then the head of a marching column emerged from the trees.

"That's not the IInd – no banners!" exclaimed the Exfil Tribune seeing the leading men emerge on to the bank's path. "What…what is that? Who are they?"

Sure enough, the two Immunes officers could see an approaching Centurion plume, cross wise as it was. A Senior Centurion by the look of it, with a guard of marching, armoured Legionaries. Yokeless – they would be the vanguard, about thirty – but that was it. No Legion pennants, certainly no eagle, no Legate – as warned – a few Tribunes lurking on horses, to be sure, but completely lacking in Cornicifers blasting away greetings and all the other assemblage to announce the full force of a Legio on the march. As the column came even closer the fort soldiers started to mutter: "Who the fuck are these jokers?" because behind the vanguard came the marching column, half of which tramped unarmoured, with yoke staves, but the yokes were 'winter birches'.

"Where's their fucking kit?" every other man said to his neighbour.

It got worse as this kitless half a legio marching (and 'marching' was being generous, Exfil Two remarked to Six at the eastern tower) were 'No scarf' men, wearing the light tan tunic of a training battalion.

"Have we actually just been rescued by an unarmoured, unarmed training battalion?" the FCL growled to one of the veterans standing next to him at the gate.

"Don't forget the Gauls, FCL, they rescued us as well."

The FCL spat with pure contempt. "Fucking balls to this! I'm glad I'm not in the XIth anymore, we can shoulder this shame ourselves."

In-between the 'No scarfs' some, actually marching, armoured cohorts appeared. All were fully geared up with some of the unarmoured novice Legionaries double-carrying an extra 'summer' yoke each and struggling, even though they were "barely the weight of a kitten!" (Six's input).

The armoured cohorts were visibly inconsistent and couldn't possibly all be from one Legion. Clasping, rigs, shields, sword hilts, pilum shafts, helmet edgings, the way things were positioned or tied differing dramatically to the experienced soldiers' eyes, like comparing a magpie to a frog.

"Those aren't even real Centurions at the back!" Two exclaimed, and his comrades noted the hated arm banding and paunches of 'training Cs'. "A training base, here? In the middle of nowhere?" Five asked up in the east rampart. "Army bullshit, kidda. Let's just see, though." replied Two.

The column was getting even closer, back up on the gatehouse; "Any ideas, Skipper?" tried the Exfil Tribune.

The Skipper pulled a face. "Best get back down that ladder, Commanding Officer." And both Tribunes descended the gatehouse rungs and took, what the veteran FCL loudly described as, 'a dubious honour guard' of Exfil Immunes out of the gate to meet the approaching vanguard.

In formation the receiving party turned and formed up in a line along the path, parallel to the eastern post of the gate facing towards the river. "It's our bloody fort until I say it isn't!" said the Exfil Tribune loudly and there was a murmur of approval from the guard and ramparts.

"Got any orders to back that up, 'Sir'?" asked the Skipper in a quiet voice.

"I was rather hoping you did, Infil Tribune, but until we know who they are, Brigetio is ours," replied the young CO of Brigetio with an uncomfortable smile.

The fresh Gaulish horsemen drew up on the other two sides of the receiving party, five apiece, creating a sort of military triclinium. The vanguard were now in shouting distance and the Brigetio Tribunes could see that, yes, it was a Senior Centurion, a 'wonky big hat', with a set covered in tied awards. The Centurion himself was paying no officers, neither his own nor the ones clearly awaiting his arrival, any attention but stared up at the men on the wall, not liking what he saw one bit.

"Remember," said the Skipper. "…we are officers, he's just a senior NCO."

"Is that supposed to be a bloody joke, Skipper? He's a full SC by the look of it," whispered back Exfil as they both stood as parade ground steady as they could remember, faces locked.

"Just don't get flustered and accidentally call him 'Dad'."

"Who the fuck are you? Sorry, I didn't see your markings under all that muck…apologies, who the fuck are you – Sirs? Which one of you is…in charge?"

The word 'dubious' and the phrase 'studied contempt' had both been fashioned for this very moment in Roman Army history.

"Where are your Centurions?" The SC just about managed not to say 'your mums'. Without waiting for a reply: "Are you perhaps lost, young Sirs?" Then, having finished with initial observations, the SC halted, saluting crisply.

The Tribunes returned the salute.

"Salve, Senior Centurion. I am the acting commanding officer here," and the young Exfil introduced himself and the Skipper.

"Immunes, eh?" the born and bred Line Centurion ground out the words. Twenty plus years within one of Pompey's crack Legions ensured the NCO understood the need for the varied specialist units within the Army but still viewed them with the appropriate measure of suspicion and dislike due to anything not presenting itself on his parade square each morning.

"Who are they then?" The SC now looked right at the floating dead and gestured for an Auxiliary to get his arse off horse to drag one of the bodies over. "And where's the administration building?" he respectfully demanded looking over the gate, noticing a template inconformity with regards to Army fort constructions.

"Actually – first – who are the dead people?"

"We were in the middle of an attack on the fort when your column arrived, the corpses were the first wave."

The SC grudgingly pulled a face of half approval, asked the garrison strength, got the answer, asked the question again believing the Exfil Tribune to be an imbecile, then asked to speak to a Centurion/Grown up, was told there were none, made a mental note to ignore this obvious lie and search the fort thoroughly for one of his colleagues. A wet, armoured, corpse was dumped at the SC's feet by a pair of Optios, and he proceeded to inspect the thing, mostly through prodding it with his vinestaff.

It was at this moment the four mounted Tribunes trotted forwards, freshly minted and shiny like coins rushed out at an Imperial ascension in times of political uncertainty. Completely unlike the Skipper and the Exfil Tribune who were sweat-dirt greased and wholly unacceptable as legal tender.

"Salveaaa…Tribunes? Am I to understand you are part of the Eee-leventh?" asked the leader, twenty, and a drawl you could net fish in.

"They are Immunes all on their own, Sir. Why – I haven't found out yet, shouldn't be anyone here, but we shall get to the bottom of it, mark my words," the SC answered for the Immunes pair to save time. While the four new Tribunes tried not to look quizzically at each other as regards to *'Wtf R Immunes?'* their Centurion checked the belt marking and scale jerkin of the bearded dead body, finally taking a knife and cutting off some damp blonde braids with ornate silver clasps.

"Ahhhh, I see. Immuuuunes!" The lead XXXth Tribune exclaimed unconvincingly and his three chums gave a non-committal nod in their brother officer's direction.

"Optio!" One of the halo of four Optios that hovered in constant proximity to the SC moved to take the braid and look at it. The SC Optio turned the hair one way then the other. "I'll talk to Ulles but it looks Cherusci to me, mercenaries probably."

"Long way from home," grunted the SC.

"Uh, Excuuuse me…could you, perhaps, report to uuus, Senior Centurion?" the lead officer asked, thinking now would be the time to assert the authority of the Tribunes, *'…draaaw a line, so to speak, marching is all very well but at our destination the men will looook to us fooor…leadership!'*

"Sir, report arrival at Brigetio, enemy action has recently terminated, hostile forces having been driven off by the garri…soldiers here. Sir."

"Thank youuu, Senior Centurion."

A gaping chasm of silence opened up.

"Yes, Verrrry good…" and in a loud voice the Legion Tribune, turning back to the column, shouted, "…Leeet us take up our new home, men. Fooorward!" No one moved. The Exfil Tribune coughed.

"Perhaps, Sir, the Immunes officers might like to know who we are and a demonstration of authorities to enter, otherwise they shall be forced to resist the walls under Roman civil and Army law. Sir!"

The Skipper decided to rescue the Legion Tribune even though he hadn't had the courtesy to dismount.

"You are not the Legio IInd, are you?"

This was one of the only three times the Skipper and Exfil ever saw the SC smile, once would have been enough.

The mounted Tribune pulled himself up. "We are the XXXth Legio!"

"Who?"

"Fuck knows."

The assembled officers ignored the gunners' voices up on the parapet but the SC made a note for later.

"The Leeegion XXX is being newly formed by the Emperoraaa, himself!" explained the Lead Tribune.

One of his three colleagues, who would one day attain the role of Pro-Consul, had the awareness to add, "…After the Senate demanded that a new force be created to subdue local hostile enmity against Roman soil."

The Lead Tribune nodded in annoyance. "Quiiite so. Brigetio shall be the foundaaation of aaaa…"

"He's going to say 'glorious'" a voice – Two's (who had come out of the east tower for a proper look) – said up on the palisades loudly.

"Silence there!" roared the SC at the fort. *"Fucking Immunes."* He then muttered not too quietly.

Lead Tribune paused for this interruption, then continued "…of a… formidable…new chapter in the Aaarmee rolls of Rooowme."

A further silence.

"Shall we perhaps formally present the XXXth's credentials to Brigetio's Commander, Sir?"

"Yes, eeees. Let us do thaart."

Another Centurion-abyss of quiet yawned while the four Tribunes searched for the document bag and then, with icy realisation, came upon the memory of packing it while half-cut into the baggage train some nights ago because it was a bit heavy.

The Skipper had had enough and remembered why he volunteered for sitting in a wet hedge, deep in enemy territory, with seven men he trusted implicitly.

"This is a hostile situation: we have just fought off an attack and you are carrying Training Garrison recruits with no weapons. Senior Centurion, produce the good copy please."

The SC immediately responded. "Optio, release the good copy for the Immune's Tribune!"

Instantly an Optio pulled a sealed scroll from a bag and showed it first to the Senior Centurion, hands held deliberately behind his back, who then, having looked, said, "I view the affixed seal unbroken and bearing the signet of Army Group West. Note the date, Optio."

Another Optio was already doing so in addition to the names of all present. Next the scroll carrying Optio turned to the Immunes officers. Both the Skipper and the temporary Fort Commander looked very closely at the scroll and seal, because this was an Imperial order pertaining to a Legion movement and change of command. There was no taking it back or getting it wrong. "As acting Commanding Officer of Brigetio Fort, I adjudge the seal unbroken and bearing the seal of Army Group West."

The Skipper repeated the phrase with 'second in command' inserted, then the item was passed up to the Lead Tribune whose gloved hand fumbled it slightly but managed to recover.

'See that officer fumble? Was that an omen and, if so, what does it mean?' was a much returned to topic of Legionary conversation for the next few, hellish, weeks.

The XXXth Tribune then paraphrased the half-heard wording of receipt to an acceptable degree.

"Break the seal, Sir?" the SC 'suggested'.

The Western Army Group seal was broken and the Lead Tribune read aloud the orders. He had a good speaking voice despite the time he took to employ it; "The Seeenate, people and First Citizen of Rooowm, the Emperor Traaaajan, instructs Army Group West to require, on this day, er…thank you, Optio…the arse-embly, under the oarrrrspices of Jupiter and Mars, of a new fullll Legion to be four-med from existing legionary men and weeeeell trained Roman citizens, of which full detailing can be found within appendix section. At eventual ennnndorsement, the body, representing all that is rightfully granted to Roowme for the protection of itself and its allies, shall be known as the XXXth Legio."

Normal, but then…

"The Ooofficers, Centurions and Senior Legionaries are to make all best endeavooours and haste to assemble at the Garrison Fort Brigetio, to have beeeen vacated by the existing Legio XIth and to ensure the security of the Pannonian wiver border, to execute its due-ties underrr self-governance until such time as joined by a leading officer and allocated within a greateeer formation."

'What?' thought the Skipper, the Exfil Tribune, the FCL, Two and a shoreman holding a pilum so laxly he nearly dropped it.

Skipper tried to catch the SC's eye but the Centurion was steadfastly staring at his officer like an angry pa before confirming, "I hear the order said and judge it to be true and rightful."

The three mounted Tribunes repeated the phrase, then the Skipper did but, crucially, all eyes were on the Exfil Tribune. There was of course no dispute the acting CO would say anything otherwise, except if he did…that was a civil war.

The Exfil Tribune dived straight in and did well, sounding like a commanding officer.

"I hear the order said on this day and judge it to be true and rightful. Therefore, I cede command and possession of Brigetio Fort to the yet to be inaugurated XXXth Legio, represented and witnessed by the Senior Officers and Senior Men present. Welcome to Brigetio, XXXth Legio, may Jupiter, Mars and Fortune bless this Legion. The Emperor, Senate and people of Rome!"

The last phrase was repeated by all and then the SC stepped out, eyeing his Lead Tribune but pointing towards the gatehouse suggestively: "Sir?"

The officer took the hint.

"Pleeeease proceed, Senior Centurion."

Everyone who was senior: Training Centurions, Optios and the FCLs from the seasoned cohorts was gathered around the Senior Centurion in a mob, who then outlined what he wanted before sunset:

I.   Auxilia cavalry to patrol the bank two stadia each side of the fort and one in depth behind. Continue visual contact parallel to any hostile forces still present over the river

II. Walls manned immediately and a significant, visible force at the dock '…and get those bodies out of the water and in a room for a proper view!'

III. Training Battalion 'graduates' ('Noscarfs') stay outside and given one hour's rest and a biscuit

IV. Marching Baggage train, tail trailing at least one hour under full guard, priority unload to areas designated before arrival – storage areas to be identified and cleared ready for the season basics coming up behind by separate convoy, expected five days behind

The SC Optios were immediately into the fort; the first men of the XXXth ever to step foot in Brigetio walked purposefully, surveying what they found ready for the allocation of a full Legio and its marching stores.

A wait occurred before the Optios came back out. Meanwhile the SC eyed his Tribunes, ruminating on how to expedite all the work to be done. "Sir!" he said to the Lead Tribune, "With hostiles still in the area do you think it's a good idea for the Gauls to be out unsupervised?"

The mounted Tribunes jumped at the hint. The senior officer had to stay, of course, but within a moment the three other young men tore off on their horses, two west, one east to cover the baggage train and oversee the three patrols of campaign-veteran horsemen from the great cavalry plains of the Massif Central.

Having successfully rid himself of the encumbrance of small children on moving day, the SC began to work with his returned Optios on a schedule, following their inspection of the fortification. The Skipper saw that all four Optios looked like they had been with the SC for a very long time, were professional staff who had abandoned ambitions to the Centurionate in exchange for serving one of the most senior enlisted men in the whole of the Roman Army. The quartet were currently unreadable but, even so, when eventually they 'invited' the Immunes officers to join their Centurion it was with a 'certain look' of friendly warning. The Exfil Tribune and Skipper knew what was coming.

"Well, well, well. A fire, I hear. How bad, Optio?"

"To the ground, Senior Centurion."

"Ah, and there they are. Thank you for joining me, Sirs, a few questions if I may," the SC said, greeting the fort's original Tribunes.

"Did the enemy set fire to your admin building, because I didn't see any smoke when coming up the road a moment ago?" and for emphasis, kicked the piss-wet corpse still at their feet.

There was no other way round the truth.

"They didn't burn the admin building down, Centurion, it was…before," admitted the Exfil Tribune.

"Ah, another, previous attack valiantly fought off?" The Exfil indicated in the negative.

The Senior Centurion's eyes bored into both officers and ran through numerous scenarios, settling on the least favourable.

"Did…you two…burn it down…yourselves, Sirs?"

The Skipper, looking north tried "Shall I take my men and see if there are any…?"

"Oh no, Sir. You've done quite enough already and, if I may continue…how did you manage to burn down your own administration block?"

"Whaaat's going on there, Senior Centuurion?" came a horse-top enquiry.

"Nothing, Sir. The Tribune Immunes and I were having a little chat. Now, let us go inside, young Sirs, and see what's left of your first command then you can explain all about why I'm missing a building."

The Noscarf Legionaries of the XXXth had just finished their oat biscuit when the Deployment Master, the primary Optio of the Senior Centurion, began getting them back on their feet to impose 'the system.' A fortified cart park was then dug out in the field behind the fort. As each ox or mule-hauled vehicle then arrived from the marching caravan it would slowly pull up at main gate, its load assessed by another of the SC's NCOs. Most carts were ushered past the gatehouse, circumventing Brigetio via the west wall to be stationed in a particular area in the park depending on contents.

Roped channels were thrown up with efficient signs to denote routes; 'cook stores channel IIa', 'Fourth Cohort gear follow 'XI to c' sign', 'trestles into Sundries Vb'. 'Immediate and essentials' wagons were allowed to turn left into the fort to be unloaded straight away. These vehicles passed three hundred legionaries inside the fort going at the burnt out ruins with hooks, grapples and spades. A few hours later brooms and mops went into action diluting the black dirt and dust into the, newly enlarged, parade ground.

Whitewash was also immediately deployed on the buildings even though the SOG had only just redecorated, the spies having removing all of the disgusting drawings left for them by the XIth on departure. After some discussion amongst the deployment team, the Legio's limited marching rations were piled high at one side of the parade square.

"I don't like the double handling…" the SC remarked to one of his Optios. "…but with the main fucking supply column out of contact, the rations need to be inventoried again then placed in secure rooms. Get to it and find a couple of rural types from the Noscarfs to keep the birds away while you do so."

At the SC's insistence Skipper was to stay close to the Centurion ("In case there is another h'accident, Sir") but with nothing to do the Tribune watched the dots now moving about on the eastern hill, the men of the entire River Immunes wandering amongst a mess of their sprawled kit. Discovering the Infil team was bunked up inside the old General's quarters, one of the senior Optios had given them *'a word to the wise'* to fuck off out of it before the SC discovered their billet arrangements.

Equally, the Exfil boat men were deemed 'in the way' and while the hydraulic workshop and boat sheds were left alone, everyone who wasn't XXXth was exiled up to the hill. The veterans made it up the slope first, before even being asked, decamping with their gear and all the best food stores and blankets. As the rest of the river teams arrived, big cauldrons were already on the go bubbling with pottage.

"Lunch in half an hour, gents!" the FCL announcing to the newcomers.

Meanwhile Gaul Auxiliary horsemen worked the south bank relentlessly, backwards and forwards to the point where the Exfil Tribune decided it was safe to go get Werewulf team and find the extraction boats. The SC was immersed in shouting at drovers so with a word to a gate Optio, the Exfil lead slipped out of Brigeto, gathering a retrieval team from the hill. Riding back up the river road from the east, Gauls reported to him that the three catamarans were safely moored just a stadia or two downstream, having floated by the front of the column earlier to mutual bemusement and then pulling up following the receipt of 'safe' signals. Chasing the Gunboat had been a big boat of angry that quickly fucked off to the northern shore having spotted a Roman prey item of quite a significant new dimension.

After tenth of an hour, Exfil Tribune came upon his catamaran squadron with one of the XXXth officers, the political one, who was nibbling something unwise, dried and local proffered by the Lead Pilot. "These yours, old man, would you like them back?"

"I suppose I better," the Exfil Tribune retorted to his 'colleague' and jumped up on the Gunboat's running board to greet the crew.

"Good work, gunners, even you lot could hardly miss at that range."

The gunners laughed hard, still pumping from the engagement and well pleased with the result.

"And well done, Lead Pilot."

Lead Pilot smiled widely and passed on the small smoking brass pot to a co-pilot who took a big drag. "Did you see the guy who was keen to enlist, Sir?" the Lead Pilot growled, all red headband, long up-brushed hair and a waistcoat full of pockets containing boat-related items and a large amount of contraband.

"Turned out he couldn't swim, though, so we had to let him go."

"What happened to the nasty boat full of shouting idiots chasing you?"

The Lead Pilot frowned for a second. "It just…disappeared, Sir…"

"It fell off when they saw the column and headed downriver," clarified the Fire Caller.

"Just…gone," the pilot continued, popping his lips, before taking the pipe back.

The new Tribune of the XXXth listened to all this with interest, absorbing life at the front for a book he would write later in order to secure his reputation as a citizen of both action and letters. Pleased at gathering some 'colour' he wisely threw the dried, allegedly edible, item away and asked with a wink, "Fancy a pull, Tribune?"

The Exfil thanked his brother officer then they got to work.

The Legion Tribune's Gaul minders dismounted and with the pilots assembled a tow to a lashed together horse team. One by one the three boats were pulled up to the Brigetio launch dock where the Shore Team busied themselves hauling the River Goats up out of the river and stripping them for a clean. Fishing bodies out of the berths was a task deliberately given to a particularly green XXXth unit of Noscarfs who retched and winced through the job. The Exfil Tribune then took direct command of the Xboat and had it pulled way upriver, past the fort, before pushing off again. Crossing to the north bank where Werewulf's spotter team emerged from the reeds, jumped aboard in a touch and go before following the current down back to the landing ramps.

"All right Werewulf?"

"All right, Sir."

"That was quite something, Werewulf, you and the scouts. Couple of hundred men tramping overhead. Well done."

"Any food, Sir?"

"Head up the hill, FCL's got a pot on. We'll meet you there for a debrief once the boats are secured."

An hour later with the three catamarans lashed to the quay, all Immunes were eating hot food and drinking watered wine, looking down on the work within the fort. As they ate, the Exfil Tribune, Skipper (released from the SC's gaze following an inadequate explanation of pyrotechnics) and FCL dictated a joint report of the recent events and actions to Comms. Two separate reports, in fact, the first cataloguing 'events' leading up to the action, the second on the action and handover.

As the day rolled on empty carts filled up the new wagon park at the fort's rear with unhitched animals penned in clusters. The huge amount of fodder that had been carried with the convoy, reserved just for conveyance, was being dished out to the grateful beasts. Drovers worked on their animals and vehicles, repairs and checks, salves and carpentry. Inside the fortification, with manpower to do it, all the remaining burnt timber and rubble was being piled for salvage or discard, good bricks stacked up carefully. A few more shackled, burnt bodies had turned up, the Skipper noted. Fresh Legionaries carrying lumpy old blankets unhappily out to the cemetery were watched with a scowl by the SC – more questions were coming, of that there was no doubt. The Skipper felt he didn't really want to leave this hill.

At dusk, the progress made was remarkable and a runner arrived up the slope, panting, to summon the Immunes off the hill.

As they wandered down with their kit, the specialists passed legionary work parties re-digging the palisade ditch down to at least a couple more feet. Night fell fast and with it the Gaul Auxilia were also trooping in, patrol by patrol, entering the fort as the Immunes made their way through the gate. Menicitrix exchanging a few words in one of the dialects with a troop Decurion.

An Optio with assistants was waiting for the river teams inside the gate and both officers followed the NCO to the west of the fort. Here, in one of the previously deserted laundries, a new wooden plate had been affixed to the outer wall indicating the area was now the main command post and administrative centre. A second SC Optio came out to meet them.

"Tribunes, salve. Your men will be taken to their new accommodation. It's not up to the standard you're used to, but…" he said with a wink, "…we've got you all inside."

The Skipper thanked the Optio. "Thought we'd be lucky to get a tent."

The senior NCO gave him an appraising look.

"You fought today, Tribune, and well by all accounts. It was the SC who made the decision: men who fight sleep inside if there's a bed."

"So, he's not all bad then, Optio?"

This got a laugh. "SC's waiting in there for you and the Exfiltration officer. I'll see to your men and gear, Sir."

The Skipper and the Exfil Tribune walked past the door guards and signed in at a desk, something neither man had ever seen in the XIth. Down an oil lamp lit corridor they were led by a heavily tattooed Macedonian Legionary into one of the old tub rooms which bustled with Legionary administrators, Training Centurions receiving schedules, scroll holders being hammered together and wax and papyrus uncrated with corresponding stylus and ink. At the centre of the activity was the Senior Centurion flanked by two XXXth Tribunes, the Primary and the 'Politician' who'd given the catamarans a tow. As ever, a pair of SC Optios were also hovering.

There were two large tables, one covered in dockets – the visible representation of various systems – but it was to the other trestle the SC pointed to on seeing the officers enter. "Sirs, we found this. What is it?"

The second table was a mass of – now baked – clay and singed paint. It was a relief map painstakingly worked up over years by the Infil team and kept in the XIth's General's old ops room: amazingly, it had survived the fire, albeit in a less malleable state.

"It's a representation of our area of influence as worked up by my team and our predecessors," the Skipper answered, knowing the SC's real question was '*Is this a load of bollocks?*'

In the centre of the table was a model of Brigetio, the Danube in blue paint – the water was the responsibility of the Exfil Tribune, different shades marking currents and shoals – and then a significant amount of land leading off in all directions. Drop points, ambush spots, lookouts, viable launch areas all marked and coded. It stopped Eastward at the bend south to Aquincum. Beyond the central river, clay lumps were moulded for the hills overlaid with marked paths, settlements, farms, proper roads, improper roads, marshes and anything else interesting the Infil team had ever stepped on, all rendered into the map.

The Legion Tribunes were leafing through a charred data slate still chained to the table, which held the expanded key.

"This might be impressive work, Tribune." The SC then eyed the Skipper.

"Is it accurate?"

"Our General felt so."

The Senior Centurion pulled a face and stared some more, bending over the table.

"What are these?" He pointed to the northern edge of the relief, way up in the 'Red Zone': flat plains carved out of the forest with three little conurbations made of stones – one larger town and two villages.

The Skipper moved to the northern edge of the map for better pointing. "They are, Centurion, the main Macromanni settlements in the region. The town's military strength is in the file. These, however…" and the Skipper pointed to a series of markers halfway between the north shore and the dwellings, "…are insurgency camps. Mixture of mercenaries and locals being trained, unfortunately, by Roman deserters."

Senior Centurion grimaced but he'd been around.

"From the XIth?"

The Skipper shook his head and suppressed any anger at the accusation towards his old Legion. It was a fair question.

"No, they weren't of the XIth and we never worked out where any had run from, tattoos burnt away. My bet is they've been floating outside the Empire's borders for some time, hired mercenaries who will train any local war chief's soldiers. Paid for from further afield than the Macromanni coffers, that's for sure."

The Political Tribune asked, "Dacia?"

"Yes, we found coin. My previous…commander…"

SC interjected, "And it is still to be determined what you orphans actually are."

"The previous command had all my reports, but we made copies."

Senior Tribune looked up at this.

"Coooope-ies? Maaaay we have them?"

The Skipper and Exfil tribune exchanged a nod. The XXXth were the new border Legio and the Infil's real job was to provide information for Brigetio

Sector security, not gather intelligence exclusively for the Special Operations Group.

"I'll have them sent to you."

"Thank you, Sir."

And the SC then pointed back to the small, stone settlements. "But the presence of nefarious hostiles in the area is hardly news as evidenced by your recent good work, all of which are currently drying out on a big sheet next door. These towns and villages are what I want to know about, not their military strengths or any of the other bullshit going on in the area. What's the status of their stores post-winter?"

The Skipper considered this question.

"It's a breadbasket, the whole region. All the villages and the town hold silos, the last tithe to the chief went in September so each place is carrying seeds and first crop harvest – we saw turnips being pulled two weeks ago. Last year was a good harvest, bumper with no hail. Can I ask why you are interested in the crops, Centurion?"

"Because it turns out we don't have any fucking food, Sir." The SC whispered back under the noise of the busy room.

The SC made a gesture for all to follow so the four Tribunes and one Optio made their way to a long, private, rectangular breakout room with a newly assembled trestle upon which burnt oil lamps. A great pile of scrubbing racks and lime-stained paddles were still piled at one end but would be gone in the morning. Nothing more was said by the command group until bread and pottage arrived then the orderlies dismissed. In the flickering lamplight, the SC started serving, "I'll be mother" – just weird. As he ladled glop into wooden bowls the Centurion revealed news.

"Our main season stores convoy is not coming, I found out an hour ago. It was supposed to be trailing a week behind our march from Aquincum but we never had contact with it, none of the Auxilia falling back in rounds ever saw the damn thing. This morning before we broke camp, before we arrived here, I instructed a patrol to go all the way back at double speed until they found the train. Nothing. Hundreds of main supply column carts gone. So the Gauls, somewhat amazingly, did something sensible and carried on back to Aquincum. They met a Tribune there, I've got his name for the 'One Day' box, who barred the Auxilia from entry to the town. An actual Roman Auxilia! First of all, I thought it was this bitch of a merchant pissing us about but no, much as I'd like

227

to see her nailed to a cross, it wasn't. Our stores were taken and 'redeployed' by the IInd Adiutrix as soon as the transfer receipt was signed, the convoy only making it a mile or two up the road."

The Exfil Tribune looked at the XXXth officers. "The IInd has nicked all your supplies?"

"Well, you're eating them as well, so how about 'our' supplies, Sir?"

"Thaaaaank you, Centurion," the Senior Tribune interrupted as he took a bowl and spoon.

"If I maay: We have been instructed by the Proviiincial Army Command to make dooo via rather a curt note. Our food supplies are needed for the advanced Legions on the eeeeeast border. So then, we shall 'make do' as Romans should…doooo. The Adiutrix is a senior Legion aaarfter aaall."

The young Exfil officer frowned and chewed his bread more slowly.

"An entire Legion, make do? Let me ask something that's been on my mind when we transferred command this morning. Your designation is as a 'border' force awaiting…designation. Self-governance, wasn't it? Is the XXXth carrying unique command?" The two Tribunes of the XXXth looked blank.

The SC said slowly, "We ARE carrying unique command, not sure why. Although I don't believe the subject was ever specifically acknowledged by the IInd's General in Aquincum when the orders were shown months ago. Unless I am mistaken…?" he turned to his two Tribunes.

"Weeee read the full oarrrrr-ders as written, Senior Centurion."

"Did the IInd General say anything, Sir?"

"Noooo, he welcomed us to his command and saaaaid he was looking forward…Whaaaat? Whaaaaat's the matter?"

"So, he never actually acknowledged that you aren't part of his sector purview? What do you call it – acknowledgement of command?" began the Skipper.

SC grunted; he was allowed to belittle and torture his officers but no one else was. The Centurion banged the table hard.

"Look at us Sir, we are four Tribunes and one permanent Centurion. If you fancy your chances of arguing a point of law with the Military Commander of an entire province, be my guest but, with all due respect, you seem to have been discarded by both your previous employers so I wouldn't take odds. Unless, of course, you are about to reveal you're actually the Emperor's nephew, which I doubt as I've met him, then our supplies are staying nicked."

Skipper eyed the SC.

"Are you just carrying marching rations, five days' food from arrival?"

Grudgingly the SC admitted the Infil Tribune was right.

"We've cut that and can last for ten. The XXXth are going to have to go foraging. What's around our side of the river, in the Green Zone?"

The Skipper shook his head. "Not nearly enough, the border was ravaged in the last war. A full requisition 'with receipts' would barely yield another month's fodder and in the process you'd kill off the entire local populace within eight months. The Governor, and this is technically Upper Pannonia, so the proper Vindabona Governor, wouldn't sanction that: it's Roman territory."

"Barely," grunted the SC.

The Political Tribune finished his oats and greens, "Surely we should then send to Vindabona for supplies, no?"

The SC shook his head.

"No, the river's too dangerous. How much traffic have you seen since the bend, Sir? That's right – none. As for Vindabona, we are an independent command so should self supply, no recourse to provincial stores. Somewhere there must be some money to do so but the time it would take for a full resupply? A season, perhaps. Sure, bits and pieces will trickle down from the IInd but they'd let us half-starve. Eventually we'd have to abandon the fort and run for Aquincum within a month…"

Political Tribune got it. "…to be formally taken under the IInd's Sector Command, necessity overriding Army Group West's views on the matter all the way back in Rome. Then we'd have no independence and be redeployed at will."

"Well done, Sir."

The Skipper spoke up after a few moments, reflecting on a likely sequence of events that would lead him back to Aquincum and the SOG.

"Your earlier question over the map, SC – well, there's enough stores over the river, outside the sector, to feed the Legio well into winter. Half a year's worth, even at full strength. You'd have to strip the north but, while we are nominally in truce with the Macromanni, we've got an excuse. As you've seen, Senior Centurion, the insurgents have been building up since the XIth left and getting more confident. Always moving over the river on to Roman ground, somewhere behind us will be Sarmatian horsewomen lurking, ambushing and burning. It's why you were sent via the river road, not through the forest tracks."

The lead officer pulled a face. "Hooorsewomen?"

"Yes, brother Tribune, it's a cultural thing. The point is, King Decebalus is pulling in trouble from far and wide."

The SC scowled, "Like the Cherusci mercenaries you left floating in the dock, Sir?"

The Skipper tipped his wooden cup in acknowledgement then thought out loud. "If you are planning an invasion over the border that's illegal. However – proactively suppressing… banditry?... and confiscating supporting stores, that could work. I think we are jumping ahead of ourselves though, Centurion. Your troops will need weapons first."

"Thank you for that elucidation, Sir."

The Skipper ignored this growl from the NCO. "The weapons aren't on the hijacked convoy back in Aquincum, I take it, otherwise we wouldn't be having this conversation?"

The SC held up his hands with a nasty smile. "No, you're right there, not back in town. I don't know where our field tools are. They are 'arriving', I am told, possibly from the heavens. But in the meantime, as you say, we are getting ahead of ourselves. There is a worse problem than no food and no weapons."

"Really?" The Exfil Tribune exclaimed, thinking hard.

"Our men," the Senior Centurion said.

"And for that reason I'm going to ask you good, unattached Sirs for help, because we've got less than two weeks for a rapid induction into the real Army. Unless of course you want to fuck off and go find whoever you belong to?"

"Happy to help, Centurion." Replied the officer of boats.

And the Exfil Tribune carefully scraped the last of the food out of his bowl with a new looking spoon. As the FCL said, the boy officer was a remarkably fast learner.

Chapter Twenty-Two

Third Secretary Gallan, Sadiki small warehouse, Aquincum Town
Consistent summer weather – stinking hot
Pannonia Inferior province of Rome

Third Secretary Gallan of House Sadiki had good Greek. His mother tongue was modern Greek, he had scholastic Greek, dialects of Greek – even tonguetwisty Macedonian. He was born in Alexandria within the – yes – Greek colony but his grandmother was…ambitious. So, despite all that innate Greekness, the two brothers (Gallan being 'Major') were packed off to Athens for a first-class formal education. Elite schools meant money, Gallan's family had money, three generations serving within the Sadiki trading house in positions that mapped the rise of the familial enterprise. Great Grandfather had been the unpromising start of the recent micro-dynasty, a dissolute sailor whose enthusiasm for gambling was not matched by any luck or ability. Built on these uncertain foundations, or indeed as a reaction against them, the family's status had soared.

As the Sadiki merchant house grew, so did the influence and aspirations of Gallan's family, all down to the work of an ambitious young couple – the Third Secretary's grandparents. Bookkeepers, buyers, administrators, wages clerks, security, killers: every useful family member allotted a place in House Sadiki, incrementally increasing their blood's importance – the pinnacle of which was Gallan.

Useless Great Grandfather had worked on the trade galleys when not 'investing' in unsuccessful chariot teams and cultivating feelings of bitter resentment that his lot in life should have been 'elevated'. To this day the little clay model of him in the family shrine held a coiled line in one hand and dice in the other.

The fortunes of Gallan's family changed through one of those peculiarly successful marriages that sometimes appear from nowhere: Grandfather (Great-

Grandfather's son) and Grandmother. Young, proto-Grandmother had had an even more disastrous upbringing than Grandfathers: failed family goats' milk businesses, confiscations, writs, patriarchal beatings above the normal acceptable practice and, in common with her future father-in-law, her Pa's unevidenced-based belief in the performance of competitive horse teams.

The couple met at a creditor's office paying 'late interest' on their dads' behalfs', fell in love immediately, and after passing the hurdle of not been murdered by Gallan's maternal great uncles, Grandfather made a proposal and they were married. An uncertain and unlikely future awaited them in a one-bed slum flat with its single window looking out directly on to the city's west wall, just an arm's length away. By this point Gallan's great-grandfather had been sacked by the Sadiki merchants and the colonial Greeks' family stock was at an all-time low.

Then came war, a horrendous, bloody war. For many a lifechanging opportunity, as the black Army joke goes, but in amongst the chaos a different type of opportunity presents itself to some. Near to starvation and relying on handouts, Gallan's young grandfather waited in the dawn mob with his two mates ready for the dock foreman to pick day workers. Grandfather was feeling positive as his new brothers-in-law worked in the grain association and, fed up with giving coin to their younger sister, had assured him they'd do their best by 'faaaamily'. By midmorning, unpicked for work, it was apparent the brothers-in-law had failed to wield significant influence at the quay. So, Grandfather and the two chums stood around the forum to see if they could get on a jury; a fat chance of that but worth a go. Life looked dismal. They sat on the steps of the court steps and waited to be moved off.

"You, you and you!" barked a voice at them.

"That didn't take bloody long!" moaned the tall, red-haired friend. The trio made to get up and be shooed away for cluttering a civic area.

It wasn't a guard, however, it was much more ornate, shiny and very Roman.

"Now, now, now. Look at you, fine fellows!"

This was how Gallan's grandfather was introduced to the Roman Army. Having shared in the collective and tacitly acknowledged lie with the recruiter that, 'Yes, I can ride a horse', Grandfather was invited to take up the opportunity of a campaign term, following a brief period of fun on horses – "Back by second flood, mi' laddos! Every girl likes a cavalryman, eh?"

"Where?" Grandfather had asked. The Recruiting Centurion scowled at him – the campaign itself was subject to the upmost military secrecy until time of departure, apparently.

Grandmother had not been pleased; "You know the new General has just arrived and who he is, off to join his bloody dad to go and get slaughtered by a bunch of pissed-off Jews. They already massacred one legion and you can't ride a sodding horse! By the way, I'm pregnant."

Grandfather's answer was that they would either starve to death or have to move back in with her parents. Seeing there were few options avaliable, she gave him a kiss, made lunch and that afternoon both went up to the Nicopolis garrison where Grandfather was entered into the rolls. Grandma went with him to enter her name into the widows' fund (strictly voluntary contributions in the Auxilia 'because it's so safe!' assured the Recruiting Centurion) and partly to know where to find her husband if he immediately deserted and was arrested. "Got to be practical with a baby on the way!"

"Thanks for the support, luv."

"Don't be soft."

She took the enlistment cash, after deductions, and he disappeared into the garrison. An acknowledged fact of life is that when a first baby came along you must immediately move house, which Grandma did, and suddenly start doing things you have never considered undertaking before, like join the Roman Army structure.

Unlike his two friends Grandfather wasn't stupid, far from it, and approached his new duties with the right attitude. It wasn't that he was a natural horseman, it was the fact that he could listen on behalf of those around him then make them do it. So, Grandfather's arm got given a band and a pay bump – after deductions. Two more months' training passed before one last happy leave looking out of TWO new windows with views across the southern quarter.

"We've arrived, luv!" Leaving a bag of coins behind early the next morning, Grandfather went back to the troop, had a brief glimpse of the General saying something in the distance, and boarded ship.

On board it was disclosed they would be going to Judea, which they did, and a good war followed for Grandfather, not for the Jews or an awful lot of Romans, admittedly. Grandfather rode around a lot, his aptitude for getting troops to do what the officers wanted was noted – he was given another arm band and ordered not to volunteer for anything within the first week. He had a couple of fights –

lots of dust and hit his funny bone once, not a bad result all told, as the smaller of his two friends caught it. Saw a lot of the countryside and then was transferred as a 'reliable man'. Grandfather was good at people and good at mathematics – *'bloody Greek, stands to reason!'* had been the recommendation given to the Roman engineering officer on reassignment.

"Let us see!" had been the response, and many did see as Gallan's forebear was put to work on a ramp. A big ramp, a very, very big ramp up to a Jewish fortress on the top of a mountain. Every day and most nights Grandfather ran around under arrow and sling-shot 'putting out fires' literally and figuratively. Cajoling men or pointing out a formulaic-combined-weight-error which would lead to a spectacular splintering implosion of timber if left to its own devices. His worth was only accelerated when the Roman Chief Engineering Officer went down with the 'local malady' of being hit in the lung with an arrow.

Being a Roman the Engineering CO hung on stoically and Grandfather was one of the trusted, key men who relayed orders and often created them when the delirium associated with blood poisoning took hold. Finally, the edifice was finished and so then was the Judean fortress. Grandfather was brighter than even his new ramp-mate, engineer comrades so didn't take up the offer of entering the fallen stronghold after it was taken. His new mates returned ashen-faced, telling a story he already knew and now would never have to un-see.

Against all expectations Judea was gradually being subdued, Grandfather was offered a permanent commission to the Auxilia, complete with spousal package. Just at the point of making a decision on the commission news came that the lyre player was dead. Like when Grandfather had been a boy and Race Week came around, uncertainty rose its head, except this wasn't about losing seven days of dinner on, 'Blanco' this was Imperial uncertainty.

That's when Grandfather met General Vespasian. It was brief, he was formally commended, promoted again, given a sizeable purse of coin and asked for an assurance of personal loyalty to the commanding officer. Given the circumstances Grandfather gave it and within weeks was onboard a fleet 'with' the Farmer-General and a lot of other soldiers heading for Alexandria (and home).

On arrival Grandfather was asked to 'accompany' the General Staff and found himself being a Greek 'local' liaison up at headquarters, especially with regards to the port and grain shipments, which is where he met his old man's boss's, boss's boss. In fact, 'the old man' of the House of Sadiki, being clever

234

himself, didn't say, "Oh, you must be thieving drunken So-and-So's son!" and instead listened attentively to the benefits of loyalty and the necessary, responsible steps this military staff were making to enact a 'stabilising' Roman government, to wit: stopping grain shipments from Alex and thus starving the Imperial capital. The liaison job seemed to go well as General Vespasian was quickly made Emperor of Rome, its entire populace and Empire.

Grandfather met the Emperor of Rome for the second time who said, "Well done," and gave him another commendation and a bag of gold then asked if he wanted to stay on in the Army. Grandfather did as he had been instructed by his wife and said, "No", citing a two-year-old.

The Emperor of the known world nodded and turned to the merchants gathered within the Emperor's quarters and pointed at old man Sadiki: "Give this man a job!"

The Sadiki head bowed low replying, "It was my firm intention to do so anyway, if you no longer needed this very capable individual."

The Emperor stared at the merchant for a moment searching for 'side'.

"Well, now you've got two reasons, eh? I'll throw in a newly-made eunuch as gratitude." That last sweetener turned out to be an unexpected boon to House Sadiki as the cut boy, despite being a Jew – who as a race were notoriously bad with money, instead obsessing on theology's finer points of grammar in-between prosecuting family vendettas over a goat fence – turned out to be some sort of business savant.

And off they went, Grandmother driving the charge of education, betterment and strategic placing of relatives within House Sadiki because it was all about "Family, family, family."

Gallan was the apex of the family's intergenerational progress: fiercely intelligent, diligent, articulate, numerate, good-looking, a natural polyglot – he would soar. By the time he and his brother departed for Athenian education the family complex had more windows, all with views, than slaves. The brothers arrived at Athens via Rome, spending a month taking in the Imperial City, but more importantly, his shrewd grandmother had deduced, to leave for the great centre of learning with a boatful of first-estate scions also attending the new Greek school.

Aboard ship rank quickly dissolved and the young men, whose families ran Rome, became firm friends with the dashing Egyptian-Greek and his brother. Gallan's stock only rose higher on arrival in Greece as he could negotiate accommodation, find nightspots, buy food and ask for directions rather than just be able to recite long passages of Herodotus with a terrible accent.

"Did he really make it all that way across the sea in a fanny, Cato?"

"A fucking dolphin, Gallan, as well you know."

"If you say so, but when you meet the girls tonight don't get confused and end up fucking a porpoise."

"You are doing this on-porpoise, Gallan."

Pop toga'd, top-ancient-Greek-bants.

The work at the authentic Greek school, as recently constructed by Imperial Rome, was challenging and stimulating, the discussions fierce and oratorical.

The young men attended the new cultural centre each day, the building built by the Emperor Trajan as a gift to a bemused Athens and at the general request from first-estate Roman fathers because, *'If we're spending all this bloody money on Athenian schooling our young men cannot just be left to sit around olive groves all day with Greek...ways. They need to be supervised. Inside a proper building.'* The young men, being mostly Roman, enjoyed the great marble space designed to recreate a purely imaginary high point of Athenian culture built by the city's – effective – conquerors. It was all reading, writing, debating constantly, declaiming, exchanging tales of their upbringings, taking boat rides, exploring the mountains...the list went on.

They actually ran to Marathon (horses back) and took mules to Thermopylae. While the band of brothers wanted to go to Sparta everyone, mostly Athenian, said it was shit-hole now so they didn't in the end. Great teachers they met who were, although diluted forms of Aristotle, mostly original and startling different in their ways of thinking and questioning everything: "Maybe Arion did ride a womb, is it allegorical, young master Cato? Yes, a fine idea, this will be the afternoon's discussion; the natural birthing, safety of the dolphin-womb. Gallan, you are sniggering, please start..."

And in amongst this fascinating paradise where the denarii FX rate allowed all of them to live like kings...

"...or perhaps tyrants would be more apt..."

"...or Emperors?"

"No, not that Cato, that's definitely too much, even for Athens..."

...Gallan had his most extraordinary meeting. With God's son, who was actually real, and alive, despite being nailed to a cross a few Emperors before.

God's Son changed Gallan's life forever. He had, however, inherited his grandfather's nous and kept the fact quietly hidden from the rest of his friends. Slipping out to attend the 'quiet' meetings at all hours was a strain but easily camouflaged.

"When are we going to meet this girlfriend of yours, Gallan? My father was a Consul, Cato's grandfather spectacularly disembowelled himself for reasons too political to mention in polite company: are we not good enough now, eh?"

Gallan would just give a sly smile and his notoriety and prestige only grew with conjecture over the Greek's 'slipping out', consensus settling on their 'Didactic Orations' tutor's young wife with the massive tits, which the Roman students all believed they had seen despite her being heavily veiled and behind a screen at a welcome drinks-do in the first month of arrival.

Returning to Alexandria Gallan declaimed, showing off new skills, the censored adventures of Athens to his family at the lavish homecoming dinner, all to great acclaim. The warm letters had already started to arrive from both his new friends and, more importantly, their father's secretaries delighted with the assistance afforded to the patrician scions navigating a challenging period of education. Gallan having helped return his buddy's all literate and completely unstabbed to death in a dive bar.

At the end of the welcome dinner, his grandmother kissed Gallan on both cheeks.

"Well done, Grandson, you're a worker, always knew it. Now listen, boys will be boys, so until you get it out of your system have fun with your 'brothers and sisters' but be discreet. I don't mind what you do but remember, lad, it may not be illegal but it's certainly frowned upon. I'll give you a name of a friend of mine who is reliable if you really feel you have to. Don't blush, I've been around a bit, good to have a secret society, good for contacts, your great uncles are all in one of the biggest but don't say anything coz' I'm not supposed to know. Have your fun, you're a young man, we'll find you a wife then you can settle down."

His grandfather had just given him a wink and placed a fat gold piece in his grandson's hand.

"If I were your age…go and have some fun," then followed his wife up to bed.

"How did she know everything? Everything?"

"Because she's Grandmother," his mother had said drily, not even bothering to ask why her son asked, then also went to bed.

So now here in Aquincum, gainfully employed by the House of Sadiki, Gallan spent several hours looking at the fish he'd been given by a boy, worrying about the message from Eleazar which clearly alluded to his darkest secret. Then, even though he hadn't a clue why, Gallan began to scour the town for a local 'presence'. He surveyed the walls, the baths and public places mostly for certain Greek letters, signs or one of their myriad variations. These secret indicators could be very discreet and the Third Secretary spent half a day pondering the significance of a particular notice until he decided it really was just an overwritten advert for carp. He despaired.

Up to this point Gallan was doing well within Sadiki, everyone had said so, helping to negotiate the difficult passage of the Master's disappearance.

"Known Master since he was a small one, lovely toddler, lovely man, just hasn't…got it. Know what I mean, Grandson? So, he's gone for a little holiday." Gallan had nodded bemusedly.

The House had leant on Gallan's family heavily when the Master *'went on his travels.'*

Grandmother and the Lady Lassalia holed up in conference for whole afternoons and mornings.

"Anything we should be worried about, Grandmother?"

She had patted him on the cheek. "Just you continue to do the good work you are doing, learn the ropes, there's no rush. All you have to do is what you are asked to do as soon as you are asked to do it. You're a clever boy, you'll go far."

And he did go far, first back to Rome, then Syracuse and Leptis Magna before finally to Salona as one of the Lady Lasallia's personal bagmen under First Secretary Eleazar. "Trust him, Grandson, the eunuch, he's all right."

That final midday of comparative normality in Aquincum everyone from the House of Sadiki were celebrating the dispatch of the season's supply convoy. They were done with the Army Special project and could go home to Salona to make a 'real bonus'. The staff saw the Lady had taken her chariot off on a joy ride, so opened the good wine to toast having just successfully delivered the company's first, full military contract in over a decade. The old joke about it not being a good party unless you end up getting arrested turned out to be less funny when the actual Roman Army surrounded your building and a civic Proctor read out a court dictate, co-signed by the Governor, preventing anyone from leaving or destroying any documents under pain of imprisonment or a less than civilised death.

The Lady Lassalia and Eleazar were both gone, so Gallan calmed everyone down and climbed up to the principal's balcony, had the glassware cleared and then watched the slow progress of the returning two-hundred-plus wagon train. Dispatched by Sadiki only a few hours earlier, the convoy trundled back through town on to the holding field outside their small warehouse but was now guarded by a large detachment of local Garrison troops. The House of Sadiki's most junior-senior employee, Gallan stood on the balcony trying to work out what was going on.

A Sadiki signal was spotted from the large warehouse across town, the one held by the shell company. With a sinking feeling, Gallan was informed in blinks that the cover was blown for the other storage depot and 'military' were inside. The Greek Third Secretary turned to go back downstairs when the boy appeared, waving from the edge of town, a loyal, useful boy, it turned out. Gallan waved back. Days passed slowly inside the cordon with nothing to do but worry and the food and drink got low, because the Legio IInd weren't messing about when they said no one leaves or enters. The local lad kept coming back, however, making the signal spot by the white jars at the back of the baker's on time, each night, until the office security man made that first link to the outside world via the sling.

On the third day of confinement, Gallan finally learnt the Lady Lassalia was under arrest when the court Proctor arrived, flanked by an unpleasantly tall armoured soldier of some description, informing the office that their Domina/Boss would soon provide written instructions as to what to do and "That it was in everyone's best interest to cooperate."

So Gallan waited some more, the only distraction being the Emperor's Nephew trying to enter the little warehouse, to be firmly rebuffed by the IInd's cordon. Hedgehog had waved a little sadly to Gallan up on the balcony, before disappearing back to town.

Then, after a full week, a small package of paper arrived, delivered by a local scribe accompanied by – a definitely not local – black-robed, face-covered individual covered in knives. It was very surprisingly addressed directly to him, Third Secretary Gallan – not First Secretary Eleazar or the Second Secretary. Gallan thanked the scribe and apparition of death politely to then slip back inside the warehouse, pretty relieved at not being cut open at the door, to read the documents in a quiet side room. Having read the papers, Gallan did what most people do when unexpectedly having authority granted to them and sought to share future blame. Off the tightly rolled docs went, luckily only a few pages, that night slung off the balcony.

While Gallan waited for a response – and the boy was obviously still working for the First Secretary hiding in the back up office – he had a long discussion with the guard Centurion, who brought over the nasty, looming officer, about 'access'. Seeing he would get nowhere using the simple logic that to enact the instructions given to him, presumably dictated under duress at the local Governor and the IInd General's behest, he and the staff would have to leave the small warehouse to interact with the outside world, Gallan went somewhere different.

Ten minutes followed with a first-class performance of aloof, disgruntled opinion that the female head of the household was "…probably a prostitute, and his own good friends Bobo and Duck, well actually their real names are – 'major, major name drops' – had warned him about working for a woman, and it didn't matter anyway because the chum's father promised him a job in Rome…" did the trick. The tall crooked officer had, at the end of the exchange, asked resentfully, "How do you know one of the …?"

"Bexi? Oh, we studied together, his father was so good as to even put me up for a few weeks when I was last in the capital. Stunning views, but he'd barely let me leave, time on his hands now he's no longer Pro-Consul. Likes to hang out with his son's friends, feels young again, bit embarrassing really but…" The unpleasant officer listened, trying to keep his mouth closed as men he'd only ever, literally, looked up to were this…office merchant's…friends???

The cordon dispersed and Sadiki runners were sent for food while everyone else stretched their legs on the small field.

The cordon had dissolved just in time for the boy to run up the steps that morning. Gallan had been right, it was a reply from Eleazar, complete with a proper authentication seal proffered to him in an almond-sticky hand. Gallan, it was confirmed, had been selected personally by the Lady Lassalia to fulfil all instructions which were: to provide the IInd Legion with everything specified, as set out on the list from the local General. The full resources of the House of Sadiki were to be bent to the task. The second instruction was the message from Eleazar directly to Gallan, retold by the boy and coming with a meaningful fish. It shocked the clever Greek. *'Why had Grandma told the House Principals he was more than dabbling in…stuff?'*

What Eleazar had added to Lassalia's missive, translated into plain language, was that for some reason Gallan was to seek his sect brothers, if indeed there were any way out here in the Pannonias. His grandmother's words rang in his ears so he took a breath and 'got on with it'.

After his blatant demonstration of earlier cronyism to win freedom, Gallan and three of his staff were allowed to wander into town, initially in the company of the folding chair of an officer but after a series of very long and deliberately detailed meetings with the small local money men, hauliers, river hauliers, and leaning hard on a dictation scribe, the Tribune got bored and buggered off. That's when Gallan started searching the town for signs and sigils.

Mid-afternoon now, the boy found Gallan looking at the scratchings on the back of the public latrines and beckoned him to a popular bakery with a sit-down spot at the back. A familiar voice greeted him from behind a curtain – Eleazar.

"Why me? Why…the sect?" Gallan whispered through the hessian.

"I don't know…" Eleazar replied. "…but she asked for you to handle the arrangements, not any of the other senior clerks, and while you have many virtues, the only one I can think of that stands out for such preferment is your, er, 'religious predilection', shall we call it?"

Gallan thought on this. "How long have you known?"

Eleazar had gone.

Gallan finished his drink, left the bar and made at least three more laps of the town. Nothing.

No marks, no Greek riddles, no cryptograms, no fish graffiti dripping with meaning – although being a river port there was plenty of graffiti featuring significant town elders engaging in numerous activities with anatomically dubious carp. The local catfish god, 'King Catfish' of the River People, also featured heavily on walls but its pictorial creed seemed to extend no further than lurking and drowning individuals at random. Especially Romans.

Gallan sat and pondered his failure. If he couldn't find a sign, he would have to make one himself, send a signal.

On his wooden-framed bed Gallan thought hard on what to do but nothing came to mind so, as was his wont, turned to the Good Word when all else failed – one of the secret rolls kept under the mattress – and read for a bit. It was an old favourite, life relevant to Gallan as an up-and-coming young merchant trader, relating to investment opportunity as it was:

'Thou wicked and slothful servant, thou knewest that I reap where I sowed not, and gather where I have not strawed: Thou oughtest therefore to have put my money to the exchangers and then at my coming I should have received mine own with usury. Take therefore the talent from him, and give it unto him which hath ten talents. For unto every one that hath shall be given, and he shall have abundance: but from him, that hath not shall be taken away even that which he hath. And cast ye the unprofitable servant into outer darkness: there shall be weeping and gnashing of teeth.'

A small lantern of the mind was lit – the tale of the talents was a favourite, and not just of Gallan. It was one of those teachings everyone knew, whether huddled around in a small cave or sipping wine on a patrician-wife's triclinium.

If the House of Sadiki had taught him anything it was that: greed engendered an excellent delivery system for news.

First thing the following morning, Gallan walked down the steps of the little warehouse where a single guard waited with the overly tall officer.

"Where are you going?" the crane-like man spat.

Gallan greeted the Tribune formally and outlined that House Sadiki had to move a substantial sum of money for the Governor and so would need to visit the local merchants and moneylenders to discuss terms. The officer grunted and said he would come. Gallan, of course, agreed and headed to the biggest merchant in town: Holgur.

The advantage of having a Tribune in tow was that they didn't wait. Holgur saw them almost immediately at his house.

"You're not seeing her!"

Gallan bowed deeply returning a good sneer, "I have no wish to see her, Merchant Lord."

This went down well. Gallan was unsure if such a thing as a merchant lord actually existed but it hinted at far away exoticism where traders could be princes. Whether true or not, Holgur lapped up this exciting glimpse of a broader world behind his frontier military zone of fish and nothing.

"My only wish is to execute the instructions given to me for the reinstatement of funds and logistics to the named parties," Gallan added, with an aside to the Tribune, "I am a Roman citizen and, quite frankly, this is not my money, or indeed rightfully the Lady Lassalia's as I understand. So why don't we help these funds on their way to the rightful parties?"

242

"You understand right, Greek," the looming Tribune replied with his most friendly grimace.

"So, to do this, I may need help. I have Athenian-backed treasury notes, temple guaranteed, that need liquidating and guaranteeing locally."

This had all got Holgur very interested, the little Gypto-Greek shit on his doorstep had turned turncoat on his mistress and was sitting on a big pile of cash that everyone was going to get a bite of. Following the monumental fuck-up regarding the court cases that morning this was a big bite Holgur was definitely going to take.

"How much?"

"A lot. I'm not sure if it can be handled here."

"Try me."

"Notes for a thousand librae of silver."

"Jupiter!"

"It will be quite a complicated transaction. I'm sure costs will be incurred and I would have to be…"

"Don't worry, you'll get your cut."

A less than pleasant guttural sound emerged from the Tribune. Holgur reassured him:

"The IInd will have what it needs and we won't forget you personally, Tribune. That's a lot of silver, ten talents?"

"Yes, I need it in ten chests specifically. Everyone involved needs to be very clear on that. The silver will be used to purchase new supplies and, given the circumstances, it would be best deployed through…local traders, perhaps? The question is: can you help me find enough silver and then choose the traders who will best make use of this 'investment'? I've met most of them but I need some…guidance."

"Leave it with me! Ten chests it is."

The news spread like wildfire, ten talents of silver was coming into the Aquincum market, a huge sum. Holgur made it known he had it all in his gift and spent the day telling everyone, sucking up 'preferred supplier' bribes like King Catfish himself (who he had secretly prayed to that morning). "Very important this Sadiki man knows where the bitch's cash is going – that it's being spent well. Has to be spent wisely see, that's what Secretary Gallan says, and I'm helping, all for the good of Rome, of course."

'Ten talents…precisely.' At noon, Gallan found himself in the bath bar eating and drinking for free with a full menu of 'sisters' and anything else he might like upstairs, all available gratis. Association members happened by continuously and purely coincidently, joining the Alexandrian and regaling him with stories relating to financial probity and return.

Gallan was convinced the news of the very specific amount of silver had spread the full course of the town when a small girl with a basket of mackerel asked him if "…He was the man with the ten boxes of treasure?" and "Could she have a boat of her own?"

The news had indeed spread wide. In the Lower Pannonian Gubernatorial Office building, the IInd's General was trying to hold together a shitty border against the probing of a Dacian empire several hundred miles away. On hearing the news, this sector's Military Legate made it known that the rumoured money better result in more supplies turning up soon or there would be consequences, plural. Even halfway through the process of allocating the XXXth's Legion stores the General knew he needed much, much more and "…Tell those merchants they can embezzle all they want but if I don't get resupplied then everyone's going on a fucking cross!"

'Last of all me,' the IInd's Military Legate thought grimly to himself.

The Governor nodded in stern agreement with his colleague but also conveyed a response to this fiscal update down the chain, sending a message to Holgur that he, himself, would be *'in for one of the talents'.*

Later that evening the information percolated into the Special Operations Group's nondescript new rooms located at the very bottom of the administration's basement. SOGI discussed the money with SOGII in the secure rooms, having the scribe record their thoughts on how a portion of the monies could be put into an additional slush fund while still keeping the General in pilum shafts. A careful 'dissection' was made of how two whole talents might be rerouted and spent. Once agreed, SOGII ordered that Holgur was to be dragged in for an explanation – provided, not sought, for once. Time to top up the 'Aqueducts for Peace' fund, SOGI stated drily.

The Special Operations Group leader then half turned to the Assyrian guard in the secure room, who made a slight bow of acknowledgement and went to get Holgur, fiddling with his belt knots, counting them off thoughtfully. *'I, II, III, IV, V, VI, VII, VIII, IX – ten talents. Ten? X!'*

Ruben and Eleazar were not religious men and ruminated together on the rumours Gallan was spreading sat, as they were, in their sweating, bathhouse storage room office.

"Didn't he give away all his things, your messiah?"

"Not my messiah, that's the point, Optio Ruben. But, yes, I believe so."

"You don't think your man Gallan has interpreted the Lady's instructions to give away all the Sadiki money as some sort of redemption through poverty? Is he going to live on wheel? They do that, I think."

Eleazar had always seen Gallan as a talented, capable young man but religion did funny things to people, that's why state religion was so important, it was reliable. "If he does it better be up a very high pole when I catch him. But no, I don't think that is what he is doing. There is a higher power that governs our third secretary's life, above even his god."

Ruben considered this theological point and required enlightenment: "What's above a god?"

"Gallan's grandmother."

"Right…or is he being much more secular? Gallan's just embezzling the money with her Ladyship in clink and us in our love nest?"

Eleazar shook his head. "No, I'm sure that's not it."

But the First Secretary knew it ALWAYS could be that – graft – no matter who it was.

The Optio also thought Eleazar seemed very sure of himself. It was a lot of money and they'd flogged to death a few armourers in his time for much lesser sums gone astray.

"Why, then, are you so sure Gallan's not stealing all the silver?"

"Because we don't have ten talents of silver. The Aquincum float barely has half a talent. Our Mare-Nostrum-wide liquidity at this time is also… stretched… following Sadiki's endeavours in Project Invictus."

Ruben snorted. "What? So what's…? How's he…when people call on the money?"

The thing about running a large, multinational trading house across the Empire is that you couldn't control everything. You could try, that was partly what the mandatory flowers and decoration at each outpost were about – messages of 'what is expected' and 'we see everything; the flowers, the paint, the ledgers' – but of course Eleazar and the Lady Lassalia couldn't possibly do so.

"We just have to trust Gallan, the Domina picked him and...I'm only a slave."

The next day Gallan finished another free lunch and wandered the town, making a point of doing some little things just in case he'd caught anyone's attention: alms for a beggar, reading on a bench – a certain text that never usually left the hidey-hole gouged out of his bed, conversed with some bemused fishermen in an overly friendly way, walked into the Danube up to his knees and gazed meaningfully about, bought a loaf of bread to share with some urchins.

Then Gallan walked back towards the little warehouse to dry out and see what happened next.

What happened next is that he was picked up, thrown in a large sack and carried off down an alley.

Gallan was terrified and in a sack. *'Had they found out he didn't have the silver and the temple notes were forged? Was he going to be tortured and ransomed ("shit! Sadiki didn't have the money!")? Was this sack the First Secretary's work – had Eleazar assumed his plan was graft so was going to have him put in the river? Was it Holgur who'd torture him for fun until he just handed all the funds over? Which could be quite a long time, philosophically speaking, as there weren't any.'*

The sack was placed carefully on a chair, lashed to the seat, then the top opened. The Alexandrian was in a small room with no window, the only light a few tripod oil burners.

Two black-robed figures regarded him with their face scarfs pulled down. These were the Assyrians Gallan knew, the desert tribesmen everyone muttered darkly about as belonging to the 'spies'. He'd half met one at the door of the little warehouse, escorting Holgur's scribe with the demands. Now in this lightless room, bound to a chair, the Greek watched a shadow come towards him, padding forward to pull up a stool and form a guarded smile under curious brown eyes. It spoke softly.

"We are supposed to be watching you anyway, but have become intrigued, ourselves. We would like to know something. This silver you have..."

'Oh Lord Jesus and Yahweh help me because I don't have any of it!' thought Gallan. A little furrow of thought crinkled the dark tattooed face before asking in a measured voice, "...if you were to give it to us, Greek Secretary, these ten talents...what do you wish us to do with it? Should we keep it safe for you, or for its...owner?"

'I can only give you some, it's yours, don't kill me!' the Greek was about to blurt out, trying to formulate the argument that he didn't actually have all the silver but was sure he could get it if enough time was…

Hold on! 'Should we keep it safe for its owner?' A classic shakedown line but…the questioner leant forward, almost expectant – not greed but something else, almost…hopeful.

Had Gallan's plan actually worked?

"No…" tried Gallan, "…you should not keep the silver safe."

"Ahhh…" The Hatra turned to his colleague for a moment then spoke carefully, raising a blue-inked hand to chin.

"…But why not? It is a lot of money. Should not such an important sum be kept hidden?"

'Kept hidden? Surely not? Assyrians?' Still, keep it going…

"Something so important should never be hidden, it should be properly…used?"

The Assyrians turned to each other again. "And how would we use your…money?"

"It is not my money?"

"Then whose is it?"

"My Master's?"

"Not your mistress?"

"My Master."

"Then it is your duty to keep the money secure for your Master, surely?"

"My Master would not give it to me if…He…did not want me to use it in His name…"

"And what is your Master's name, Greek?"

"My Master's name is…"

A shot of fear, a choice.

Gallan resolved himself and gave the name of his Master. It was not the name of Sadiki or Lassalia.

All three paused. The Assyrian smiled.

"Brother!"

The other standing man smiled likewise, turning the twelve knots of his belt.

"Let us first say thanks to the Lord our God and his disciples!"

Still tied to a chair, Gallan agreed. "It is right we give thanks and praise."

'Fucking too right...'

His bonds were cut and the two Assyrians, with Gallan, prayed together. Then a story was told by the desert tribesman of illumination, of being ordered to render a dangerous man under guard from Antioch to Rome, a man who'd spoken to them.

Locks tumbled and Sobe turned on her cot, looking up with dread. She always half-expected Holgur but it was just the shadowy guard. Nothing unusual in that except, for the first time, the robed man spoke, a whisper.

"Sister, you do great work. May the Lord look down on you and keep you safe. That may not be enough, though, so I will help you."

'Fuck! Right, wake the fuck-up.'

Sobe sat bolt upright, hair everywhere. The Assyrian had pulled his cloth mask down and was looking at the prisoner, not unkindly, but expectantly. The Lady Lassalia's brain whirred, memory recalling snippets and half heard jokes at dinner parties.

"The Carpenter King looks upon all of us, Brother."

A moment of slight perplexity before the warrior seemed to relax, reflecting on the words as he did.

"Yes, yes. He does. That is good you remind us of the humility of the messiah, a simple carpenter. Who indeed shall inherit the earth, Sister?" *'Who indeed? No idea!'*

"Humility is so important." Sobe tried.

The guard smiled again. "I have met your man, the Greek Gallan, he is well. Your position, however, is very difficult so we asked Brother Gallan if there was anything we could do. The Greek sends you these for comfort."

The Assyrian pulled out a scroll which Sobe Lassalia opened. Definitely no concealed knife, not that she'd asked for one, instead just densely-written Greek. A scan of it showed that it was some sort of religious text with case studies, but a laundry list would work as a cipher and Gallan had marked certain letters with a flourish. She suppressed a smile. *'Grandmother was right – bright boy'* then thought, *'What to do next?'*

248

"Is there anything more, within reason, I can do to ease your suffering, Lady?"

Theatre time. She pulled up her dirty gown, covering her head in the way her mother used to at temple. "There are more texts…Brother… that Gallan has which would bring me consolation in these times. May I write them down?"

The Assyrian frowned. "That is difficult."

"The words of Christ are always difficult, in their simplicity."

'*That was bloody gold!*' she thought later.

The guard considered this, with more frenetic brow work.

"This is true. May I tell Brother Gallan which texts you wish for?"

A little embarrassed he added, "I would also know who opens your heart to the Word."

'*Fuck no. Right – deploy some humility, they like that.*'

"I am the one who must learn from you but, I must admit, have some caution despite your kindness. My faith must now be alone as I am, directly with Him. For do you – we – not follow a single Lord?"

A perplexed frown of tattoos in response.

That waffle was more like dodgy copper than gold, but it worked and the guard agreed Sobe could pass a note to her Third Secretary.

The note was covertly sent back to the little warehouse, the cipher used was from the epistle Gallan had sent Lady Lassalia through the new Assyrian back channel. The Greek read the slip and messages were hurriedly sent out with the boy. In the time it took 'me lado' to run to the baths Eleazar understood what the real plan was, and the gears of the House of Sadiki turned in earnest. They were going to supply much much more stuff, much quicker, than even the IInd Legio had asked for. It was all very clever but a careful letter needed to be sent out East by Eleazer, to Dacia itself.

In the days that followed, Gallan worked harder than he ever had, instructions flooded out of the little warehouse in order to fully enact Lassalia's stratagem before anyone local started asking about promised hoards of silver. At night, the Greek was now invited to the local 'community'. In a storage barge sitting out by the island, his brothers and sisters gathered: Assyrians not on duty, fishermen, one of the money men he recognised, a baker and his wife, even a minor civil servant from the Governor's office. As the newcomer Gallan was invited to speak and it was from a mixture of faith and pragmatism that he chose a reading from a single loose pamphlet tucked inside his most valuable possession, a codex that grew fatter every month.

"I do not issue orders to you, as if I were some great person. For though I am bound for His name, I am not yet perfect in Jesus Christ."

The Assyrians hummed in appreciation, lips moved along with the words of their own, once captive evangelist, in silence.

"For now, I begin to be a disciple, and I speak to you as my fellow-servants. For it was needful for me to have been admonished by you in faith, exhortation, patience, and longsuffering. But inasmuch as love suffers me not to be silent in regard to you, I have therefore taken upon me first to exhort you that ye would run together in accordance with the will of God."

"…so said Ignatius of Antioch," ended Gallan.

"Yes, yes, he did," murmured back the robed Hatra captain, remembering their conversion thoughtfully.

Chapter Twenty-Three

Far from the world
Summer
Danube river convoy

The river convoy wound its way on, the day watches saw small hamlets, dyers hanging wool in oranges, yellow and blacks on string lines in the sun, cattle drinking, children working as they should do, and a small barge being pulled up stream by a team of two oxen. A broken-down old shack appeared ahead late one morning and Centurion Chief Armour Galba decided that there was an opportunity for drill. The handheld maniballistas were loaded by the armourer guards and, as the decrepit old building came into range, the Legionaries began to release bolts with a string of thwacks, reloading and then firing again. The shack was on a slight bend so the range was a mid-distance shot. 'Guns' was directing fire from a mid-fleet barge and, predictably, those men were the most accurate, the bolts smacking into damp rotting timbers.

As more bolts started to find their marks, shattering the cabin, a young couple were suddenly seen running from the building in a state of much dishevelment, which brought a loud cheer from the Legionaries until they were told to settle down and continue the practice – strictly on the target. Drilling on tied hay bundles in Vindabona, the armourers weren't half bad. The boat, however, gave the men an opportunity to get the feel of shooting from a moving craft and by the end of the live-fire drill most of them were getting the knack of it. The Centurionate watched, huddled down under their awning in the lead barge, and made small bets.

This diversion soon ended as they passed out of viable range and when the sun was at high noon a tower became visible behind a row of lime trees ahead. A square wooden tower: two Legionaries could be seen patrolling at the top. Bullo stood nervously on the bow giving coded flag signals. The nerves came from about twenty Centurions underneath him lounging in their tarpaulin hide, shouting useful comments:

"He's not bad for a blacksmith!"

"Arm straighter, boy, and slower – say in your head 'one on Messalina', change signal 'two on Messalina', change signal…That's it, boy, that's it!"

"I can see up your kilt, son. Go on, Big Balls! Have a wave."

Bullo turned scarlet.

First Spear Felix had woken up.

"Ignore them, sunshine, just keep going. Carry on like that and we'll have you back in the line as a Rank I."

This last comment was the most off putting for Bullo but the young armourer cadet pressed on with the red and green day flags.

"Receipt signal coming in!" Bullo shouted back to his boss, and he and the flag assistant recorded what the return signal man up on the far flag tower, sent. The tower had a gangplank that protruded out from the covered platform allowing flag positions to be clearly seen against the sky.

Heartbeats passed as the signal assistant checked the message:

"WELCOME…RESUPPLY READY…HAVE IMPORTANT MESSAGES."

The hulking, black shape of the Centurion Armourer came forward for a look.

'"Important messages", no less,' Galba thought, turning the expression over in his mind.

He played with the phrasing and didn't like it. All or no Army messages were important, depending on how you looked at it.

'"Important" in a flash signal?'

"Check codes?" the Chief Armourer requested forward from halfway up the barge.

"Codes check but they are old, two month's," the signal assistant shouted back.

'Welcome?' All a bit friendly.

Under the tarp Felix was staring up at Galba, listening to the exchange and chewing jerky blankly.

'A resupply "ready" to do their job? Keen. No one liked 'keen' in the rank and file, it would have to be a young officer to be that keen, but in a lone tower on the frontier? Possible, but again, you'd have to be very ambitious and/or stupid to take that posting. The fact was, you didn't always have to go where you were sent if you were a. An officer, b. Had some nous about you.'

Galba made a decision. He clambered up some crates and waved to the new convoy Captain in the stern; "No stoppie, no stoppie. On, on…"

And the great muscled arm of the black Centurion Armourer made a forward chopping motion with the vine staff, metal plates clattering. Galba spent the whole time fully armoured now, not just in case of trouble. The new plumed helmet, he realised, had a purpose; people could see it even if they couldn't see him, could see where his head was moving, where he was looking, and also gave the impression that he really was a Centurion. There was something about the helmet and the new rank marks that had stopped his set being just protective clothing any more. The rank seemed to be seeping into him, and with a whole menagerie of Centurions in close proximity, Galba saw every one of them wore the plates or scales like an uncured skin. Natural and pungent, looking as comfortable as bear fur on the wearer, complete with the aroma of warning and death.

The new Captain was a happy, compliant, replacement for his brother and the lead barge pulled back into midstream, followed by the other four boats in the trailing convoy.

"Incoming signal!" shouted Bullo sternwards.

The signal assistant checked the cipher: "STOP, MANY STORES, IMPORTANT ARMY MESSAGES."

'Army messages' was the decider. The Chief Armourer couldn't be sure but it didn't smell right. He signalled twice downriver to the convoy.

"Return signal to tower, Boss?"

"No, Bullo, get down from there. Everything back in the signal box. Good work, son."

The barge carried on: all its passengers looked up at the southern outpost drifting by. More figures in Roman uniform appeared, silhouettes moving up on the covered gatehouse but noone came out, no one shouted from shore. Convoy and Tower watching each other in silence under the baking sun, crickets chirping the only noise.

It was after passing the tower that the river people began to gradually disappear from the sector. Fishermen became less frequent, carters had vacated either bank. For the whole afternoon, all they saw was one tinker who warily eyed their drifting by, staring but making no attempt to sell them anything. Unnatural.

The river became truly wild, all aboard could feel the depths, sweep and nature of the great course as being very old. Strange eddies moved each barge in unexpected crosswise currents and the bargemen worked forcefully on the guide oars all day, wrenching one way and then the next, in directions counter-intuitive to the landsman's eyes but always just about struggling the craft back to where they needed to be. Even Galba agreed the convoy had to stop for rest eventually, so under the early evening sky the barges pulled up and staked themselves to the bank, not the south bank but the north. While south was 'Roman' land, as dusk ended that sides terrain became difficult with mud and foliage but on the north bank the convoy found an open, defensible space to pull in at.

Once the complicated business of securing huge trade barges to a wild shore was concluded, Galba resolved himself and approached Felix at the front of the craft with the other Centurions.

"First Spear, I'd like to ask if you could…"

Felix waved an entrenching tool at him.

"On it already, Boss. Come on lads! Let's fucking dig something long, straight and quick."

Every Centurion sprang up and taught the armourers how to dig a staked ditch properly. It was a work of military art, all sharp right angles and consistently half a pilum deep. The senior men seemed to love the work and had some sort of competition going.

As the camp was prepared, three fortified sides against the bank moorings, lights were spotted, static pinpoints less than a mile away. Galba weighed up another decision and decided to balance the day with boldness against the earlier pragmatism of passing the fort. Stores were running low.

He asked for Centurion Alba and shared his thought.

With a nod, Alba took three Centurions and four armourers at double pace down the track. Camp was made secure, lines ready to slip on the barges in a few moments, twine and tinkerbells set out beyond the ditch and fresh earth palisade, campfires set and bedrolls laid out on the soft ground- softer than a barge deck or crate at any rate. Galba made the river camp in the image of a mini legion overnighter but maintained his command post up on the lead barge, rather than moving to the encampment's centre. A permanent lookout was also set up on the CP's elevated crate stack, scanning the south bank as much as the north as night fell. Two-man picket stations were determined with the outer cordon return paths all pinned out with white sticks.

Just before night, an edge of concern began to creep in at Alba's continuing absence. Galba looked down the track to the lights thinking of what to do when a sentry shouted back that cart noise could be heard. A trundling came towards the Roman camp down the inland track and Alba appeared with an old man and his grandson on a wagon.

"It was a bloody dairy! I bought the fucking lot with two silver bits – got to love the exchange rate in shit-hole nowhere, might retire here."

"Got to conquer it first, Alba."

"Plenty of time for that, First Spear. I could always desert."

"You'd be doing the Roman Army a favour."

"Thank you, First Spear."

"My pleasure, Centurion Alba."

It was a mountain of cheese and, rather comically, just four loaves of bread. "I'd usually say the loaves should go to the Centurions but that doesn't really help us much, does it, Boss?" said Alba to Galba as the stores were distributed.

"How about we give it to the armourer cadets, Centurion Alba?"

"Now that is a good idea. Hey! Oi, Big Balls, take this and share it with your mates."

And Alba chucked the breadbasket at Bullo who looked as happy as a young man could outside of a seamstress-packed alleyway.

"Now..." continued Alba once the orange-rinded wheels of cheese were unloaded from the cart. "...I take it you don't want me to kill these two and go back to the dairy and finish the rest off?"

With a jolly smile, Centurion Alba indicated the old man and the boy, both completely oblivious to Latin.

Galba thought on this. As usual, Felix was always a certain distance away observing the exchange between his two senior subordinates but said nothing, nibbling at some goats' cheese the FS had cut off.

The Centurion Armourer declined Alba's offer. Yes, the cheesemakers could send a runner to 'unfriendlies' or, equally, killing the dairy workers could provoke unnecessary unpleasantness. He wasn't a field commander, indeed he was in command amongst four score and ten or so of such experts, but killing people who'd just sold them cheese didn't sit right.

"Probably best, Boss. Right then. Fuck off, Grandad!"

The old man and his grandson got Alba's gist and turned the cart round, making their way back up the track.

It was a good night in the field, the watches were alert and tried to outdo each other in professionalism, old legion pride fully on display. Cadet Armourers stood their two hours' stag terrified, not so much of what was lurking in the dark but of the particular Centurion each was paired with. The outer pickets were all made in silence but the ditch and mound watches passed differently: war stories, really dirty jokes, a list of all the girls that had been fucked with descriptions of each, a history of personal wounds, advice and admonishment – but bonds were made as the young armourers soaked the Army in from the most distilled source possible.

Old Sibius stood a turn with a like-minded, horribly burnt, Centurion and they enjoyed compiling a combined tally of all that was wrong with the modern Army, so much so that they sent the relief back to bed and stood a double. The armourers were Immunes, not Line soldiers, but *'It's a funny fucking thing…'* they were *'…all right'* the NCOs decided almost to a man.

Nothing happened. Just before dawn camp was broken, staves pulled, breakfast cooked and the barges pushed off within an hour.

Through a morning river mist the convoy saw one, maybe two, people back in the trees, possibly mounted. A semi-submerged body was later observed, all in black, caught on a north shore thicket. Burnt-out shacks and hamlets appeared on both sides of the river, sunk boats and debris. One craft was spotted on the river but on seeing the convoy its occupants hightailed it to the bank, hauling the skiff out of the water after them. Some of the men were itching to let off a bolt here and there but each time something was glanced, real or imaginary, the Centurion Armourer would calm tempers down, climb atop the high box and chop twice down river, pointing with his vine staff: *'Forward'*. The mood grew unpleasant and that wasn't just due to all the cheese that had been consumed. No one really laughed, as they would have two days before, when one Centurion spent most of half an hour with his arse over the side moaning about dairy.

'*Keep buggering on, eat the stadia!*' Galba muttered from time to time. The convoy entered a dark-watered stretch of the river, slower, reedy. Huge willows hung everywhere, enclosing the stream into a tunnel of drooping foliage. Big ripples appeared in the peat-black mirror and then huge walloping splashes broke the surface. The bargemen seemed spooked and bade everyone to be quiet and crouch low, each rudder man moving back a little from the gunwales and looking behind him at the stern wake as much as in front.

"What's all this about?" Bullo asked one of the more friendly, off-duty bargemen who was awake, staring in concern from under a mouldy blanket. The riverman made a series of odd gestures; whiskers and a meeping. Bullo suddenly got it.

"Hey, lads, I think they are afraid of the catfish!" the armourer cadet shouted, laughing.

The bargeman hissed him silent but, as if on cue, a huge coal-dark shape rose out of the murk parallel to the lead barge, easily about half the size of the boat. It broke the surface, skin like charcoal smoke arching over and over. Galba waved at his men not to fire but to be still. The creature's mouth opened under the water, pink and grey and the size of a small cart but then, with a slap off the surface, that sprayed up on to Roman and sailor alike, it was gone. Several armourers, sailors and Centurions glared at Bullo who himself remained frozen to the spot for at least three stadia until the grey sky appeared again from under Grandfather willow.

Night came with the convoy still moving, making good time. The new lead Captain indicated to Galba this stretch of the Danube River was slower and deeper than day one. Through darkness the barges kept fore oars breaking, the torches lit and spotters out on the bows, the convoy making it to dawn without incident and, relieved, set up for breakfast on the move. Which didn't, however, happen.

"SIR! Men on the water, it's…a bridge!" shouted Bullo from the lead bow, a station he'd now adopted as his own.

Laying under the boat's bow gunwales, the Centurions began stretching, casually gathering sets and weapons together.

'*Bridge?*' thought Galba as he ran forward, '*There is no bridge*' but sure enough, there were heavily armoured men standing on the water, drawn up in a shield wall blocking the width of the river.

"IT'S A BOOM! Anchor, anchor!" the Centurion Armourer shouted back from the bow.

In a moment oars were rapidly sculled in reverse and lengths and lengths of expensive anchor chain let out to get drag on for the overloaded barges. As the convoy slowed, boatman drove stake poles into the riverbed at the bows and somehow hammered them as they ran back down the still-moving boats before lines were wound round the drivers and the craft shuddered to creaking halts. Galba knew their station in the current wouldn't hold for long tied up on the hastily driven staves, but it gave him time to think. As the convoy stopped shouting came from downriver. At least two hundred warriors bellowing from a makeshift boom-pontoon made from anything that could float, all lashed together. "Ah…that's where all the local fishing vessels have gone," observed Alba, poking an unhelmeted head up over the barges front under Galba's armpit. "Don't sound friendly" Felix responded from down in the bow gunnels where he was having his set's back straps done up by an Optio.

The glint of spears, pitchforks and hooks also twinkled from the banks, flanking the mass of coloured shields and weapons on the boom, the latter individuals having the look of real warriors. The Centurion Armourer pulled Bullo down from the front and, after studying the makeshift construction more closely, sent the boy back for Workshop. As Galba waited, he glanced below but Felix's back was turned, the FS just carefully doing his boots up extra tight, never looking up.

Workshop Lulla made his way to the bow and looked out at the small army of hostiles.

"Fuck, Boss!" he said blanching.

"Never mind that, look at…"

However, the Centurion Armourer was cut off. Horses appeared at their sides, bone-armoured riders decked out in feathers with lances and bows appearing directly adjacent to the convoy on either bank. Long, long arrows, bigger than a ballista bolt even, came whistling in with great accuracy and power. The Centurions sprang up now and ran about creating shielding, each NCO pulling an Armourer or two behind him or covering a sailor. A shower of splintering noises and thuds exploded into shields, crates and the barges themselves, then a glare as fire-traced shafts came in.

"Bucket teams!" shouted Cadet Bullo, instinctively giving an order regardless of appropriate station in life, and men ran everywhere calling fires and getting them doused, the shields trying to move with the fire crews for cover.

"Guns! Guns!" Galba shouted back to the Artillery Lead stationed atop the second barge with his men.

Guns waved his straw hat in acknowledgement and then gestured to the banks.

The armourers primed the handheld, bolt throwers and popped out from behind scutum shields and gunwales.

The long arrows came in thick and fast from feather tassel'd bows, concentrating on the lead boat. The Roman maniballistas were slower returning fire, however.

"AIM YOUR SHOTS, AIM YOUR SHOTS!"

Galba was standing straight up on the bow now, screaming back at the maniballista operators, bone-tipped lengths of painted wood flashing by him from both banks.

"You look good up there, Centurion."

Galba glanced down at the speaker, Felix, who was clambering up with another Centurion, both with their oval shields. The line NCOs braced themselves just below the bow perch and lifted shields, just in time to cover Galba as a whole volley of arrows came flying at chest height.

"Ooof," Felix grunted, the other Centurion fell back slightly from the impacts but recovered instantly. Shaft heads drove straight through the shields, one at least half a foot the wrong side but they were strong enough to 'take the edge off' as Felix would later put it.

Down midships an old, old Centurion with half a face burnt off two decades ago – Sibius' new mate – placed his hand on a young armourer Cadet's shoulder, whispering to him and his friend, "Just breathe, lads, steady, and when you are ready just…slot them. Get the first hit and it'll all be fine, mark my words, no hurry."

Advice followed, bone armour splintered in red mist as bolts punched a bareback rider off her mount. A fetlock was shattered on another creature, tumbling horse and rider into the Danube with a great splash.

"That's it, lads! First engagement, is it? Good, you're doing well, boys. Now, same again when you're ready. Just fire and reload."

Other Centurions took a very different, louder, approach with the armourers but all roads led to effective Roman fire control.

A piebald's stomach was shot right through, two other riders driven back to cover from the bolts, a human abdomen ripped open, a thigh shot went straight through human sinew into a horse pinning the rider through a somersaulted crash. Incoming fire on the bow slowed, then stopped.

The light cavalry could be seen riding away up a hill inside the treeline.

Galba pointed at Workshop. "Lulla, get back up here!"

Without a ranged weapon Workshop believed his best contribution to the Roman Army was ducking under the bow gunwale. He now clambered back up on the bow to find the First Spear smiling, arm bleeding from a minor laceration, "It's nice down there, isn't it? Hope you didn't shit yourself on my spare cloak?"

"No, First Spear," Workshop replied sheepishly. The First Spear and the other guard Centurion stepped down from the bow to let Lulla in.

Galba pointed; "Lulla, the regulars in the centre, not the shite to either side. The hundred or so men in the centre, see?"

Lulla peered, "Yes, I see them."

"Well?"

"Horrible cunts who want to kill us?"

"Look properly!"

Workshop kept looking; "Wha...Oh!"

Galba could feel the First Spear's curiosity behind him.

"Yellow and black checks with a green line, right?"

"Yellow and black checks with a green line, Boss. And that is a white bear skin on a pole in the middle. We're a long way from home, though, Centurion Armourer."

But Galba had made up his mind. He turned to Felix.

"Alright, First Spear, I've got a plan but I don't think you or our brothers are going to like it."

Felix half smiled.

"You found cheese in a forest, Boss. I'd follow you anywhere."

"We need boats, small ones, and a horn player, size immaterial."

"Oi, Alba! We've got a job for you, Ex-Cornicifer of the Xth!"

It was a very strange sight; two of the barge's jolly boats – coracles in fact – lowered into the river containing fully armoured Romans. The warriors on the boom watching the launch at first presumed it might be a sacrifice of some sort. They launch, Galba and Lulla were in one boat paddling away – the boatmen had refused to help – Felix, who said he wouldn't miss this part of the best 'leave' he'd ever had, and Cadet Armourer Bullo crouched in the other craft smashing the water inexpertly while Alba, standing in the back, was blowing into a squeaky copper bull horn they'd found for use in mist. He blew the refrain again and again: short, short, long, short. Alba had to concentrate hard as it was hardwired into him to blow the Xth's long, long, short, long, but with a will of iron he stuck to his instructions. The light little boats skimmed away from the anchored barges down towards the boom, all the while Galba shouting for the need to hit the centre.

"That's the centre with the heavily armed professionals, is it, Boss?" screamed back Felix over the rushing river.

"Yes, First Spear. You need to hit the centre!" Galba shouted.

"Luring them into a false sense of security, are we?"

As they flew along the middle current, whoosing down on the boom, the Centurion Armourer fought down a sense of panic.

'What was he doing? We should just have crashed it with the barges and fought like a proper Roman Army. My new brothers must think I'm incompetent or mad. And very shortly dead.'

He pushed all that down. Black and yellow with a green stripe, he knew that design and it made a sort of sense: exiles.

Closing with the pontoon, the Centurion Armourer saw a lot of frantic weapon waving from the rabble on both banks. Galba could also now see the levies were packed in, all the way back into the forest: that was a lot of rabble. *'Fuck!'*

Alba's horn kept sounding as the Centurion-Cornicifer bobbed up and down in a half stand upon Felix's coracle.

"The middle's having a think, aren't they, Boss?" shouted Lulla.

Sure enough, no hand waving from the middle warriors, all heavily armed with real war gear and consistent markings. On the pontoon boom, near the white bearskin on a stick, a conclave of large men in a lot of gold was being held, the largest of which had a long plaited yellow moustache and a spectacular helmet.

"Lulla, There! The white bear on a pole, paddle for it!"

The Chief Armourer's coracle slewed sideways and First Spear's boat somehow managed to slip in behind them. Bullo was petrified of the catfish as he paddled, and was just praying to drown or be killed by the warriors they were flying straight towards. The First Spear saw all this writ large on the boy's chalk-white face.

"I hate fucking boats, Cadet Armourer, do you?" Felix shouted to his paddle buddy, as he suddenly jolted upwards, nearly falling out of the coracle.

"Yes, First Spear!"

"Good man, you'll go far. Do you know who Marcus Agrippa was, boy?"

"No, no, I don't."

"He was a wanker and when we get out of this, we'll share some wine and I'll tell you why."

"Yes, First Spear!"

"Shall we invite Centurion Alba and his horn to our little party, Cadet?"

"Er...er..."

The horn spat out another shrill refrain from behind them.

"No, I thought not either."

Fifteen, then ten feet away and spears were being lowered but at the last-minute Galba could see they were reversed.

"Grab them, Lulla, grab the butts!"

Both men crouched up, grasped a couple of spear shafts each and braced themselves to the coracle, it was a bone-crunching smash into the boom, the small boat splintered immediately but, clutching the pike ends, its little crew were quickly lifted high up and vaulted onto the makeshift bridge before being grabbed by huge-fisted hands and steadied with no immediate stabbing. Behind them, Felix simply stood up, lifted Bullo – fully armoured – up by the back of his rig and jumped forward carrying the boy through the air onto the floating platform.

Alba's alight was even more deft once the other two jumped for it, riding the back of the coracle as the front hit the boom and the craft was sucked under. Horn in hand, the Centurion flew through the air landing on his feet into a group of tabarded, longhaired barbarians who clapped him on the back, impressed at the acrobatic feat, and didn't immediately kill him either.

Galba regained his balance and the checkered warriors allowed the five Romans to move together, they were curious and appreciative of the morning's entertainment, even if in all likelihood they were about to kill the legionaries. The pole with the white bear bobbed behind blonde heads and men were pushed out of the way by bodyguards with heavy longswords, as the very tall man in a plaited yellow moustache, helmet, earrings, torcs, clasps, bangles, rings – all worked in gold, no silver to be seen – came through.

The big, jangly man regarded all five of the Romans.

"And…who might you be?" He said in accented but clear Latin.

"Great Prince Herminaz, it is good to see you so far from home!" Galba got in, quick and friendly like.

The big man drew a blank and squinted. "Forgive me…Centurion…? I meet so many people…"

One of the hauskarls whispered in the prince's ear.

A glow of recognition.

"Ah, yes, of course…my goodness…Chief Armourer Galba of the VIIIth August Augusta, who are my friends and have many arrangements between my family. You have been promoted since we last met, Chief Armourer, a Centurion – my sincere congratulations to you!"

Getting correct rank and station right was an obsession for the prince.

"Thank you, Prince Herminaz, rightful heir to the Cherusci throne, fatherling to the inner wood, lord of Aig, the Groves and Saer." Galba had had all this drummed into them by the VIIIth's Protocol Tribune for the presentation ceremony a few years ago. Not the 'Rightful' bit though, that was a bit of on-the-fly improvisation but seemed prudent given recent historical circumstances.

Prince Herminaz nodded in a grimly appreciative manner, tinkling a little as he did so. "Always so courteous, the twice-August. Now, let me ask: how are you? I must admit I am a little surprised to find my friends from the VIIIth on little boats in this benighted part of the world. Your compatriots are…?"

He turned to his hauskarl who whispered again and genuine recognition now dawned; "Indeed, of course. Senior Armourer and head of the great fortress workshop; Acinious Medius Lulla!" The prince pulled an enormous sword from his scabbard, Felix and Alba flinched slightly but the other three, the VIIIth-men, knew what was coming and didn't move. Bullo himself had worked on the fucking thing for three weeks.

The prince turned the sword admiringly. "It still cuts as well as the day your general presented it to me, I swear I have not had to sharpen the edge once and I have killed many, many men with it."

Everyone nodded in firm agreement with the formal lies, at least the former part of the statement regarding whetstoning, the latter involving killing was almost certainly true, his father being one such unfortunate and the reason for the prince's exile.

"None of them Romans, though! Hahaha!"

They all joined in with the prince's little joke, then remembered where they were. There could have been an embarrassing silence but a prince is a prince and so he just carried straight on.

"It was the horn blast, from this man that gave me...pause." Herminaz gestured to Alba with his off hand.

"Oh, how I heard the blasts of these Romans in little boats approaching, just as I was...of course, ready with my men here to lend immediate...assistance to...but then I hear 'pap, pap, parp pap' that's how it goes is it not, Cornicifer?"

Alba nodded his head enthusiastically, happily feeling no need to correct the warleader as to his current rank (Some would have, they would have been dead.). "Pap, pap, parp, pap', yes...it reminded me of childhood days..." and he clapped Galba on the shoulder beaming, "...when the famous VIIIth Augusta came to my family's fort, killed my uncles and half the people, taking me hostage."

Felix touched his sword. The prince pretended not to see, exclaiming; "But! It...was...the best thing that could ever have happened to me!" and the prince eyed each of the Romans with a complicated form of total sincerity. "Tell me though, what is the VIIIth doing here, in Pannonia with these large, civilian-looking barges full of valuable things...I imagine?"

Now the prince looked as hungry as a wolf, or perhaps a monstrous catfish, staring upstream at the convoy. He was being paid by 'whoever' but obviously the Roman supplies were the bonus. Galba thought that in the current circumstances the only thing to do was come clean but lie comprehensively.

"We have been mobilized, I am part of an advance party and the entire VIIIth is moving from the Rhine border down here. They should be just behind us."

"I see, I see..." nodded the prince seriously, obviously not believing a word of it, but that wasn't really the point. Galba and Lulla were used to dealing with the Cherusci and Chatti on an almost daily basis: sometimes it was about telling the truth, sometimes lying a bit, lying a lot, having things stolen and turning a blind eye, gifts, favours, overpriced supply agreements, buying things you didn't need, employing the useless or employing the capable who were, on some level, spies. In the end, the calculation you had to understand was that: it was all about honour in some strange way. Like knowing a good tune but not knowing why it was such.

Right now, the Romans may just get killed and dumped in the river with all the supplies taken, but on the other hand, they were of the VIIIth Legio. Lulla had also made the prince's sword and Galba knew that had something significant about it to do with both honour and wyrd. Meeting on a river would also have meaning to the Cherusci noble who had an indefatigable belief in destiny, specifically his own.

These points were indeed exactly what the prince was mulling over: it was a lot of equipment in those barges, he had the full manifest, and an opportunity to kill some Romans well away from home while getting paid in Dacian hard currency for the pleasure. On the other hand: that horn noise…the Norns had presented him with a choice. Perplexing. Except the great Cherusci lord realised there was no choice, this was a moment of destiny only princes and, may the gods see fit that his bastard brother meets a bloody end this winter, kings are presented with.

Just to hammer the point home to his men he hoisted his great sword, unsubtly named 'Spleen Wolf', high in the air; "Look well, my children! Before us, met on this wide flowing river is the Roman's Vulcan of the VIIIth, who smelted my great sword, for ME, Prince Herminaz, true heir to the Cherusci throne, which as the Fates guide has cut down men, fell foes, tearing their backs with its sharp teeth!"

At this moment, another gap in the warriors appeared, as if on cue – which it probably was. Galba saw the Germanians had a shaman in tow who was now shaking violently, foaming and putting on a pretty good show before freezing, eyelids opening to reveal black eyes, as a babble of cryptic sounding agreement spewed forth.

"Yes, yes, very good. The gods have spoken!" The prince acknowledging the necessary religious sanction before moving onto business.

The aristocrat turned earnestly to Galba. "Now, how can I help?"

Galba nodded his thanks. "I was wondering if we could surrender to you?" The prince understood at once and began issuing orders.

First the Cherusci lord was raised up by the feet to address what he termed to Galba as 'this local filth', and announced to the bankside levies that the Romans had surrendered to him, prince etc etc. Great cheers, especially from the local Macromanni who had been nervously watching what was going on and been in a state of high anxiety since dawn when the goat-milk boy galloped in announcing the approach of Roman Army boats.

Bullo was also hoisted up by Felix and Alba to make signals, acknowledged by the convoy who set about Plan A's prearranged activity. First and second barge slipped their temporary moorings and made for the north shore by the pontoon entrance, boats three, four and five for the opposite bank.

The Cherusci kept their station in the middle of the pontoon instructing the flanking rabble that all barges were to be made secure on the bank and 'ONLY THEN!' would they sacrifice the Roman war leaders to the gods'. Following a short service of thanks – a gesture to the royal shaman – looting, sacrifices and slave taking could then commence. This was all said in the local Germanian dialect but Prince Herminaz made sure to have the announcement translated back to the Romans in Latin by one of his personal staff. At the end of the speech, Herminaz gave the five Romans a wink gesturing to the translator. "Just so you know what's happening, I mean, I can barely understand this shower myself half the time. Wouldn't want there to be any misunderstandings but, well you know, it's all part of the 'deception'!"

First Spear Felix gave Galba a look of *'Well, we shall see.'*

With the last barge tied up and a few words from the shaman, the bank levy whooping themselves up into a killing frenzy, Prince Herminaz gave a great roar. He grabbed the back of Galba's rig and shouted, "For the gods and fate I make a sacrifice this day as my name is Kal Herminaz, son of King Tagura and true King of the Cherusci!"

The prince was lowered to the pontoon planking then strode along the boom dragging Galba to much cheering until he made the edge of his men's shield wall, shuffling edgewise to face the locals. The prince gave another roar, Galba tried not to shut his eyes, and planted Spleen Wolf down the right clavicle of a local cheering idiot with a wicker shield and pitchfork, all the way to, yes, the spleen which erupted in a great spout of jutting blood, bright red, coating the noble and Centurion Armourer.

This was taken as a good omen by the Cherusci and with another shout from the prince, Germanic warriors joined voice to their leader and started slaughtering their distant cousins down both sides of the pontoon. At that moment, maniballistas released volleys from the barges into the bank levies, still all in a state of half-drunk frenzy. Centurions, armourers and cadets leapt off the boats, tearing into the confused horde on the banks who began wailing as the news caught up.

Atop the pontoon, Galba tried to get involved but it was very crowded and none of the Cherusci warriors seemed to want to rotate to the back.

"Never learn," Alba said, sword still sheathed with thumbs in belt, so they stood watching from the centre.

"Where's First Spear?" Galba realised Felix was not by them.

"Over there enjoying himself," Alba pointed.

While the prince fought north along the pontoon, First Spear Felix had somehow got to the cutting edge of Germans moving south.

It was a sight to behold, sheer focussed killing. Despite knowing the man briefly, Galba had warmed to Felix despite the strange command setup. He would probably have a good relationship with the FS if they all survived, but from this day on he'd never forget the other side of First Spear.

Cut hamstring, shield boss punched forward, sword already in adjacent man's armpit, shield edge smashed back into knee, followed by overhead stab, three rapid boss smashes into four men with spears, pushing stunned into the water, one fell, heel stamp staves head in, other two off balance—about ten stabs in less than five second, all chest and neck, reverse dagger hold into next man's kidney below the leather cuirass, charge forward with shield and pin crowd behind, two steps back quickly—enemy loss of balance, they stagger, in again with fresh gladius stabbing finding arteries, hearts, necks, liver, one straight through the ribs into the lungs.

No glancing shots or wasted effort. In the end, the levies facing Felix tried to turn tail or jump into the river, the First Spear didn't relent for a moment, totally committed, sinews firing, killing panicked men from behind or those trying to surrender. Killing like a First Spear who knows every dead enemy reduced the risk of one of his men being killed either today, tomorrow or a month or year later.

The only real order Galba heard Felix issue in their whole trip was on the boom, "Cordon, cordon, cordon!" and the south bank Centurions created a three-sided receiving space that bottled up all on the banks and bridge. The armourers were sent off to chase down any running for it into the forest.

"First Spear wants everyone dead!" a Centurion had called out after them and the Immunes jumped to it: hunting down running men, the wounded trying to limp or crawl away, a bloody three-on-three fight in the treeline which left all the enemy dead and one of the few mortal casualties of the day for the Romans, but the armourer died face front in a real fight so that was acceptable. At the north bank, Prince Herminaz led the charge and slaughtered with less efficiency but a high level of noise and enthusiasm.

At the end of the almost total slaughter, when the leaders came together, Prince Herminaz declared a glorious battle had been won pertaining to the loyal and ancient treaties between himself, personally it appeared, and the Emperor Trajan. The dead of both Cherusci and Romans numbered just three, one Roman two Cherusci. The second Cherusci death had been caused by a hit in the head with a maniballista bolt, but it was no time for silliness, war was war, and the prince had the head cut off by a hauskarl and dropped surreptitiously in the river while everyone pretended not to notice. The man died a damn hero and no one was going to interfere with that.

"What shall we do with the other bodies?" Galba asked the prince.

The prince seemed a bit nonplussed by this question; "I have no idea. I am not sure of the custom here. You have to understand they were my allies and I trusted them before they traitorously turned on my flanks and attacked my good friends the Romans who I threw my body in front of to protect."

First Spear nodded in happy agreement with this neat summation - the 'official' report to be filed eventually. "Perhaps, leave them where they are, great prince?"

"I think it's what they would have wanted, best get on. Now, if by any chance the VIIIth have any changes to their itinerary and arrival is somewhat delayed…" The prince looked at Galba neutrally. "…know this, Chief Armourer Centurion; no matter what, I am here to help. The same goes for you, I think, is it…First Spear?"

Felix bowed. "It is, Great Prince of the Cherusci, I am First Spear Felix."

"Of the…?"

Galba looked at Felix and they both agreed that now and only now was the time for truth, "We might be going to join a new legion, the XXXth, in Brigetio."

The prince was absolutely delighted with the news.

"Then you will need guides and local friends, trusted parties who understand Rome, not like this scum, paid by the Dacian king…I hear…and their Sarmatian cavalry bitches, that I've heard tell, infest the area…"

'Which you recently commanded'
'Bitches? Like actual wome…'

Instead, First Spear replied, "That is exactly what we shall need, asteemed prince, might you be able to escort us east in this hour of need?"

The prince thought seriously on this.

"I was supposed to return home on important religious business…"

'To murder your brother'

"…but, of course 'sigh' my duty must always be to Rome. Tell me one thing though…"

"Of course," said Felix.

"If you are First Spear and he is a Centurion Armourer, why was he giving the orders? Please tell me as I do like to understand the Roman Army in order to aid my assistance to it."

'Or attack it'

Felix grinned and bowed again. "I would be delighted to, prince of the Cherusci, but could I tell my grandchildren I have shared a drink with yourself after the great battle of…"

"Absolutely, quite right, quite right my Kameraden!" the prince roared, liking the import conveyed by the Roman FS, "As for the battle, I really have no idea where we are…"

The hauskarl muttered something in his ear.

"No, no. That sounds awful. Come, let us set my tent up and think of a great name for this important victory."

Chapter Twenty-Four

Salona docks and other places
Starting with a pleasant summer sea breeze
Dalmatian coast

Decimus Terentius Scaurianus walked the Salona quay unhappily. Amongst the porters and bustle of trade his five body-men, nominally lictors once again, followed at a discreet distance, un-toga'd, weapons hung from thick belts with visible indiscretion. Weaving through the trolleys carrying bales, slave-runners, merchant reps and sailors the ex-Pro-Consul felt discontented. Scaurianus wanted to be 'home', in Rome on the Consul's seat he'd just vacated after only eight months.

His exalted position in life was owed to being capable, useful and flexible. Ability had got the man to where he was today from being the second son of a farmer but Scaurianus' virtues were also the curse of his life.

The ex-Consul had never had any interest in roads, but interest was a luxury only for those born of a higher status so he had manufactured interest when opportunity presented itself to the ambitious young man years before. Roads had been a first stage from which to demonstrate ability and delivery. Scaurianus could build a road well and, more importantly, could keep them built. In his early life, after building a couple of the bloody things, word had got around about the competent project manager, specifically into the ear of a well-connected, young civil servant.

That civil servant then slingshoted 'Scauri' around the Empire repairing the work of various Governors' immediate relations and/or clients when their graft-heavy, slipshod affairs were washed away after a few light summer showers. As Scauri's administrative patron put it, after one lengthy 'repair' job covering some fifty odd miles, "I'll say thank you but no one else will. You don't get nice commemorative plaques saying *'so and so did builded the Via Nowherea Minoris really goodly,'* that's not for you, Scauri. You just do the repairs, even if those repairs mean rebuilding the entire thing so it doesn't evacuate down the slightest of gradients when a small herd of pigs try to walk on it. The point is, there are people who will know about the achievements of Decimus Terentius Scaurianus and these are the people who actually run the Empire. I know, I'm one of them, be reassured by this."

Scaurianus hadn't been reassured, but was surprised to find he was wrong. His ability with roads led to elevation, not as a reward, Scaurianus quickly realised, but because where 'They' wanted him next often necessitated certain social or civic preconditions. The nature of all the work thrown at him was highly challenging, seemingly impossible. If there was someone who could do the job other than *'the Pleb'*, they would do it.

Once that person ballsed it up, Scaurianus would reluctantly be brought in, having passed through all the appropriate social hoops, loans and nominal religious offices to be rapidly made eligible to sort the mess out. All through Scauri's career-journey the young, then older, civil servant seemed always to be at his side.

Scaurianus' civil servant was indeed 'The Scipio', a patron who took an interest in most aspects of the project manager's career, even seeming to enjoy his self-appointed role as mentor to the 'amusing social project'. When Scaurianus needed proper togas suitable for Roman society he was, for instance, sent to a particular tailors' generations of 'Africanus' had always patronised. A small, exclusive, place where the Scipii had got their civil, campaign and in-exile clothes run up in for hundreds of years. How to eat, how to drink, a suitable wife, people watching and a running 'who's who' where the descriptions vastly favoured preceding dead ancestors than current events, were all provided by Scipio to his protege.

"But you are blissfully free of all that family history, like the Flavians you just have a long lineage of sturdy sons of soil in your comet's trail."

"I thought the Emperor Vespasian was descended from Apollo?" Scaurianus had remarked back drily to Scipio, sitting together at the Athenian building site one afternoon, eating lunch in front of a massive half-built school for rich twats.

"Well, obviously Vespasian was descended from Apollo, he was an Emperor. Was it Apollo, though? Seems a rather refined choice for an individual famously exhausted by the liberal arts. Would have thought he was a Mars or Jupiter man – demi-god-thing – myself."

Then came the Army projects which Scaurianus also had no particular interest in.

"And that's why you shall be so good at it!"

Again, Aulus Scipio Pallo had been right and Scaurianus found learning the military ropes easier than creating an embankment through clays. His secret, kept hidden way deep down, was that managing a legio, by which he meant commanding but could never quite shake the habit of language, was actually quite straightforward. Like a road you were told where it had to go and you just had to get it there. The trick was that you didn't actually have to do anything with the Army itself, that's what the Centurions were there for. Scaurianus found that most of the problems in the Army stemmed from a contradiction between this view and the senior officers or governor he found in situ.

What you did have to do was: keep the Legio fed and equipped, relay or come up with orders in the correct spirit and watch the accounts. Then in your spare time meet and greet local stakeholders thus creating a buffer between trained killers and politics – occasionally you might actually also learn something useful. At home, Scauri had a room full of 'official-present-clutter' his wife moaned about but didn't dump in the Tiber as the children seemed to enjoy all the huge blue-glass eyes, tiny painted spears, masks, hats with bells, sashes, clay horses, enamelled phalluses and tasselled bags presented to him over the years.

The main point of conflict for a competent commander was not armed conflict itself, it was keeping the Tribunes busy, shuttling them continuously from job to job between the CO and the senior NCOs.

"In my view, Sir, the principal purpose of the Auxillia is to take the young officers for a nice, long, ride in the countryside with some chance of coming back or not getting lost…"

…had been the words of the Gate Centurion when newly appointed General Scaurianus had drawn up at a certain mountain fort unannounced, saying: "Give me one bit of honest, useful advice for my first day, Centurion."

Scaurianus smiled at this memory, he'd replied that the NCO should be disciplined for such insubordination. The man had saluted, agreeing, but asked if the General would like to meet his junior officers first, before making formal judgement. The Legate was looking forward to seeing Centurion Felix again, as soon as several hundred miles of tracks and a mountain range to the west were traversed.

What Scaurianus really liked doing was holding civic offices.

"You'll hate it, it is all dinner parties and bureaucracy!"

Aullus Scipio Pallo was wrong this time. Civic duties were indoors, purely cerebral and involved just the intellectualisation of problems while the tiresome business of delivery could be overseen from a chair once a capable staff was put in place. Having grown up sleeping outside in summer under a lean-to and then with the cattle during the winter, winter defined by the old Terenti measure of their having to be at least a foot of snow, the farmer's youngest son embraced Imperial civic life warmly.

He also liked parties. They were, again, inside or near inside with food and drink all on tap and the conversation was rarely about pigs. One of the formal offices in Rome Scaurianus had actually sought of his own volition had been the 'Curator of Ancient Monuments'. "Why on earth do you want to be in charge of gluing the willies back on old Greek marbles the day after festival end?" Scipio had not really pursued the answer to his question of 'Why…?', the civil servant never asked a question to actually get an answer, instead working on the basis that he already had the information or was completely uninterested in the response. Scipio knew the answer to 'Why' his trusty and capable 'find' wanted the position, even though he had just been greeted with a shrug.

Consequently, the Scipio acquiesced to the request and had Scaurianus nominated to the curatorship in the year of his 'protege's civil Tribunate.

Most curators of the public monuments were either ancient bores, without the organisational ability to keep the willies, arms, nipples etc glued back on properly, or the first appointment of a coming young man who wasn't quite ready – i.e. thick – for anything more advanced. This second group of men were efficient at maintenance but periodically had to be reminded which willy didn't go on which Venus. What the post brought to a man like Scaurianus, however, was cultural credit.

By the time Decimus Terentius Scaurianus arrived at Salona he had held the curatorship for eight years, a record. Taking an entirely new approach the staff of ancient monuments was significantly beefed up from the usual classicists and men who could mix seven types of fixing mortar. The castrations, beatings and bodies fished out downriver by the Portus construction crews with 'look but don't touch' carved into their backs marked a policy shift and the post-racetrack grand tradition of wanton destruction of civic, foreign, adornments rapidly found other outlets. Foreigners and other Romans mostly.

Suddenly all sorts of people were invited to 'viewings'. Aulus Scipio Pallo had thought the idea hilarious and thrown his weight behind his client's initiative, inviting all the 'best' people.

"Pallo, why am I standing in a square looking at a statue, is it 'a Thing'?"

"I have no idea, but that odd little man over there is going to explain the statue to us, so get a drink and settle in, Quintes."

"But Scipio, it's a centaur fucking a girl!"

"I believe there are many levels to it."

Against all odds the cultural evenings had become 'a Thing', mostly due to the intersection between people like Scaurianus – all freshly minted social insecurity – and the Scipio's class – bags of social security but not a sight of anything minted freshly or otherwise for a few generations at least.

The curatorship of ancient monuments brought Scaurianus ('the Pleb') a great big gravel dump of culture into the sinkhole of no formal education which, once sanded and paved over, allowed the route of the via career to move forward arrow like and unhindered.

A new 'get-to-it' Emperor brought Scaurianus the Consulship, the full Pro-Consulship before turning fifty, alongside an ancient Brutti who felt continually exhausted by the effort of his monthly alternation of Imperium, leading to a frenetic signing of paper at the first of every other month once 'the Law Farmer' (Scauri's unflattering nickname around the hard marble benches of the senate) resumed his powers.

The Scipio had explained the reason for the tired Brutti dragged reluctantly off of an estate: "We felt it a marvellous opportunity to get some things done, Scauri, but one of the Establishment needs to go on with you in case it all gets a bit much and you suddenly feel like becoming a god, invading the sea or worse still, enacting constitutional reform."

Eight months of fascinating, wonderful work followed without a hint of Scaurianus losing his mind. A complete overhaul of public works, treaties to stabilise borders, closing various patrician tax loopholes balanced out with restricting applications to certain positions thus cauterising urban social mobility.

"In case your younger self tries to take your job, Consul?" Pallo had asked innocently on reading the last draft legislation.

Then in month nine of his tenure Consul of Rome, Decimus Terentius Scaurianus had come before the Emperor Trajan who commended him on his excellent work, awarded him various estates, treasures, titles – then sacked him. Which was unexpected. Consul Scaurianus made the point that he still had three months to go and there was much still to push through. He didn't make the point that, by all rights, what the Emperor was suggesting, or that he was suggesting it, was completely illegal. This was for two reasons; the first being of obvious consequences and the second that the patrician of the Ulpia and all Rome was seeking genuine help. The curse of Scauri's career pursued him as the Emperor apparently 'needed him somewhere else urgently'.

In the throne room Scipio had, of course, been present and pointed out, in a particularly patronising manner to the Consul, what an honour it was to be thought so well of, by his Imperial Majesty. Even so the Emperor and the scion of the great Scipii had, however, carefully approached the subject of *'What'* they wanted Decimus Terentius Scaurianus to actually do. A further list of rewards for the Terentii were gone through first: automatic bursaries and awards codified for the Consul's young sons, more farms, rights, exemptions granted through loopholes the Consul had been about to expunge. Soon to be ex Pro-Consul Scaurianus knew it was going to be bad.

Typically, a former Consul, especially one who excelled, having served his full term got a Governorship in a plum province. "And that is very much in your future Consul…" the Emperor had emphasised. "…but first, I need some help…"

And it was the 'I need', not 'Rome needs' or 'The senate needs' or 'duty requires…' that made whatever was coming next as mandatory as hitting the ground following an assisted trip off Jupiter's window ledge. Why the Tarpeian rock metaphor had sprang to Scaurianus' mind at this point was not difficult to work through.

"An Army Legate, with full powers, but not actually the General of a new Legion? Have I understood that correctly?"

He had.

"May I ask, Lord, why?"

"All will become apparent soon, Consul!" were the mysterious words that ended the audience with the First Citizen of Rome.

Pallo had told him straight afterwards, of course, as the Scipio boarded his ship back to Salona. "Shouldn't have bothered with the peace treaties, then?"

"Toodle pip" was all Scauri got in response as the Scipii bireme pushed off.

Now, many months later, following an afternoon's aimless wander of Salona docks, the Legate and the civil servant had a nice evening dinner together and within a few days they were on the eastern road, riding with lictors in tow, to burn every imperial horse exchange from Salona port-city to Aquincum Town.

Part Three
Heat

Chapter Twenty-Five

Brigetio Fort
Before a summer dawn, e.g. really early
The Pannonias

The forming XXXth Legio certainly had the numbers – with leftovers even once you selected clerks – and it was the first time nearly any of the veterans had come across such a thing as an 'over-strength' legion. For the 'Noscarfs', the birdshit-white tunic'd novices, they didn't know any different.

Pre-dawn was accompanied by the rumble of cartwheels and hooves signalling the wagon train's departure. Meanwhile the senior men of Brigetio Fort assembled outside the new, western administration building (the old laundry) around a single brazier.

"Just so no one gets confused, let's just run through it again." The Senior Centurion said in barely disguised contempt, at the early morn' briefing.

"Eight legionaries make a contubernium, ten contubernia a century, two centuries a manipulo, three manipuli a cohort, ten cohorts a legion. If any of you…" And by 'any of you' he clearly meant the four new Tribunes brought up with the baggage. "…have any further issues remembering this, one of my Optios will be happy to furnish you with an old, filthy Army rhyme to help. Today is about…cohorts and cohorts usually have Centurions, so in place of not having any real ones…"

He didn't even bother to look at the training Centurions lolling about fatly insulted at the edge of the standing group. "…I am assigning certain individuals to these posts, you know who you are, you are all here. Today is back to basics, I want urban and rural split. I want pre-existing Line units split." All assembled had the good sense not to groan or object.

The triangle was ordered struck and kept up its three-sided din until the last sleepy head was turned out of his cot. Morning triangle meant full kit and out first, from the various fort barracks, ran the actual proper Line legionaries.

Transferred entire centuries from other legios and the odds and sods of conturbernia also grudgingly let go from across the Empire. While the Noscarfs who, even without any armour to adorn themselves with, were still in the barracks fucking about with their hair the Optio 'funnels' went into action. The Senior Centurion stood dead centre at the assembly entrance to the parade ground, his parade ground which no man, woman -gods forbid- or beast could enter without his express permission or passing by him, the area's newly painted perimeter of white stones being a sacred and inviolable boundary.

The SC greeted the running, armoured men holding a torch against the last dark of night.

"Say goodbye to your boyfriends," he shouted to each unit approaching him. As they passed the senior NCO, four Optios pulled individuals away from their old Legion comrades and directed them to the commanders standing, also torch lit, at ten points on the huge square.

In one area stood the Skipper, in another the veteran Legionary First Class, then the Tribunes flanked by a Training Centurion each, Infil Two had been given another spot and the rest were taken up with certain others deemed worthy. The Exfiltration Tribune was excused, he was still young and needed to work on the hydraulic systems and boat repairs.

SC's Command also had a special task which would keep the Exfil officer fully occupied. This task had already started earlier in the dead of night, with Werewulf slipping over the river to inspect the burnt-out ferry.

Back on the parade ground, eventually the effluence of a training battalion flowed out of the barrack rooms (if they were lucky, or tents if not, given the space issues relating to a fifth of the fort's buildings reduced to ash). Of the first eight humans that appeared only one red-haired, failed carter-escaping-creditors 'volunteer' who was hiding behind twenty-five years more service under the eagle (not that the XXXth had one of those yet), managed: two sandals, clean off-white tunic worn correctly, single thick belt, knife, wooden training shield, wooden training sword, yoke with one wooden entrenchment tool, water bottle, waxed ration kerchief and a back satchel actually on his back (ready for weights). The rest of his chums were told to 'fuck back off out of it' and sort themselves out under blows from the vine stick and prods from the Optios' staves. The SC now asked the happy hero; "So what is it, 'Red', urban or rural?"

"Carter, Sir."

"Fuck me, your dad was a carter? Right. Was your mum the whore your dad fucked in town or his imbecile sister he fucked on a midden heap back home?"

"Don't know, Sir."

"Stop calling me Sir and stand on one leg."

The ex-carter wobbled after thirty seconds, "Good news, I can tell you who your mum was, she was a town whore. You are 'Urban', Red. Optio, all carters are urban today."

"Yes, SC!"

The Optio grabbed Red by his shoulder, took a paintbrush and smeared a thick line of green down the man's front and back, the sticky liquid having been found in a lower store area: a sealed, vast vat of the stuff even the XIth couldn't be arsed to take with them.

Newly minted half-legionaries continued arriving to be either allocated a cohort or sent back, the SC Optios spotting returnees: three time and four time and even a handful of five-time failures marked down for punishment details at the end of the day. It took a whole hour before some assemblage of cohorts was achieved, mostly split along the lines of proper, full, Legionaries mixed in with either, exclusively, green striped urban Noscarfs or rural Noscarfs.

The rural Noscarfs were going to have an infinitely better day and two or three veteran Legionaries were put on punishment when caught trying to surreptitiously shuffle out of their green striped units. Rural were fit and stupid, urban sly and shit – who needed working on. Pure Army truth.

The SC didn't bother having them form up, it would waste more time and make him cross, crosser, but just gave all assembled the standard *'useless pack of cunts'* speech and let the unit heads begin their work. He left it up to each group what they wanted to do, just making it clear what HE wanted: a body of men who could go on expedition in less than two weeks and mostly come back again.

The new XXXth Tribunes were given the rural Noscarfs but the Skipper was allocated a green stripe cohort. "Think of it as a mark of your experience and capability, Sir." the SC had said in the briefing, having announced this infirmary pass.

Some unit heads split their men into smaller groups to begin conducting circuits of shield drill, marching, line orders and fun with heavy pieces of burnt timber from what was left of the old administration building. The Skipper, however, just started running towards the continuous rumble coming from outside the Fort with a friendly shout of , "Come on!"

Out through the gates, the Infil officer took a right towards the huge convoy of empty wagons rolling out from the park towards the southern bank, travelling back home east. These were contractor vehicles for the marching supplies, not the Legion's carts. With them going any 'expedition' out north would rely on 'Marius' mules, the men themselves humping 'kit and a quarter'. The Skipper deliberately ran through the convoy of unladen carts pulled at a pace by the rested haulage beasts.

It certainly woke his boys up. At the bottom of the hill Skipper saw his first casualty of the day amongst the men huffing and puffing behind. Trying to find a gap in the carts the men tried to dart through the caravan. But the flanking unit of Gaulish Auxilia guarding the convoy all the way back to Aquincum, no doubt with at least one good night out on the town if they were allowed by the IInd, decided to 'help'.

The cavalry circled their horses in the way of running infantry, knocking over Noscarfs and pushing others off balance with the butt of a lance, all the while shouting Gallic abuse and curses. The Auxilia left the armoured, full Legionaries alone but fucking about with Noscarfs was perfectly acceptable Army practice. A way of paying back hundreds of years of war, oppression, enslavement and enforced civilisation. It was also fun. Predictably one idiot Noscarf fell over and had his arm crushed by a wheel, two Scarfs cursed as they picked him up and hauled the screaming man off to the gate where medics would put him back together again, or not.

The Skipper didn't head up 'his' eastern hill but ran south, past the emptying wagon park taking a wooded path through the rising, back hills. Soon the men were lulled with the rhythmic jog on flat ground and as dawn rose, they passed the southern village. Farmers were taking their cattle out from the stockades to graze and the white-powdered quarrymen made for work at the limestone faces a mile or so away. The villagers looked on in some surprise as the Roman Army appeared on the track. SOG had taken no interest in this side of the river despite it being about as full of marauding interlopers as the north.

It had been months since the Infil Tribune had even seen the place and he could sense the whispers and stares as they ran by. The headman, all got up in orangey-yellow robes, came out to watch the cohort run. Some villagers, the romantics or mercenary, would already be scurrying out to secret places in the hills to tell undesirables of the news but most, the Skipper thought, would be talking about money and opportunity. *'Was a legion back at the fort?', 'Would they see the days of top up stores needing to be bought?' 'Should wine be purchased and if so in what quantities?', 'Do we clear the chickens out of the old brothel and give it a lick of paint?'*

Most certainly the talk would be, *'Are they staying?'*

One clear-cold night last winter the Infil Tribune had stood on the old XIth General's balcony watching the glow as this village went up in flames. SOGI had refused to even see him when the Skipper ran over to the House requesting a sortie. Instead SOGII told the Infil officer that '…it wasn't in their operational remit to interfere in the Green Zone…' but, in the morning he was to lead his team to find out what had gone on.

Creeping up in the freezing, misty winter morning the Infil team found out what had gone on; the once thriving village had three buildings burnt, the old headman's body still lying in the central track, a foot and a hand cut off. Dead local women and a few children: the raiders obviously trying to find out where the hidden winter stores were. No men, though, they would have made it into the forest and hidden. Without them the farms and small money from the quarry would die followed by everyone else.

The chaotic aftermath of a raid, horse tracks and a lone jay feather were the only sign of the marauders.

So now, back on this early summer morning the surviving villagers and a new headman, the old headman's son (mid-twenties, forked beard and highly commercial), talked and conjectured. The eight hundred odd Roman men ran on by the village's wattle pens, armour or training equipment bashing and clanking. Even the actual Legionaries seemed to have forgotten how to move 'quiet and efficient', the Skipper thought grimly.

In a third of an hour, the scratch-cohort ran through commuting quarrymen who stepped off the forest path to let the soldiers by. All the white-dusted villagers staring while holding carry bags or picks depending on seniority and wealth. Shortly, the bright wall of the quarry face glared out through the trees, a rising sun reflecting harshly off fresh cut stone. The Army formation slowly emerged out into the clearing of the surface works.

The Skipper had no translator but didn't even need his limited local speech, he gestured at a tailings pile of waste rock and nodded when the foreman obviously said, "I want it back!"

The Noscarfs were instructed to put their 'armour' on and heaped up handfuls of stone into their body satchels sewn with strong, deep pockets. Each actual, armoured Legionary checking the weight carefully as no regular would let these unarmoured fuckers get away with a thing. Front and back bag packed full of rock, heavier than actual armour as the wooden training gladius and shields were weightier than the real equivalents, off the eight hundred all went again, this time to a hill, in fact a set of hills known as the 'Quadril'.

The Quadril had been the XIth's since time immemorial, you didn't run it, you 'danced' it. 'To dance the Quadril'. The XIth, a fully functioning elite Legion founded by Caesar himself — 'yes, that one and don't you forget it' — expected a century to dance a Quadril once a month at pace: there and back. At each season's start the dance card would have two cohorts dancing a double back-to-back, if a cohort failed to complete by the water clock running dry, they returned to do four spins of the dance floor two days later. For selection to certain units, especially one of the three Infiltration Immunes teams of the XIth, you could be dancing all day and all night until the Skipper was happy or you really weren't.

"So, potential suitors…" the Skipper announced at the base of the exercise, standing upright hands on hips, to the already panting men about him. "…let me tell you who you are dancing with. First there is the 'Vestal'," he pointed to the hill directly behind them.

"…The virgin hill, your first, treat her with respect or it's going to be a long day. At the bottom of her you shall find a stream, anyone drinks and they go back, from that point take the hand of Tarpeia: it's scree and long drops each side. She is treacherous as the view is beautiful, don't look at the view would be my advice, it's a long way down. If you make it alive over her, be ready to meet the noblest lady you will be waltzing with: The Lady Livia, four hundred feet higher than her nearest rival. If I catch any of you on the log cutters' winding paths, you go back again. Straight up, straight down. Finally, you come to Messalina, so-called because she will fuck all of you and remember it is a competition: winners eat dinners, gentlemen. Large parts of Messalina are a climb, the downward leg of the first evolution will be one of the most agonising things you will have done in your life. Do we have any goat herds amongst you?" Two armoured Basques from the XVth, obviously brothers, put their hands up.

"Good, I expect you both at the front helping. Everyone else: watch them. Up, up, everyone on their feet. Now go!"

And off the Skipper raced straight to the top of the Vestal inside a a fifth, in fairness the Basques were not far behind so he told them to go forward and wait, one on the reverse of the Vestal and one on the slope of Tarpeia to give advice/prevent death by falling. Then back down Vestal the Skipper bounded shouting encouragement. The armoured troops tended to be older than the Noscarfs but were still at the front of the ascending human sprawl aided by a life in the Army. Surprisingly, though, third up was the young, redheaded ex-carter keen to disprove his lineage.

"Good, Red, come on, come on, straight to the top and straight over, don't stop." On summiting, the Pyrenees-born soldiers showed the freckled boy 'quick feet' and 'bounce'.

More men came up, lumbering. Infil Six was with them and knew what to do, moving up and down the line shouting abuse. The Infil Immunes could do this all day and much worse. The line strung out, the usual stragglers emerged; a baker's assistant, a court-discharge and a cooper. Skipper knew the last one was destined for the carpenters but at the moment they just needed Line soldiers.

"Come on, come on. Straight back, hold your straps if you want but keep breathing, keep breathing! In through the nose, out through the mouth."

A Training Centurion who had been assigned to the cohort passed out from the heat as the sun rose.

"Leave him, he's not XXXth, we'll get him on the way back," ruled Infil Six.

Hours of crashing about, vomiting, dropping kit down gullies, a few good kickings when inevitably packs were checked for weight and bottles for water levels. A few jokers crept up the 'soft' charcoal burners' track on Livia, not realising a ravine separated it from the final up-down. All on report for punishment, Six's rib punches just a warmup for later.

Soon the men learnt that while small private hells were to be had on each hill, most regarded Lady Livia as by far the worse. The Messalina slope was horrible on aching knees and the Vestal got less fun the more time you spent on her, as the joke went. Tarpeia kept your mind busy with outright fear of going straight over the side, but holy Lady Livia, wife of Augustus and goddess Empress, where did you start?

She went on for ever, the false ridges breaking the spirit as every time you thought you had made it, another, shallower gradient appeared, another ridge until your soul 'knew' that the climb would never end, that it would persist through time until the nemesis of the world. She looked massive as well, opening at the bottom of Tarpeia, Livia suddenly reared up and there she was: this immense slab of rock and forest looking down on you, unassailable.

Men actually prayed to her in supplication through salt-flecked lips before starting. Descending was equally eternal after the initial amazement of remembering what 'down' was again, on and on it went. Covered by the forest, the scrub, she demanded every last bit of commitment and belief. Much like the woman herself.

For most of the men, the first dance would never be quite over, some part of themselves would always be left on the Quadril panting, lost or just running. Last, dying thoughts of many men of the XIth and XXXth, either lying in a retirement bed, on the winter cobbles of the Subarru, in the infirmary coughing or bleeding out in a wet field, pondered some part of Livia's slopes.

At the tail of the first run what was left of the cohort's minds eventually found themselves running down the last gravel path where, at the bottom, a standing stone stood with four ladies crudely carved into it, and the Skipper waiting.

"Kiss the stone! That man there, go back and kiss the stone. Well done! Come on, last push, that's it, kiss the stone. Right now, you can go, get some fluids down you."

In the clearing below 'Messalina's' last down-stretch stood a batch of forester huts. Old women came out with cheese, bread and flagons of dark local beer. Skipper nodded at Ancient Neg, tossing her a purse.

It wasn't actually a bad first effort, thought the Skipper, the training battalions had done a reasonable job, even if one of their NCOs was likely dead from heatstroke somewhere behind them.

"Right, very good. Now, the dance is only half done and it wouldn't be polite to keep the ladies waiting."

One Noscarf cried and went through a few turns of "I can't do it, I can't do it, Sir!"

Threatened with SC report, he was up and running with the rest in a sixth hour. The afternoon saw some competition as Infil Two turned up with his lot of rurals, yet to dance.

"Fancy a race, Skipper?"

The Skipper considered the pros and cons of a race. On the one hand, Two's men, whatever they had been doing and it wouldn't have been gardening, had not yet endured the Quadril. On the other, they hadn't yet endured the Quadril.

"Done, Two. Take a tenth my lot; salt, meat, bread and we show these bastards how to dance and I won't have to court martial one of my direct subordinates for beating a superior officer!"

Two snorted at this.

While the Quadril would never be fun, this was as close as it got: last man in loses. With a savagery the Skipper's men hauled up the weakest of their group and rinsed Two's rabble by thirty men in. The ex-baker had to be dragged off Messalina 'like a gladiator on heat', but gave the stone a big slobbery kiss at the bottom before hyperventilating which gave everyone a big laugh. Old Neg had the long stores dug up and did a brisk trade.

In the late afternoon, back at the Fort's parade ground, Skipper led the first combat evolutions for his eight hundred odd. Combat drills were the part of training most of the men loved, an opportunity to bash the shit out of each other with swords and shields. That's what they thought before they started, anyway. The problem was that in battle many men either got completely carried away (killed stupidly) or lulled, with the bang and thump of sword on shield, into an unspoken tacit agreement with the man opposite to mark time.

Controlled aggression had to be captured. The milling circles broke out, groups of men forming a boundary waiting for their numbers to be called, then in went two fighters. Practice swords, no shields – punishment duty for blocking – they went for each other flailing. Teeth knocked in, smashed noses, knuckles and bruises and welts with the occasional bone break. Losing the fight like a cornered animal was preferable to winning like a prize fighter – that was made very clear by Six. Soon two-on-two fights began then mini skirmishes were set. Sometimes the millers wore just tunics, sometimes with armour or the rock packs, sometimes just with shields where the men were expected to smash the enemy into submission.

"I've killed more men with my shield than you've had shits, lad!" the SC remarked to one Noscarf loudly as he passed one of Skipper's milling circles. This had truth to it but it was not the truth of the hard disciplined, Roman training story the Senior Centurion was currently trying to portray to the men. He'd been a mad, bad dangerous fucker when young. Pissed most of the time but a blind eye was often turned because sometimes you needed that, when everything was fucked, the overlap gone and it all got a bit different.

Standing on a mound of bodies just with a shield, not even his shield, he'd lost his, staving in all comers with their wicker squares, all slashing and frightened eyes. He'd put down a lot, the SC had, when he was a young man, when he drank. The older NCO now standing here would have flogged the boy he'd been. But they'd been different times and the fact was, when it all went down, you needed men who would wade forward up to their waists in offal and sharp edges.

At the end of this Brigetio training day the emerging Legion came together and mass formation drill was conducted, the more switched-on commanders having practised within their cohorts during the hours beforehand. The Skipper had done so marching about late afternoon, testing individuals' command and response as well as breaking the men up into sub units, to represent a legion then getting them to move about a bit.

The first evening of *'Manoeuvres at full Legion Strength'* though, was a "Fucking Colossal Cluster Fuck!" as adjudged by the Senior Centurion at close. Fifty individuals added to punishment when it was quickly established that knowing 'left' from 'right' would be the next morning's work, certainly for the particularly awful Seventh Cohort.

Finally, as the light faded, drills ended and punishment rolls were read. About a quarter of the fledgling Legion were on report, which wasn't a problem as there was a lot to do: latrines to be emptied, walls scrubbed, floors scrubbed, digging – endless digging – of trenches, rocks to be broken, port staves sunk for the Exfil's work, foliage cut back on this and the far bank. All of it to undertaken under torch staves as night fell. Either sweating filthy inside the Fort or under the Auxilia protection if outside the walls.

The worst crimes of the day were dealt with immediately in the square with all watching. As the only real Centurion, in his view, the SC was the one who should administer punishment on the XXXth and he wanted to make a point. Beatings with stave, floggings with whip, four men stuffed in a sack overnight and left in the Danube's shallows tied to the pontoon – pitch black, freezing, claustrophobic screams rang out until kicked back to quiet again by the stoned pilots emerging from their smoking lodge house nearby.

Then another morning, more of the same in front of the Legionaries, day after day, all on half rations. Every other cohort had now found the Quadril and at any point, day or night, there were at least a few thousand dancing. White sticks now marking the route so defaulters could run it in the dark, one already dead off Tarpeia's hip by day three and a score injured before the week was out- up and down, up and down. Sometimes running in kit, sometimes marching with yoke and two days simulated rations - also known as more rocks.

Further formation movements in Centuries and Maniples for the cocky: 'S and Ds' painted in green on some sandals. Unit contact drills shield on shield, readjustment of the front man to the rear, shuffles – whistles screaming all the time. The correct way to get a body out of the way, hamstring cut-push and stamp, diagonal attack and pilum throwing. Endless hitting of upright logs cycling through the positions of attack. Also on the syllabus came setting up mini camps blindfold, cooking the right way, folding a blanket the right way, fighting rust and anti-concussion cheats if in a fight. A thousand little tricks and traps to learn.

The headman of the southern village appeared at the Fort a few days sniffing an opportunity. The small-chief claimed he could sell the Romans food.

"A biscuit's worth of flour and a fucking leek I reckon." The SC had commented to his Optio after the interview.

To everyone's surprise, a day later five oxcarts arrived with grain for the Legion mills, dried meat and turnips in great abundance. The SC paid a bit extra and said, "Do it again."

"I wonder which one of the neighbouring villages is going to starve until the harvest comes in?" commented the Skipper when the headman had gone.

"Who gives a fuck, Sir?" and the SC signalled for the produce to be taken into one of the three well-guarded storerooms, the food split up in case of fire, theft, rot or major rodent incursion. Evil-looking cats and a borderline hydrophobic terrier were also flogged to the Legio quartermasters by commercially-minded village children.

Through all these daily evolutions the XXXth Legio were watched. Brigetio's Infililtration team knew something lurked in the hills behind them, once even catching sight of Sarmatian horsewomen trotting across a far ridge in the Green Zone. Half the Infil team made counter-patrols through the forested valleys, always keeping a careful line of sight with the new signal tower erected at Brigetio, on the Senior Centurion's orders. With so many unarmed Legionaries outside the walls, it was a dangerous time. The Gaul Auxilia also looped continually on patrols but two squadrons always stayed within the walls.

Three times Infil Comms had signalled back to the tower before burning a dye pack. An experienced Auxilia controller stationed up-tower would release the first, waiting, squadron in the stack. Racing the cavalry out of the gates towards the area indicated with smoke, from which to then take a bearing towards something suspicious. No contact was ever made but horse prints were found every time. Still, the Romans were difficult to attack, even unarmoured a Legion was a lot of men and the fort's environs were now a hive of activity.

Instead, the odd arrow occasionally flew by and traps were found on Messalina during the fourth day. Sharp sticks and caltrops discovered on the high, narrow path– Roman caltrops gathered up from previous engagements – but they were soon cleared away. Just giving a welcome edge, in the SC's view, to the daily evolutions.

While the line cohorts trained, the Exfiltration team were hard at it on the river, their special new task was to build a viable pontoon bridge right from the port to the opposite bank for Embarkation Day, counting down quickly through the minus' as it was. The young Exfil Tribune had made an adjustment to the original plan, which was to build directly out from the pontoon, that the SC had grudgingly acceded to. Instead, a downriver area two hundred yards away from the gate was selected as the crossing point, where a spur jutted out into the steam that would reduce the needed span. As the Legion didn't have any pontoons in store every foot was going to count: even adjusting the crossing area, they needed five hundred and seventy-six strides of 'not water' altogether.

The Gunboat would not be cannibalised but the two other pontoon craft would give Exfil their first seventy feet. On crossing the river at night, Werewulf found that the attacking mercenaries had, as expected, done a shit job of burning their ferry with it having sunk before the fire did any real damage. Raised, repaired and floated back gave the pontoon another hundred strides.

General river traffic had completely dried up from the west, an ominous sign that was the talk of the senior staff's evening briefings. The Auxilia begged to ride out further to scout in force but were reined in under dire warnings because, *'Well, everyone knows what cavalry are like!'*. "Justifiable contact to pursue is not a child with a sling, get it?" the SC had made clear to the Gaul Decurion, then later muttered to the command staff, "They'd be in fucking Vindabona by dawn if I didn't threaten to nail them to a tree."

The Exfiltration crews scoured the local banks for anything that floated. Abandoned boats from the attack were found in addition to various canoes, coracles, skiffs and rafts confiscated – with receipts – or nicked outright if left unattended. The edge of resentment from the river people was blunted as they were all put on the payroll with wives, kids and men all now building rafts for the Roman Army. That they were brought under guard to the Fort and couldn't go home was less popular, but that was military contracting for you. Soon birchwood rafts piled high, fed each night by punishment details bringing in more timber. Still only three hundred and sixty strides, though, with five days to go until embarkation.

The alarm triangle rings, the thick, black iron triangle had rung the alert at least twice a day for the last week. Everyone came running, Exfil Tribune cursed and launched his Gunboat, Auxilia squadrons galloped back at full pelt. Panting, sweating Noscarfs halfway up Lady Livia turned and found a new pair of legs. All streaming back to the Fort to take positions.

Sometimes they were sent straight back out to drill again by a disgusted SC, glowering at them under the parade ground awning, or sometimes to file out on to the wagon park for formation drill on the rough-churned ground and, on rare occasions, to be fed. But there was something about the sound of THIS triangle, though, that made even the most exhausted urban recruit, face down in a muddy ditch, sprint that extra bit faster.

Atop the signal tower, Auxilia signaller had screamed down a message, just before furiously hitting three sides of beaten ferrous with an artillery spike:

"North bank signal, upstream Auxilia; codes match, message; *'approaching force – south bank infantry on shore and boats.'*"

From the western river the Auxilia alert patrol galloped back into the Fort a sixth hour later, soaking from having swum their horses back over the Danube. In the Fort the Senior Centurion, two Optios and the young Tribunes met the dripping cavalrymen, who stated that they hadn't seen anything, but had acted as a relay for the pathfinder team further upriver. *'Unknown Forces ETA third of an hour'* was the only useful thing to be added.

The SC, XXXth command trailing, ran up the palisade, passing the gatehouse rungs to the eastern tower, a position affording him the maximum view upriver. Cohorts were streaming into the gate below. All ten Line units conducting controlled marches now, the SC was pleased to note, rather than looking like a starving mob of wasters on grain dole day.

From the east tower SC bellowed orders, "One quarter and we close the gates, send riders back for stragglers, if not likely to get in they are to wait at the far treeline behind the fort for orders." The politically minded Tribune affirmed and even called him "Sir!" in the excitement. *'Silly sod!'* the SC muttered under his breath.

The Skipper had got inside the gate with his cohort, having spent the morning pushing trees over in groups of eight. Running past the dock he saw the Exfil Tribune was launching the three catamarans out to the middle of the river. The Gunboat crews priming their dual artillery pieces for action, veterans loaded up on the support craft, spears up, ready to deploy where needed.

Tenth of an hour passed and flash signals came in from upriver. The Pathfinders, made up of the Infil team minus the Skipper, Two and Six, but carrying Werewulf and his Exfil scouts, had been working with the Gaul cavalrymen on the far bank since before dawn. Playing cat-and-mouse with a pack of light scouts, no more than boys, sent to keep watch on the Fort armed only with a spear and a knife each. These Macromanni lads were fast but the pathfinders were hunters and two of the boys lay dead with throats cut, beaten out of treelines by the Gauls on to the blades of waiting gladii.

Having relayed the 'Unknowns' via the Auxilia cavalry the Pathfinder team had now relocated to an upstream position for line of sight with the fort's communication towers, spotting west. Comms was now flashing signals back to the tower furiously from the top of a ridge.

"Signal upstream!" shouted Brigetio Fort's Auxilia signalman of the watch, from atop the new tower. "Codes match..." the message was relayed to the eastern rampart where the command stood. "Reads: *'Unknown force, C+, boats and shore infantry approach, shore is 'G' for Germans.'"*

"Right, this is it!" the Senior Centurion shouted at the top of his lungs, "Get the last of those men in and tell the Tribune of the gate to shut the doors. Scarfs behind the door, Scarfs up on the gatehouse, every fifth men on the palisade is a Scarf. Everyone else in the towers and down there behind the gate guard...if that all has your approval, Sirs?" the SC ended, turning to his Tribunes with a hard look. It did.

The runner pelted away from the SC along the palisade to Brigetio's gate tower, where the Skipper was stationed. It was the same runner as during the previous week's attack, the Infil Tribune noted, but looking slimmer, less out of breath and delivering orders concisely with all relevant information.

Skipper listened to the message then shouted out the Centurion's orders. He then checked the gate house gunners were ready, they affirmed and ratchet slots clanked metallically as the heavy crossbows were armed, swinging around to the north west on their pinions.

For a few hundred heartbeats everyone was moving. Then the gates swung shut, the thud of the double bars dropping into iron brackets seemed to be a signal for instant stillness. All at once Brigetio's troops magically locked into position, in formation. The SC was very slightly impressed by this as he made his way out of the tower along the palisade before stopping halfway.

"All right, boys. Looks like we are going to be having a fight and each one of you is now ready for that fight, I guarantee it. We are going to win this fight, I know that, doesn't matter what you've got in your hand, in fact. You, boy, come here."

A startled Noscarf looked up from his station on the rampart. "Give me that!"

The mesmerised soldier relinquished his training shield and wooden stave to the actual, real, Senior Centurion, receiving in return an ornate gilded, ivory-pommelled sword and the oval bronze shield with the Medusa head, all the eyes of lapis. He couldn't have been more surprised if he'd been given Perseus' war gear.

"Yes, that's much better. This is all I'm going to need! Bring those back bloody or not at all, boy. WE are the men of the XXXth legion, WE are going to destroy anything that turns up in a moment and knock off early for double dinner. How's that, lads?"

"OOH OOH OOH!"
"What did you say?"
"OOH OOH OOH!"
"WHAT DID YOU FUCKING SAY?"
"OOH OOH OOH OOH OOH OOH OOH OOH OOH."
"Goooood! For the Emperor, Senate and people of Rome!"
"FOR THE EMPEROR SENATE AND PEOPLE OF ROME!"
"FOR THE XXXth!"
"FOR THE XXXth!"

We're all going to die...
"Good speech," Two remarked to the Skipper up on the gate rampart.
"Get down with the men, Two."
"Sir."

The Auxilia signalman up on the new observation tower shouted down again: "Signal from spotters. Message: *Unknown force making signals, repeat making signals, unknown codes. Code: Ulpia, Dextro, Sevrus, Crix.*"

The SC was back on the eastern gate with the command group in a flash and, frowning, he turned to one of his staff. "HQ signaller, how old are our codes?"

"Three weeks, Centurion."

"Check if last month's match."

Two Tribunes were up with the SC.

"What do you think it aalll meeeeans?" the Senior Tribune asked.

"It means we don't know, which means that we are going to kill anything that comes down that river even if it turns out to be lepers with a noisy bell, Sir."

"Codes are not last month's, SC," the HQ command signaller reported.

"When was the last change?"

"Three weeks for our sector, Centurion. Picked them up from Aquincum cypher office just before we left."

"Perhaaaaps we should…" the Senior Tribune started.

But the SC cut him off. "These look like proper Army codes and it still could be us that's behind. Do you have the codes for all of last year, Flags? Yes? All codes should be consistent before spring so we need one to sort out a bit of Roman trust, or not. Flash repeat through scout relay to unknown force – message: 'code month to use – Balearic Blues v. Sodius Greens win. Circus Maximus.' GO!"

'Fucking Greens!' a Scarf murmured from a guard rail.

"Blue monkey cunt," the SC retorted, slightly amused. To a level racing banter was one of the only things permissible across ranks and outside of Army jurisdiction.

"Signal gone, Senior Centurion."

They waited.

Tower shouted down a repeat to the command flag who checked the code tablet.

"Signal from scouts…relay from unknown force, reads: 'Green twat but copy, month code – Aldix, Centaur, Hecate, Excelsior' end message."

"Check September, Flags." The SC ordered.

"It is the code for last September…it matches the book, repeat matches, Senior Centurion!"

"WHO…?" roared the SC. "…The fuck… is this…coming down my river? Tell gunners to be ready but artillery up. Tell those boat rats out there the same thing."

The two Tribunes finally got it.

"I seeeeeee, Centurion, verrrry clever; because it was a chariot race you used. But suuureleeey the enemy might know something of charioteering…perhaaps?"

"No, Sir, trust me. If you're not Roman, Egyptian or Jewish you can't, not if you're a barbarian. Something to do with the brain. Barbarians can never really understand chariot racing like they can't swim, see in the dark or turn up to a fight wearing proper armour not completely shitfaced."

"Whaaaaat about the British, Centurion?"

The Senior Tribune's eyebrows conveyed he had made a clever point.

Still staring upriver the Senior Centurion fought down a little flash of pure fear, rain and the smell of burning meat.

"The British don't race chariots, Sir. Pray you never find out what they do with them."

The commands flag legionary interrupted, "Hand signal from Exfil boat lead, SC, checking codes ma…"

"He's right fucking there, man! I can see him on his little boat! What's the fucking signal?"

"Visual contact. 'G' for Germans."

The SC started running furiously for the gate with the command, shouting: "Ready boys, ready!"

Shields rose with one mighty crash, stance made, pilums, metal swords and wooden staves up.

Just as the Senior Centurion made it to the gatehouse and halfway up the ladder, Top tower started shouting again: "Signal from Xboat: 'R', repeat 'R' for Romans," relayed the trailing Flags.

The SC swung back on the gate ladder and screamed down, "What did you fucking say? How did you get 'Germans' before…No: clarify."

He swung up to join the Skipper. The signaller came up with them who immediately ordered two Scarfs to push a gangplank out for clear visuals, having taken the decision that accurate relay standing on an extending plank of wood, fifteen feet above the ground in front of two primed heavy artillery pieces while awaiting the arrival of an enemy in force was a safer option than another 'clarify' from his 'wonky hat'.

Flags signalled, teetering, to the Exfil Tribune on the Xboat; "Confirm signal…Romans. Confirm…Germans…"

The Exfil Tribune just shouted back from the middle of the river, "Roman boats, German infantry parallel, south bank!"

"Bollocks!" swore the SC.

"Whaaaat should…"

"We wait, Tribune, because we don't know. So, we wait. You are from Tuscany, is that right, Sir?"

"Oh, well yeeees, just outside…"

The SC mumbled an update to the Skipper while pretending to listen. "If it all goes to shit it's down to you, me and the young officer in the boat there who seems to be able to handle himself, got it, Sir?"

"Received and understood, Senior Centurion." Replied the Infil Tribune, arms crossed peering West.

"…Whooose olives, funnily enough, were commended to my father by none other thaaaan…"

"That so, Sir?"

Slowly the first barge, a big black thing, hove into view weighed down with cargo crates. A few men dressed as legionaries hovering about its sides. At the front stood a great black anvil of a man wearing a Centurion's helmet.

"Obviously not German, but doesn't look like a Centurion to me." The SC muttered gripping the gnarled wood of his heavy vine stave. More barges appeared and slowly the lead boat began turning into Brigetio's quay.

Suddenly a tarpaulin was thrown back revealing armed men.

"GUNNERS!" The SC screamed at the sudden movement.

The HQ signaller dived down flat on the plank as the two, primed heavy artillery bows were levelled down right where he was standing, about to fire. The Gunboat did the same, wrists made to turn the firing handles.

Almost immediately the SC screamed again, "HOLD, HOLD!" and literally jumped in front of the gate artillery. The Skipper saw it and threw himself at the nearest ballista, knocking the gunner out of the way, smacking the butt down, just as the bolt left the canal flying a finger's breadth over the Centurion, out over the river to the far bank.

The Senior Centurion looked back and gave the Skipper a nod.

"What…whaaaat's going on Senior Centurion?" the Lead Tribune demanded shrilly.

"I think, Sir…" the SC said in a measured tone, eyes now locked on the approaching boat in front of him, "Our depot supplies have arrived, and training is about to become a whole lot more serious. If you could stand everyone down, Sir." The SC caught a wave from the idiot who'd dramatically thrown the tarpaulin off, now standing next to the purported Centurion at the approaching bow.

He saluted back, eyes hard. "You missed, SC!" came a friendly shout from the barge.

The SC spat then clapped the shaking gunner twice on the shoulder, ordered the gate open, took a sip of water and went to meet a man he had never met, but had certainly heard about. The Centurion thought about this as he descended and allowed himself, just one last time before the chain of command exerted itself, to mutter, "Macedonian goat fucker!"

Chapter Twenty-Six

Dacian border crossing point, the new bridge
Summer rain
Eastern squirrelly edge of Pannonia Inferior Province of Rome.

Far, far to the east of Aquincum Imperial horse relays were being expended at pace across the still shitty roads as SOGI and his team rode hard towards the Dacian border. This current chain of events was set in motion a few days before by an express rider sent from the IVth's General. At the bridge garrison, unusual activity had occurred. All the way along the Roman-Dacian boundary continual raiding and attacks had been a fact of life – this was not usual activity. The Special Operations Group had always been glibly comfortable in their 'strengths and intentions' assessments of Dacia but what had turned up at the new bridge – nominally completed to foster trade and cultural exchange between the recently treated empires, ha, ha – was unexpected: actual trade.

When the news came into Aquincum on a lathered mare the Governor and General of the IInd looked to the Special Operations Group for answers, the SOG had none and so it was 'suggested' they went quickly to gather information themselves. In person. It smarted, the SOG Lead constantly worked at the interrogation cells and now he was expected to actually go and find things out himself. All that time with hot irons wasted.

On the sixth day of hard riding, the senior members of Special Operations Group arrived at the bridge in a downpour. They entered the border post's gates flanked, being a hot border as it was, by an Auxilia patrol who had picked the spies up long before arrival at the river station. Trotting through the mud up to the outpost's tower, surrounded by unpleasant Thracians, SOGI found the IVth's Military Legate waiting under an awning atop the 'tall fort' steps. "Over there," the tough looking old man said, pointing to the other side of the river. A Tribune wandered over in a brown waxed cape, looked at the arrivals dubiously, then marched SOGI across the fresh timber of the new bridge. The General had already gone back inside.

In the rain SOGI saw that the accompanying officer was not a young callow boy on the first rung of a career but a Tribune who had rotated back into his role continuously. Perhaps gone a bit native, got a girl. A huge purple scar across the throat but still fluent in all the local languages – that type. The maimed officer was a survivor of 'both Tapaes' due to skill in the latter and blind luck in the former disaster against King Decebalus of Dacia.

On the other side of the bridge, the Tribune introduced SOGI to the man in charge of the unusual event. The man had been kept waiting at the border for SOG to arrive, all green wound turban and good serviceable, boots. Green Turban explained his business, national status as a Dacian, and produced supporting documents.

SOGI inspected the massive wagon train behind Green Turban, the papers and his citizenship status – accredited Dacian holding a royal token. The spy ran a hand through thin, wet, hair and had his accompanying specialists ask questions of the drivers themselves, before inviting the caravan leader in for a 'chat' over at the IVth's crossing office. Green Turban happily acquiesced, bringing a secretary and a caravan guard in tow.

All did not go well as the invitees waited in the anteroom of the border control building, the 'tall fort'. The SOG's Assyrians were all ready to pounce and drag the guests down into the below cells for 'the chat'. The IVth's General, however, was very clear on what constituted 'a chat'. The General emphasised the 'facts of life', halfway through a shouting match in the operations room, by having his personal bodyguard enter the outside anteroom and remove the Assyrians from the building. These were Dacian citizens acting for the King's brother, Rome was not yet at war with the Empire to the north nor would the General start one by torturing their neighbours.

"I mean, we all know the bridge isn't there so we can sell melons to each other but that's what it says on the legal 'barrel.' So, if someone actually wants to sell melons to us, I'm not going to be the one to upset the melon carts."

The General also added that, as part of the Dacian export permits noted, a portion of the convoy could be relinquished here, at the border, and was specifically marked for the IVth. While the caravan's inventory contained no melons it did have actual, useful things like grain, metal, tools, pig cages and dried meat. The Legate had no idea why, as he wasn't expecting a resupply.

"But, never look a gift horse-cart in the mouth, I say. If you want answers from our little Dacian chum, cheese and wine is as aggressive as it gets."

SOGI threatened the General with arrest for obstruction of the Imperial mission, reminding him of his duties to Rome, of the vital work the intelligence group were doing at the express command of the Governor and sector commander, the General of the IInd.

The IV's General's reply was as old as the Seven Hills: "But none of them are here, laddie. I am, though, and I don't see any of the fine men of the IVth Flavia Felix facilitating any of that. Give it a go though…Tribune?" The General raised his clasped hands back towards the professional Tribune sitting behind him. The other man did not move, just stared hard at the chief spy in silence, cutting the fine skin off a peach with a long, thin knife.

A voice instead rasped, "I'm good General. Now you lot seem like clever fellows…"

His voice grated like a sled over gravel. "…a riddle; what comes after four? Now you want to say five but you'd be wrong, it's six. You want to ask why, don't you?"

SOGI stared back, cold and wet, he really didn't. "Let me tell you then. Because the answer's: 'Legions', see? As there is no fucking Vth Legion any more, isn't that right, General?"

Peach skin flicked across the table at the SOG team. "That is right, Tribune, all got wiped out in a nasty dark forest with not enough kit. That's the elephant in the room."

A throaty growl that could have been a laugh, "The Vth's emblem was an elephant, it's the General's little joke. See how it's funny?"

Peach juice flecked SOGII this time. "I'm taking those supplies so when less welcome visitors eventually come roaring over this bridge we've built for them to attack us from, into Lower Pannonia, the IVth have got a chance that the Army list won't be 'One, three, six, seven…' understood?" was the General's final word on the matter.

The SOG rode out at speed for Aquincum a few hours later, having watched the mysterious first wagons trundle south over the bridge towards…Aquincum.

Chapter Twenty-Seven

Merchant Holgur's hospitality suite, town of Aquincum
Evening judging by the cockroach's activity
Pannonia Inferior province of Rome.

Sobe Lassalia had by now been in the dark cell for several weeks. At first, she wondered if 'her' room was just a cleared-out store cupboard but, judging by the heavy bolted door, now believed 'her rival', as Merchant Holgur naively styled himself, seemed actually to have built himself a prison cell within the family home. A prudent outlay of funds as it had obviously been well used. The whole fingernail she'd found embedded someway up the wall towards the sole grating supported this view. Slaves, business rivals and possibly even Holgur's own wife had been in here: a small, sad prayer was etched into the plaster below the fixed wooden bed. A pathetic little text asking for forbearance towards the frailties of womanhood. Sobe had carved out a more forthright injunction to Isis into the plaster for future inhabitants of this sordid place:

'Life, death, love, hatred, light, darkness, return to me, to me. Hear, Lady Isis, and receive my prayer. Thee, thee I worship and invoke. Hail to thee, sole mother of my life.' She had time on her hands after all.

Then as an afterthought Sobe added a little something from the 'New-Jews' pamphlets just in case the place was searched by the Assyrians.

'Let your light so shine before men, that they may see your good works, and glorify your Father which is in heaven.'

Essentially the same prayer told differently, Sobe thought, which told you something about religion.

The food and water came intermittently into this dark place. Sometimes the Lady Lassalia was allowed an oil lamp. Tucked away in the bottom of her bed roll were the radical Jewish texts brought by the black-swathed guards from

Third Secretary Gallan, which Sobe read over and over again, ready for the nightly visit.

Holgur tried to 'visit' Lassalia at night but an Assyrian guard always stood at the cell door, unwavering in their rotation. All the merchant's protestations, suggestions to go and take a break, threats, orders, bribes just batted back by unblinking eyes just visible behind the headscarf slit.

Tonight, once the drunk, sweaty merchant stormed off again, the door begins to open. Lady Lassalia theologically steeled herself, taking out the hidden sheaf of papyrus for a last crib.

There were two Assyrian guards who took turns to watch her, but it was always the same man who came late at night. On entering, he would enjoin Sobe to keep very quiet before kneeling and removing first the weapons held on his belt, the one with the twelve knots of the disciples – not the seven tribes of the sand – then unwound the long black head scarf. He was darker than Sobe, of about the same age he wore inked lines on his face, clan tattoos, all in deep blue bisecting the lips.

It always starts with a prayer, "Would you lead us tonight, Lady?"

Some evenings she would lead prayers, sometimes he would begin. The second option was better as the more he spoke, the more she learnt and filed in her growing mental references regarding the cult of Jesus the Jew of Nazareth. Nazareth helped, she had run pomegranate there for years and, although having never visited the place, had some vague conception of the town – bit of a shit-hole, but in an area that really liked pomegranate.

"Please…" He asked again: it was her go, apparently.

What Sobe had realised early on to her great relief and advantage, was that this young cult was somewhat disjointed and lacked the uniformity of an established, proper religion. Where you were told what's what by a priest and the holy number of crocodile's teeth was the stuff of doctrine. Furious attempts were obviously going on to share information – thank goodness – to spread this creed but it was still early days. Lots of overlapping groups passing new bits of the good word from town to town. Just this week the Assyrian had, with great excitement, taken receipt of fresh teachings from Gallan by a man named John, who had been busy.

Lady Lassalia's strategy to pass off as a follower of the Jesus prophet and messiah was to rapidly bluff out the gaps in her knowledge.

She took a breath, lifted up her head, arms outstretched, "We beseech ye…"

"Why do you aways lift your head, Lady?"

"We lift them towards god, towards the sun…son, son of god."

"Ah, I see. But surely, we must humble ourselves in obeisance towards the ground, for is it not right that as the Christ was a simple carpenter…?"

"In his temporal being, yes, but resurrected surely Jesus sits within heaven at the right hand of God?" Fingers crossed.

The Assyrian thought, then nodded. "Yes, I see now. Please continue."

"We beseech thee, O Jesus, the Lord God, the Father, and Mother Mary who…"

Another interruption: "Why do you pray not just to Jesus, who is the embodiment of God, and God himself? Why also his mother, she is…just his mother?"

This seemed a very strange question: Sobe had never considered it would be otherwise.

"Because Jesus is born of a union of earth and spirit culminating in the birth of a being that bridges our mortal souls from earth to God. In honouring Jesus, we also acknowledge his lineage in both the mother and the father. Without them all, there is no Jesus, there is no birth or, therefore, rebirth."

Stupid fucking question, without Isis how could there be life? All self-respecting religions paid tribute to the lineage of their representative on earth, otherwise you could be following anyone.

Again, the Hatra thought hard and then smiled. "Yes, yes, I…we are still learning of our faith. Continue."

Sobe took a deep breath.

"Right…and the three being one and one being three…" She paused but thought he seemed to be getting it.

"…bring the light of the Lord to the world, banishing all darkness as dawn rises through the…"

She just lifted this bit from the welcoming of the sun but he didn't seem to know any different so Sobe carried on. It must be admitted that the House of Sadiki had never been particularly devout but the young Sobe Lassalia had leant more towards her mother's religion, a true Egyptian, than Dad's. Her pa, who would occasionally go through frenzies of candle lighting to the usual Greek pantheon in times of stress, including 'regional hero' Alexander.

'Not sure Alexander was that great at accounts. Now: Anubis, that's a god who can handle a ledger' her mother would bitch as yet another goat was wasted by the family's patriarch.

Sobe got to the end of the prayer without further interruption and Egyptian and Assyrian both knelt in silence, deep in inward contemplation. *'My right knee hurts. Has he brought bread?'*

"My thanks lady, that was very…poignant. Where does that prayer come from?"

Face frozen like stone, Lassalia answered, "God."

Hard to quibble with that one.

Eyes open now, the Assyrian nodded in realised agreement but did not meet Sobe's gaze, instead looking at the corner of the room, always head tilted to one side away from her when discussing matters of religion. The desert tribesman would, of course, still be used to a religion of man and religion of woman, as was the normal course of things. This co-religion of everyone in the same room was probably just a bit too sexy.

'Would that help or hinder this cult's survival?' Sobe pondered, watching the Assyrian's cocked gaze fixed on where she kept her deification pot.

'Sexual tension always a plus when selling something' she decided, based on long experience.

"Lady, I think this prayer sums up the revelatory light of Jesus's presence but also his teachings. An example of the truth that we must live well in the darkness to live everlasting. That by doing so, yes, we shall be resurrected through not just our commitment of faith in the afterlife, but that, also here in this mortal world a light, even if it is just a candle to what will shall be next, can also be lit. Do you agree?"

"Yeah."

'No idea, could be.'

She was pretty sure God made the sun come up and that's why it wasn't night all the time and consequently there was plenty to eat. Plus, you can see it, a basic proof of God. She wondered if Jesus himself drove the chariot of the sun now he was, well, reborn. A reward perhaps or would it be a chore? As a girl she loved playing *'riding the chariot of the sun'*, up until her first trap had totally gone up in flames with a sound beating to follow.

"Does the Word of the Lord made flesh and the truth of the resurrection bring you great comfort at this time, facing death as you may well be?" the Assyrian asked earnestly.

"Yes."

'Although smuggling me out of here would be more useful'

However, she'd tried that avenue early on and got a sermon on the dignity of their precious Ignatius travelling to Rome under guard – by the Assyrians – willingly. Travelling joyfully despite knowing that in all likelihood he would be executed. In short; *'if we didn't spring the man who converted us to Jesus we aren't going to stuff you in a laundry cart.'*

The Hatra may have used much more allegory saying this but the message had been clear.

Ever serious, the Assyrian continued: "I would ask, as it troubles me, is there not a contradiction in both Jesus's message as to being a poor man, a messiah of the spirit, yet we hear often that Jesus is of the House of David, of King David, an attested king in the secular world. The two messages point in different ways…"

'Jesus wisely liked to have a fallback position of rank?'

That question was, however, too far deep in the murky depths of actual learning and Sobe cut it off at the pass.

"Let me stop you there. Did not your Ignatius say to you – when you asked similar questions about the links to the Torah and scrolls of the old Jews – that we should not be concerned with anything other than what is in front of us? That we should not ask endless questions trying to conjoin the stories of the Jewish people with Jesus' teaching? I think it was, I must say it, almost a rebuke, wasn't it? When you asked such things while the Great Teacher was feeling the effects of sea travel?"

The Assyrian thought back to the moment with a pang of pain and shame.

"This is true. He was being very sick and annoyed. Those words, I must confess, were not the exact ones he used either but very similar in tone. I hope that you do not think I am…"

"Of course not. Now, has our mutual friend from the House of Sadiki shared any further teaching?"

"Oh yes, indeed, Brother Gallan has a great wealth of writings and teachings. These new ones have just arrived, they are extraordinary, I have never heard them before. They are also written by John…"

"Would you, if we are very quiet, read it for me?"

The Assyrian touched her hand for just a moment. "It would be my greatest of pleasures, the work you have done, how you have bent your great enterprise to share the word of Jesus…"

"Jesus, his father, and mother Mary."

"Yes, yes, of course. This work you do is an example, madam. Now where shall I begin?"

"At the beginning."

Because otherwise the cipher code won't work.

"In the beginning was the Word, and the Word was with God, and the Word was God. He was with God in the beginning. Through him all things were made; without him nothing was made that has been made. In him was life, and that life was the light of all mankind. The light shines in the darkness, and the darkness has not overcome it…"

He actually jumped up.

"Yes, ah, yes! Now, I see now. The light, the light! Forgive my earlier questioning…"

"There is nothing to forgive. Now, I'm going to make some notes, please continue."

'Seven, twelve, twenty-one…'

Sure enough, Gallan had subtly reworked this writing and after a while there it was.

'Good,' she thought, reading the message.

A day later, in the afternoon, a larger prayer meeting was being held in the Aquincum bakery. The usual followers were in attendance including at least six of the black-clad Assyrians. One of the killers led the meeting and for the life of him Gallan couldn't understand why all of a sudden, they were praying to a list that seemed to comprise of Jesus, God himself, even though Jesus was the representation of God on earth and, even more bizarrely, Jesus's mother. He waited to see if Joseph or any nephews or pets were going to turn up but thankfully not. Gallan just kept his head down and prayed. When you watch half the congregation taking off long-curved swords, knife belts and garottes at the beginning of every 'community', it reinforced a certain ecclesiastical compliance despite all the friendly 'brother and sistering' with warm smiles and big hugs.

They were big huggers, the Assyrians, everyone got one, even the women, although it all felt a bit forced. But the others in the group seemed to warm to the appearance of the mother Mary, everyone likes a mother, no harm in that, the Greek secretary thought.

The new texts from the writer John were also very popular and easy to get hold of in the spiritual, if not temporal, sense. Gallan was thanked for providing them before the readings. His Aramaic was getting so much better and this one, Gallan considered, was a really good stab into Greek and he'd managed it in less than a week sat around in the little warehouse waiting. Even the subtle changes to accommodate the book code had not been particularly challenging.

At the conclusion of the readings by any that could translate Greek, including a wizened old slave man probably taken from the northern regions of that sprawling country, the congregation left in ones and twos, discreetly as you could in a small town, until it was just the Sadiki man and the Assyrians.

"A most illuminating sister, your Lady, I must say. Please Gallan, take this, an entreaty to the light of hope no less from your mistress."

The black-robed guard handed over a slip of papyrus containing Lassalia's scrawling hand.

Gallan turned to go.

"My brother Gallan, it is a very intriguing code you both use, most ingenious."

Gallan froze and a hand rested on his shoulder, "What must we do, to be the works of God?" the guard whispered, readjusting the headscarf over his tattoos.

Gallan saw it was an actual question and luckily thought and memory released the response, "This is the work of God: that you believe in him who he has sent."

The guard nodded. "That is correct and it was good you answered as such. For you are spreading the good news, Sadiki man, you and your mistress. Even if perhaps the reasons are not wholly of the nature of evangelism. The harvest is plentiful but the workers are few, Brother Gallan, so we shall not tell anyone, not the Romans – but tread carefully, little Greek, and do not think we left our desert cunning when we found faith, do not think we are just…guards."

Gallan swallowed. "I thank you, Brother…"

Third time unlucky trying to prise a name from the deliberate pause. Instead, he tried honesty.

"The men you work for make me very afraid."

The Assyrian moved to the flour door, flanked by his Hatra band with all knotted belts now tied on, as he went saying: "And so they should, but Brother, the man we work for does not reside in the Governor's basement. Be careful, little Greek, and may God love you."

Chapter Twenty-Eight

Sweaty horrible office in the baths, Aquincum
After their Domina's chat with the Hatra
Pannonia Inferior Province of Rome

First Secretary Eleazar of the House of Sadiki read the new, papyrus slip with Lady Lassalia's handwriting upon it. An update from Gallan following the latest community back channel. The young Greek stood waiting in the dripping bathhouse hidey-hole, having struggled through the crawlspace at sunset. Eleazer thought hard before revealing the great plan to the other two men, the only bit of which Optio Ruben centred upon was:

"So, we are actually going to leave this room, and go outside?"

While Ruben might have been an armourer, he still thought of himself as a soldier. Weeks stuck in the two-room safe house had tested him though, with just an occasional peek through the shutter slats, a narrow view of the Governor's Building opposite, being the only glimpse of an outside world. The use of the bucket was nothing, the rising fumes as summer came upon the world was a usual Army inconvenience.

It was just that in the normal course of events you were surrounded by your comrades sharing the hardship. In the bottom of a ship or a field, a glasshouse (although not for a long while), ditches or the infirmary. A civilian eunuch had been a different creature entirely, one who wrote, spoke, washed and obsessively snipped at his hair – a perfectly crafted white-grey affair – in patterns that grated. Eleazar did sleep, Ruben had seen him, but it was upright in the chair held together with rotting pegs and string. The Optio found this annoying for reasons he couldn't quite determine.

"Yes, tomorrow morning, Optio Ruben, we go outside, early," Eleazar confirmed.

"And surely to be instantly arrested? IInd legionaries have been searching high and low for you, First Secretary," Gallan asked.

Ruben once again mulled back over the word *'deserter'* in his mind. No one knew where he was, no one could claim him. Except in a bad way.

Eleazar arched his back, stood up and without warning stripped off to his loincloth. "Possibly, but we must look our best. Have these clothes washed if you would, Gallan, and returned for morning-dark, same with the Optio. Have that boy also provide Ruben with whatever unguents are needed to make all that leather and metal gleam."

The bundle of soiled fabrics was passed to the Greek Third Secretary.

"I think we can leave the unguents, but tell the boy I'll need oil, wax, a brush and a cloth."

Gallan bowed. "I shall do so. Do I come with you tomorrow?"

Eleazar considered this and looked at Gallan in a manner that made the young, clever Greek feel currently more naked than the eunuch. Eleazar then began to pour three cups of wine.

"I thought we were going to be arrested, Gallan? That worth a risk for a seat at the top table?"

Gallen didn't need to think. "Yes."

Grandmother answered for him.

Ruben stared at the young man and spoke.

"Hardly anyone comes out of a Roman prison. You do realise this, Third Secretary? No one escapes either, not unless they're meant to. One way trip down, down, down if this goes pear-shaped. Garrotted or chained to an oar. You would not do well at an oar, despite being a Greek."

Eleazar offered Gallan a cup. "He knows. So then, be here first thing with the laundry and I also need this…"

He pulled a scroll from the table. "…notarised a second time, with seal. Get the old magistrate to do it, I hear he's not working much at the moment. The sons are taking up the slack at court from what I see through out shutters. Flatter him and pay him well. Tell the learned judge it's part of the Sadiki reparations – which it is."

"What exactly is it, First Secretary?" Gallan asked, taking the already heavily waxed tube.

Eleazar raised an eyebrow but allowed the question.

"It is the culmination of her plan. It is opportunity and danger. It is several hundred approaching wagons. That help at all, Third Secretary?" *It's our trap.*

Gallan half bowed and crawled away through the plaster hole to his tasks. The boy waiting for him in the bath bar finished a fig and took the laundry for scrubbing. The Third Secretary then headed to the magistrate's house, philosophising in a half-hearted way on the boy going to a place for cleanliness while Gallan repaired to the renowned mire of the law.

Chapter Twenty-Nine

A short walk outside to the Aquincum Administration Building
Following a very early bath
Pannonia Inferior Province of Rome.

The Aquincum bath house annex was lit by oil lamps when Gallan arrived early the next morning, holding a package of washed, folded clothes, a military care pack and a thrice-sealed, twice notarised scroll. Let in by a bribed bar slave at morning dark, the Third Secretary made his way through the crawl hole into the damp fetid air of the Sadiki's fallback office.

Eleazar asked for the scroll to be placed on the table and inspected it. Notarising an already sealed and notarised scroll to register that it was sealed and notarised was rather more about theatre than strict legal necessity. But in the First Secretary's experience of working in the provinces it never hurt to have more brightly coloured seals, stamps and ribbons than less. Admittedly the Governor and the General of the IInd Adiutrix were proper Roman but both would have to tread carefully with regard to local customs and process. One of the great secrets of the Roman Empire was how much its sprawl relied on the immediate locality to survive.

Each province was provided with an administration building and that was about where Rome's help ended for a Governor. Taxes were expected to flow to Rome not the other way round, so it paid to pay attention to local ribbons, stamps with naked men jumping over bulls and seals of herons, sphinxes and in one case an actual seal with a crowned seal holding a spear. The amusing seal seal had been the only thing to commend that deal, Eleazar often reflected.

Following Ruben's scrubbing of military accoutrement the trio took themselves through the crawl then walked out of the dark bar space to the empty bath house proper. Paying off a surprised slave holding a broom the men had a proper dip in the blissful, half lit empty silence of a pre-open facility. Cleaned and clothed another coin was passed to the side doors night-bull and out into the street's first light they went, freshly burnished. Ruben squinted at the rising sun and open sky but hardly had time to get used to outside conditions again. He, Eleazar and Gallan walked briskly and in a businesslike manner the short distance across the road and up the colonnaded steps to the doors of government.

Upon reaching the huge portal, the three were immediately let in through the small day door by guards, Roman-looking as the party was (as any proper petitioners would), and reached the Porters' Office.

"Too early, unless you have a specific appointment. Do you have a specific appointment?" the imperial porter asked, a man probably brought from one of the Governor's own estates as his accent was obviously 'born of the Boot'.

"We don't, but I think the Governor will want to see us."

"Because you are a very important eunuch and doing very important things, I don't doubt."

The porter picked up a large wax frame full of the day's schedule to emphasise the point. "Because there is a warrant out for my arrest, I believe. I am the slave of the House of Sadiki who is Eleazar the First Secretary."

The porter, principal monitor of the comings and goings of the entire provincial administration, knew exactly who Eleazar was.

"Well, that will do it. I'm sure a space can be opened up in the Governor's diary, although as to where the meeting will take place, that's not up to me."

He didn't have to grin nastily.

The tall vulture of a Tribune was the officer of the morning watch and stood in the outside atrium area listening. He glared at Gallan, ignored Eleazar then looked at Ruben: "Who are you, Optio?"

Ruben came to attention and announced himself.

"Then why aren't you with the XXXth?" the officer asked, looming menacingly.

Meanwhile the porter sent a runner inside, then addressed the small party. "I think you had better come in."

Two IInd Legionaries closed in behind the trio to emphasise the 'better'.

They didn't go straight to the cells but instead stayed on the ground floor, walked through the formal atrium, all flowers and fresh white civil servant togas, through the official areas and into a columned courtyard with a water feature. The Governor was not a 'ten things before breakfast' man obviously as, on the other side of a nymph blowing a water horn, the Civil Legate was still eating with his wife and three young children. A 'second family', Eleazar knew: the

Governor had an elder son in the Senate and a daughter married to one of the Decimi twins who were doing their very best to spend a rich father's vast fortune in one lifetime.

The Governor cut a slice of milk cake and listened to the administrator who had taken receipt of the party from the porter. In tow was the nasty-looking officer, like a carrion stork Gallan had once seen at an oasis in the deep sands. Pannonia Inferior's Imperial representative gave the party a half glance then whispered something to the assistant, who came over and ushered them through the next door.

Still no dungeon, just another anteroom with one entrance and a high window. The door, however, was locked from the outside and the three men waited.

Chapter Thirty

Holgur's house, Aquincum
Early the same morning
Pannonia Inferior Province of Rome.

Just after the same dawn, while her colleagues sat waiting for the Governor or 'other arrangements', the Lady Lassalia was still asleep, seeing no reason to change her lifestyle habits especially given the limited natural light in the room-cell. The door quietly unbolted to creak open, Sobe opened an eye. Not Holgur, not the Assyrian, but someone new: a girl.

"Come!" the young woman whispered and gestured outside.

Sobe pulled herself up, sat on the edge of the bed and considered this offer, before taking three cautious steps to the door frame. No guard. Could this be *'killed trying to escape?'* but leaving the room is just too tempting so the prisoner crosses the threshold and starts footing it along the corridor's boards behind the girl-slave.

'Why bother with the pretence of escape? If the tables were turned, having waylaid a few Assyrians from outside of the cell, then it would just be happy days rushing in with a few thickset men and a pillow,' reconciled the darker parts of Lady Lassalia's mind.

Sobe follows the girl and is not murdered, instead led to a room with a home bath full of shelves packed with oils and unguents. Her filth clad clothes are cut at the straps and Sobe took a few small steps into paradise, the wooden tub, warm with lavender and rosemary sprinkles. Oils are poured in from rough-hewn bronzes by the girl. Submerged, Sobe awaits footsteps rushing in to hold her under, but it is still just the girl. The bath is bliss, the water warmed from the pre-dawn cook fires. Normally, Sobe took freezing water when she wakes, warm baths before noon being a clear sign of physical and moral weakness, but she believed current context warranted an exception. Is this wash just a precursor to assault by Holgur?

He doesn't seem that picky though, more a pushing the scullery maid face down in the dust under the washing lines 'man'. Emerging from the water the girl then scrubs: she is a good scraper but Sobe's skin is delicate from weeks in the dark, soon it is red raw, bleeding in places. Long, dark matted Egyptian hair is massaged, oiled, dunked, then partially combed over and over again. The girls knew her job, with a comb passing from scalp to splintered ends after five rounds. The tub is black with dirt when Lassalia steps out and is towelled. A new dress, one of Sobe's own dresses, is clasped onto the body with two brooches, the ones she was arrested in. Sobe eyes the girl.

"Invited to breakfast with the family, child?"

The girl won't make eye contact but ties the lacing, a shake of the head. *'Intriguing.'*

"Where did you get my clothes from?"

"I am the right hand, Lady."

"Come again?"

The girl looked up this time, imploringly.

Now Sobe had it.

"Ah, got it. Thanks be to Jesus?"

This was Gallan, her boys were obviously moving the game on. Took their bloody time about it, though. The new convoy from the east must be close now and the scroll reveiled.

A broad enraptured grin from the girl. Sobe didn't think she'd ever felt happier than this little slave looked at that moment. A bit sad really.

"Was 'meek' a deliberate mistranslation of 'naive'?" Sobe wondered, not for the first time in previous weeks of study. She'd have to ask Gallan if he'd changed that bit just to fit the cipher.

'Well, Jesus, thanks for the clothes.'

"Makeup?"

The girl shook her head.

Obviously Nazareth Mary was not involved in this decision, she'd have sent makeup. Or possibly just a pomegranate.

"Then it looks like I'm ready for whatever this is, girl."

The slave then made three knocks at the second door, it opens with the faithful Assyrian brother entering. First embracing the slace in thanks he bows low and beckons Sobe to leave. Giving a wink to the slave girl, Sobe followed the black-clad man out. Down the set of back steps of the house they go, Sobe's calves having to work following the confinement, bypassing all the main domestic areas to an open street door. Here the second Assyrian guard waits, stood over a prone body that was just about still breathing, one of Holgur's men, chocked out by the looks of it and the whistle in the breath.

"I thought you weren't going to help me escape?"

Assyrian Brother kept her walking.

"You are not escaping; we are escorting you somewhere. Efficiently and without fuss." She steps over the body.

At the threshold to the street, Sobe took in a deep breath of fresh air before Lady Lassalia raised herself up to her formidable height and went back out into the world like a pike from the reeds. Now it was time for execution.

Chapter Thirty-One

Governor's main office, Aquincum
A long, warm day in a room full of bodies and information
Pannonia Inferior Province of Rome

The Governor's office was in silence, the big man himself looking at a ledger the account administrator held open, the reader engulfed in self-pity.

Looking at the Governor was the Military Legate, General of the IInd Adiutrix and Regional Commander, who was having to fight down his loathing of Lady Sobe Lassalia, merchants in general and civilian authority even more so than usual because the Dacian border was now in thorough confusion.

SOGI leant against a wall with SOGII, because spooks always find the edge of the room and never go anywhere without at least one special friend. Having ridden into Aquincum during the night after a week's hard journey from the bridgehead, the intelligence staff's stance wasn't, however, the all affected cool it usually was. This was mostly due to a good deal of shouting from the General, especially as the SOG Lead had begun the morning meeting hinting that he'd be requesting the arrest of the IVth's General.

The plan to plug the logistic holes in Pannonia Inferior through confiscation and extortion of the House of Sadiki was not going well.

"Are you going to open that?" the General asked for the third time, eyeing the thrice-sealed scroll, notarised both locally and 'outside-province' with more tassels than the IInd's Legion standard. The document tube had been produced an hour before from the now 'secured' First Secretary of Sadiki who'd just appeared on the doorstep from nowhere. Embarrassing. The Governor turned the cylinder over in his hands: it was not addressed to him and if he did break the seals…it was obviously a trap. It was obviously to do with the massive convoy of supplies trundling their way towards Aquincum, west from the bridge checkpoint.

An administrator came in. "All are assembled in the anteroom, Governor."

The Civil Legate nodded and looked down again at the sea of negative in the province's accounts.

"Close that," he instructed the accountant, and the ledger – the working, up to date, wax real one (as opposed to the senate submission last month) – was snapped shut.

Ignoring the General's glare from the other side of the table His Governorship walked, the office door was opened by junior civil servants and the embodiment of provincial authority strode into the waiting main room to find various parties awaiting an audience, with him. Everyone stood. He surveyed the crowd knowing that having them all put to death was illegal and unfeasible but felt a longing pang of empathy towards the more infamous dictators.

However, he was not Sulla and protocol demanded at least one, flat, welcome.

"Cornelius Ulpia Mako, it is so good of you to come at such short notice."

Hedgehog bowed.

"Sir!" one of his lictors muttered, reminding Mako he was the Emperor's Nephew. He straightened quickly.

"Right, yes. Morning! Good morning. It was a pleasure. Well, I was in bed but…not doing much else…not that I am not happy to help, whatever it might be you need my help with. Can't think what that could be, hahaha. Probably need a…actually no, I'm not sure I'd even be any use at…"

The Governor ignored the babble. Now going from right to left he went through the other individuals assembled.

"Not you, you or you," his digit indicating the local merchants. Holgur was already incensed, having arrived to find a Lady Lassalia not locked in his/her cell but standing in front of him, actually standing, bathed and clothed in the Governor's atrium. A friendly salutation from her just made it worse.

"But, Sir, this…"

A flick of two fingers had Holgur and the local businessmen 'ushered' away by waiting legionaries.

"You, Lady Lassalia, please come in. Ulpia Mako, if you would join us and…who are you?"

The looming crooked Tribune answered for Ruben. "He's under military arrest. Deserter from the XXXth."

If this Optio was under arrest, then he probably needed to be in the room as well, in fact. "Who is currently under arrest here? Raise your hand."

Ruben, Eleazar and Lassalia raised their hands.

The Tribune's long arm also shoved Gallan forward. "I have just also placed this Greek bastard under arrest for aiding and abetting."

"Everyone under arrest, please come into my office."

The Tribune opened a wide lugubrious mouth but the detainees were already walking inside to take places around the negotiating table.

Much later, same day.

"We have been at this for eight hours," the General stated flatly. By this point, he'd exhausted all other avenues emotionally and logically.

Around the table the Governor was conducting a whispered side meeting with the accountant and Eleazar who was explaining something. Optio Ruben was no longer under formal arrest and the vexatious ugly Tribune had been dismissed, from both the room and building. The dismissal had occurred at around the time, which felt like ancient history, of the furious lunch exchange.

Explosively the IInd's General had made his views on, and level of interest in, the fate of a random Optio quite clear. The question of Optio Ruben's court martial had just become annoying for everyone and before the haranguing Tribune was thrown out the General reconfirmed the order, given by Chief Armourer Whoever-the-fuck, for the junior NCO to continue formal liaison with the House of Sadiki.

The Tribune was a damn fool anyway, if this part of the Western sector really had deserting Optios then they were all fucked – Optios were the ones who kept the books. Depressingly, the General also found the new Optio was less annoying that his own staff, having a firm grasp of actual facts or numeric questions occasionally thrown his way.

"Who knows how many carts of grain for the IVth at quarter strength for two months?"

"How much bacon does a maniple need?"

"What length of leather is needed for legion repairs per quarter?"

"Which is the nearer fabrica of the two?"

The slightly fey Optio had it all at his fingertips. Each time the General knew the answer sounded right, the older staff officer behind him giving a confirming nod that the ball was in court without having any specific idea himself.

The young Greek secretary had also proved useful, able as he was to lay out the various legal avenues their discussions danced around without the impediment of actually being lawyer, so Gallan was also de-arrested.

By late afternoon, the only emotion left in the Military Legate's armoury was a simmering, underlying fury at his own – not that it was his really – Special Operations Group who had comprehensively failed to do anything useful and were now stating 'possibilities' at any point when they were asked something. Somebody should come out of here arrested and the General had never wanted a nest of spies in his midst but the concept had been foisted upon him. *'Could he arrest them?'* he mulled.

Actual lawyers were also in the room. The old magistrate and his eldest son had turned up and were proving extremely useful, being a focal point for both sides of the 'negotiation' to vent all disbelief, incomprehension and general spleen at.

Of course, the Governor's real nemesis was the woman in front of him and she was like a remorseless siege operation (definitely the investor end) during the hours of discussion. At some point, the General had even stopped calling her 'woman' or 'thieving bitch'. Over time the 'you's' had then caved into 'Lady' and even 'Lady Lassalia'. The General felt the realisation of this transition must, on a smaller scale, be like that of the Romans at Cannae coming to terms with a fatal encroaching envelopment.

'Those bastards came from north Africa as well,' the Military Legate realised, looking at her, reflecting bitterly that if he wanted to salt the earth of every Sadiki office in the Empire, he'd probably end up having to transfer the mortgage on his villa to the woman first, in order to purchase the materials necessary.

The Lady Lassalia leant forward on the table, hands clasped and jangly (throughout the day of constant messengers her worn jewellery had seemed to grow and, although the General wasn't an expert on such matters, he was pretty sure she wasn't wearing makeup this morning). Looking now like a high priestess of Isis, solid gold bangles rattled for attention:

"So, boys, what it comes down to is – do you want me to open this?" She waved the tasselled scroll addressed to her teasingly in their direction.

The recording clerk scribbled, minuting her words – this reporter's presence was also one of Sobe Lassalia's victories against the Roman administration. Hours at the beginning of this interminable session had been lost on the matter of 'minutes'.

The Governor had initially dismissed the clerk on the parties assembling within his oficina maxima.

Sobe had immediately refused to say anything without formal minutes, in inked and sealed papyrus, and threatened to go back to her cell at Holgur's.

This led to the Assyrian guards leading (not dragging, the IInd's General noted disapprovingly) her out of the meeting down to the lower holding rooms of those 'certainly in trouble' following a furious eruption of Legates.

An hour passed in discussion upstairs and a message was sent that she'd be allowed back up.

She had refused to go unless the clerk was in attendance.

Messages passed that *'minutes couldn't formally be taken for security reasons.'*

Sobe had answered with *'A Dacian army running over a starving, badly-equipped frontier is a bigger security issue.'*

The Governor had threatened her with arrest for treason.

Lady Lassalia requested trial in Rome with Mako as her representative and would call witnesses.

More morning passed in the heated exchange of scrawled notes giving time for Eleazar, who'd been left upstairs in the meeting, to use his expertise helpfully. Quietly working with the administration staff he'd sidled up to on wider fiscal 'problems'.

An hour before lunch the discussions restarted with the Lady Lassalia and minutes clerk back in the Governor's office.

Just as they started SOGI demanded his entries be struck from the record, again, on a security basis.

Everyone groaned.

The Lady Lassalia pressed the SOG Lead unrelentingly with leading questions, traps where his silence trod a likely path to indictment if the record was ever read aloud in the Senate back in Rome.

The General had watched in grudging respect: SOGI had obviously decided a cool, stoic hush was his strategy with the Sadiki woman – *'fucking spies!'* He hadn't bargained for how the gaping void of quiet would be filled.

"…Why does the man who does not want to reveal his identity to the meeting of the Imperial Governor of Pannonia Inferior tell us of his view on the via Metz?" Lassalia rumbled in a hard, clear voice.

"No response. Please minute my question."

"Has the man who does not want to reveal his identity to the Emperor's representatives received any funds from key contractors historically connected with the IInd Adiutrix?"

"Silence. Please minute my question and the response."

And she'd fucking broken him, broken the lead intelligence officer. As the treason-intimating questions built up in the formal minutes the spy's silence burst like a dam. Suddenly a stream of threatening invective, spittle – the works – spilt over. The General had always thought the bastard was bloodless, but no, she'd picked that scab right open. It was the most revealing thing either Legate had ever seen produced from the SOG in eight months of torturing lumberjacks and innkeepers' daughters.

SOGII had to pull his leader back, assisted by one of the Assyrians. Sobe just stared back, sitting still with an eyebrow arched, fingers interlinked, then said:

"So, let me get this response clear, I've been called a…"

And repeated exactly what the spy had just spewed out with a "Please minute my clarification," to finish.

The Governor had been an unpopular Pro-Consul and had consequently been assigned his dues by a disgruntled Senate committee: a Governorship in a region only recently recovered from war, full of an expensive army to run and no funds to do it with. Up until this point in the Civil Legate's career finance had been the sole province of his various administration staffs who, if left for long enough, would eventually find a solution. You didn't get taught finance in a Greek oratory school, and the civil servants, Army clerks, bandsmen and Optios saw the wheels just rolled. Every month you'd glance at a summary document and ask, "So, is everything all right?"

Except here in Pannonia Inferior nothing was 'all right', or even slightly right. Provinces didn't go bust, it was the equivalent of losing an eagle, but they were very close now in Pannonia Inferior. In three months, the Governor hadn't had a hot bath, not being able to relax for an instant as he felt the warm water swell his veins, it was like a physical premonition.

Over the day some conclusions had been made by the Governor: *'Money is what this woman dealt in, it seemed to run in rivulets around her, she wore enough of it, and she spoke its language. What's more, it seemed to listen. Hmm.'*

Many hours now since Sobe had verbally tortured the head spy and here she is waving the scroll around provocatively asking if it should be opened. The Egyptian seemed to be circling them, the Military Legate felt. Each person had a spirit animal, the General knew, and hers was a ruddy great big bejewelled shark. As a young man he'd clung to a raft for three days. One by one, the young Tribune watched the other men hanging from the shipwreck disappear under without warning. That was how he felt now. Fucking boats, he hated boats.

When previously asked, Lady Lassalia steadfastly refused to have any knowledge of what was in the sealed message, the Dacian convoy's appearance or why she was in the room. Her deft manoeuvring away from liability was infuriating and the Governor and SOGI eventually had to give up their facile entrapment attempting to establish her pre-knowledge of working against the interest of the state, i.e. *'Could they just confiscate the Dacian convoy?'*

It turned out having Lassalia locked in Holgur's cell was the worst thing the Governor could have done.

"Because while you accuse me of all sorts of things, if it comes to court how could I have plausibly known anything, being under military lockdown? Unless the security was so lax I, a woman, continued to conduct business right under your nose, Governor? Even the newest of advocates would make you a laughing stock and my lawyers, I can assure you, will be very expensive. So, shall we go back to the hypotheticals of what we do next? Concentrate on the future not the past? Option one as I see it is…"

The room had listened, all knowing it was Case Study Three that was the only viable option with items One, Two and Four always threatening disasters comprising of either courts or military failure.

Case Study Three is 'She, the named recipient of the scroll, opens it in front of all assembled as witnesses'. So, does she open the letter? Once the letter is unsealed, being notarised by a Roman lawyer, two lawyers due to the silly old sod of a local magistrate, it has been deemed read by the legal recipient.

The Governor made a decision.

"Open it. Would you mind opening it?"

"Are you sure?" she said with a wink.

"Yes."

No, he wasn't.'

Everyone girded themselves as freshly lacquered nails reached for the papyrus roll and cut each seal with a thumb talon, bisecting and destroying the wax. The Lady Lassalia didn't even bother to scan but read the words out loud from memory (the House of Sadiki loved a template).

"Written at the Imperial Court of Dacia by his royal…"

"What does it mean?" the General asked at the end.

The Governor adjusted himself in the seat and tapped a stylus at his notes, then looked Sobe straight in the eye, returned straight back with smiling interest. It felt like a test because it was a test, the Governor reflected, of all the 'nuances' to this business.

"Well, Brother Legate…" the leading man of Pannonia Inferior began. "…it is rather clever. All the supplies which we demanded, our original lines having been disrupted due to, let us say: unforeseen circumstance, are on their way to us."

"I got that bit. Good."

"Well, yes, they will arrive by the unexpected eastern road convoy in the next couple of days having crossed the Dacian border at the IVth's position, at the new bridge, and we need to find rather a large sum of money to pay for them."

"This is the part I don't understand. We all agreed: the House of Sadiki screwed the province's supply lines, they pay for it, as previously made clear."

"No."

"No?" The General hadn't quite understood all the ins and out but knew it would be a 'No'.

"It would be…unwise…to confiscate anything," SOGI added slowly, deciding to have an opinion, one that was as popular with the province's military head as proposing the arrest of the IVth's General.

"Oh, would it? Am I being unwise, 'Marco' or whatever name it is this week?"

The General then turned back to the Governor.

"Is this due to the bit about the loan or loans?"

"It is." The Governor continued, "On taking receipt of any supplies we need to pay the sum requested in this letter to the House of Sadiki, but the invoice is not to the House of Sadiki but to Prince Comoscius, one of the senior Dacian royal family. House Sadiki are instructed within this letter to act as 'royal' agents for the money who upon receipt of the payment, from us, are then automatically loaned the gross amount back by Prince Comoscius' branch of the Dacian Imperial family."

"I say we just keep the money…"

"…And because, General, this business has been originally contracted between Sadiki and the supplier under Roman law, originally witnessed by the lawyer Crysis of Antioch, whoever he is, then opened and witnessed on Roman soil with the transaction occurring on Roman soil, with a Roman administration or 'us' as parties: acting with impunity would be dangerous because, in whatever form, the money for goods supplied technically belongs to a Dacian citizen, or one of its ruling factions. This is political." The Governor took a deep breath and looked around.

"Let me also stress this to everyone here on 'my' side of the table that 'we' are duty bound to uphold all articles of this transaction if we choose to take receipt of the goods, up to and including ensuring the paid funds do not go missing from these good Egyptian merchants, thereby upholding commercial law and cross-border agreements in the Roman Empire. I should further stress: anyone considering an informal action to retrieve funds involving 'informal routes' should also be advised otherwise. Included within the transaction principles from Sadiki is this young man here to the right of me." The Governor gestured to the Hedgehog.

"He is apparently a co-signatory of the deal and a full, male, Roman citizen. For reasons I will not bother go into he cannot die or be made bankrupt."

"Cripes, no! Well, I bet could manage the last bit if I gave it a go, haha!"

"Quite, my Lord. A straight default on an arrangement involving both the civil and military administration would also badly inflame things over the border. Trade lobbies across the Empire would cry out in protest. Non-payment of funds for goods, monies which are at least in principle to be sent to the good Dacian prince, would strain relations at a difficult juncture between our two nations. Nations which are, in principle, at peace following recent treaty agreements from the last war. It has been impressed on me at the very highest levels this status quo is to remain such for the time being. A practical question now, for our friends across the table…"

The Governor gestured to Lassalia across the marble top.

"Are the supplies rolling towards us over the border quite correct in quality and quantity as per our initial request?"

The Lady Lassalia didn't flinch.

"Anything the House of Sadiki says it will provide, it will be done. Ask around. In fact, I threw in ten percent more grain than you set out to me in that charming meeting all those weeks ago, the numbers didn't quite look correct, a bit low." She looked at Ruben for confirmation, but the Optio was staring at the wall.

"Oh, they fucking did, did they?"

The Governor coughed. "Thank you, General. I thought so. We are indebted to you, my Lady."

SOGI leant forward and looked around the room. "This arrangement puts coins into, let us be clear, our enemies' coffers in some form. Why is a senior member of the Dacian royal family supplying our Army with food when they know full well what we eventually intend?"

This time the Governor snapped. "Money you fool! No intrigue, no grand stratagem, no bizarre conspiracy because it's just…money. If the King's cousin can make some coin shipping food across the border, he'll do it."

SOGI threw up his hands. "But Sadiki keep all of the money here, as its loaned back to them…"

"Jupiter!" Shouted the Civil Legate in exasperation "The prince knows Sadiki are good for it, he's probably already been paid."

The Governor caught a slight smile of smugness at the corner of Lassalia's lips as she sat scraping a last bit of grit out from under a long, green copper painted, nail.

'Yes, already been paid, including a fee for the protective loan, no doubt.'

"And…" the Governor continued. "…we know nothing of what the leader of the Special Operations Group has just stated regarding Roman 'intentions', minute that. The Dacian Empire are peaceful allies of Rome under the last truce."

Lassalia flicked the bit of dirt, if not at SOGI then certainly in his general direction, before taking over to explain everything patiently as if to children, which she detested.

"Our enemy are putting food into their enemies' bellies, our enemy are taking our coin, seems like a fair trade. Maintains the status quo. Given the current state of affairs you should be jumping all over this offer, I understand it's nettles for breakfast up on the frontier, is it not? Everyone's a winner."

General and SOGI exchanged a glance.

'How does she know we're down to nettle soup?'

So, boys...

"Are you going to turn down provisions of this scale, at this time? At this time of year, the only other place you can go is through the Mediterranean and those routes might be...problematic."

With three starving Legions in the field, the IInd's General suddenly felt that retrenching to one point of fact was all that mattered.

"I want my supplies, now."

"Quite so, Brother Legate. Turning down a full resupply is not an option. Let us say we abandon and forget any previous misunderstandings relating to supplies and hasty payment plans."

Sobe smiled like a crocodile.

The Governor now glanced mournfully at the account's ledger being pored over by Sadiki First Secretary and the office accountant. Quite how the Sadiki secretary had gained access to the province's books throughout the course of the day, the Legate wasn't sure. 'But', his financial controller has said at lunch that 'actually, the eunuch's quite helpful' and the Governor would take any fiscal help where he could get it right now. Which led to a very real problem: Pannonia Inferior had no real money left (Neither did the House of Sadiki, for that matter, but Sobe's magic was that the Governor would never have guessed that in a hundred years).

The Civil Legate coughed, "My 'only' issue is how do we satisfy the sum in question. It is made out to coin and metal in the full amount as stated. This might be..."

Bangles and rings jangled and clinked in a manner that conveyed this would not be a problem and, given the Sadiki contacts with all the great temples across the known world, an arrangement could be made. It was highly expressive jewellery.

The General butted in. "So, let me get this right. We are going to end up in debt to the House of..."

The Lady Lassalia would never let a negotiation be derailed at such a late stage unless, of course, she wanted it to be.

"Let me ask another question, General, or two. The first is: have you ever had a supply request met with such speed? I thought not. Secondly: Prince Bugger-Lugs over the bridge is only bringing in four months of consumables…what about everything else? There seem to be lots of bits of metals and things you boys like, continually."

"By 'boys' you mean the Imperial Legions of Rome?"

"Them's the ones. What's happening with all the other stuff after four months?"

SOGI tried to take up the repeatedly discarded baton of cold menace.

"As you were instructed, the western trade routes are to be opened up once again, by yourself, and trade will flow as before."

"Except that ain't gonna happen." She always liked a bit of Aventine Latin at these points in the proceedings. Touch of the gutter.

"Is it not? Why?"

"Because I don't bloody well want it to, it doesn't suit me. Unless there is suitable appreciation shown."

This rattled some cages. '*Sod this!*' the General decided and slapped the table.

"I am defeated."

The whole room turned to the military man, looking at him. Generals didn't say that, like cats didn't quote Horace.

"What are you suggesting, Lady Lassalia? For a simple soldier like myself."

The Lady Lassalia liked victory and she radiated good cheer.

"I do everything, darling. Well, myself and the good people of the House of Sadiki. We'll find something for the local suppliers to help out with, as subcontractors, but we just take responsibility. It's going to be a busy time for you and our pledge is to deliver on time, to budget, everything that is needed. You just pay us back over time, we'll run up a schedule…all good. Usually, Sadiki doesn't do long-term military contracts but we're getting the hang of it now and as I always say, 'never do anything once'."

Eleazar looked up from the ledger to take his turn closing the deal.

"There are thirty-five independent contractors which we believe can be streamlined, I believe with…savings."

"How much saving?" asked the Governor, sitting up.

"Considerable. Plus, we can supply all the finance to do it in large tranches, getting bulk discount."

"Done!" said the General.

The Governor smiled and nodded. "Done."

'Done!', She of House Sadiki thought. Roman Army backed debt to reinject some liquidity back into life. Keep the money moving…

"You see, everyone is happy. God loves a cheerful giver!" and Sobe gave the slightest of glances to one of the Assyrians standing behind SOGI, who made the slightest of nods in appreciation. Doesn't pay to be too cocky, Sobe knew, even when they think you are being cocky. "Now, let us leave the finance-lawyery bods to do all the paperwork and we'll get to know each other a bit. Not you though, Spy, I know you already, or your type, of old."

And with the principals grateful to finally escape the negotiations, a completion dinner was hastily arranged. The Governor, General and Lady Lassalia spending an evening of civilised company together with the patrician's family, as respectable folk of station. Sobe swapped perfume recipes with the First Lady, presents of sandalwood and a roll of silk arriving the next day wrapped in a green-peach Sadiki bow. The children listened in awe as the tall Egyptian reeled off her three best, horribly grisly crocodile stories. The Governor ended up pouring his heart out on the fiscal demands of this border role and "…how he had been promised somewhere nice in the east! Sobe was incredulous: "Such opportunities here, Governor! Perhaps I could help point them out?"

Which was how Gallan and Eleazar ended up on long-lease sabbatical, starting the next morning, to the primary office of the Governor. Unearthing general fraud and enhancing the Governor's specific fraud while all the while boosting tax receipts fivefold.

"It is like a holiday day, every day – all so easy!" was Eleazar's view after the first afternoon, which had three errant tax collectors nailed to river posts by the following Tuesday.

At the end of the dinner, the family retired to bed leaving Sobe and the IInd's General. They lounged opposite each other on the triclinium drinking. She was an impressive woman, there was no doubt of that and the Legate was feeling the strong stirrings of hate turning to…something else. He steeled himself and thought of the final days of Mark Anthony.

"Now you are a bad boy and I need to go to bed."

"Which bed is that?"

"Well, that's blunt and to the point, General!"

He bristled.

"I meant, are you not still under some sort of arrest?"

She just looked at him and laughed, "You are actually quite funny once you get under all that stress. Massages! That's what you need, I'll send my boy to you tomorrow. He's sixteen stone if he's an ounce and that's just his hands, you need some of those knots stretched out. Seriously, managing stress…"

Pannonia Inferior's Military Legate lay happily befuddled as an Egyptian-Greek women lectured a Sector General on managing tension. Once she'd finished the list of tips and things she would send him, and they were having lunch together the next day apparently, it was time to go.

"Let me walk you, if I may, to your…'little warehouse'?"

"Sweet, you nearly said 'lair', didn't you? Come on then, do you have a litter?"

"This is Aquincum."

"Well, I could use the walk. In these shoes, though, I'll need to lean on Rome's might. Are you up to the task, General?"

"We serve the people."

"Really? Good, because I'm quite pissed after a month in a cell."

On the way out the couple picked up shawls, bodyguards and torches from the doormen and walked into the street.

"Smell that night air."

Lassalia took a breath in looking up at the stars, the heave of her bosom pushing deliberately into the Military Legate's arm. He didn't move, it was his duty not to.

"Are you married, Lady?"

"Yes, my husband is travelling. Has been for some while."

The General couldn't help but think of the dark river whooshing to their left when she said this.

This senior soldier's gaze then left Sobe's, she was still looking up at the firmament, to the orange light glowing from high up in the administration building's upper windows.

"They're still at it, I see."

She grunted, "Leave Eleazar to it, he loves all that detail. They'll be going until dawn, I reckon. Not that they need to but I'm sure you know what it's like getting men together in a room, even men without balls. 'We pulled an all-nighter!' Bloody waste of time but keeps them happy. Come on, I'm going to bed under military escort."

"Excuse me, Your Honour, but that woman is under arrest and in my protection!" The couple squinted into the dark as five shapes emerged.

"Merchant Holgur!" the Lady Lassalia exclaimed in joy.

"You are coming with me, woman! General, I have an order here from the Governor himself to hold her…"

"It has been rescinded, merchant." growled the General.

Holgur made to protest but Lassalia cut him off asking the General sweetly:

"Could you ask Merchant Holgur a question?"

"What, my Lady?"

"Ask him if he's a Roman citizen."

"Merchant Holgur, are you a Roman citizen?"

No Assyrians around Holgur now, Sobe noted, just toughs.

"General, I…"

"Are you, Merchant Holgur, a Roman citizen? Don't look at her, look at me!"

"I…I have not yet had that honour but operate…"

"Is that a 'No', do you think?"

"I think it is, my lady. What would you like me to say to him next?"

"Nothing, but you can kill him for me."

"I must protest, I am protected by the laws and that woman is…"

"Kill him for me."

"Are you serious?"

"Yes."

"No, I'm not going to kill a man in the street because you…"

"What are carrioballistae platforms, General?"

"W…What? Well, they are purpose-built artillery carts able to…"

"I'm bored already. Did you pay for twenty of them last June?"

It was a very sore point.

"Yes, I did. Why? What do you know about that?"

She guffawed.

"Well, nothing, no one does, because they never arrived here. Pin that. First: friend Holgur, during my recent stay with you enjoyment was curtailed by the smell of fresh paint emanating from recently renovated areas of your house. The new dolphin mosaic I glimpsed 'in transit' this morning is exquisite. Looked to me as though it was the work of an Ravennian, especially brought in, I presume?" Holgur blanched against the dark.

"Exquisite and costly work. Believe me, I know unnecessarily exquisite building work when I see it, and your shale dark blue dolphins are 'It'. Why do I mention this decoration? Good question, well done me for asking it. Here's another good question, which is also the answer to your question, that I just asked for you - keeping up? Don't worry, here's the punch line: Did you write a nice note of thanks to CP Baxci of the XVth Legio for underwriting your rather gaudy home renovations? You see, I've had 'Holgur/Aquincum' on a red flag list with all of our Sadiki offices for a while now and, funny thing, it came up way, way out east. These carry-io-things must be doing great service in Parthia which is where the fabrica dockets trace them to. Which is odd as payment was made out by our own..., go on, have a guess?"

"Er..."

The gladius was out and in Holgur three times before he could say another word: kidney, heart and throat.

"CUNT!" the General bellowed at the shocked, falling body.

The thugs were running away before their master's body hit the ground. The corpse stayed there all night and day in front of the administration gates. Dogs chewed at it, Holgur's widow eventually had to be ordered to retrieve her husband, an order complied with utilising the services of a grateful Bait-vendor and a small fish cart.

Halfway back to the little warehouse now "You see, it's all that pent up stress, darl. We need to sort that out. Now, what a lovely evening for a stroll, the starlight really brings out the blood on this dress. He was a pumper, wasn't he? That's stress for you. Take note, General, embrace the calm."

"You wanted me to kil..."

"And you made a decision to say no, but then you just went and killed him anyway, just like that. It's not Holgur I'm worried about, he's fucking dead, it is you, General, making decisions under stress. Right, you boys, has anyone got a medicinal flask for your General? Come on, one of you must," she said, turning to the military lictors.

"Decimus," the General half commanded as they walked off and fiery spirits were produced by Decimus to keep the summer 'cold' out.

The Lady Lassalia took a swig.

"To new friends!" she toasted.

"To new friends!" her latest client concurred.

Chapter Thirty-Two

A roadside shack up a summer mountain
Scalding clear sun, cold air
Dalmatia-Pannonia Inferior Province crossing.

"Goat's eye, anyone? I don't want to hog them and there's only two. Somewhat obviously."

Legate of the XXXth Legio, Decimus Terentius Scaurianus declined the object proffered on a knifepoint by 'the Scipio'. Instead, he kicked at the loose dirt that comprised the road-stop bar's floor and chewed an ear of black 'mountain' bread.

Summer proper was here, and the party had taken a midmorning rest after four hours of hard, not fast, riding winding up the slope path towards the ridge. The dilapidated but well-stocked road-stop was situated just below the apex, taking custom from drovers and traders before the travellers made a descent either west or east. Eastwards in our party's case. The two 'Principals' sat at the bar's best crappy table, recently adorned with a leather cloth thrown over the cockroach eggs and ingrained dirt by the civil servant's body man. A perfectly sensible precaution as stomach ailments were the enemy of careers working in such places. They'd get the shits at some point travelling from Salona to Aquincum but all efforts should be made to alleviate the worst impact of dodgy road fare, i.e. death by evacuation.

"Nice edging, isn't it?" Scipio remarked of his tablecloth, which sported a badly pressed border of either a hunting scene or possibly rats screwing, depending on the light. The civil servant crunched the eye noisily to emphasise the point.

"Real nice," Scauri absently replied and stopped destroying the alleged 'road's' edge with his foot. It would be another ten miles before they crossed the pass and dropped back down onto a nice bit of straight SSG (Sand, Stone, Gravel) grade II. The Military Legate cut a cheek off the boiled goat's head placed in front of them by the ancient potboy, making a sandwich with dark grainy bread, a pickle and half an onion. From a small pouch, the administrator took a pinch of travel salt, sprinkling it on the breakfast before closing it.

One of the party's newly aquired military Tribunes brought two cups of boiled wine over to the unstable table. The proprietor of the shack was sulking in the back despite being paid 'corkage' because it had been made very clear no one was drinking any of his ditch piss arrayed in flasks behind the counter.

'Mrs' hadn't got the memo, however, so came over beaming despite the shouts from her husband, with two tiny cups made of wood and poured crystal clear liquid into each, beckoning the guests to take the hospitality. Both men peered at the drinks.

"Well, it is going to be a wait while the horses cool…" Scaurianus remarked as he got up, took an ember from the cook fire and, lighting a straw match, placed it in the cup. The drink went up with the fury of a small sun before the match even made it to the meniscus of the local fire water. "Nothing could live in that."

The Scipio smiled.

"Dear lady, you spoil us!" and he downed the drink in one.

Scaurianus sipped at his cup once the flames died down. The Legate then flipped her a coin that could probably buy the entire local village visible at the bottom of the gorge, and beckoned for Mrs Shack Stop to leave the flask and bugger off. He also bought her hat as a souvenir and put it on.

"Important to 'blend in'."

"I've never found that to be important, Scauri. Quite the opposite."

Scaurianus sighed. Scipio wore thin after a few days on the road. So, they drank in silence surveying the mountain vista as the sun grew hotter and the flies swarmed about. No breeze at all even this high up, just the sound of the lictors chatting at the long benches behind, and Mr and Mrs having a furious row about the coin.

Scaurianus was just working up the energy to have one of the lictors go and enforce some quiet on the couple who sounded one recrimination away from '…and then the knife was just in my hand!' when a shout went up from the forward scout.

"Rider, east road."

So far, a few caravans had passed through and an Imperial courier. They'd watched these travellers make their way past on the road, no one stopping. The Scipio had questioned whether the reluctance to take a break was due to the presence of resting Roman soldiers or the reputation of the establishment. Within minutes the new rider appeared, black horse, black-swathed rider, but this one did stop. With a flourish.

The Scipio got straight up and wiped his hands. Scaurianus raised an eyebrow. "Someone you know?"

The aristo civil servant smiled happily and picked up the flask of regional firewater and a cup.

"Just playing the good Roman to a traveller on the road," Scipio was already walking towards the dismounting rider.

'Bollocks!' thought the Legate.

Scauri considered the dark wrapped figure that had just appeared, and it brought back memories of the desert. Particularly a hot dusty day when he'd been listening to the fallout from a particularly vicious worker fight. A fracas not at all like the current couple's squabble behind him at the bar. In that desert friction was never anything to do with something sensible like a coin, booze, dice or women but usually the religious connotations of a mountain neither stonemason had ever actually seen. He'd had to have one Jew and one Samaritan nailed up on a cross next to each other for a day and a night to promote inter-people relations. It had worked for a whole fortnight of comparative peace.

Just after that workplace hammer fight the Hatra had wandered into camp for the first time, offering their services with regards to logistical security. It was a service Scauri the road manager paid for immediately in hard coin knowing it exactly for what it was.

Scauri took a sip of wine as he thought of that particular extortion. He should really write all this down for posterity at some point, people would be interested in this stuff, surely? As he mused upon a memoir the Legate watched the Hatra rider refuse Scipio's flask, instead passing a document tube down while talking hurriedly. After just a twelfth-hour the desert tribesman, a southern Assyrian from the far sands at that, turned horse around and rode off fast in a cloud of badly compacted dust, returning down the east road.

The Scipio sauntered back over to the road-stop bar with the new leather document cylinder, sat down and started to leaf through its contents. After a while he said, "Aren't you going to ask me what that was all about?"

Scauri shrugged. "I imagine you are diligently keeping abreast of important events and happenings relating to the province's cultural scene which your office oversees. A new cheese festival that urgently requires the formal acknowledgement of the Roman Empire, perhaps? The rider, I suppose, is part of an inter-Empire social exchange programme to aid better understanding of each other. Consequently, the Dalmatian Cultural Office has been allocated couriers that look exactly like a certain, infamous, type of desert killer usually associated with other parts of the administration. But then I'm sure that's exactly the type of misconception you are keen to confront and break down, Scipio."

The aristocrat kept reading but hum'phed.

"You're no fun. Play properly. I do the jokes."

The Legate poured two more drinks and sighed. "From Aquincum?"

"Five days old. Like most things in life problems seem to go away if left to themselves."

"Not with roads."

"A fair point, but apparently all is now well with your supplier."

"The XXXth have their supplies?"

"No, but your supplier, she's out of clink."

"Oh, good. Nothing else?"

"Nooo, no, no."

'Liar.'

"I think, Scipio, we better get going."

Scipio nodded and took the evil flask of spirits, thanked the proprietress and her husband, had their wrists untied from the bar by a lictor and the party mounted up. As they rode off the civil servant watched his courier race away east in order to reach Aquincum before the man who thought he was the Assyrian's 'boss' noticed an absence, but then that was one of the principal advantages of having employees with full face coverings. The rider also took a new message with him to Aquincum because, thinking about it, not supplying the XXXth with food (as suggested in the received missive), might indeed have merit. Some plausibly deniable advantages could be gained relating to the very secret, special cargo that would eventually need to use the river down from Vindabona. It would cause poor Scauri some stress but, then, that's what he was kept around for.

Chapter Thirty-Three

Brigetio Fort, new home of the XXXth Legio
A fine summer morning
Southern bank of the Danube, Pannonias'

"Bad news, Boss."

That's how the Chief Armourer was greeted before lunch. The uncrating of the supplies had gone suspiciously well up until this point. He knew it was too good to last.

"What is it? What's missing?"

Workshop was the harbinger of bad tidings.

"Nothing's missing…"

This was going to be complicated.

"You best come and see."

Currently Centurion Chief Armourer Galba was ensconced in multiple dockets. Trying to guide men and equipment into those inadequate spaces allocated to the Legion Armoury by the SC's Optios. The forge itself had taken all night just to get off the barge and they were still looking for the special curving anvils, each weighing as much as a man, but now magically disappeared. Galba had spent the last few days being told to come and view things personally and was not now interested in the entertainment value his horrified and surprised reaction afforded spectators in the immediate area. These were just usual 'niggles' however.

"Just tell me what the problem is, I may not have much of an imagination, Lulla, but try me."

'Workshop' Lulla leant on the door heavily, arm crooked up. "It's the sets, Boss." A cold fear rose in Galba's stomach. It was always the bloody sets.

"Do we have armour, tell me we actually have armour, Workshop? Because, when we loaded, many of the crates had 'Armour Sets' branded onto them. You checked it. You checked it?"

"We do have armour, Boss, and, yes, I did have the crates checked."

"You had them checked or you checked them yourself?"

A deep breath. "We have all the armour we need – more, in fact."

"Well, isn't that good news? Now answer my question. Who checked the crates, Lulla?"

Lulla didn't answer. They both knew it was the armourer cadets.

Here it comes…

"Remember we thought one of the boxes sounded rattly? Well, that's because it was filled with…the fittings…"

Galba was out the door before Workshop could either finish or get out of the way. The Centurion had actually broken into a trot. Lulla hadn't seen that before: it was like watching one of the massive workshop tables, now being assembled, do a little jump in the air all on its own.

The main workshop was a bloody mess but then it was being unpacked so Galba tried to ignore the evil that was loose hammers and tongs lying on the floor, on the actual floor! Through a side door he came to the large storeroom currently being used as an un-crating area. Cadet Armourer Bullo and one of his chums stopped what they were doing. The young man was holding a linen bag.

"Give me that, boy!"

Galba took the bag and peered inside. It was a mass of loose bronze rivets, buckles and clasps. Levelly the Chief Armourer asked, "Where did this come from?"

Bullo pointed to a huge wooden box.

The Centurion looked in and saw it was filled to the top with hundreds of similar bags all with the Fabrica stamp of origin inked on to them.

"Oh, Jupiter and Vulcan help us! Show me the segments."

Lulla leant on another crate, looking in he reached down and pulled out a handful of steel plates, all with neat little holes in them. Galba took them and inspected the component parts of a set of lorica segmentata armour. It looked like the remains of a good lobster after a really good eat.

"They sent them unfitted. Of course, they did. Workshop, have you ever known such a thing?"

Lulla shook his head.

"Used to happen all the time, quite common in fact, made sure a Legion's Armoury was up to the task."

'*Obviously Old Sibius is in here,*' thought the Chief Armourer, but didn't respond. It was his penance for not checking...everything...himself. Instead, Galba turned to the hateful old git.

"Can you fit a full set of this template, Sibius?"

"Of course, I can, I'm an Armourer. First Class before you were..."

"Right, good. Do we have harnesses?"

"Yes, Boss."

There was an edge to Workshop's voice. "Do they need to be fitted as well?"

"The leathers all been cut and cured, so it's just a case of..."

"Sewing several thousand leather strips together? Well, that's alright, then. Do we have jackets?"

"We do have those."

"Do we need to stuff them with eiderdown or are they twenty miles of linen and a huge crate of fucking geese? I mean, how did this bloody happen?"

"Not paying attention to detail."

"Shut up, Sibius."

"Boss, the jackets are fine, quite good quality in fact."

Galba looked down again at the curved plate he held, running his hand across both sides before giving the metal a quick lick to be sure. "These are the inners, what do the hard steel plates look like?"

"Er, we haven't found them yet but I'm sure they're probably in those boxes at the back..."

"'Probably-sure' is not a thing, Lulla. You two cadets, stop unpacking. Armourer Cadet Bullo, get everyone into the main workshop in a tenth of an hour, all except Guns."

Workshop coughed.

"Armourer Cadet Briscos is sharpening at present, could we perhaps...?"

"Leave him to sharpen every edged weapon of an entire legion until he goes stark raving mad and gets the nips?"

"That was the plan, Boss, unless you can think of an alternative because what you are about to do..."

"Right, let Briscos sharpen an entire fresh-forged batch of weapons, then, but that's his career done right there."

"Builds character, he'll be all the better for it. An Armourer shouldn't get above whetstoning a sword or two," stuck in Sibius, who was enjoying the situation so much that the earlier rebuke had just washed off him.

Within the hour's tenth, all the Armoury team were assembled: the workshop, Menicitrix and his fitters, even the carpenters. Guns was left to his own devices as his crew worked up the artillery pieces outside in the park, from the massive siege onagers on down.

The doors of the workshop were bolted and the Chief Armourer gathered the men round.

This is when he really needed Ruben - there would have to be a system.

"This Legion is marching in just days. The XXXth on its first outing will be moving into hostile territory. This legion WILL be fully armoured and armed. Right now, our journey to get there is through several hundred thousand clasps, rivets and hooks. Who, here, has fitted a full set of this template?"

The Lead Armourers and, surprisingly, Bullo put their hands up.

Despite Sibius' continual claims that the Legion's standards were going to the dogs, Galba and the department heads, including 'Guns', got together every time a template update came through and did an unfitted set each over an evening with wine and cheese. Old Sibius was never invited because it was fun.

"Sets are now the priority, everyone will be teamed with a lead fitter, including myself. You get to watch one, then we watch you do one, then off you go. And, believe me, we shall be running full QA. Men's lives are at stake. Any questions?" Old Sibius put his hand up.

"Yes, Honoured Sibius?"

"What about the helmets? They alright then, because you haven't mentioned the helmets, Chief Armourer?"

Galba looked to Lulla. Workshop looked at the floor.

Fuck.

Chapter Thirty-Four

Brigetio Fort
The same warm morning
Pannonian frontier

First Spear Felix was having a hot drink under the western Command Building's outside awning. The brew was piping hot even though it was nearly noon with the sun blazing away overhead, but old habits from northern postings died hard. Sat behind the First Spear on folding chairs were his own set of Optios, wax tablets everywhere, in quiet conference with the SC's staff. As the Centurions ran a Legion for the officers so too did the Optios have their own ways, not to be interfered with by the 'big Cs'.

On Optios: the Optios of the 'little Cs', century Centurions and the like, were one man apiece and mainly did the rolls and hitting people when their bosses weren't around to do it.

'Little C Optios', kept the books, directed formations, swept up stragglers, recorded the endless punishment lists and equipment checks working with the First Class Legionaries – of which the XXXth had fewer than virgins. The 'big Cs', however, kept a staff of 'Big L Optios' who could hit and move a formation with the best of them but spent most hours focused on Legion-sized, mind shattering (as most normal legionaries saw it), detail. Of looking ahead and pre-empting what would be needed and what could/inevitably would, go wrong.

They weren't clerks, that was different. Clerks were the dichotomy of the Army. Literate, numerate Legionaries too useful or useless to be in the Line, depending on a point of view (the Senior Centurion was unexpectedly on the fence, if asked). A handful of these creatures were already picked out and formed up in pods inside the new administration building, scratching and jotting away on huge old lime-bleached trestles.

'Big L Optios' usually came up with their bosses – they were hard fighting, adept Centurion material – but mostly so fully engaged in keeping many thousand men, horses and supporting infrastructure going that there was little time for ambition. Such were the men on the folding chairs at the back of the awnings shadow.

Stood next to the FS in the morning shade were the SC and the Infil Tribune, the 'Skipper', who in that peculiar Army way had somehow become attached to a new enterprise without having any real orders to do so.

"So, how are we feeling today?" Felix asked his colleagues, looking out at the parade's current evolution of bruised 'eighties'.

The Senior Centurion screwed up his face.

"I just saw the Chief Armourer running, First Spear, saw him through the Armoury door."

"Right, well, that's not good."

The FS turned back to the seated group. "Optio, remind me to go and say hello to the forge Immunes later. Let's leave it a bit, though, perhaps Vulcan smiles on us and the Chief Armourer just really needed a shit."

"Wasn't that sort of run, FS, more of an 'Oh, shit!' than 'need a shit' jog."

"No, no, I expect it wasn't, SC. Anyhoo, we'll give the Chief Armourer some time, maybe he'll sort out whatever snag has been encountered."

"Wasn't that sort of run either, more a 'Fucking, fuck, fuck!' big man sprint."

"Alright, Senior Centurion, you've made your point. How are the men?"

"Hungry, First Spear," Skipper replied. "Half rations and a manic training schedule is making people really quite sad and fumbly."

"Do we cut again?" the SC asked. This got the Optios' attention, all eight of them pricking their ears up ready to process an important logistics change.

Felix swayed his mug in the negative. They had a plan and it wasn't to eke out a starved existence until food magically arrived up road or down river. No help was coming any time soon from Sector Command in Aquincum, this morning's Auxilia package had made that very clear. If the XXXth were going to eat, then it was up to them to hunt. This all meant, perversely, having well-fed troops.

"Your man at the village, SC, the orange clad chief from down the road, anything more we can get from him?"

The SC was taking receipt of more turnips later that day, all things being equal, and said so.

"Good. Stick with the plan, in a handful of days we go 'a-foraging' over the river."

The Skipper winced at the First Spear's powers of understatement. "I just worry a bit that…can you actually forage at Legion strength, First Spear, or – is it more of an invasion?"

Felix grinned.

"Doubt yourself now, Sir! It's just what you said to the SC before I arrived: 'WE can certainly carry out a diplomatic, peacekeeping visit to a friendly neighbour. Very eloquent, if I might say so. The SC and I have got it all written down, an officer's view. In case, you know, anyone asks. Later."

"Oh, good." The Skipper grimaced. They were Centurions, he wouldn't stand a chance if it all went bad, legally speaking.

Felix now turned to the Optios. "In fact, let's cast the die, once we are over the river it's all or nothing. As of tonight, full rations for all Line units, sustained until we leave. No reserves."

The SC couldn't fault the decision but didn't like the risk. Nothing as back up but the men were, right now, just the right side of getting flaky. Being fed properly would give them a boost.

Half looking at the parade ground activity, Skipper thought back to the late-night discussions around the clay map table. First Spear constantly questioning both himself and others trying to form a workable assault plan. Each inch of the map table, each representation analysed: "Could you get a mule up it?", "Scree or fixed stone?", "Is it scrub like bushes or scrub like small trees?"

Luckily the Skipper knew most of the answers but Point and Werewulf had been kicked out of their cots in the dead of many nights to run through area detail until sun-up. At each morning's exercise, though, Felix looked fresh as a badly scared but vibrant daisy.

Skipper tried it on again.

"What's the route north, First Spear?"

Felix shrugged.

"My Tribunes are out on important business, Sir, you will have to wait until they return to ask them."

A 'fuck off'. The Skipper wasn't surprised.

But Felix did go on a little, last night's session meant he owed the Infil Tribune something back, he wasn't just another prick waiting around for a thumb. "The town and two villages, as the SC has already identified, are the targets but we need to secure all of them and, this is crucial, get back alive with enough food to make it worthwhile. This is not news but, I realise Tribune, it's a question of unit cohesion versus speed. Using just the main cart track to the west for the haul back? With an entire Legion and slow moving vehicles commandeered from the target area? That's the bit I'm struggling with."

A low cough.

"What about a Numidian caravan? Foot up and back with…assistance." the SC muttered.

Felix gave him a level stare and the two Centurions eyed each other thinking hard.

"You done one, SC?"

"I've seen one, FS."

"What was it like, Senior Centurion?"

"Fucking awful."

The Exfil Tribune had no idea what either man was talking about, they were not sharers and he wasn't going to ask – it obviously alleviated the need for carts, whatever it was. No carts meant the XXXth could insert and return through multiple routes. Over the hills and marshes, to the great plain each target sat within and back again. That made some sense.

Skipper gave it a go, "A split force with no carts, then, First Spear?"

Felix turned back to the Infil Tribune, half-confirming, "Three avenues are possible if we enter and return all on foot."

Skipper knew the routes the FS referred to.

"You'd have to stagger them to make a rendezvous on the plain. There's a large chunk of the outward where the main west track and centre path cannot conjoin. Western force would be on its own until they clear the valley and marshes. That is two-thirds of the journey."

Felix took a sip of his drink: cloves, fat and an egg. He'd got a taste for the brew long ago in the high ranges, lived on it for three weeks once upon a time on the side of a mountain. That had been hard, brutal work, but a period that made his career. Although Felix could never quite admit to himself that he preferred fresh cut 'Mountain Fat' in the drink.

"Good to know, Tribune. Keep thinking, someone has to. Anything else on the men, SC?"

"Glad to have the Centurionate with us now, put it that way. Getting there."

"E-day does not budge, SC."

The trio continued to survey the huge parade ground. Centurion Alba had booked the main area for the second half of the morning. There was now a proper training system, with wax entries of course, devised by the SC and operated by his Optios.

Alba had been given First Cohort, the senior command and traditionally the smallest but best formation within the Legion, although its new Centurion made the point that:

"At this stage, I can only say there might be a one in ten chance we aren't the shittest. But their erstwhile leader has done a good job so far. Skipper, you have my thanks."

Felix doubted First Cohort would be shit, Alba would make them the best because that was First Cohort's role. All ten cohorts of the legion had been rotating around the local area every hour since dawn. Parade ground sessions were tiring but at least there was no log lifting here, instead Alba had drills within drills going. A circle with four centre men having to instantly respond to different points of attack on a complicated sundial carved out in the dirt. Behind them a tortoise was having rocks thrown at them enthusiastically by their tent mates all the while being commanded to readjust and manoeuvre through a flagged course – sometimes backwards.

Quarry stone and sand had started to arrive from the southern village for the Fort's eventual repair and reconstruction. The material had been piled up into an artificial hill at the SC's specific instruction. In full pack, an 'eight' was now forcing their way up to control the top of the mound against a defending strength, who successfully kicked and punched the 'attackers' down to the bottom again – no one had taken the hill as yet. In another area training pilums, just big heavy bits of wood really, were thrown at different distance markers. Three launches then immediately into locked shields to 'present', then a two-step shuffle forward in formation and back for retrieval of the projectiles – the First Century Optio all the while screaming abuse and pushing backs with his long stave. A 'bucket' was also up and running: turns taken by an eight on an eight fighting in a dug-out pit, pumped each morning with river water and slurry from the latrines.

Just a straight-out fight, wins notes noted by Alba's primary Cohort Optio with the most demerited group digging out and covering the 'bucket' at day's end with the rest of the losers. Cleanliness was all in the Legions so the bucket marked a full evolution of drills and the exhausted, bloodied men would quick step out of the gate to take a dip in the river. All fighting spars, tunics, weight rigs or armour meticulously cleaned down ready for the next set exercise.

For the First Cohort their time almost up on the parade square, lunch would be taken from the stewards at kitchen trestles and eaten on the hoof as they ran off to go have a 'dance'. The Centurions really liked the 'Four Ladies', the Skipper saw, and the tradition of the Quadril was sucked up into the XXXth as though they'd been here forever.

"Let's go for a walk," said Felix, indicating the Optios were to stay behind planning for mice and other such things. The three men ambled out from under the awning to cross the parade ground.

"How is it going, First Cohort Centurion Alba?" Felix shouted cheerfully.

"A finer body of men I have never commanded, First Spear."

Felix appreciated the lie, it was what was expected in front of the men.

The First Spear took the comment in with a smile, watching a Noscarf scream from a kick in the goolies. The Falsetto was then thrown down the hill of construction rock by some great lummox. The bigger man was a Scarf, rural build, taking out a sob story of three seasons of drought and a repossession on what was probably some ex-store clerk given the 'court's discretion' following 'misunderstandings'.

SC's Cohort formations had stuck, the Centurions just taking over command on arrival from the hodge podge of assigned leaders. First Cohort were previously the Skipper's men, the Infil Tribune himself thought with no little pride. In the bucket, he could just make out some orange hair under the swill and 'Red' looked up grinning. All that pushing trees had paid off and the boy stood triumphant over a vanquished eight. Low shields, working as a unit, Red's mates had been patient and built-up momentum knocking the other men down into the soggy filth.

With a wink to the ex-carter, officer and senior NCOs walked on through First Cohort's exercises, the last evolution of which featured some Scarfs having a lot of fun. All 'blued-up' pretending to be unspecified 'wild barbarians' they jumped up and down with spear lengths as a maniple of Noscarfs tried to 'put the kettle on'. Novices attempting to encircle and corral their crazed enemy into one spot. The Noscarfs weren't actually doing a bad job motivated, as they were, by weeks of abuse from the established, armoured Legionaries.

"Don't fucking kill him!" Felix took a moment to shout at three Noscarfs battering an armoured man past the point of submission with the heavy wooden practice shields. They took no notice of the First Spear as Felix knew they wouldn't. "Tribune!" he instead shouted to one of the Legion officers who was supposedly controlling the kettle. The officer took note and started to frantically blow his whistle but it took an Optio wading in unhappily with his staff to prevent a serious training accident.

Once through the parade ground Brigetio's command party ascended the gate parapet, nodding to the ballista gunners now always on station. Below them, the Skipper could see Red running out with his tentmates for a wash, trying to find a good spot to disarm, disrobe and clean themselves and kit in the 'busy' area. A challenging task given Centurion Alba's standards, that was made worse with what now lay before the fort.

Two new palisades had been extended forward from the east and western Danube-facing fort towers all the way to the river, enclosing the bank for security purposes. In this area filled full of mess, every minnow wrangler and his family from the entire sector seemed to be hitting something with an axe or hammer or just living noisily around the temporary lean-to' propped up against the northern fort walls.

"YOU, THERE! In the designated latrine area."

A boy of six looked up, grinned as he wiped his arse with his hand and gave the Senior Centurion of the XXXth Legio the universally recognised sign of having a tiny cock. He didn't even bother running off, instead his mother joined her little lad and started screaming unintelligible abuse up to the parapet underscoring the words with a ladle.

"That type of thing carries on and we can tie all the dysentery corpses together and walk to the other side," observed Felix. "The thing is though, SC…"

"Dysentery is no respecter of rank or role: I am well aware of that. I'll sort it. Where's that fish fucker who's in charge got to?"

The Skipper ignored the disrespectful description of a fellow officer and instead just pointed to where the young Exfil Tribune, stripped to his waist, was tying off a birchwood raft before it joined the huge pile of the things behind him.

Brigetio fort's whole front bank was designated as the preparation area for 'E-days' scratch-pontoon. New moorings had been hastily assembled off the dock, webs of single planks and step lines allowing for precarious movement across a growing fleet. The huge armoury transportation barges had been impounded, not a popular move with the rudder-men (even the amiable brother), and with the captured ferry these craft formed the nucleus of a great, emerging creature. Painted numbers were already appearing prominently on the main vessels as Exfil's grand plan to create a crossing point began to take shape. Attack and vulnerability to fire were major concerns, hence the palisades. That still left the riverside open. In the middle of the river, the Gunboat and Xboat had dropped as much chain as they could and were just about holding station, the crews rotated and supplied by a jolly boat from the shore crew.

Each day, fire arrows came whistling in from the far bank and were answered by the clack and thud of the boat Skorpions firing in return over the river. Small boys and girls with pots of water would run around the construction area screaming with delight as they put out the small fires, the fun occasionally spoilt by Mum or Dad getting one in the chest while asleep. The Auxilia cavalry made a few patrols but the north bank was becoming more dangerous and with a hiatus in infantry transportation, due to the cannibalisation of boats, the Gauls had been pulled back from the opposite shore.

Most of the craft, especially the rafts being constructed, were all stored on shore stacked up in great teetering piles. The whole thing was distinctly un-Roman, an anathema to the SC and even past the point where Felix could still be amused at how much annoyance the situation was causing his direct subordinate. The river people were locked inside the palisade except when released to cut extra wood or forage from the surrounding area under guard. Plank shacks and awnings piled up against the north fort wall and a daily fight was had as the veteran spearmen moved the overnight sprawl away from the main gate.

Cooking pots were always on the go with pottage doled out when the women decided it was time. Rubbish was strewn everywhere, broken clay shards, food leavings, rags and a fine sprinkling of flammable timber cuttings. Any attempt to impose a collaborative system fell to nothing, families and communities grouped together and the fights between them were spectacular and sudden, mostly prosecuted with fish gutting knives as ancient grudges between 'those upbend' were played out with 'Grandfather Rik's bastard lot up by the big willow'.

The women were some of the worst, initially a single Legionary or Auxilia had been sent out to ensure foraging parties didn't run off into the forest. That guard trebled as it became apparent that neither the wives nor older children could physically move thirty paces without trying to flense each other. Two corpses had already been floated down the river with a little candle by the old priestess, funnily enough that was the only time anyone got any peace as the whole river community came together and offered prayers to King Halach, the giant catfish god who sat in final judgement of souls at the bottom of the deepest part of the river.

First Spear Felix noted that the 'unorthodox' legionaries who made up the Exfil pilots attended the funerals, knew all the words and dropped a biscuit or some part of their meagre ration into the stream as the river people did, then danced a lot. Immunes were a bit strange, First Spear knew. He'd been one once, up in the mountains. You get set apart from the standard, had to in order to do the job and that was the age-old problem as over time odd habits sent you a little…different, it was difficult ever to go back to the Line.

Up on the parapet Felix took a sip of his now, lukewarm drink with the cloves and the fat. He had found his way back to the Line formations though, found a path back in a particular way, which reminded the First Spear: the second ice store needed clearing, it was full of flour at this moment. He'd known the room as soon as he saw it. Second ice stores that never held ice, sometimes it was called the 'east prison', which never had a guard or 'the lower arches' or the bone-dry, spare aquifer. Nobody went near those places, you just didn't. Unless invited.

"We eat a lot of fish here, don't we, Sir?" the First Spear remarked to the Infil Tribune, watching another small fleet of boats head in, nets full, trying to find docking space.

The Skipper smiled and nodded. The XIth had indeed eaten a lot of fish, the XIth had lived off fish while at Brigetio and not all of the river people were now set to crossing construction. Selected fishermen set out each morning, pulling their boats up stream to find the best pools, a steady stream of huge river salmon and carp bolstering the camp rations, not even close to sating the XXXth's appetite but keeping it alive. The fishermen wouldn't run either as the pay was just too good, not just in metal but the Exfil boat carpenters were grudgingly released from essential duties to mend and improve some of the small craft as payment in kind.

"YOU!" The SC was shouting again at something up on the fort's palisade wall, "You there! Yes you! I'll have someone's hide for this. Get that native off the wall, get the fuck out of my camp. Guards!"

The SC's ire was directed at a small dark man hiding under a vast, battered straw sun hat who had somehow got into the Fort. The hat looked back from its place up on the palisade gangway slightly bemused but continued eating a raw onion as the SC bellowed.

"What the fuck are you doing, Armourer?" the SC screamed at the Legionary who was just standing, at ease, behind the little fisherman, "Giving him a fucking tour? Get that swarthy bastard off my fence and you're on report!" The armourer stared back grimly.

Felix pretended to look the other way and tried not to smile.

Instead of leaving the rampart the little boatman shuffled in his thongs, hitched up his canvas trousers and pulled a rag out of a flouncy, orangey-yellow braided shirt three sizes too big for him. He placed the rag on a bit of stick he was carrying, all the while keeping the onion clasped in his teeth, then raised the cloth and gave two short waves.

The Senior Centurion was puce, "What the fu...!"

THUD, THUD, THUD, THUD, each huge crash followed by an immense roar of rushing wind. Just for a moment the Skipper caught a flying black dot just before the SC was knocked off balance from the force of rushing air. Not everyone ducked, some river people just ran around screaming in terror. The little man in the hat was the only person to stay completely unmoved, just looking inquisitively at the far bank - even the armourer behind him flinched.

The gatekeeper gunners swung about in fright, the two catamarans rocked as turbulence pushed down onto the river. The briefest of lines was described on the far water, spray thrown up, before a massive series of crashing, earth flinging, explosions erupted from the opposite bank. Foliage, water, mud and dust everywhere followed by a few falling trees. The noise then continued in a more subdued tone, the clatter of fast rolling, bouncing, boulders making their way through vegetation.

"OUTGOING!" Felix shouted, somewhat belatedly, watching the carnage.

Someone was mewling over on the far bank: they could hear it all the way across the river. Then a few figures could be seen wandering about in the dirty haze, dazed and confused. One was dragging a long spear by the end, completely bemused, tip trailing in the dirt.

Down at the pontoon the Exfil Tribune shouted across to the catamarans on station, all Skorpion gunners on the midstream boats opened up, bolts flying, cutting down the enemy roused out of their observation post. He had the fire continue into the dirt cloud for a few more rounds to make a point.

"Whatever that was…must have been at nearly full depression, a head and a half above the parapet." as the only officer present the Skipper felt he should say something about what they had just witnessed.

The FS shrugged jovially.

"Effective though wasn't it, Sir? Artillery is assembled, I see, and the gunners do seem to know what they are doing, although some warning might be good in future. Ever heard of the VIIIth, Skipper?"

"Old Rhine Legion that's fed all of our armoury, is all I really know."

The SC, despite himself, was enjoying the far-shores chaos. He hated Infiltration units, the enemy's only marginally more than their own, but decided to give the strange Infil officer the benefit'.

"The VIIIth are famous, can slot a bolt through a needle and place a full-stone right on your sister's lap. Their artillery is, I grudgingly admit, the best in the service. How we got them I have no idea. But that still doesn't excuse…that…"

The Senior Centurion looked back at the little Hispanic who had now replaced the green rag with a red one and was making a series of signals to a fire director sat up on the new obs' tower behind them. The enormous siege onagers could just be seen way back in the park, poking up over a barrack. The shots, the Skipper thought, must have passed over every meaningful building in the fort, glanced over the north fence before dropping down precisely on target.

Felix wandered over to the side of the tower parapet to communicate along the palisade directly.

"Lead Artillery Armourer! That was an effective test, well done."

A satisfied bite of an onion under dark glittering eyes confirmed this opinion.

"Maybe a little warning next time?" A wide smile and a nod was returned.

Felix decided he'd had enough excitement for the day and went off to talk to the bakers about a cracked oven. He would also quietly mention the ice store full of flour bags to their 'Rolls'. If he did that now, he'd have time to get into full rig and go for a dance with Seventh Cohort who were troubling him. Before descending the gatehouse ladder the FS, however, took a moment to consider Guns' exciting local shirt.

"Senior Centurion, when your man with the turnips arrives tell him to find some of that orange cloth they all like round here. A lot of it."

The SC looked back at the First Spear with a disapproving eye raised.

"That's going to be our colour, then, FS?"

"I think it is, SC, I rather like it."

It was plain what the SC thought, a crisp clean white scarf of the 'Wild Parthians' tucked into his rig.

"Bit optimistic, don't you think, FS?"

Felix laughed then started down the companion ladder.

"We'll go and have a chat with Centurion Chief Armourer Galba after lunch. It will all work out. I mean, if we've got 'scarfs' then we must have armour to stuff them into, stands to reason. In fuck-all days' time we are walking over that river, the men deserve a scarf, Senior Centurion. Do you understand me?"

"First Spear."

THUD THUD THUD THUD, and this time the SC and the Skipper just crouched a little.

"TELL US! FUCKING TELL US YOU FUCKING LITTLE SHAMBLES OF A MAN!" screamed the SC.

Chapter Thirty-Five

Armoury of the XXXth in heavy discord
Brigetio Fort
South of the river

The plinking of little hammers started mid-afternoon and didn't halt morning, noon or night.

The plink, plink, plink of precision metalwork echoed unceasingly from the Legion Armourers' workshop. Noise from the whetstone its constant accompaniment, grinding and keening up and down.

Two hours into the great endeavour First Spear Felix, fully kitted out ready to follow the increasingly dubious Seventh Cohort over the Quadril, approached the Armoury. Two Armoury guards, Scarfs, once from the XVth by the looks of it, addressed him apologetically.

"If you could keep to the painted white lines, First Spear, Centurion Chief Armourer's orders."

Felix returned the chest salute and indicated to a trailing Optio that they were to do as instructed. The workshop's double doors were wide open, for light the NCO imagined, and as they picked out the freshly-painted white stripes guiding them into the gloom, he could see why there were instructions not to leave the 'path'. Every inch of space within the long rectangular room was taken up with the assembly of armour sets. Around the white lines the floor was gridded with green paint from the vast tub of leftovers, previously used to paint urban recruits. That had stopped now as the urban troops were finding an equilibrium with their rural brethren and also due to the red angry rash the stuff left on a man's skin.

Over in one corner Felix saw Galba was engaged in an angry discussion with a wiry old subordinate, a group of cadets were watching the bad-tempered exchange. You got to be First Spear by learning what to ignore so he and his Optio stopped at a 'T' junction where the white lines intersected, and looked around.

"You see it, Optio?"

"I do, FS."

"Reckon it's all of them?"

"I do, FS."

"Never seen anything like it, have you?"

"I haven't, FS. See that, FS?"

The Optio pointed a stylus to a square bench at one side of the room where four one-foot stands were being worked on.

"Helmets as well, then. Right."

Both men stepped back as two armourers carrying curved metal plates and sacks jostled past, they nodded to the First Spear but nothing more. No salute. That's how serious it was.

"First Spear."

Behind them Galba appeared, just wearing a grey tunic and holding a large tablet and stylus, the writing implement looking odd within the Armourer's massive hands and forearms. A heavy, battered work belt hung around the Centurion Armourer's waist just like every other man in the building. Favourite hammers, tongs, picks, chisels, set length and a hand drill hung off it.

"Going well then, Chief Armourer?"

They just looked at each other.

"Afraid it's still three days, Galba, we just don't have the food."

The other man sniffed and nodded.

"I should have checked all the…"

"Bollocks. It happened, just another Army fuck-up. Do you have everything you need?" Felix instantly saw that it was a stupid question.

"Alright, anything you need that I can help with?"

The tablet came open, Galba looked at it, as you always checked your notes before answering a superior 'taking an interest'.

"Space, First Spear. We are arranging a system where component sets are gathered ready to be picked up by one of the teams and worked on. To do this we need to get ahead of ourselves and only a quarter of the parts are even out of the crates."

Felix addressed his Optio. "Who's on the other side of that wall, it's a barracks, right?"

The Optio took a new tablet out of his satchel and reviewed the scratchings quickly.

"Some of Fourth Cohort."

"Put them in tents but issue some wine to show I still love them. Do it now and get four of the biggest buggers they have to take a borrow of Armoury mallets and knock a bloody great big hole through the wall."

"The bunks, FS?"

"They go as well, don't be polite about it, just get them down and we build new ones at a later date. Get it swept properly as well, there'll be loose rivets to find, no offence CA. Right, next, Chief Armourer?"

"I need light, this is going to be night and day. Food and water for every watch or the men will be leaking buckets which leads to rivets popping out on the march, let alone what happens if we get into a fight."

"When we get into a fight, Centurion. Optio, tell the kitchens: galley team on at all times. Same rations for Armoury as Line."

The Optio spoke as he etched in shorthand.

"Centurion Armourer, have one of your men let me know how much oil you're burning per hour, we'll also set some braziers up. There's enough wood chips out front to stage a reenactment of the Golden Palace's finest hour so we have material to burn. I'll get a covered wood store made up at the side of the building."

"Obliged, Optio. Can I get an eight at all times for QA as sets come out?"

"Done, they'll welcome the break."

"Not sure about that. I'm planning to have each set marched for an hour up and down the rubble parade hill, torches set up so even at night they'll be at it."

Felix laughed. "Still 'Done' but they'll just hate you for it, Centurion."

"Such is the lot of the Armoury. I have a list of other items, here you are, Optio. We have the first sets made up if you want to take a look, FS."

"Lead on!" and they walked towards a table flanked by the angry looking old Legionary blacksmith, following the appropriate white line against a constant stream of armourers and cadets carrying metal, leather, tools and arming frames.

"May I introduce you to Legion Armourer First Class Sibius, First Spear."

Galba half waved at his subordinate unenthusiastically.

The man looked old enough to be Felix's great-grandfather. The First Spear also thought the similarities didn't end there as the NCO's angry old progenitor had died standing up while unnecessarily re-digging an irrigation ditch 'properly': they'd found him in the sleet, stone cold dead but still bolt upright, claws grasping a shovel.

Anyone who subsequently worked at that spot claimed they could hear a shade muttering about 'half measures' until Felix's pa got the priest in to sort it.

"Good to meet you, First Class Armourer Sibius."

Sibius just looked Felix's armour up and down, "That's Cronius's work, isn't it?"

Felix blinked and smiled.

"Yes, yes, it is. My goodness he's been dead for…well, anyway, when I knew him, he was very much Chief Armourer Cronius. God, I was terrified of Cronius even when I received my…" A huge snort interrupted the flow.

"Chief Armourer? Chief Armourer Cronius, you say? My goodness, who'd have thought…? Not me, First Spear, I can tell you. Seen much action wearing that thing?" Galba's fury began to bubble.

"A bit, yes."

"Well, you must be a lucky bugger, First Spear."

Felix looked hard straight at his Optio who was staring blankly ahead.

"I must be," Felix replied lightly then turned his attention to the work in progress at this workshop station.

"Is that it, then?"

Before them on arming stands were four immaculate, fresh completed sets, already buffed and shining. First Spear walked round one of the stands, it was perfect work. A design of segmented armour he hadn't seen before, a few adaptations, cut curves for better shoulder rotation, and as he prised open the segments he saw that there was not a full leather harness. "All the plates hang off each other? I see just a few strips."

"Should have been done years ago, all perfectly possible," snorted Old Sibius.

First Spear continued his inspection. It was beautifully assembled, much better that any Fabrica-fitted set would be. Each rivet, clasp and tie in exactly the right place knotted with Thracian bows. The overlapping hard plate slightly offset from the 'soft' plates allowing full protection with a wide range of movement. That was the thing about the Old Sibiuses' of this world, you needed them – not too many, but then Vulcan only ever allowed so many master smiths into the light. The sets' perfection begged a question, though.

"You did these, Armourer Sibius?"

"I did, First Spear, showing the boys how to craft a full fitting."

Felix took this in and made an assessment of what was going on down at the Armoury benches. No other full sets were anywhere to be seen. He now knew what the bad temper had been with between Chief Armourer and the ancient wiry creature. Galba knew his business and was obviously sorting the issue out but sometimes a First Spear could give a little 'encouragement'.

"And how long did it take you?"

"First Spear?"

"One of these fine sets of lorica segmentata, how long did it take you to do one?"

"Well, to craft anything it's not about time but…"

"Because when I came in here you didn't seem very happy and your superior didn't seem very happy."

"If you say so."

"I fucking do say so."

Felix gave Old Sibius a look even the old man found difficult to hold. It wasn't angry or hostile, nor did the gaze threaten violence, but then looking down a deep well doesn't either. Just the certainty of cause and effect if you fell in. Both would still envelop the unwary in darkness when not stepped back from very lightly.

"You have a station system here, Chief Centurion Armourer Galba?"

"I do, First Spear."

Felix kept his gaze on Sibius. "This is fine work, old man. You will do what you can, I know that, show these boys the perfect example, but – we do not have time for the pursuit of the ideal set of armour. In a clutch of days, a demi-legio worth of sets will be ready and marching into a conflict zone, the whole XXXth Legion of which you are now part of. You don't get to handcraft each piece, that's for another day. Just say 'Yes, First Spear'"

Old Sibius was a second-lifer, the Army was his home.

"Yes, First Spear."

"This armour…" Felix pulled at his own rig. "…has saved my life, Sibius, more than a few times and every night I pray for the Emperor, my Legion, my family, and a few others amongst which is Chief Armourer Cronius. I'm not saying you couldn't do better, there's no doubt you could. But, see, out there, north over that river you and I know there's the most beautiful and ingenious sets of armour someone like me, a little field runt, could only ever dream of owning. That nice German prince we brought in the other day for instance, lovely stuff. I

359

bet, though, you could do even better than his rig. Point is, Chief Armourer Cronius could arm an entire Legion, you could not. Which is why you are only a Senior Armourer, because that's where the Army needs you. The thing about Cronius is, or was, I reckon, that he wasn't half as capable as your actual boss here. I like your boss, but even if I didn't, it wouldn't matter because he has so far impressed me. I know what you are thinking, but then you didn't check the armour crates either. So, the message is…"

Old Sibius shuffled. "Get on with it."

"Get on with it! There we are."

Felix took one last look at the frame. "This is excellent work, though. Boys – learn from this ancient – but listen to this one," the SC said, turning to the watching Cadets and indicating Sibius then Galba with his vine staff.

"Yes, First Spear!" the Cadets responded, and Felix made off for the door. Hovering was not going to help anything. Galba escorted him out.

"Hope that was alright with you, Centurion?"

Galba half smiled, all armourers were prickly over their domain but Felix had done it the right way. Pity it had to be done at all, though.

"Might have a bit of good news, though, First Spear. Have you seen the artillery is up and running?"

Felix grinned. "Nearly took my fucking head off, Centurion Armourer! Pretty impressive, close up."

"Go see them tomorrow morning, at the artillery park, might be interesting."

"I will, what I've seen so far scares the shit out of me. The VIIIth's reputation lives up to itself. Apart from the bit about fondling deer, that is, but I'm sure when you have some free time…"

The Chief Armourer managed a snort.

"I don't need to say it, do I, Chief Armourer?" the First Spear said quietly to Galba, looking at the floor.

"No, First Spear, you don't. Three days."

"Good. I mean I've ordered the bloody scarfs."

Galba laughed for the first time in a while, "Oh well, definitely we'll have the armour done then. I'll tell the lads to get off the dice."

"That's the spirit, Centurion."

Chapter Thirty-Six

The following dawn, Brigetio Fort
Artillery pens
Danube border

Not much surprised the First Spear but next morning, upon reaching the fire support corral, he had spilt liquid hot, cloved, fat over his hand in astonishment. The Skipper, who'd been invited along by the NCO hadn't however burnt himself in astonishment. Offered a mug by the FS he had instead, after the initial sip, accidentally spilt the evil contents on the ground when Felix was looking the other way.

Rosy fingered dawn was just appearing over the eastern river hills and Guns was already at it. The man seemed to live off onions, one currently held in mouth while measuring an angle, and in the cool air he had replaced his straw hat with a bright red knitted thing that seemed to be beloved by moths. Huge canvas sheets were everywhere and the FS and Skipper walked around the massive black shapes of onager catapults, then past the Fort's existing Skorpions and Ballista - weapons that had apparently been removed from their mounts for a refitting. First Spear asked a single, accompanying Optio if he'd given permission for this refit to happen and when he got the answer filed it under 'no record could be found at this time'. The decision to look the other way was influenced by the row of new Skorpions and Ballista brought up with the VIIIth artillery train, all black-veneered wood with strange protrusions and extra wires. They exuded menace, but that wasn't the surprise, that was four towering silhouettes on wheels.

"Carroballistas!" Felix exclaimed before adding a low whistle. There was no record of such things in the XXXth store but somehow, there they were: four great-ballista, big brothers of the Skorpion field pieces, each mounted on a proper suspension wagon. 'Gunwagons' that, with the right crew, could even fire on the move, at a pinch…if desperate.

Felix had seen the mobile fire support platforms before but these wagons seemed to have hinged stabilisation booms fixed to the carts, obviously ready to swing out and plant the cart firmly to the ground. The FS also saw the booms had large wooden screws, presumably to counter even extreme gradients and be able to fire accurately from a slope. First Spear Felix couldn't have been more excited, even if the spilt, burning horse blubber hadn't been eating into the back of his hand.

"You ever seen these, Tribune?"

The Skipper shook his head as they neared the specialist vehicles. "When they work these carts make a real difference and that isolated western insertion route can take them."

The Skipper was keen to learn and by full dawn, Guns indicated the wagons were ready to test. Horses were used rather than oxen, a team of four, and in each cart two Artillery Armourers went along with a couple of big Legionary 'winch monkeys' and drivers to run through static drills.

After an hour of range, the Skipper and First Spear left them to it but came back to the corral at lunch for a 'field test'. The exercise began with the Gaulish Auxilia sent swimming over the river as a lure, riding the north shore unsupported by infantry. Meanwhile two of the gun wagons trundled out of Brigetio's gate, turning along the bank road west, the other pair going east.

Very soon word had got out, hostile horse and foot patrols appeared glad of a return to the 'happy time' ambling about the far shores, running down unsupported Roman patrols well away from the evil rock throwers hidden within the stomach of the old Fort.

Felix and the Skipper were with the eastern wagons, now pulled off the shore track and positioned in a small copse by the bank – 'duck hunting'. Seeing an Auxilia patrol being chased back to the river by whooping levies and Roxolani cavalry, the Gunwagons had quickly pulled up to a halt opposite, opened stabilisers and hunkered down in the small trees. Some fine tweaks made, winches spun, and the mobile artillery loaded thick metal bolts into deep canal grooves. Both sets of gunners, loaders, teamsters, Guns himself, Felix and the Skipper nervously peered through young, green branches towards the opposite north bank. Watching the noiseless figures of an Auxilia 'tied fly' patrol, glinting in the bright sun. These Gauls were racing back to shore, but not too fast, chased by a large group of enemy spearmen frantically trying to envelop the Decurion and his chums.

The Macromanni spearmen thought they'd caught the squadron, who had drawn up and dismounted 'in a bit of a panic' at the shore. Cavalry all waving arms frantically for an imaginary exfiltration. With much excited horn blasting the enemy shield wall closed together at a walk, spears lowered as the levy came out of the scrub onto the shores grey stones. Guns took ranges and gambled, leaving both heavy holts primed (no swap to parcels), and Apollo smiled upon them. At a signal massive iron-pointed staves thwacked out of the runnels and flew across the Danube, dropping perfectly down onto their marks. Ripping two splintering holes, three lines deep at least, into the spearmen.

Faint screams could be heard by Skipper, Felix grunted with satisfaction. Across the water shock had also arrived, enemy formation discipline breaking down looking for the 'What?' and the 'Where?' of about ten dead and maimed men who had just been running alongside a moment before. The Macromanni quickly gave up wondering and ran back to the scrub in panic, only for the Roman Auxilia cavalry to turn from their shoreline pantomime and ride the fleeing levy down mercilessly.

"Bravely vanquishing the enemy as they ran away!" the Skipper remarked to the wagon gunners above him as they watched the Gauls scythe down the fleeing enemy, which got a predictable laugh. Prince Herminaz standing off to one side of a spoked wheel just pulled his bejewelled beard and spoke quietly to a flock of Cherusci advisors gathered about their lord in a huddle.

First Spear Felix had also made sure Prince Herminaz had come along to the live-fire test, getting an eyeful of the new weapons. Just to impress upon the Cherusci 'allies' what Roman engineering could do. It worked to a degree and the prince certainly stopped complaining about not having enough gold at the officers Mess dinner that night. Not that the First Spear attended such things, but each night, after dinner the Tribunes always sidled over to the planning room saying things like: "Look, I was talking to the prince over dinner and he may have a point so is there any way we might…"

Obviously, the answer was always 'No, Sir, we might not', but neither the First Spear nor the SC and their staffs presently had time to formulate the different types of 'No'. Fending off the good ideas of royalty and commissioned officers left with wine for three whole hours was not a luxury the NCOs of the XXXth currently had with a handful of days to go before 'E', so shutting the prince up was useful.

That particular night, while Prince Herminaz sat sulkily in the drying-rack-adorned silence of the officers' wardroom reflecting on the day's display of Roman technology, next door the assembled men of the NCO Mess listened to the Armoury noise coming from outside as they drank and chatted. At every eleven triangle, before a few hours of snatched sleep, the First Spear held a drink with the senior men. All NCOs bar the Skipper and the Exfil Tribune who were, and felt, honoured guests amongst the professional Army personnel. A chance to relax a little and informally take stock in the quiet-ish dark. Galba wasn't in attendance as he rarely left the armourers' shed, the only sign he hadn't deserted was the dinking sound of many hammers and the whetstone grinding.

Centurion Alba pulled up an awkward hessian bag from beneath his stool.

"Last of the crates were finally unpacked today and…look what I found." He shed the bag revealing a long-curved brass horn.

The Centurions and Optios groaned.

"Got to have a Legion band to keep the morale up!"

This got a grim laugh then, puckering his lips, Alba played half of *'Monkey Trousers'* badly until the SC threw a cup at him.

"Give me that!"

And unexpectedly the Senior Centurion took the horn, gave it a disapproving onceover and a wipe before launching into, *'My Sweet Persian Tulips'* – perfectly and hauntingly, a tune that was the favourite of old Pompey's Legions, from which the SC came. It was said the tune played to the last as Crassus' expedition was overwhelmed. A legend went that the last sip of water in the whole doomed Army was given to the lead Cornicifer so he could keep playing as the Parthians cut them to pieces before taking their, famously well off, Legate for a more expensive drink of molten gold.

The NCO Mess drinkers listened to the tune in silence then sat still for moments after the last long bar was played. The SC coughed and threw back the horn.

"Piece of shit, needs pinching at the neck."

"I'll see to it," said one of his Optios looking into his drink, homesick, the Skipper would have thought if he didn't know better.

Felix shuffled on his chair. "Very good Alba, we now have a new morning job for the officers. One of those Tribunes is probably musical." Polite smiles, rather than outright laughter, in deference to the Skipper and Exfil.

"Find the musical one, best players from each cohort to then be selected, a little competition for Command Cornicifer. Find any twat who can play a pig whistle and get them up and running for manoeuvres at midday." Optios made notes.

"So that's what we shall be marching to sorted, but what are we marching under, First Spear?" Alba asked, now serious. All eyes turned to Felix. This was a question that had been coming and needed a proper answer.

The Skipper noted the Centurions collectively responded as one to Alba's enquiry and the reaction was anticipation mixed with discomfort, all directed towards the FS.

Felix lounged back on his folding chair, wine in one hand, a single outstretched leg, and gazed back levelly.

"Yes, I've been thinking about that, and it is not the duty of the Centurionate to decide such…things. The XXXth is currently just a number, as you are all well aware. It has no eagle, or General, and so is not officially formed. All we've done is had a Tribune read out the order of assembly at Brigetio but that doesn't mean we are on the rolls. Good news, though: what we do have is a lot of orange cloth, thanks to the SC's headman. It's the one thing that seems to be in abundance in this part of the world – if only we could eat orange cloth! Combine orange cloth with ancient precedent and we have some…cover."

The SC spat. "The Tribunes are going to have to ask, First Spear? Like old Rome? That's what you're thinking?"

"They are, SC. So, tomorrow: Senior Centurion, Alba and myself will be in full ceremonial kit. If I might also ask the two officers present to join us in their best clothes?"

Both officers shrugged, bemused.

Alba then turned to the Skipper and Exfil Tribune explaining what was expected of them, for the bending of old, old Army laws to cover their current predicament. *'An asking'*, like back when the army were seasonal farmers because there was no eagle yet. "Then, you see, Sirs, we'll need to get an embroidery circle going," Alba finished off as though it was all quite self-explanatory.

A military fudge and the first away
Brigetio Fort
All the good stuff happens at dawn

A readying Danube border.

First thing, a ceremonial parade party brushed their faces with red clay dust, always kept in kit by an FS for religious matters and marched in perfect step to the usual morning briefing at the Admin/old laundry. The stern, crimson-faced and thoroughly polished marching six bore three long spools of fresh orange cloth between them, lying on a crisp white sheet, shouldered within one of the Legion's treasury crates. The four XXXth Tribunes were waiting for the normally quite, informal daily meeting and were taken aback when the group entered stamping in full 'parade' with face paint.

While the officers gop'd, First Spear addressed the Lead Tribune with his full title and made a prayer to Jupiter, Neptune (incorrectly, but out of deference to the river) and Mars then exclaimed: "We are not a legion but of Rome, not an army but to go into battle. As Tribunes of the XXXth we beseech you, as the Emperor's representatives to let us be marked, let us march under banners of the XXXth if not an eagle itself, as is our right!"

None of the Tribunes really understood what was going on. The Senior Centurion stepped forward and pointed towards the administration doors.

"You will have to ask us to march, us and the men, I mean, Sirs. There are no golden Eagle standards here. Each citizen out there will have to be reassured they are not committing treason for there is no compunction to march under orders to war."

The Lead Tribune blinked. "Aaaask?"

"Ask, Sir," the First Spear restated, hard-faced under the red mask of war. "As officers of the Army you will have to ask us to march under a banner extraordinary with all the responsibilities thereof." This ceremony hadn't been conducted for several hundred years but the words the NCO's had come up with last night sounded proper. "We have no Eagles from the Emperor or Senate."

Two blinks.

Felix assured the officer in a softer voice now. "It can be done. This is your time, Sir, grasp it! Make us banners, on this cloth with the simple numerical of the XXXth upon them. We need them to march, the men need them to follow in the field and for reassurance."

The Tribunes squinted at each other realising the import of what the NCOs were saying. Marching about and fighting off attacks was one thing, an expedition across the river with an unsanctioned force could be seen as a Rubicon even if nominally going away from Rome in direction. The matter was weighed up in a huddle of whispers but the Lead Tribune's pure ambition won out over common sense.

"You shall have them! However, First Spear Felix, I'll need sooome men…to make our baaaanners…" The SC noisily hit his breastplate three times with his vine staff, looking straight forward.

The First Spear explained to the startled officerlings:

"That cannot be, Sir, we cannot touch the banners. The banners cannot touch the ground. If any enlisted man touches the banner, he has taken an oath. All must be sewn in this room and blessed for the asking by yourselves."

Four Tribunes stared back as the ceremonial party in dismay "Weeee have tooo…Sew?" The box of cloth was then reverently placed on an old laundry table. Formal salutes (unreturned due to shock) and the ceremonial party began to march away noisily in step.

"Like, actually…with a needle and things?" asked the Political Tribune, watching the extraordinary group tramp off through the administration offices doors.

"I don't! I have to play the horn today, I've got a note from the Senior Centurion.' exclaimed the third officer happily, running off to pick up his new trumpet and leaving quarter of a mile of rough tangerine coloured cloth behind with his colleagues.

Outside, at a trough, the iron-clayed men were signalled to kneel, the First Spear made a prayer and then they stood. Two of the party began to wash the clay off in the horse water. The SC did not go to clean his face. That wasn't his old Legion's way, you didn't take leave of Mars, he took leave of you and the clay would fall off at its own pace. In fairness, the red masked visage of war seemed to suit the SC well. Instead, he growled to his scrubbing superior, "Well done, First Spear, that'll give the young gentlemen something to do."

First Spear spat out some wet straw that had got in his mouth and began to dis-armour, a waiting Optio hovered to take his rig. He had office work to do.

The Skipper also stood back from the water asking, "Was all that true, First Spear? That your Tribunes must make the banners themselves due to ancient tradition?"

Felix gave the Skipper a look and instead turned to the Exfil officer. "How's the bridge, Tribune? Long enough yet? I mean, in its component parts?"

The Exfil, scraping with a handful of grass at his cheeks, shook his head. "Two more days, First Spear, but we should start cutting the last gang planks for the pontoon this morning."

Felix nodded, now turning back to the other Tribune, "Infiltration ready to go, Skipper?"

The Skipper had also left the warpaint on, nothing to do with tradition but because he'd have to daub up soon anyway. "Off in an hour."

"Boat?"

"No, going to do our best impression of Odysseus legging it from old One Eye," and the Skipper nodded to an Auxilia squadron preparing to go out. The Infiltration team from Point to Comms was already assembling their gear next to the riders and Two was having a heated exchange with a squat Gaul in a silly bronze hat.

The tunic'd First Spear made for the Skipper to follow him back inside to the new administration building where they then stood at the clay table. Next door a yelp sounded as inept things were being done with chalk, pins and shears.

Officer and First Spear looked at each other – a plan had been finalised late last night. SC began:

"Let's go through it again. We are going to split into three, Route Gold is here in the centre, Silver to the east and last but not least, Bronze to the west. Bronze is the only road that'll take the mobile artillery, right, Sir?"

The Skipper nodded. Bronze Route going north was the sole carriage road from the river, meandering up over the hills to the west of the intersecting valley, with marshes in-between it and Gold and Silver routes.

"I need at least half a day's markers across all three, Skipper, think you can do that?"

It was a lot of ground to cover. All three insertion points to be marked out covering a deep zone into hostile territory by the second dawn. "Best get going, First Spear."

Felix grinned. "Good luck, Sir, I know you'll do it."

A good Army lie, and the Tribune buckled his leather harness to go and supervise the assembly area. By the gate, Infil team stood up at their Skipper's approach and pulled on the last of their rig straps. Other than Point, each man had added a roll of canvas wrapped, white painted marker sticks to the top of their packs.

"Making friends, Two?" Skipper asked nodding at a scowling Auxilia.

Two just spat.

The Skipper walked over to the lead cavalryman and made sure the orders were clear and understood at the top, represented in this case by an unhappy Decurion. As each Infil team member then formed up by an Auxilia horseman a very different set of legionaries was assembling on the other side of gate. A motley band of Noscarfs and Scarfs with the youngest Tribune in charge, each holding a musical instrument.

"You've got to be fucking kidding, Sir?" said Two as *'The corn of my fathers'* started up across a heartbeats interval in different keys.

The Skipper couldn't help a chuckle.

"That's right, chaps, nothing like a loud, rousing song to start a covert Infiltration sortie."

"Fucking Army!" said Two, then shouted, "Horn Wankers!"

The line of cavalry walked out from the gate. Each Infil team member marching shadow step, bank side, in time perfectly with a horse's front legs, as the cornets blared across the river.

Chapter Thirty-Seven

The XXXth's pungent, exhausted Armoury
Brigetio by the Danube
The Pannonias

Galba had been warned off the morning's administration briefing by Felix, something official was going on, which had been a relief. His hands and back ached, the eyes were sore but despite having not slept for two days the Centurion Armourer was a man with a mission and a scheduling chart to support it. It wasn't a bad chart, could be better. *'Bloody Ruben, bloody deserter!'*

The Chief Armourer surveyed the painted grid thrown up across the far, long wall of the main Armoury workshop. Time, targets, QA throwbacks, a big painted 'box' with "STOP. Look at me!" – on it were scrawled cheats, tips and newly-identified problems with the component sets and helmets. This box had a caricature of a scowling, top heavy Roxalani horse woman to ensure male eyes were drawn to the key updates. Cadet Bullo couldn't draw tits as well as Ruben but like everything else it was 'make do and mend'. Most of the guidance was also pictorial – areas to be pre-filed, holes drilled out, clasps that needed the slightest of bends with small pliers – they were armourers not clerks.

Morning inspection of the Armoury began as men rotated in and out of cots for four hours' work or sleep, all oblivious to the constant, ambient clamour. The cord framed beds themselves were located outside the main workshop to save space. Unconscious bodies stacked under an awning, half chewed food still in sleeping mouths. One watch down then forcibly roused by a bunkmate, rotated and returned to the work benches.

Workshop Lulla's yellow, drawn face briefed the Centurion Armourer that they were behind on assembly but the QA was holding up: both plus and minus factors down to Sibius' supervision but Galba had a plan to catch up. Twice a day the chief allowed himself a walk through the great ragged hole of the armoury wall into their new release area. Amongst all the other items racked in the vacated barracks this was where the fresh sets were kept, ready to be sent out on the backs of overly-excited young 'eights', a First Spear Optio assigned to oversee the task.

Two more sets, the Chief Armourer saw on his inspection, and there would be a new Six Century Batch: sixty-four complete, QA-tested, sets of segmented armour with a fully-assembled helmet accompanying.

Galba watched, arms folded, as an eight from the Fourth Cohort were being pushed about by a Senior Armourer, the young men strapped into the first full 'releases' to Line. This knackered, Legionary eight, had instantly cheered up when given their first armour, an excited set of small boys receiving a full set of deadly killing implements was exactly what it was and looked like. Once the armour was placed on each Noscarf – helmet on head, serial marks taken from the freshly stamped pieces – the newly adorned would be dragged outside the old barrack to a roughly punched-out window and issued with a fresh shiny gladius, pugio dagger, a shield taken from the hanging rack and two pilums before being kicked on to the painted line for inspection.

All eight men now stood at attention as the weary Senior Armourer on duty and a Cohort Optio signed and counter signed for the kit. Army bureaucracy completed to mutual satisfaction, the last thing to happen before this newly-fitted group left for duties was a blessing from the SA, thanking Vulcan and commending these men to Salus, goddess of protection and wellbeing. Then the eight Noscarfs marched away at the double to spend some quality time finding out what life in a full rig felt like, the novelty running out before lunch in this case. Galba strolled outside watching the 'tent' clatter off as the next, babbling, eight of Fourth Cohort Noscarfs were herded into the fitting room.

Workshop appeared next to Galba, having his breakfast watching a QA unit testing sets straight out of the workshop, running up and down the quarry stone hill. A Cadet Armourer ran with them, scanning for loose fittings and picking up rivets before trying to ascertain where they came from. A little fittings anvil was stationed by the main door of the Armoury with an Armourer and a pack of spares. Any QA defaults and the offending man – *'What did you fucking do to it, you twat?'* – would either be instructed to lie in some uncomfortable way across the anvil, wincing as the hammer banged down directly next to his head or softer parts, or the set would be removed entirely for the defect to be reattached or adjusted.

"Having a little holiday, Lulla?" Galba asked.

Lulla ignored this and chewed his porridge. "Right Boss, we're generally good out here on QA but when we get a problem it's where it always is – the upper back clasps. Thing about losing the full leather frame is that there's little give, everything's got to be right first time or the set just shakes itself apart."

Galba had also noticed this. "Ideas?"

"A few. I'll get Old Sibius on it, I think it's a sequence problem. The benches need reordering so the back clasp gets fitted earlier."

"If you are going to do that, I want you to make a few other changes. That whole lower inner-outer plate overlap, ditch the rivets. Just tie the inner hanging segments and make fast to the outer, riveted, sisters."

"Sibius will do his nut."

"It will save a lot of time and you can tell Old Sibius that if the sets actually come back from over the river, he can do them all properly then, but only then. For now, it is cheap and cheerful leather ties. Tell the release fitter to communicate the changes, when the time comes, so at least each tent head knows what the ties are. You know Legionaries, they'll fiddle with the bows if bored or they think personal adaptations can make equipment betterer."

"Had porridge, Boss?"

"Nah, later. Have you looked in on our sharps, boy? Thought not. Come on, time to face our crimes." Lulla passed his bowl through the weapons receipt point and followed his Chief Armourer. They walked around the building and the grinding, whirring noise of the whetstone got louder. At the back of the Armoury, both men first saw the guard that had been stationed there following attacks on the continual nature of the great wheel by sleep-deprived Line Legionaries billeted nearby. Behind the guard, perched on a high stool, an assistant working a handle kept the great circle of quartz turning.

Next to the turner, Armourer Cadet Briscos had a gladius held in his right hand, holding down the blade with the left onto the rotating stone, sparks flying occasionally. Sharpening has its own music as the angles scraped out tunes whining up and down the scale. Cadet Briscos didn't acknowledge his superiors, his mind was far, far away, eyes looking on to a different landscape.

Galba picked up a blade from the 'done' pile – perfect work, razor edge, no chips, minimum wastage. On the other side of the great whetstone was the morning's 'to do' pile: gladius', daggers, pilum points and arrow heads.

"How long's he been going?"

Lulla looked sheepish.

"He's got that knack, in the groove. Shame to interrupt…"

"Not a single break? Has he eaten anything?"

"He's had a drink, I'm pretty sure of that. Otherwise, he'd be dead."

Galba made his way in front of the wheel and said loudly: "Armourer Cadet Briscos, you are doing a fine job there I see."

The Cadet didn't flinch, just worked the gladius side to side, the assistant pumping his arm on the handle.

"Briscos, how are you doing? Do you want a break?"

Briscos moved, the blade came off the whetstone to be efficiently placed on to the pile to the Cadet's right. Turning back to the wheel Cadet Briscos held open a hand to the left, all the time eyes fixed forward, down towards the sharpening target on the turning stone. The assistant paused, having heard the chief's questions, holding a new, blunt sword freshly de-coated of storage wax and looked at the Chief Centurion awaiting guidance. Briscos just sat there, eyes locked at the wheel, the stone turning quietly on its own momentum, with his left arm held out.

"Cadet Briscos, do you need to stop?" Nothing.

"Vulcan has him!"

"Shut up, boy!" hissed Lulla to the assistant.

The Chief Armourer looked at the assistant and then looked at Workshop.

'Ah, thats how it was.'

Just an exhausted mind? Perhaps.

"Give him the blade." Galba muttered.

Taken, it was placed immediately, grinding and screeching, a ladle of water poured over the wheel by the assistant who then went back to turning. Backwards and forwards the edge went.

"Lulla?"

"You've seen it, Boss, don't tell me you haven't. Sometimes the forge takes one of us!"

The best armourers had an obsessive nature and tiredness, stress and the attraction of letting your mind go blank of all of life's problems other than the double clasp in front of you was a lure for a certain type of person. Galba looked again at Cadet Briscos, glazed eyed running the new blade at a high angle.

'Or maybe Vulcan does come for some of us,' Galba thought.

Afternoon, aided by the clanging iron triangle, brought the entire XXXth Legion together for formation manoeuvres using the newly selected Cornicifers with their horns. The SC was in his element, i.e. it was a bloody disaster. "A sharp, a fucking sharp, like this…"

A blare from the Centurion's horn which he carried in a fist menacingly, "…but even if you pack of cow-fucking rural morons though it was a flat, which it was, why were you all shuffling left? No? No idea? Seventh Cohort, why are you trying to hump Third Cohort? No idea either. Well, this is the guide – follow the Senior Cohort even if they are doing the wrong thing. Tribune of the Third Cohort, were you doing the right thing or the wrong thing? Would you like a clue, Sir?"

The Tribune mumbled.

"Well why didn't you do the right thing, Sir, if you knew? Let's try again. Avanti!"

Meanwhile, inside the administration block, First Spear sat with his Optios, clerks, 'Cookie' and 'Rolls', the head baker. Even with the fish and supplies coming in from the village's headman they were coming close to being all out, four more days were all the food the XXXth had, stores now run down to keep the men working and training. Felix also nonchalantly asked if the old ice store was now completely empty of flour sacks. Rolls confirmed he'd checked it that morning and given the floor a good clean.

The FS nodded a thanks with a motion of the hand, which was returned, then made a last review of the consumables tablet.

"Full rations tomorrow, breakfast the next morning and the rest of the flour gets put into marching rations."

Closed the meeting.

The penultimate night before E-day came for the XXXth. Now the punishment details were reserved only for the stubbornly lazy and stupid – Seventh Cohort in the main – but the First Spear instructed all defaulters would be set just to QA testing during the night on the parade hill, no floggings at this juncture. Tribunes' Mess commenced early in the admin block while the men ate fish stew – a good day on the boats – in their barracks. The sound of fights and singing from the river people's camp outside alternated as reliably as the seasons, the dink of small hammers and the turn of the whetstone all now the familiar sound of Brigetio Fort. At the end of mess, three Tribunes and prince Herminaz took wine outside the administration block where a small concert had been arranged for them. The SC and two of his Optios also came outside, joining their offices to listen and nodded thanks for the offered wine.

"The First Speeear busy tonight, Senior Centurion?"

SC just nodded with a flat "Sir," in response.

The new legion band started up.

'Etruscan Hills' was pretty good, depressing as it should be. 'Monkey Trousers' was getting better even if only manageable at half speed. The SC had put a total ban on 'The Sweet Tulips of Persia' three bars into the morning's go at it, threatening to castrate the entire ensemble if he ever heard another note being played by them.

After a few more songs an interval in the music was had during which the Lead Tribune made commands and the appropriate Cornicifers blew manoeuvre signals with accompanying responses made back. The new, Lead Cornicifer all the while sweating like a Sicilian nightclub soloist in August, as each order was thrown at him. Barely a mistake, though, although the 'bloody Seventh' horn player hoarded most of them. The interlude even got a polite round of applause, although not from the SC who just bored his eyes, like ballista bolts, into those he judged to be 'lacking aural proficiency' (read: 'fucking shithouse!').

The concert restarted with a medley, arranged by the musical Tribune also conducting, of the Legion songs from each organisation that had contributed men to the XXXth, except, of course, 'The Sweet Tulips of Persia'. 'Sulla Owyn' for the XIIIth, 'Apollonius' for the XIth and 'My Mother's Garden' for the VIth amongst others.

Hearing familiar tunes, the men of the Legion slipped out from their barracks or tents, ones and two then whole eights as the concert went on, all standing in the parade ground's dark at a respectful distance listening. Oh so discreetly, the SC ordered a certain amount of wine to be broken from stores and handed around. With each song, the men sang the words softly, not the marching lyrics, but the real ones. Some of the Scarfs shed a tear, Noscarfs learnt the words to new tunes as they hummed uncertainly, soaking in the traditions.

No one bickered or fought, the men gravitating to friends new and old, mostly staying in their new eights, the SC noted with approval. Even the punishment duties had stopped running the hill and watched, an SC Optio caught his boss's eye who gave a nod that defaulters should get a cup of wine. Some of the younger boys looked around for missing tentmates but were hushed up by the older ones. At the medley's conclusion, the SC turned to Lead Tribune:

"Last day tomorrow, Sir, best to bed but how about we go for a chat first?"

"Of cooourse. Whaaaat's wrong, Senior Centurion?"

"Nothing. I didn't mean you and me. I think you call it 'mingling', Sir." And he pointed to the Legionaries drinking and laughing in the parade square.

"You meeeean, chat with…the meeen?"

"Sir."

The Tribune, to be fair to him, took on the novel idea, filled his cup and grabbed a large skin from a mess attendant to do refills. Whether he could fight was still to be seen but the patrician certainly knew how a drinks party should work, the SC thought. The Senior Centurion did the same and walked into a group of the Seventh, no shouting or berating; "Get this down you, boys, now who's a 'Green' and who's a prick?". The Centurion exchanged good-natured racing banter with the Legionaries. No place better to be right now, he thought.

Out in the open air with the men, not messing about in the fucking dark.

In the sweltering, oil lamp lit, evening-Armoury, Galba was hammering a rivet into a shoulder segment. He scowled watching Menicitrix and then one of Lulla's workshop team slip out. He could have stopped them going. Old Sibius sauntered over to the wide trestle and joined the Head Armourer. Instead of pointing out why his chief was doing it all wrong Sibius pulled up a high stool and poured two cups of watered wine. Galba took one and they drank. Sibius stole a glance as another Armourer passed on his work to a Cadet and quietly left the room.

Galba eyed the old man. "You never got the touch, Senior Armourer?"

Old Sibius made a snorting laugh. "Ha! Three times, but that's not for us. Not for real armourers. Don't need to tell me anything about dark sweaty rooms and fire. A real Armourer should always be doing."

"Surprised I'm still here?" Galba asked, permitting further comment.

Old Sibius just looked at him. "No, no, Centurion Chief Armourer, I am not. You…are a real Armourer, you're just not a craftsman. You could be but you chose not to."

"That why you don't like me?" tiredness made him petulant.

Old Sibius turned his cup. "I love you, boy, known you since you were a little Cadet. Just…you should be better."

Both men stared uncomfortably at their beakers.

"Anyway, enough of that. Back to work…Cadet Galba."

And the old man hobbled off to annoy a group of last stage helmet assemblers.

Galba felt a knot of…then picked up his hammer and – why not? – focussed in and bounce hit each rivet dead centre with a little extra care.

The senior baker crept down dank, cold steps towards the reserve ice store. He'd overseen clearing it of grain bags himself, ignoring the under-bakers whining about why they "'ad to move everything as easier darn' 'ere than over t'side." Rolls'd told the lad to get on with it then washed the floor himself, after morning ovens – that was his pleasure and service.

At the bottom of the stone-flagged flight, Rolls peered across a colannaded basement vault. A sole grill providing the only light from an evening sky. As the baker's irises swelled a shape emerged in the gloom, a dark, red-robed figure waiting by a shadowy portal across the way. Hunched into the ice store opening, itself. The creature wore an all-white mask of a man's face with two gold eyes, half-cut to see out of. Rolls crooked his finger and stood still.

"Who are you, stranger?" the masked figure asked.

"I am a soldier, striving along the road."

"Pass, friend."

The baker approached the strange sentinel and passed into the dark portal behind.

The shape of Centurion Alba was waiting in the shadows for his turn, a few other shades were also lurking around the pillars of the basement, the approach always needing to be made alone.

No one else moved so Alba pulled his hood up and made towards the ice store. "Who are you, stranger?"

"I am a Lion, wreathed in thunder."

"Pass, friend."

Alba tried not to realise who the gatekeeper was, but he recognised him. The pleasing thought that this was to be run like one of the old, proper lodges was not something that could be fully suppressed, Alba smiled, despite himself, on entering the black. The keeper of the door, one of the lowliest of services, was a Legion superior rank.

Next the FCL of the veterans appeared. "I am a Persian, moon sickled."

One of the four Tribunes, a new initiate inducted by his uncle in Rome.

"I am a raven, I hold the cup ready to be filled with light."

An Optio.

"I am the bridegroom, veiled you cannot see me but know me by the ringing of a bell."

All were greeted as 'friend' and when no more came, as the tenth hour sounded from beats of a triangle way above in the watchtower, Felix took one last look into the shadows and, satisfied, bolted the door before making his way to the doorkeeper's bench seat.

Inside the stone benched, rectangular chamber two small candles to allow seating were extinguished by a black gloved hand and about thirty men sat in complete darkness, silent for many heartbeats.

A lone, low, steady voice asked a slow question. "Where are you?"

Thirty or so answered in unison. *"I am lost in the dark."*

"Where does the dark abide?"

"In the night of the world, in my heart I give succour to the dark."

"Are you one who wishes to reside in such a state, to give comfort to endless night?"

"No, I am one who seeks the light."

"Will you take the light?"

"No, it must be given by he who has it within his gift. Through rebirth old night shall be banished, made anew through the lightbringer."

"And what will you do with this light?"

"I shall use it for the sowing of life, it feeds the running river of brotherhood, feeds the grasses and the oxen of the plains."

"Can you be given this light as a man?"

"No, light can only be given to 'we', a brotherhood, together as streams running to a great river."

"Are you ready for such a commitment, to receive this light of brotherhood?"

"We know not this; it is in the gift of he who holds the light but we pledge to strive for the gift."

A long pause.

Alba waited on tenterhooks, squashed between an artilleryman and one of his own Cohort Legionaries.

Old lodges could just end there, right now. A signal to the masked gatekeeper and the door could be flung open for the assembled to leave and reflect on their failure to be granted the ritual of light, of assembly. Old lodges sometimes deemed the meeting unworthy or unready.

It depended on the Father.

All was still silence in the tomb sealed, dark confines. Breathing fell in step, not a shuffle or scuffle. The slight warmth of the man next to you on a hard stone seat.

Flames suddenly shot up as oil-soaked braziers erupted in yellow-white fire, sparks of burning light and blue sparks burst at all points in the room, the assembled men shielded their eyes with arms, trying to look at the light they had asked for, to look at the figure before them. A solid golden sun mask, a red Phrygian cap, body wrapped in a long blue, silver starred cloak. Mirthas had come to them this night.

"Brothers, here is light! Behold the world, behold hope. Men of the XXXth Legion's lodge, a beginning!"

And the hymn was sung, low and deep, high and pure, voices winding together like tributaries. Flagons of the legions last wine now passed around by black-hooded 'Ravens'.

At the plainsong's rumbling end the Father stood at the head of the chamber robed in stars, the golden mask of the sun looking at each and every one of them, before speaking.

"Brothers, as is fitting for the birth of this new lodge of our Lightbringer, I bid welcome to new Initiates." A clap of the hands like thunder, green sparks crackled up from the braziers. Alba grinned taking a swig of red, this was going to be fun (as well as poignant with meaning, of course).

The gatekeeper moved from his seat to a different, side, door and unbolted it. Three naked, shivering men were led out by him, each blindfolded. Terrified Noscarfs who had not the first idea what was going on – other than being given a 'tap' to be somewhere at a certain time, muttered to them at some point during mess, or on the side of a hill or inside a sweating tortoise. Only one seemed to have any composure and Alba was glad to see it was his red-headed, new Signifier.

"We begin the trial of welcome!"

The room returned to a not particularly hospitable pitch black.

Dawn broke on the last day before Embarkation. Up high, Guns perched on the wheel head of an Onager, half watching men creep out of the old ice store steps back to their barracks in ones and twos. He then deliberately turned away and watched the sun come up, cutting garlic cloves into slivers and placing them onto his tongue. The artilleryman half smiled hammering a peg in, he was pretty sure the sunrise didn't need any encouragement from half-pissed fools with a rolled-up tunic. Admire the work, that was all that mattered. He did like a funny red hat, though, Guns thought with a chuckle.

Chapter Thirty-Eight

The Infiltrati over the river
Late summer's morning, some cloud.
Border country

Point struggled for breaths, gasping and clawing at the swimming horse's harness strap. The scout's head suddenly dunked under the dark water as the Auxilia mount was dragged downwards by a fierce eddy, side strapped man thrashed the river trying to get half a nostril above surface. In the green, gritty murk Point tried to hold a breath but the air was smacked out from his lungs by an undulating, equine shoulder. A thick Gaulish hand grabbed the scout's hair, yanking the breathing parts of Point back to the choking surface. That was the last drowning. A few grateful breaths later the red bey horse juddered, hitting the bottom of a steeply inclining riverbed, before rising from the Danube and making shore.

The Auxilia rider made straight for the north bank treeline and, once under cover, the cavalryman cut two straps, dropping Point to the floor where he immediately went prone under a bush. Hardly stopping the Auxilia kept riding, coming out into an exposed glade half a stade on, then making a great show of circling to wait for the rest of his squadron. One by one each cavalryman did the same, emerging from the water then releasing their slung Infiltration Operator before moving away at a gallop to the open grass where, once assembled, the squadron then rode off noisily with brightly coloured pennants waving. All just like another scheduled river crossing, the Gauls pulling attention and shadow units away from the Infil team as they galloped off in a wide circuit.

Point worked his way around the little wood's immediate perimeter in crouched bursts. The Infiltrator Immunes were about three miles downstream from the fort, over on the opposite bank, by 'Silver Route'. The idea was to work this insertion route up into the hills first, snaking back to do 'Gold' with a final push up marking 'Bronze's' cart road upstream.

The Skipper made a two-tone whistle of the wood lark, hand signals came back from various areas of scrub, hollows and trees around him checking-in. They were all there, no one left for the fish or carried away by the cavalry in a fit of enthusiasm. Point signalled back to Skipper that all was fine and a con-fab was had on what next.

Huddled in, Point, Skipper and Two agreed the plan was good and the Infil team moved two hundred strides downstream keeping to the treeline, parallel with the main river path. The eight stalked quietly but quickly, Point higher up on the bank slope and forward of the little force. Nothing exciting was encountered and soon 'Big Oak' was seen, the shoreside starting waypoint for 'Silver Route' all hung in superstitious ribbons and carved swirls. For five hundred beats they waited, in the gorse behind the great tree, scanning each way.

"Go!" instructed the Skipper: Five and Six scuttled over the road and hammered one of the larger, white stakes from their packs into the riverside bank. It went in deep so just the square, lime painted head was showing. The stave only needed to be there for a day and hopefully it would be missed by those not looking for it. Back over the dirt road Skipper himself drove another stake into the embankment, along the path from the oak to 'open' up the winding tinker track. With the entry pegs in, up the hillside went Infil team, following the small trade path which was now becoming 'Silver Route' with each white stick marker pushed into the ground at two hundred pace intervals. The Immunes only paused to jump off the track for a girl herding geese, the Romans lying stock still, so close to the path Four could have reached out and stroked a grey-dappled, white wing.

Despite the goose-girl quick work was made, sticks planted for several miles until Infil suddenly dropped down at a signal from their Point. Crawling forward to the scout, Skipper sighted hostile warriors on a packed mud clearing ahead. About fifty local levies, and the same again in armoured mercenaries of an indeterminate but well-armed nature, all holding weapons the right way round. Point glimpsed a feathered head and nudged his Skipper: Roxalani irregulars at the rear. The women were nestled like evil deer behind a thicket of roughly cut, levy spears. Both Infiltrators watched quietly until the Sarmatian women abruptly turned their mounts and galloped away into the forest's shadows, hopefully off to chase the Roman Auxilia decoys that were now supposed to be ranging deep into the north hills.

The Infil team sat in cover observing the levies' construction of a roadblock. This piece of ground formed a junction where the tinkers' path from the river joined one of the main commercial tracks. Carts were being upturned for barricades with the local spearmen running around hauling fresh cut branches out of the treeline to pile up on the wagons. Whoever was running these, less than friendly, Macromanni had worked out what was going to happen next. 'E' day obviously wasn't much of a secret. Possibly the small armada of boats piled up on the Brigetio dock gave it away.

Either way the team were three miles still to go marking Silver, as per the First Spear's instructions/suggestions. The Skipper made hand signals and Infil melted eastward into a wide loop. Crawling and dashing in twos until they came well up behind the barricade on the northern road. More sticks pushed into mud, on the eight went for hours, making the assembly area's wooded edge well after noon. In the blazing summer light, Skipper scanned a huge open plain with a derelict farmhouse at its centre – the broken-down old dwelling was where the three routes of march would converge before making a legion-strength push against the conurbations now visible to the north.

The area seemed very 'busy' Skipper concluded to himself.

Following a quick exchange of views the Infil team crawled flat out of the cover then, very slowly, slithered through the long grasses of the huge meadow stopping to spot riders, civilians and local infantry moving about in the distance at all points. Getting off the exposed meadow took hours on the stomach before they reached the central ruin. Once there, Skipper had the team slip one by one into the burnt-out farm, crawling under black beams to slide up against the remaining baked walls of the long rectangular structure.

"Take a breather, everyone," Skipper instructed.

Point climbed up high on to a couple of remaining rafters and was edging around old, scorched turf for a shufty. As the scout observed, below him rations were being eaten, liquid taken on and compulsory aniseed sweats sucked. Up in his eyrie Point took a passed-up biscuit and surveyed the plain, nibbling. Off to the north he could just make out the main target, the Macromanni town with its thatched yellow roofs shining in the afternoon sun. All around the resting team stuff was happening, but none of it the usual farming stuff you'd expect.

"Point?"

"Lot of movement, Skip, none of it good, but none of it is coming our way."

"Wait until dark, Sir?" said Two, crouching in what must have been the old fire hole, sipping at a leather flask. It didn't much sound like a question and the Tribune eyed him, before popping a boiled sweet into his own mouth. "Clock's dripping. Thoughts, everyone?"

'Can't move about in daylight with all these goings on, Sir' was the consensus.

"Alright, fair enough. We've marked Silver, gentlemen, but still got a lot to do. How about this – rest for a few hours then we go again at dusk, just when they like having their sausage?"

Two glared back. "And if they're not having their sausage, Sir?"

"Well, we'll probably end up joining them for sausage, but we'll be in the sausage."

As the sun lowered, the Tribune climbed up to Point, still wedged in the roof beams, and officer and scout began to look at shadows plotting a safe course through the plain-grasses towards Gold's exit. Once at that track-mouth, Gold exit could just now be seen at the meadows edge, the team would then have to quickly weave back to the Danube's shore, working all through the night without rest.

"Come on then, time to get marking," the Team Skipper quietly announced to those below.

Usual grumbles - "Don't all roads lead to Rome?" "What's the point? First Spear couldn't find his arse-sponge even if it was stuck up his arse." - as the Infiltrati packed up ready for fun at night.

Chapter Thirty-Nine

Reception room, Governor's Administration building, Aquincum
Very warm in the daytime, river stinks
Pannonia Inferior Province of Rome.

Both new arrivals to town entered the office. The patrician civil servant had quickly toga'd-up having ridden into Aquincum at first light, and now made a minor adjustment to the garment's fall as he surveyed the proceedings before him. A hive of buzzing activity within a very nice, large, sunlit – yet cool – room on the main floor of the principle administrative level. And not just on the principal level but actually adjacent to the Governor's office of Pannonia Inferior. This room, any Imperial civil servant knew, was always referred to as 'the work room', as opposed to the Governor's office itself which was designated 'the playroom'. The amusing shorthand was a private navigation aide for the Empire's organisers if one were to walk into any official complex across the Empire and needed directions from a local colleague. It seemed the 'work room' was currently being run by a private firm of Alexandrian merchants.

'Novel, yet somehow unsurprising!' thought Scipio, surveying all the activity.

"Dear Lady, I heard you were in a spot of bother, but I rejoice that the news of your demise is greatly exaggerated! Perhaps I misunderstood 'your demise' for your new 'demesne'?" Scipio thought that was rather good.

The Lady Lassalia looked up from bending over Eleazar's shoulder and gave a hard stare towards the room's unexpected entrant.

"I ain't dead, Scipio."

"And in robust funds, I am led to understand. Rejoice, rejoice!"

The Lady Lassalia never wasted her breath on retorts like *'No thanks to you!'* just stored experiences for future action.

"We get by, all in the sodding service of the Emperor, eh?" she quipped, getting a snigger from the government staff who were enjoying the new management's moments of outrageousness, if not the continual in-detail examination of what they were supposed to be doing. Staff numbers had thinned in the previous weeks.

"Fuck, yes!" the Scipio replied, not wanting to relinquish his usual role as most risqué member of any group, but it sounded a bit too affected, which annoyed the civil servant as he said it.

The Lady Lassalia stood to her full imposing height, jangling as she did so, and took a cloth to wipe ink stains off her hands and an extremely expensive plum stola.

"What are you doing here, Scipio? Salona run out of snails and oysters?"

He loved her crassness. "I'm here to rescue you!"

"A little tall for a Legionary, aren't you? I've become quite an expert on such things, did you know that following my survey for kit purposes the average height for…"

"Bored. How's our Legion?"

"Which one? The House of Sadiki has got a whole swathe of the bloody things on the books now. IInd, IVth, XIth…"

"Now you are just showing off, Sobe!" but the Scipio considered the Lady's update. He'd rushed here because of reports she was imprisoned and the logistical situation had become impossible, the whole of the frontier about to slide into ruin. It actually turned out she was un-imprisoned and now overseeing the whole logistical situation.

"Right you are though, my Lady. How are things…generally, then?"

"Much improved, penpusher!" growled a menacing male voice.

Silhouetted by the morning sun a large, armoured figure flanked by a more jittery offering rose from a round desk at the work room's far corner and turned towards the new entrants. "Now…" the menacing silhouette growled "…do you mind telling me who you two are and how you got in here before I slap you in a cell for espionage?"

Scipio was delighted by this.

"General, I hope you are well. I am Aulus Pallo Scipio, forgive me, I hadn't realised it was you. As for espionage, obviously enforceability is all context."

'That was funny,' Scipio thought and he laughed before also greeting the slighter backlit outline next to the IInd's General.

"And a good morning to you, Lord, we met of course in Rome. How are things with you?"

"Scips! I'm a blooming magistrate! A job!"

"Your uncle, I know, will be delighted."

Lady Lassalia had gone back to looking at Eleazar's views on local timber 'spillage'. There was one thing to be said for a private-public sector partnership, being able to dispatch a maniple of fully armoured Legionaries to resolve supplier disputes was faster than the courts. As she read the notes,

"It is, as usual, lovely to see you, Scipio, but we have work to do. In answer to your question on how things are going…"

"Which the good General is, I am sure, about to succinctly answer…"

The Patrician was loving every moment of this. Sobe continued while reading, not looking up. "…is that everything's fine, we've stripped out all the bollocks, got these buggers incentivised…"

A glazed nail flicked a grade III round the ear. The clerk started, but then grinned with pleasure in front of his shiny new golden stylus and goblet before him on the desk.

"…and the whole sector will be up to full strength shortly, and by full strength I mean actual, real, full strength rather than this bullshit."

The Alexandrian merchant lifted a wax tablet full of numbers from the GIII Scribe and waved the denotations suspiciously from between two fingers.

"In two weeks, the western road trains start coming through."

Scipio looked at the General for confirmation. "What the Lady says."

"Haha, brilliant!" the Hedgehog usefully added.

"And the XXXth Legion?" came a new voice from the doorway behind the Scipio, the speaker's crisp white toga fitted perfectly by the type of aides often employed by those who had worn a hessian sack during their formative years.

The General squinted, then made a salute.

"Decimius Terentius Scaurianus, greetings, last Pro-Consul."

"General." Scauri returned.

Polite half bows.

Lassalia decided this exchange merited a break from logging and stared over at the compact, grey-haired man who looked as if he should be wearing a well-made builder's jacket rather than a dazzling white rug. She did, however, also notice the bands of purple at the sheet's edge and decided the 'bloke' was worth knowing.

"Anyone going to introduce me? Where are your manners, boys?"

The Scipio fell back on series of measured, didactic movements hammered into him a few decades ago under some olive trees.

"Forgive us. Lady Sobe Lassalia of the House of Sadiki, may I introduce you to Decimus…"

"Yeah, I got that bit, but who are you?"

'Last Pro-Consul'
Eleazar tried to whisper a warning.

"Your Boss?" Scaurianus answered neutrally while searching through his exceptional memory of contractor dockets (he had most of the originals kept in crates at home, much to the annoyance of his wife, 'just in case' he ever needed to refer to exactly how much clay cost in Numidia fifteen years ago, in spring.)

Lassalia decided to poke. "Improbable but go on."

"I am the Senior Legate of the XXXth. You are my supplier."

"And you're a bit late to the party, aren't you, sunshine?"

The Scipio coughed. "My dear, the man in front of you has just been the year's Pro-consul of Rome."

"I don't follow politics."

Scaurianus wasn't offended, she was right. He was late.

"Anyway, it's sweet, we have two Generals now, you'll have someone to play with, big boy," the Lady Lassalia addressing the last comment to the Sector Commander, a long defeated and assimilated province of the House of Sadiki.

Before the IInd's General had a chance to respond *'yes, my Lady',* Scaurianus needed to clear up the continual misunderstanding.

"I am not a General."

This got a searching glance from the General of the IInd, who'd been girding himself for an argument about 'Independent Command' with, probably, a direct equal. Scaurianus was not a Sector Commander but being a General who was one of the last Pro-consuls, well…it was a fine balance of Imperium. Except, apparently, the notorious social climber wasn't a General.

Scipio wanted to gloss over this bit of the detail.

"It's a long story I'm sure the IInd's Legate does not want to go into…" *'Oh yes, 'he' very much did'*

"…suffice to say honoured Scaurianus is Acting Commander of the XXXth Legio, on the way to his Legion right now."

"Who is the XXXth's General, then?" The General asked, eying the General who apparently wasn't a General, thinking hard while he waited for an answer.

Scipio moved things along. "We heard there were some supply issues…"

Lassalia signalled for wine to be poured by a civil servant, a man whose duties had been assessed and redefined as appropriate to ability in the early days of the mass, Sadiki, secondment to the Governor's office. Taking a drink, Sobe spoke,

"There were logistical issues, but solutions have not just been found, but enacted."

Scaurianus took a goblet but didn't drink.

"We rushed here…" he began, ignoring the snort from Lassalia. "As our understanding was that the new Legio's season-consumables, all of them, had been confiscated by Sector Command. Even though, as I'm sure the General of the IInd Adiutrix has previously been acquainted with, the XXXth holds an independent jurisdiction on the border."

An uncomfortable pause as the General of the IInd Adiutrix felt no particular need to confirm what he was or wasn't acquainted with.

"Did the House of Sadiki have some delays, perhaps?" Scipio asked in a measured, concerned manner to the Lady Lassalia.

"We delivered to the XXXth on time and in full."

The two Military Legates' eyes were moving to lock.

"Where's the Governor?" demanded Scaurianus.

Lady Lassalia waved her hand, batting away the point as immaterial.

"Honoured Governor's having a whale of a time supervising the construction of a new villa."

"It's got a massive, massive pond. More like a lake. For fish, one of those big catfish is the plan. Who's going to catch it? I don't know, not me. Crikey!"

Sobe smiled indulgently, "It is a very, very big pond, Ulpia Mako, isn't it? But back to current affairs: as I said earlier, commercially things are starting to pick up here in…er…? Sod it…", she clicked her fingers and frowned.

'Aquincum' muttered First Secretary Eleazar from the desk, fulfilling his role as comedy straight man.

Scaurianus processed the information and evasions from the House of Sadiki. The ex-consul also took in the presence of the Emperor's Nephew. Indeed, he'd noted, it was 'the other one', Imperial-nephew-wise.

'Always start with a solid, simple foundation' Scaurianus thought: "Are my men being fed?"

Sobe Lassalia knew the next moment would need to be managed. "Have you eaten yourself, Legate? You look like a man who needs some sugar, have a date." She waved for dates to be brought and continued:

"All the various problems are being sorted. All is in hand, there was a supply bump but now it's all being flattened out."

The ex-consul knew there would be a lot of 'detail' behind this statement but pushed on: "Well then, am I to understand that Brigetio Fort has now been supplied with a season's worth of food?"

"No. But that's a good thing."

"No? Is it now?" the Legate replied levelly at Sobe. "Because I am a very stupid person tell me, how then, is it that the supply problem is 'sorted'. Explain it to me, O' supplier of mine?"

She flashed back a complicated half-smile.

"Because, while initially the XXXth were prevented from being supplied, now we can supply them, I don't want them supplied."

Legate Scaurianus set his face into a dangerous, not very indulgent smile.

Lady Sobe Lassalia responded by becoming very tall.

Scipio, fascinated by the exchange, was put in mind of his father's story about when Caligula released leopards at a dinner party: shocking, random and involving fierce dangerous creatures confined in a single space.

The civil servant drew a reflective breath and decided he wanted in on the fun.

"Perhaps you might provide a few nuances to us public sector rubes, My Lady?"

'You bloody know about this, Scipio.' Scaurianus realised, but didn't allow himself to get distracted, however, as he had just made another connection – a docket from long ago.

"I bought gravel from you once."

"Satisfied?"

"Yes."

'On time, to budget suppliers' stuck to the memory like honey.

"And because of that you get to explain your reasoning behind keeping supplies from eight thousand-odd men I'm responsible for, starving just a little way north of here, Merchant Sadiki." and the ex-Consul took a first sip of wine while waiting to discover what plan he'd just trodden in. It was good wine.

The Lady Lassalia had someone clap their hands and the room cleared of administrators other than her own, then she shouted a name at the top of lungs which brought in someone new to this impromptu afternoon party.

"I believe this belongs to you." She beamed.

A slightly louche, smiling Optio sauntered in, wearing half a uniform, clutching a wine glass and tablets, "Morning, Lady, what's occuring?"

"Ruben! I think this is your Legate, not a General apparently, officer thingy."

The Optio in question followed Sobe's words and gaze, then in rapid series of movements disposed of all drinks and folders to a side table, snapping to shocked attention.

Scipio smiled; this was better than leopards.

"SIR!"

Scaurianus just closed his eyes. "Optio…?"

"Ruben, Sir. Recently of the VIIIth Augusta Augusta, now Senior Armourer Optio of the XXXth…designation yet to be affixed."

"Optio Ruben, a pleasure to meet the first of my command. I take it you are not a deserter?"

The Emperor's Nephew stepped in. "No, no, that's been clarified. He is definitely not a deserter, some people thought he might be but actually he is a loyal servant of the Emperor!" Ruben tried not to sag at this 'helpful' explanation.

"Well, I'm glad that needed to be clarified in my absence, Optio Ruben…no, don't, I don't want to know whatever the…whatever has been going on here…Just what IS going on here?"

Sobe's general tactic for life was never to answer questions directed to you, but be sure to answer all the ones that weren't.

"It's actually quite clever…"

"Oh, I have no doubt of that."

"Told you she was good."

"Shut up, Pallo."

"Yes, shut up, Scipio." Lassalia snapped, to the patrician's double delight.

"The XXXth has been without food while I have endeavoured to sort out a number of issues including temporary incarceration, mine that is, by what we shall term – an enemy of the Roman people."

"He's properly dead. Thwak, currrk!"

"Thank you, Imperial Nephew. Now I am near to solving the supply issues for the whole sector. So, to recap: the XXXth were illegally deprived of supplies until this enemy 'agent' was neutralised."

"That sounds like bullshit."

"It is honoured ex-Consul but go with it. The XXXth have been sending their little Tribunes and horsey-Gauls to us every few days whining for supplies and as of two days ago we could have delivered them."

"But you didn't."

"An opportunity has arisen. Last week, when one of those fresh-faced Senators' sons from the XXXth turned up in person, he got a bit hysterical and told us that without the supplies they would all starve."

"This is news?"

"No, but what the XXXth officer then revealed, or threatened us with, is. At first, I couldn't believe it: 'Initiative' in the Army! It turns out the industrious little men of...possibly your?...Legion have set about creating a fallback position. To quote said Tribune, but sped up a bit for convenience: 'If I don't get our food the XXXth will go north, across the river into Macromanni territory and forage the supplies ourselves.'"

The IInd's General took an involuntary breath in, he'd taken a lot of soothing by Sobe on this one. Scaurianus just about manged not to flinch. Sobe Lassalia continued to enjoy herself.

"Right now, the river down from Vindabona is essentially closed for normal merchant craft due to 'massive political instability', which means not really belonging to Rome anymore. The southern hills are also leaky with raiding horsemen or persons and only one in three overland caravans get through intact. But then your stranded men, full of this initiative-stuff, presented me with a solution. By not supplying the XXXth at Brigetio the entire Legion will attack north all of their own volition and consequently, if successful, secure all the supply routes needed to establish a proper bridgehead at the Dacian boarder out east. Who – the Dacians, I mean – have incidentally..." she turned to the IInd's General. "...have just woken up to the fact that one of their royal family is supplying the Roman Empire. Their king has now cut off that trade."

"Literally?" asked the sector commander.

Sobe thought about the head in the bag.

'Well, that loan can be effectively written off' was her comment to the horrified, now Second Secretary, Gallan who was holding open the courier sack this morning.

"Not much room for reopening negotiations, let's put it that way."

Sobe answered the IInd's General, but smiling hard at the ex-Consul.

"With Dacian consumables gone for good, everything now has to come from the Imperial trade routes. That means we need the rivers and roads to the northwest back under control."

Listening, Scaurianus wondered how exactly the province had ended up being run by the private sector. He once again tried clarification on this aspect.

"Tell me, Lady Lassalia, in-between choosing tiles for a new aquarium, what does the Governor think about a Roman force pushing over a treatied border – treatied by me personally as Pro-Consul, just as an incidental point of interest?"

"I'm sure if we asked him, the Governor would point out a Legion with independent something-or-other is not his responsibility. The XXXth acts autonomously I believe, isn't that right, General?"

"Completely correct, my Lady. If any of my Legions were to be deployed into Macromanni territory, it would get political."

Scaurianus stood up and prepared to get back out of his toga and into riding clothes.

"I'll be off then, thanks for the appraisal and the wine. Would love to stay but as the unfounded Legion I'm supposed to be in charge of is about to make an illegal crossing into Lower Germania, forgive me if I don't stay. Scipio, you are coming with me, as are you, Optio."

"Do I have to?"

"Sir."

"Yes, you do, I'll even call you 'the Scipio' if it helps. Optio, put a proper uniform on."

"Um, can I come? I think I probably should just…you know…help?"

"The presence of the Imperial Household is always welcome of course, Sir."

"Of course," added the Scipio supportively.

It was then that quiet shuffling from an outside corridor proceeded a new party slithering into the room – SOGI with the usual unintrusive entourage of SOGII, the Scribe and five Assyrians in tow. The Scipio barked a laugh.

"Hark, I hear the footsteps of not single spies…"

SOGI glared at the unknown patrician, marking the face down for 'follow up', and then, radiating importance, made for the IInd's General.

The General put up with silly whispering until he got the gist then cut the SOG Lead off. "Please share this news with all those assembled."

"But security clearance is…"

"I won't tell, darl."

"Do it!"

SOGI bristled but liked an audience.

"My network reports that an unidentified, large Roman force has crossed the northern border. We are working to ascertain who…"

"Dear Sobe, am I to understand that you didn't tell your brilliant plan to these gentlemen from intelligence?" Scipio enquired loudly of Lady Lassalia.

"Of course not."

"Excellent!" Scipio said laughing, clapping his hands, which earned him a second classic look of cold, professional, promised revenge from the SOG Lead.

Ex consul Scaurianus sat back down and closed his eyes for the third time, the IInd's General managed to find a new level of verbal derision for the head of intelligence, Hedgehog pulled a face at Optio Ruben with a 'Cripes!', Lassalia got up and shouted through the door, "Two more for lunch!"

Sobe then took a couch opposite ex-Consul Scaurianus, leaning forward. He, in turn, lifted his lids slowly and looked back, thinking.

"Tell me something good."

"You aren't going to be tried for treason, unless of course the XXXth get wiped out."

"Really? And how do you know that?"

"Because we really need to clear that northern border and get trade going."

"When has actual logic defended anyone from a Senate-backed trial relating to unlawful Legion movement? While I don't think Julius Caesar had just run out of turnips when he crossed the Alps, you can see my point?"

"Funny you should mention the Imperial combover…" (an Alexandrian joke that stuck) "…now don't get cross, I know you won't be tried for treason because I know why you are a Legate not a General."

"Do you now!" Scaurianus replied levelly, wondering if she was lying.

"I do, because I have recently become a significant supplier of very high-end luxury goods."

'Oh gods, she wasn't lying.'

"A one-off contract from Vindabona, on its way in just two weeks."

Big involuntary breath from the ex-Consul. *'Two weeks!'*

Scaurianus' thought process then started to hyperventilate through a sequence of:

'*Accurate? – most probably*'

'Q. *Why via Vindabona and not safe, Salona route?*

'*A. Speed and theatre.*'

Lady Lassalia was all about the calm: "Legate, please breath out. Good, well done. Here is what you should do: just stay put here in Aquincum town for a few days. If it all goes tits up over the border, then at least there's a bit of distance separating you from the Legion's antics."

"Your antics."

"Mine? Imagine! A woman influencing the Roman Army! Now: stay put, have lunch, go and sneer at the Governor's new monstrosity being built on the hill. Let half a week go by then we can all go and have a look at this fort of yours. You never know, you might be a conquering hero."

"Of an allied territory? I'll settle for not being an enemy of the state."

"Well, if it turns out you are an enemy of the state, you're still in a good place. King What's-His-Chops over the eastern bridge is practically giving gold away to treasonous Roman ex-citizens."

"Great." But internally the phrase *'Plausible deniability'* turned itself over in Scaurianus' mind. The fact was, there was no choice but to stay here and the woman knew that. The 'luxury goods' were apparently already scheduled to arrive at Brigetio from Pannonia Superior. Ready to make a grand entrance on to the Dacian frontier. The fact the entire route was a warzone seemed to have escaped the planners...or had it?

'Hmm.' The ex-Pro-Consul eyed the Scipio hard.

But then small quails stuffed with their own eggs began to arrive and so the ex-Consul ate, deciding he was all at sea in a tide of fate and deniability, plausible or not to be determined.

As the food bearers offered up their tempting morsels to all assembled SOGI circled the informal lunch menacingly towards the rude fop, Scipio himself seemingly oblivious to the approaching threat, chatting away merrily to the

Imperial Nephew on a divan. At just a few feet away the Patrician suddenly seemed to sense this dangerous presence and the Head of the Special Operations Group was gratified at a certain nervousness now apparent in the smug toff. SOG Lead loped forward out of the shadows and suggested to Mako he go get a drink. Hedgehog did what he was told leaving looming spy and reclined civil servant.

"I do wonder, who you think you are?"

SOGI liked a clever inverted phrase to leverage self-doubt.

"Well, Metes Sena Bathos, isn't that the nub of my being here?"

The civil servant's nervousness dropped like a sail, replaced by hard, blue-eyed assurance.

"I think we do need to have a long chat, you and I."

SOGI froze at the mention, out loud, of his real name. "How...?"

Scipio patted the cushions next to him, "Let us talk about that over this splendid lunch."

At a signal from their real boss, not the SOG Lead, the Assyrian guards left the convivial meal.

Chapter Forty

Out of Brigetio Fort
Summer heat rising and still
Roman border begins to push.

Embarkation day -I. At the exact moment the din of the midday triangle echoed away, the fading sound was joined by an unexpected, other, silence. The Armoury hammers suddenly arrested their ceaseless ringing and the whetstone's screech halted, causing the parade ground activities to halt in surprise.

"Knock the men off, Senior Centurion," Felix ordered, looking back at the Armoury wondering if the silence was a good or bad thing. Cornicifers sounded and the men of the XXXth were sent for rest and food while the FS gathered about him some Optios to go and investigate the dark forge rooms.

Outside on Brigetio beach the Exfil Tribune did not, however, halt his work cutting planks and tying stakes.

In a bog, way north over the river, the Infil team lay on their backs under water, sucking reeds. Above them a force of Macromanni levies and Roxolani horse crashed along Bronze Route, looking for small white sticks.

Back within the Fort, Cadet Briscos was gently helped off the whetstone wheel and brought inside where he was cradled by Lulla and Bullo. In the black, sweat-slick Armoury workshop Centurion Chief Armourer Galba brought everyone together, arm in arm they clasped each other. Senior Armourers, Armourers, Fitters, Carpenters and Cadets.

"Senior Armourer Sibius…" Galba croaked. "…Please lead us."

Old Sibius took black soot from the forge, mixing it with grease before covering his face.

"We thank you Vulcan…"

As the long prayer of the smith was intoned Sibius made a mark on each of the assembled Immunes' foreheads. The main double doors were softly shut, and the braziers extinguished. Then they slept, on benches, the floor, even hunched over sat on stools. This would also be one of the first legends of the XXXth: the *'forging of their own armour in just a day'*. Complete rubbish but also true.

First Spear Felix and his entourage of Optios had stopped short just outside the workshop doors and watching the ritual – of which he had no part of – knew that, against all odds, the Armoury's silence was a quiet denoting victory, not failure, and quietly walked away.

It was all about the right pace, a Legion, Felix knew, and now was time for a rest – even the clerks and Optios were idled. The last QA eights ran the hill before the final sixteen men of the unreliable Seventh Cohort donned their tried and tested armour, helmet and weapons.

Only the boatmen outside continued their work, but then they weren't crossing tomorrow.

Dusk saw the Fort slowly wake back up and the full Line detachments of the XXXth assembled, each man armoured, each man with a full weapon set. The four Tribunes stood on the wooden dais, the Command Centurions and Optios below, facing out. Ten full cohorts stood at perfect attention.

Lead Tribune stepped forward, the other three officers behind him holding wrapped bundles with sore, pinpricked hands.

A pause, then the officer began to speak.

"I have no Eaaagle, we aaaare not yet a Legion but I ask yooooou, each maaan, to do what needs to be done for the XXXth and Rooome. I offer theeese…"

With that, each Tribune behind the ranking officer released a cord and pulled away linen sleeves. Rectangles of bright orange cloth unravelled to be affixed to poles planted into the dais, the mark of 'XXX' stitched on to each hanging in white and black. Murmurs of Legionary approval whispered across the SC's square. The marching banners were simple but striking, the officers' embroidery circle had done an excellent job.

"Will yoooou follow me?"

'…we vow to bring the light together as one, in brotherhood, to steer, to guide the oxen to the stream…'

Rolls, the head baker stepped forward. "I will follow you, Sir!"

The veteran First Class Legionary of the Triarii stepped forward. "I will follow you, Sir!"

Then Alba, then Felix.

The redheaded Signifier of the First strode up to the dais's side and begged the Tribune for the Primus standard...

"Shoooould I give it to him?" shouted the Tribune across the cohorts, eyes wide in exaggerated indecision. Asking the men something was straight out of the histories and the officer was embracing the moment.

"YES, YES, YES!"

"Can I give this to him? Do you let me?"

'Give it 'im!' 'Now!' 'Do it!' screamed back Legionaries, almost hysterical.

The Senior Centurion knew this was all necessary and grudgingly allowed the 'enthusiasm' to continue unchecked, staring forward as various Centurions eyed him as to whether hitting should begin.

The Tribune leant down and offered Red a hand, pulling him up onto the raised platform, then the officer knelt before the Noscarf and presented the Primus banner to the First Cohort's Signifier.

"Nice touch, the kneeling," Felix whispered to the SC standing next to him.

Red snatched it and raised the standard up as high as he could, holding the base of the pole.

"THIS IS THE XXXth! WE ARE THE XXXth! MARCH UNDER ME! MARCH WITH ME!"

"Confident lad you've got there, Centurion Alba."

First Cohort Centurion Alba grimaced back, eyes still fixed forward, "FS."

"Fucking carters," the SC muttered from Felix's other shoulder.

After several minutes, the SC had had enough and barked for quiet. Order was returned, ranks dressed perfectly. Cohort by cohort the Tribunes, First Spear and Senior Centurion walked the formations followed by Optios carrying large ceremonial boxes (fabricae crates still slightly sticky with red paint). Each 'half M' was now presented with their own bright orange banner, Cohort numeral picked out in white wool under the Legio number in black, proudly grasped by the chosen new Signifiers. Every single man of the XXXth was also spoken to and a length of bright orange scarf tied perfectly around his neck by the officers or Senior Centurions. It took hours but no one minded the wait, all of them stood gleaming. Each Legionary with his first, or new, orange scarf proudly knotted and tucked into his plate.

Scarfs issued, the XXXth came to ease at the SC's order, the Cornicifers fell out from their units and fell in with the command up on the dais with their instruments. Over the last ten days a little tune had ear-wormed its way over the wall from the river people working away outside. It told of the Catfish King who, one day, fell in love with a kingfisher girl. The song was jaunty, funny and ultimately melancholy. Perfect for a Legion tune, a new song for a new Legion and the SC had set it to brass perfectly with a two-step beat. Horns started up and the Legio anthem rang out for the first time as the sun set. The men were delighted by the surprise and quickly sang along to the lyrics, led by the SC, freshly translated into Latin by the pilots who had got the hang of local whirble.

After the fifth time through the song, marching lyrics naturally began to emerge in all their razor-sharp wit and licentiousness. Fell out, newly found wine from an old XIth crate was poured, and men and officers came together admiring shiny kit. The Noscarfs-no-longer preening in their attainment of full Legionary rank, excitedly talking about what the morning would bring.

Felix stretched and wandered to the Armoury doors; one was now half-open with the Chief Armourer in it.

"You look like you need a drink, Centurion Armourer?"

"Don't mind if I do, First Spear." Galba said, taking a cup from Felix and joining the FS outside.

"You know what, Chief Armourer Centurion?"

"I didn't fuck it up."

"You didn't fuck it up. Want a medallion?"

"With due respect, First Spear…"

"Don't tell me to fuck off, it'll spoil the moment. So, listen, tomorrow…"

"We're not going, are we?"

"No. Disappointed?"

"Yes, but we're a bit broken. Are you taking Guns?"

"Yes, and the Gunwagons. You, Galba, will be in command of the Fort. As of tomorrow, you are also a First Grade, equal to Alba. Congratulations, Chief Armourer Centurion, First Class."

"Can I still take the medallion instead?"

"Fuck off, Galba. Have another drink. Hello Alba! You seem to have lost your flame haired Signifier to command." Felix said to the approaching First Cohort Centurion, while looking at Red still standing on the dais, looking for all the world like a veteran Egyptian bannerman.

"I know, rising through the ranks, that lad. Have we got a dead badger or something we can stick on his head?"

"Got lots of fish but so far we've been lucky on the desertion rate and I'd like to keep it that way."

"Fair point, although if you don't mind, I'll take a borrow of him for tomorrow. Can I have some of that wine? Hey, Chief Armourer, this shit actually appears to be staying on!" Alba gestured at a passing Legionary's shoulder plates.

Felix stopped pouring. "That's Chief Armourer Centurion First Class to you, Alba."

"My apologies. This shit actually appears to be staying on, Brother Galba. Congratulations on the promotion! Quick by Army standards, but well-deserved." The three NCOs clinked beakers.

"Thank you…Alba."

Alba grinned, then grinned wider as another figure approached their group.

"Joining us, SC?"

"Go on then, fill me up. Well, I don't know what the young h'officers will do tomorrow but they can sew. Good speech as well. You tell him to say all that, First Spear?"

"Funnily enough, no. Just told him to keep under a sixth hour and make it about them."

"We legal, FS?"

"Probably not, SC."

"Fuck it. Rome likes a winner."

"We winners, SC?"

"Course we are, Centurion Alba. We're going to send the barbarians mad with the band. Now…" He raised a cup. "Up the Greens!"

"Fuck off, SC."

"Galba is now a Centurion First Class, as per our discussion, SC."

"Good. Still a Red team cheating-shite though, aren't you?"

"Always."

Felix finished his wine. "Right, I'm going to check in with the young Exfil Tribune on the pontoon. Do we still have lots of hemp for lifelines in the back store, newly appointed Centurion First Class?"

"Will have them ready and waiting, FS."

"Are we sending Seventh Cohort over the pontoon first, FS? You know, in case something...doesn't hold?" smiled Alba.

"Don't think we should deprive First Cohort of its position of honour, FS?"

"No SC, I don't think we should. Thank you for the offer to relinquish your just position, though, First Cohort Centurion."

"Bollocks, bloody Army," said Alba. They clinked beakers again to this.

Felix began to move towards the river gate.

"Get the lads tucked into bed soon, the real party's yet to come. SC, Alba: make sure you two get some sleep before nightfall, Exfil begins pontoon assembly at midnight. I'm staying up for it."

The last statement of intent didn't need to be followed with a formal order.

"First Spear."

Chapter Forty-One

Bronze Route, western cart track.
Dead of night, north of the Danube,
Marcomanni territory.

Midnight and the Infil team makes slow progress back south along the wide limestone track of Bronze Route. Silver ingress had been marked for the legionnaires, when Skipper's men were fresh, on the first day. Gold path had then been a challenge through the dense woods, but Westerly Bronze was a nightmare. Bogs, water, exposed positions and hostile shadows flickering everywhere like night-moths. The little white marker sticks going into the ground at only one an hour, now. Since sundown the team has lain stock still, half floating, half crouching in marsh grass and black peaty water. A cavalry patrol of the Roxolani, full feathers, lances and warpaint, trotting up and down the wide road with torches pinning the Romans in place.

"Crossing's not going to be much of a surprise." Two whispered from a wet clump of grey stalks for the fiftieth time. Waiting with them in the dark was the corpse of an overly inquisitive, drunken farmer who had been making his way back from the turf-inn for the last time. He'd taken a piss off the wrong section of duckboard. Just as the son of soil realised what he was pissing on, Six had pulled his legs out from under him and Two dragged the man down under the water before a sound could be made.

Precious hours passed until the clattering of Roxolani hooves faded, cautiously the Infil team began to crawl away through the marsh and move south again. Pushing white sticks into any earth firm enough to take the waypoint markers. The main stretch of cart road was eventually reached, still glowing against the black forest with the falling moons last light. Twice the team nearly wandered straight into sentries or moving troops but Bronze entry had to be 'opened' for their brother legionaries waiting at 'E', scheduled to start in just a few hours. Three miles north from the river Skipper slid out through a bush to scuttle across the open, stone chip road when he heard a loud jay chirp…at night. Fear, the Tribune froze perfectly still. Suddenly great crashes erupted from the undergrowth at all points around the Infil stick, a shout from Three behind him, hooves and sandals running at full pelt, cries of alarm in the dark.

"Shit! SCATTER!"

Chapter Forty-Two

In the darkness Alba's Cohort were led out from Brigetio's gates by Signifier 'Red' for the XXXth's first outing. Legionaries placed lit torches all along the bank from Brigetio to the pontoon construction area as they marched. The bridge's base area was, itself, marked with a large white pole a few hundred stadia downriver from the fortification. Bank path illuminated with a line of orange flame, the Gun and X boats then slipped their moorings and drifted to a midstream point a few lengths from the shore's pontoon-start marker, dropping anchors and driving tie up poles into the mud. Secured in place, the pilots removed tinders from dry boxes, nestled within waistcoats, and lit up a flare of torches on each catamaran's quarter.

Following just behind the two Exfil vessels, a small fleet of other boats pushed off from the Fort's quay ready to be cannibalised for the pontoon. Six craft steered to the north bank, ferrying the Fifth Cohort with them over the river to establish the far, currently phantom, bridgehead. On landing Fifth Cohort's Centurion made contact with a Gaulish Auxilia Decurion who appeared from the trees, the Legion's entire cavalry having been sent to sweep the area since dusk. Flushing out and pushing the enemy back from the immediate crossing point.

The first part of the XXXth's 'foraging in force' plan had begun: the creation of a jerry-built pontoon bridge from the embarkation white poles to the support craft moored midstream, then across to Fifth Cohort on the far bank. All at night and to be completed within hours.

Approaching the white start poles on south bank, Alba brings his Cohort to a halt and, looking about, clocks the great black shapes of onagers and heavy ballistae lurking back in the trees. Each hulking dark mass sits in its own pad cut out from the undergrowth by Immunes. The artillery pieces now waited, dark and brooding, overwatching the Exfiltration Immunes busy with the first vessels arriving. Lines were run out across the river by half naked men and women, shinning up newly piled posts to secure ropes. A lattice glistening with torch and moonlight quickly netted up across the Danube, allowing Exfil Legionaries supplemented by local river families to move about across the rushing dark river with feet on one line and hands grasping above on another.

The river folk went hard at it, heavy clinks of silver in their purses for the work and a gold piece each – promised later – to agree the dropping of internecine 'vendetta' for five days. Rhythmic clanging rang out from the Fort's triangle, striking the witching hour, and, as per the Exfil Tribune's schedule, the first large 'filler' craft were now floated down from the Fort. All in a strict sequence given the ragtag vessels available. Poled downstream came the repaired ferry from the attack two weeks before. Its new pilots worked hard breaking the huge, ungainly raft as they fought to coax it towards lanterns on the southern shore.

A sizeable craft, and flat decked, the ferry's allocated position as the southern bank's base vessel would, in theory, create a good platform for the rest of the night's work, but the proximity to the bank and the running, black-watered current sucked at the ungainly square boat too hungrily. For a painful half hour the Exfil Tribune and his men grappled with the raft-beast, men in the water, on lines, shouting, arms crushed, oxen eventually having to be brought up.

Back at the artillery line, First Spear looked on, his companion said nothing but handed the Senior NCO an onion. Felix took a bite. Eating it—good for you but brought on tears—seemed to sum up the nights endeavour more eloquently than any words.

"Long night," muttered Felix, eyes streaming despite his love of a barely digestible snack.

Guns pulled a face back in reply, thinking quietly, *'The night was the same length as it always was at this time of year.'* And watching the activity afore him, *'I could go and help the chaps with the ferry but best never to teach a fulcrum, you had to really feel it, and they were getting there…'*

Once the ferry was finally secured, bullied into place by lowing beasts, the main middle section was ordered down from the fort's quay by the wet and panting young boat officer. One of the confiscated (with silver and receipts) convoy river barges floated down to be caught by the picket boats and secured to deep, midstream posts. An Immunes catamaran took a series of stone anchors from the barge, then Lead Pilot coracled the weights back upstream to be dropped with heavy sloshes. Hopefully to stop the bloody great big conveyor from going anywhere.

Once happy that the conveyer had stopped moving about Exfil Tribune signalled for the filler vessels of the southern-end pontoon to be released. On Brigetio dock the Shore Master saw the lantern flashes from the east and began: the tottering stack of rafts, lashed canoes, barrel boats, fishing vessels of all descriptions ordered off the Fort jetties in a strict sequence. And the suspect bridge grew. As a pontoon it was a horror in Roman Army terms, but a masterpiece of ingenuity given what the XXXth had to work with. That's what Felix kept reassuring the junior Exfil 'Sir' with, anyway. A much-needed bulwark of confidence against the incessant, disparaging comments from the Senior Centurion over the last ten days.

"Not sure Horatio would have bothered guarding this 'creation', but you know best, I'm sure, Sir."

Soaked to the skin, the youthful Exfil Tribune in charge of the pontoon surveyed his work atop a spare stepladder. It did have a hump, but he'd known that, knew the temporary river bridge would have an incline upwards into the middle. By knowing the pontoon would be quite shit in advance, it made things better, he told himself. Possibly. Although not at all in the Senior Centurions eyes, the officer was pretty sure of.

Even arranging the sequence of boats carefully, a host of spacers had to be inserted everywhere to maintain some equilibrium for the deck planks. Up on his rattly ladder, the Exfil officer watched an Immunes and two river women jam bundles of woven sticks into gaps and mismatches. Once the hefty looking woman with strong thighs had finished stamping a small thicket between a raft and a barge, the other women – their Immunes Legionary was obviously 'supervising' – bucketed river water up to throw over the spacers in a vain attempt at fireproofing. If flame hit the 'The creation', as the SC liked to call the pontoon, the bridge would go up in a moment. With this fact in mind, Prince Herminaz and his Cherusci warriors were being entertained by a Tribune in the quietly locked officers' Mess: they would not leave the Fort unless under the specific instruction of First Spear Felix.

At around the second hour of the morning, there was an unexpected but welcome arrival to the bridge assembly site. The armourers appeared, all of them. Silently they went where they were sent, as technical men to set about solving problems but also to lash and heave with the best of them. Galba, in a simple tunic, worked on connecting the emerging southern section to the middle barge. His focus was to work off the strain of the still open pontoon, as each time the groaning end had to bear the increased weight of a new craft joining it. Soon a pulley system was rigged back to two halyards strung-hung at the bank from a hefty tree, bleeding away some of the current's strain and the pressure each new extension brought to the fragile posts.

As craft were secured to the end of the bridge, Armoury carpenters swarmed the already joined boats affixing deck planks. The Exfil Tribune was glad of these expert wood workers lending their exhausted, shattered sinews to the boatmen's efforts to rapidly form a gangway thousands of men could march over.

Hours of intense labour passed until the darkest of blue began to tinge the eastern hills. Pre-dawn and they were on schedule. With the river Tribune running about shouting encouragement a final, intense push saw the last pontoon section to the north secured and planked. It was a shambles of poles, posts, roped barges and coracle rafts, but –

"Is it secure, Sir?" Felix asked the Exfil Tribune, who looked quite fresh having fallen into the Danube at least twice in the last frantic hour.

"Yes, First Spear, I think it is. I'll stay stationed in the middle. If there's a problem, I can work on it. If I can't fix it, then I'd prefer to be washed downriver with the wreckage than face you."

"That's the spirit, young Sir."

Felix then gestured to a signaller. "Well! Not a moment to lose! Quick's the word and fast's the action!"

Lantern signals were made.

Alba's eight hundred odd were lolling about on the riverbank scrub road either side of the artillery, fully packed, awaiting a 'Go' order. Now it was 'that time' and the First Cohort Centurion had the Optios bring the men up into marching order.

"Off you go, Centurion Alba, don't fall in." A voice came from the artillery pads as Alba approached the turning point.

"First Spear."

Felix threw the remains of his third onion away, ready to watch Embarkation or jump in to coordinate a messy rescue. First Cohort marched to the edge of the pontoon, two braziers and the white embarkation post marking its entry. The post had grown an arrow now, pointing towards the bridge marking the column turning curve – partly as a joke and partly because you could never be too careful with soldiers, especially at night. Centurion Alba halted the Cohort and made ten ginger steps forwards onto the planks, testing the footing. He turned back.

"First Cohort, we are not marching. Just walk, like coming back from the brothel with your wife and newborn asleep behind the curtain. Nobody fucking marches. Remember I said that, last time you'll hear such a funny thing in the Army."

A chuckle from the hundred at the front who then 'shat the news' out the back of Lead Century to those following. Then in a four-column the men crept, fully armoured and ration slung, gently as was possible across the makeshift bridge. After a sixth-hour of nerve wracking, creaking, paces Centurion Alba eventually met the Exfil Tribune halfway over on the big, middle barge.

"Seems to be holding, Sir."

Crouched up on a post with a torch the Exfil officer wasn't really listening, instead looking everywhere for strain or drift. The Centurion Chief Armourer was doing the same further down the pontoon. The massive Immunes smith pacing the northern shore span behind the Fifth Cohort cordon. It was an area (area, of extreme concern) he'd taken for his own once the embarkation started. Occasionally spotting something, Galba and his little team would quickly re-lash or add a timber brace. As Alba crept off the pontoon's exit he barely got a half nod from the Centurion Armourer who was hammering a joist. The First Centurion's sandals hit reassuring wet mud and he looked back at his men coming off the planks, muttering, "It's basically a bloody boat!"

The First Cohort were now across though and they quickly strengthened the bridgehead to the west, ready to shuffle up the bank into marching order as further cohorts joined them on the north shore.

First yellow glow of dawn. On the south bank new lead units were brought up to the entry point as they waited for the preceding bridge crossing to make space. Numerous overexcited NCO's were shouting commands from different directions at the men.

"No gaps, no gaps!", "Keep moving.", "Spread out you idiots", "Stop, slow down or you'll run into…" The legionaries, safe in their dense herds, mostly ignored all this barking.

Only once did an onager volley fire off, blasting a section of ridge and bringing Auxilia galloping to mop up whatever Guns had seen.

Sometimes against all experience and expectations things just worked, and it turned out the pontoon 'did'. After a fashion. Even the mounted ballista, the Gunwagons, slowly trundled over the planks, dragged by blindfolded mules and losing many a watching veteran Triari a 'safe bet'. Satisfied as to progress Guns walked out from the line of heavies and hopped up onto the last trundling Carrioballista wagon, his bodyguard/cleaner following. The Lead artilleryman would be the last man over the Danube.

Once Gun's jolted off the northern end of the pontoon, a big thumbs up to the Exfil Tribune as he passed the lad – who in turn saluted back unnecessarily in pure relief, XXXth Legion split into three (after some bad tempered shoving by north shores beach master). The trio of forces then marched off into hostile territory with little ceremony under the orange banners of, probably, Imperial Rome. With the Legion came Prince Herminaz's and his men, having been let out of the officers' bar at the very last moment just an hour before. The Cherusi contingent were all to be kept under the watchful eye of First Spear Felix and his command group on Gold.

In less than a half hour of marching Eight, Ninth and Tenth Cohort under the Senior Centurion rendezvoused with their assigned Auxillia patrol at the great oak, turned left and snaked uphill, northward. The Second, Sixth and shit-Seventh had stamped off west from the pontoon, under the First Spear and two of the XXXth's Tribunes, to take Gold Route in the middle of the deploying trident. Officer disposition into the grandly named 'GOLD COMMAND FORCE/ROUTE' had been made rearranged at a last, informal, strategic chat before dawn rise.

"Listen Alba, your jobs going to be hard enough with officers, I'll take your one for you."

"Thank you, First Spear."

Trailing just behind Gold Force the First, Third and Fourth Cohorts marched with the gun wagons, under Alba and only Alba going for the furthest west route, the cart track. The independent and isolated Bronze Route.

Chapter Forty-Three

Bored in Aquincum, summer beating down
Building dust and parties
Pannonia Inferior province of Rome

With nothing else to do, Legate Scaurianus of the wandering XXXth Legion inspected a Governor's new earthworks just outside Aquincum Town. From a small rise of builders' rubble, he stood watching the beginnings of a provincial villa in the grand style being cobbled together. The project was, if anything, a reflection of the local provincial administrator himself: inconsistent, overly ambitious, financially inept and unnecessary. Building projects reflected their owners, the ex-Consul knew, and it was only a matter of time before the ornamental carp pond spectacularly gave way. Undermining the main living areas and engulfing two small hamlets situated below the too, too narrow dam wall. It was all deeply frustrating.

Five days later and Scaurianus was no longer inspecting but directing works from the same hillock of quarry waste, wearing a big straw hat. He'd partly got himself involved with this private/public grey area of a residential property to keep busy while, to all accounts, 'his' Legion rampaged about without orders in allied territory. His new interest in the Governor's project was also due to new 'revelations' made during the intervening period of stay in Aquincum.

Having finished redirecting some concrete, Scauri sat back in his trustworthy folding workschair, that piece of functional furniture which *'accompanied him to more interesting events than even his wife'* - as his wife always remarked. The ex-Consul reviewed life's current situation once again: his active command of the XXXth Legion was a murky area as Scaurianus hadn't joined the force yet and they, in turn, were 'un-eagled'. Right now whatever the eight thousand men to the north were doing they were definitely doing it already and that was that.

The erudite civil servant Scipio, of course, had summed it up best, "If none of them come back from their little expedition it's not going to be good, but at least you weren't really in charge and after a few years on an island off the Greek mainland you'll be back. Rush up there now and it is a pig's ear, however, then a special ticket to the circus will be provided."

Of course, that last bit was for comic effect, Scaurianus had just been Pro-Consul so no undignified circus appearance for him if things went bad. It'd be the strongest suggestion of a hot bath and a knife or an assisted garrotte most probably. This Emperor was civilised, after all.

"Give it five days, darl, then I'll give you a lift up there myself" Sobe had added after that first infamous lunch on arrival. Scaurianus had subsequently been foolish enough to hitch a lift with her to the docks one morning and decided it'd be safer to travel the Brigetio road strapped to a hippo.

So then, to kill time in the evenings before setting forth towards formal command and unquestionable responsibility, there had been a party arranged. The party was for the ex-Consul, of course, where he'd been introduced to anyone who was anyone by the Lady Lassalia. Scauri calculated that the Lady Lassalia had been in Aquincum precisely three months longer than he had but by some generally accepted notion all of local society fell into line behind Sobe's loud form of social engineering. Men who had traded grain and fish for twenty years, within a five-mile radius of the provincial capital, were introduced to each other: "Now I know you two will just get on famously…" and, to Scaurianus' astonishment, the merchants happily went along with it as though a Sadiki-stamped conjunction marked a first 'formal' introduction.

Togas were everywhere – Lassalia was a stickler for that – and the ladies of the city queued up to order appropriate stolae so they could get into the social event of the year. Great lines were formed from the back of the Sadiki's little warehouse, which was churning out Capri-last-season summer wear as though Tiberius was back. Except the dresses had properly sewn hems rather than quick release draw strings – Trajan was a civilised Emperor, after all. In turn wives and girlfriends forced their men – a blind eye turned to eligibility as this was the frontier – into those great half-moon sheets of civilisation all in a range of exciting colours, particularly orange.

The Scipio encouraged this sartorial social equality mostly because, at the nightly events (three consecutive evenings in town that week following the main do) some poor sod's wrapping always fell off spectacularly or entertainingly slowly. The first-estate civil servant even had his own bright, bright orange toga

412

with a fish motif run up, "…To put them all at ease, the locals, and anyway, crisp white's so boring!"

There was no doubt in the ex-Consul's mind that his patrician 'patron' would wear the tangerine monstrosity to every soiree he attended on returning to Rome, complete with the hat purchased from the mountainous cart stop a week previously. With some sense of civic duty, Scaurianus had told Scipio to stop looking for, and trying to remove, pins and brooches on the Pannonian's togas. Scipio scowled but complied, instead now overly complimenting wearers on the 'wonderful jewellery' used to hold together the Roman civil dress. The 'joke' – Scipio's – being that you weren't supposed to use clasps for togas for reasons of stoic allegory.

"Facetious prick," Sobe pronounced at the first welcome party, watching Scipio do his rounds.

"Yup, Lady Lassalia. By the way, I have four of my lictors stationed in your – sorry, the Governor's – anteroom ready to remedy any wardrobe malfunctions. Please feel free to direct guests that way if a garment begins to become unstable."

Lassalia looked up at Scaurianus with an appraising smile and turned to the man on her arm, "You know what, General? I think he's all right."

"Pro-consuls, Roman Generals, or Military Legates tend to be, in my experience." the IInd's General observed, patting her bangles.

That got a derisive female snort and off the unlikely couple went mingling, leaving Scaurianus behind to observe the lively room of be-coloured 'dignitaries' including a woman the Legate was sure he had bought a sausage roll from earlier in the day.

Scaurianus liked wearing a toga but remembered the hours he'd spent watching the little nuances of how it was worn. As a young man he'd approached the clothing like any other construction project – meticulously. Employing the right artisans was key, Scaurianus had once borrowed an ancient Scipio tailor, for a purse of coins, to provide utterly secret tutelage on getting the great civic garment on perfectly. Perfectly, every time.

Aquincum Town was a small place so everyone was at the event held in his honour and Scaurianus worked the room. His only Optio, Ruben, was bright, educated and informative as political hostages tended to be. The fact that the VIIIth's renowned artillery train had somehow been co-opted into the XXXth was definitely good news. Imperial Nephew was just as Scauri remembered him, except seemed to somehow now be a key, undefined, cog in whatever had been going on here for the preceding period, and all had a good word for him. Suspicious. The slave eunuch, First Secretary Eleazar was kind enough to spare the ex-Consul and Military Legate time for a drink, from seemingly running both the House of Sadiki and the Province's Administration apparatus. Scaurianus asked this useful creature for a full spec. of the region and grudgingly approved at the level of detail provided.

Finishing with Eleazar, Scauri looked over the party throng for the spy he'd registered at lunch. The Spook was easy to spot as such creatures always tried to both skulk and look important at the same time. There, over by the buffet was the leader of the Special Operations Group but he looked unhappy with his new found 'twin'. It was as though SOGI had been instructed never to leave Scipio's sight, whom the local spy now trailed behind unhappily – best not to ask what that was about.

The welcome party concluded, provincially, before midnight and next morning Scaurianus took up an invite. The tour of the Sadiki warehouse and operations base was actually quite interesting, but then again, the ex-Consul knew his interests lay in planning things – the wall system and map girls with pushy sticks were definitely 'keepers' for future use. During the Sadiki warehouse tour XXXth's Legate had been left unattended for a moment and walked into a room where whispered 'chanting?' ceased immediately at his appearance.

Lady Lassalia was there, smiling sweetly over the look of murder in her eyes, exclaiming, "Ah, look at you wandering about unescorted! Can't leave you for a minute." She turned to the other men in the room "Gentlemen, this meeting is concluded. Now, recent Consul, let's go back on the balcony where I left you," and Scaurianus was ushered away from a worried looking Greek secretary and two Assyrian killers.

'Remember but don't comment.'

Ushered back up on the directors' terrace, the Lady Lassalia had half-filled their goblets – glass, the ex-Consul noted – and then reminded Scaurianus to take a trip up to the Governor's little building project. As he'd exhausted the sights of Aquincum by the morning of the second day – baths, Governor's Administration complex, fish – he did so. So, there he'd found himself at the disaster of a construction site. Local workers attempting to build aforesaid

414

Pompeii-style formal villa, scaled up one-and-a-half times too big and on a slope. The sheer ineptitude of the foundation work had afforded the experienced project manager at least a few hours of total distraction from the possibly treasonous actions of his quasi-command somewhere 'over the river'. That's when he met Pannonia Inferior's chief administrator.

"So, what do you think, Legate?" the Governor had asked, wheezing up to the top of the mound of rock, beaming at the activity below. Only a month before, the Governor had been in financial turmoil but that had all turned around, as if by divine intervention, which it probably was really, and the province was now looking on the up, fiscally. Going out and spending a colossal amount of state money on a personal villa was the only pious thing to do under the circumstances.

"It is very ambitious, Governor."

"Isn't it just. Well, I am an ambitious man as I'm sure you can appreciate, Legate and ex-Consul, as I'm sure you can well understand."

'Jumped-up little pleb.'
'He means I'm a jumped-up little pleb.'

"I certainly do, Governor."

Scaurianus would have left this entertaining folly at the 'enjoyment of watching struggles at sea' stage except that during the second night's party – some sort of aldermen do – while regaling Scipio of all the nonsense he'd seen that day…

"…he's only gone and done all the foundation calculations based on the central complex being ground-flush without any…" after a massive yawn the civil servant interrupted his client with an insight.

"Yes, that's all very entertaining, Scauri. Have you, though, considered what will happen if your – or the – Legion is successful? If indeed our brave XXXth sweep the northern area clear of hostile barbarians, thus receiving thanks from 'old King Macromanni' for cleansing his southern lands of 'rebels' and consequently reopening the upper Danube for safe travel. Trade thus free to travel from here to Vindabona, once again? Including, let us not forget, any 'special luxury cargo' that might be tricking downstream in the near future?"

Scaurianus hadn't really considered success as an option. He had been focussing more on modelling scenarios of graded disaster.

"I don't follow, Scipio."

"No, you don't because you are very good at building roads. If the XXXth is successful in their endeavour, then it will not be a 'foraging' exercise but a mighty victory for the people of Rome. Vindication of this state of affairs will be safe to come downriver and on arrival exultations at the new Legion's deed shall then be made across the Empire. But you are not the XXXth's General, just, to be frank, its administrator. No military glory for you, that's the whole point of this entire exercise. So, what happens to Decimus Terentius Scaurianus? How to reward you? A man as good at building things, making things, supporting things as Decimus Terentius Scaurianus is...is valued. Military fame is not in your birds, however, Scauri, but there is a plan and I suggest you get back up to that dysfunctional building site first thing tomorrow. 'Help out' the Governor with his mighty erection. I've met his wife and she is uniquely unqualified to do so, despite the three children."

Light dawned on the ex-Consul through a sort of smutty, murky dawn that promised heat but also rain.

"Because I'm going to have to live in it?"

Aullus Pallo Scipio grinned back. "Aha! Possibly. What do the Fates have in store for that lowly farm boy, now recent Pro-Consul and Military Legate to the Emperor? What could be more appropriate than a plum Governorship?"

"Plum! Lower Pannonia is a chaotic war-torn hovel."

"You have no imagination. Trust me, trust me..."

'Really, Scipio?'

"Pannonia Inferior is to be the centre of the Empire for the next few years because the centre of the Empire is defined by wherever the Emperor is. You, my friend, are to be 'His' platform. Cobbling together a Legion was only ever half the job. Trajan needs something firm to jump up high from, high up into Dacia and then up, up into the firmament."

And with that the civil servant went off to get another drink, back slapping all as he went, surreptitiously pulling a too heavy shoulder fold an inch the wrong way, leading to an indiscreet toga collapse for an obsequious merchant, just as the stuffed carp-pigs were brought out a tenth of an hour later.

Next morning back to the villa site Scaurianus went with vigour, many suggestions now forthcoming on how the complex might be 'optimised', all of which initially delighted the incumbent Governor. By the third day of

Scaurianus' usefulness, however, the provincial administrator's suspicions were definitely raised. The increasingly forceful 'thoughts' from the ex-Consul on how to stop the family accommodation sliding down the side of the hill if the stream wasn't moved, or why the heating system would be better smaller and less prone to setting fire to the uprights, became more like orders.

But then they were gone. At first light, seven days following Scaurianus' and Scipio's arrival in Aquincum, the senior command of the XXXth attempted to slip out of the town. The Lady Lassalia was at the front of the procession in her gilded green-peach chariot, screaming abuse as it careered around behind the fetlocks of a nervous-looking Auxilia escort, gifted from the IInd's general.

Behind were Scaurianus and the Emperor's Nephew mounted, with accompanying lictors. The XXXth Legate's fasci holders, Legion engineers to a man, were eyeing the Nephew's escort warily, having noted their military species immediately.

"Sir, about those licto…"

Scaurianus cut his own primary lictor off.

"I know, just ignore them. If we are subject to any Imperial displeasure, well…I expect we just die. Nothing any of us are going to do about it unless they unexpectedly challenge us to build a bridge to prove our loyalty to Rome."

At the rear of the mounted dignitaries was a short train. The Scipio with Optio Ruben, the Greek secretary Gallan and an unhappy SOG Lead all in one timber encased wagon.

Huddled inside the conveyance SOG Lead was that particular unhappy born from enjoying almost autonomous command before being confronted by his actual boss, who he'd never met before and who was supposed to be far away and now wasn't.

Trailing the executive caravan trundled a wagon full of the Assyrian contractors – who seemed to know exactly who the Big Boss was from the moment he arrived in Aquincum. This individuals first act on assessing SOG operations was to release all the miserable peasants from the lower administration building cells with a bag of coin each for their troubles. Then came the baggage pulled by Sadiki caravan drivers. The man and wife team kicked out of goal once the Lady Lassalia had remembered to mention the matter to 'her' General.

Northwards up the western riverbank it was. A day took them to a sharp left, as the Danube turned west, then in two days Brigetio Fort. Hopefully some Romans would be in it.

Chapter Forty-Four

Gold, Silver and Bronze insertion routes
Very hot daytime north of the Danube
Macromanni, hostile territory

The Senior Centurion arrived at the Legion rendezvous point first and ate an apple, leaning up against the broken-down farmhouse that, only the afternoon before, the Infil team had holed up in awaiting sunset. The NCO took a noisy bite watching the huge meadow before him and all that was now in it, namely a well-exercised Silver Force. To the north he could make out the three objectives of the XXXth's 'foraging' operation: the largest village, or small town, and its two neighbours dunly squatting, topped with golden thatch, in the middle of the horizon. There seemed to be lots of activity over there, dots running about amongst the Macromanni farm buildings, but that was fine. Not even a Legion could empty and transport the amount of food predicted to be in those granaries and storerooms in less than a day.

Around the SC his Optios milled about, for once having very little to do. To the outside of them were the three Cohort Standard-bearers, orange banners on poles, chatting excitedly with the Cornicifers in a very un-legionary manner – all being Noscarfs just two days before – but even the SC couldn't be bothered to tell them to shut up. Then in the outer circle was a mass of glinting bodies, mostly lying on the long grasses or sitting in the sun, the couple of thousand-Line Legionaries allocated to Silver Force. The SC chewed, reflecting that the men all obviously believed, or were too lazy to think otherwise, pickets a hundred feet out offered as much security as a fort wall.

During a stint in Judaea, the Senior Centurion remembered an old Jew's story about a sensible bloke called Gideon who had fucked off all his conscripts who weren't paying proper attention to their environment while taking in fluids. God had told Gideon to do it, apparently. Pity for Judaea their deity relinquished His advisory role subsequently. When the SC had finished his apple, he'd get in

419

amongst the discarded helmets and… *'really?'*…two silly sods had taken their rigs off.

First, he looked over towards the new prisoners. A hundred odd men who seemed to have been made adequately immobile, trussed up in staked drag ropes as they were. The captured warriors, rabble really, were being poked occasionally by the mounted Gauls who, as a long-subdued people, liked nothing better than making life unnecessarily unpleasant for a newly subdued people.

On the whole though 'his' boys had done well. It had all been deeply unsatisfactory in terms of real action but then, that was the Army for you, and the Legionaries were very pleased with themselves. As ordered, Senior Centurion had split east along the enemy riverbank, following the trip over the shit bridge, picked up white sticks at the great oak almost immediately and turned north on to Silver Route. The pathfinder Infiltrati had done well, the SC grudgingly admitted. There were many splits to the insertion track, but each was waymarked clearly and correctly with the little whitewashed pegs. That was until the sticks suddenly disappeared after two hours' morning march.

"No markers for two hundred steps, Senior Centurion."

"Absence is a telling marker in its own right. Tell the Cohort Centurions to get the men ready and send forward the Auxilia for a shufti, Optio."

Sure enough, a short while later Silver Route's cavalry screen rode in at a lather reporting enemy contact on the road. The SC followed correct Army protocol: briefing his officer and suggesting the Tribune get well behind him in order to be ready to command.

"No, Sir, back a bit further, covering our rear and flanks, that's it. Right back, further, further…"

Once that was done the SC summoned forward what he adjudged to be the least incompetent Century. The eighty formed up on his Optios' staffs then the SC pushed into the front row, nodding to the Formation Centurion at the left to begin a slow, shield up, march.

A few hundred paces later they found the roadblock. Overturned wagons and a few hundred Macromani levies with a large group of bronze-clad mercenaries. The SC ordered a stop at a long pilum's throw from the obstruction to see what would happen. In the forest adjacent to the track, the Auxilia crashed around out of sight, shouting a lot in Gaulish as cavalry always tended to. There was obviously something lurking in the trees but without understanding a word of his screen's chattering the SC could tell from the tone it was probably just farmers shitting themselves in a bush while holding a sharpened hoe uncertainly.

Front Century stood-to for a quarter of an hour under the hot sun while the SC took it all in. Lots of shouting from the barricade, then stones began to fly. The odd spear came over hitting the dirt or bouncing harmlessly off the elevated shields. One boar spear did manage to hit on target, with enough weight to splinter through a scutum. It cut open the forearm of an ex-saucier, who howled like he'd taken a groin wound. The SC rolled his eyes as the Formation Centurion screamed at the erstwhile chef to get a grip on himself as the seven and eight 'rowers' behind dragged the dickhead out through the back of the eighty, dumping him headfirst in the dust for the corpsman to remove towards the central train.

A few clangs and shouts continued from the trees but the SC was going to stick to the usual plan.

"Right boys, make some noise for the XXXth!"

Each Legionary banged his shield with a pilum shaft in some sort of unison while shouting "Ooh, Ooh, Ooh!"

"That's it, lads, make a noise so Mars and Jupiter can hear!"

The Senior Centurion was gratified the tactic worked as well here as it did in all the other places full of overly-excited twats. Not proper troops, not like Persians.

At the barricade, the Roman shouting excited the levy troops to such an extent a few hundred odd enemy, a-whooping and a-hollering, ran straight at the Roman Forward Century. Strong drink had obviously been imbibed. The SC ordered 'pilums to the rear' and the drawing of personal weapons.

Moments later, swinging all manner of spear, axe and general farming implements, the levy crashed into the Century with much enthusiasm. So, the Romans killed anyone in reach efficiently and quickly.

The SC got a couple himself but mostly shouted encouraging and instructional things to the forward linesmen. The first blooding of the XXXth was all you would wish for, taking a virgin Legion out. Attackers ran in a few more times at full enthusiasm, tried all the usual 'one massive swing first' stuff, 'shield wall leaping', 'kicking and swinging', then were quickly crushed forward into the Roman wall by their keen mates following. Essentially it was then a question of stabbing alot and making sure your left arm stayed up.

"It's much easier tha-tha-than practice dummies, isn't it, SC?" the boy next to him exclaimed excitedly.

"Yes, sunshine, that's the fucking point. Now, our kid, don't get…"

Once the mass of enemy further back could see they had inadvertently murdered their mates in front, all pulled back. Back to that distance, maybe ten feet or so, the SC termed as a 'poncing line'. The enemy shouted obscenities, threw rocks, occasionally an individual would rush forward to kick or hit a shield with a hoe before scarpering back to his mates, or not.

"Right!" the SC shouted. "Let's practise some snatch squads."

They'd done it in training and the Senior Centurion wanted to see how it'd go in the real thing.

"Fifteen!" he barked out.

Front Linesman Position Fifteen, to the SC's left, nodded, shouting, "Snatch party ready!"

As trained, the men to the Legionary's left, right and directly behind slapped Fifteen's shoulder and back in response.

Satisfied, Fifteen identified their mark, "Yellow hat with feather…GO!"

Out shot the four Legionaries, covered by two more men apiece flanking a few steps behind. Quick as a flash Fifteen smashed into Yellow Hunting Cap, crashing the Macromanni scum to the floor, and stepped over the dazed body. Fifteen's shield mates slashed and jabbed at startled members of the 'Poncing Line', who the Romans were now in amongst, the surprised enemy springing or tumbling back. The fourth man, from the second row – shield left back with his mates – punched prone Hat Boy hard in the head with a gladius pommel – 'A' for effort, the SC noted approvingly from back in the Century – grabbed a pair of floppy ankles and hauled the semi-conscious ne'er-do-well back into the main formation.

Fifteen, Fourteen and Sixteen closed back seamlessly into the ranks in a matter of seconds.

The enemy didn't like this and screamed abuse…but did absolutely nothing else.

Yellow Hat – somehow, it'd stayed on and was later given to Fifteen as a souvenir – got robustly manhandled back through the Century, each of the formation's strata taking the opportunity to land a punch until the barbarian was spat out of the back of the eighty. In the dust to the rear of the unit a couple of sweepers – detached men from the Second Century behind – gave the bloke another kicking before binding his hands and legs with ropes then dragging the now fully unconscious individual back to the prearranged holding pen, mid-column.

"Alright, that was allll right," the SC announced with his highest praise. "Who wants to go next?"

They practised snatches a few more times successfully until it went wrong.

"…F'fuck's sake!" and the SC waded forward himself to rescue the idiot who'd fallen over his own laces and was being set upon by four bastards with – luckily – shit spears.

'Still, nice to see the new armour is holding up.'

Killing two of the assailants, the NCO dragged the boy backwards into the shield line by his rig loops. The SC hauled the man to his feet, bent down and did his laces up himself, before making the Legionary go back and do it again.

"Properly, this time!"

The SC noted with some satisfaction the flappy sandaled fool wore a blue racing thread around his wrist.

"Can't expect much more from a 'Blue' can you?" the NCO muttered watching a passable second attempt at a snatch that retrieved, what looked to be, the local village idiot.

"Fu-fu-Fucking Blues!" the newly minted Legionary to the SC's left stammered back in reply.

Eventually the Ponce Line drifted back as the Macromanni watched friends and relations be consumed by the Roman Army. Now the enemy were shuffling about twenty or so paces away, the SC ordered 'Pilums forward' and everyone had a go at a firing line. It went well, an accurate and noisy series of impalings with nobody managing to somehow stab themselves in their own foot. Yes, that did happen.

It was at this point the barbarians ran all the way back to the barricades and everything quieted down a bit. The noise from the flanks seemed to indicate the Auxiliary cavalry were making ground doing whatever they were doing, as the incessant chatter of the northern Alps was now definitely further forward.

'Getting too bloody hot, time to end this nonsense'.

"Everything weeeell, Senior Centurion?" a mounted voice came from the Century's back.

'and speaking of nonsense…'

"All very well, Sir."

"Sooo…what…I meeeean, I was thinking…"

"Talk to them, Sir? Absolutely, definitely the right decision. Signifier: you heard the senior officer, up here on me, bring the translator. Optios!"

"Talk to themmm…SC?"

"I was about to suggest it myself, but didn't need to did I, Sir? Got there before me, must be getting old. Now, are those prisoners secure, Tribune?"

"Ummm…right. If there is some sooort of parley, do you think, I…I…should perhaps…?"

"Dangerous things, prisoners, need to be watched, Sir. I'd feel better knowing you were keeping an eye on them."

The Tribune turned back to the holding area down the convoy. "Weee seem to only haaave seven prisoners at present…"

The Senior Centurion just stood in the Vanguard Century's front rank like a granite statue radiating 'Roman Duty'.

"Ah, yeees. Very good, Senior Centurion, I'lllll get right…"

"Right! On me, parley party."

And the SC strode forward over the bodies, blood, piss and shit to a point halfway towards the roadblock.

Sure enough, out came the mercenary captain who, so far, hadn't moved from his fixed position behind a toppled cart. All impressive white horsehair plume, lots of bronze and a horrible black beard.

"Where's he from, do you think, Senior Centurion?"

"He's from 'I Don't Give a Fuck', Optio."

"Probably Scythian."

"That'd be my guess," the SC grudgingly acknowledged.

The Probably-Scythian stopped a few feet from the parley party and nodded. The Romans nodded back and tried a few languages. The Legion translator settled on something workable with the Merc.

"Ready to go, Senior Centurion," confirmed the translator.

The SC looked at the captain appraisingly, who did the same in return. "Tell him…to fuck off."

The translator felt underused.

"Is that…all? You don't think…?"

"Just tell him that, sonny, exactly."

The translator sighed a little and spoke. "One of the medium purses, I think…" the SC muttered to the Treasury Optio next to him, who ostentatiously brought out a leather bag of clinking metal.

The captain did a half grimace and shrug. "And a small bag…"

A small bag was also brought out.

The captain then began to make a continuous nodding motion with gestures before speaking some amenable-sounding babble while waving at the bags. Before the translator did his stuff, the SC answered very loudly and slowly.

"Big bag silver bits, small bag Roman aurei."

Big smile from the captain. He'd got it. "Make sure you get a receipt, Optio."

As the receipt was made out and the purses changed hands, the translator asked, "How did you know what he said, Senior Centurion?"

"I speak fucking mercenary, mi'laddo. Universal language of cunts."

With the tally receipt done the captain spoke again, pointing back to the barricade. The translator looked at the SC, who in turn nodded that he'd appreciate a little help shifting the obstruction. More chatter, a question.

"He also asks us if you would like him to kill all the others back there for another big bag." The SC declined the offer but pointed at the mercenary's belt.

"Is that a bag of apples?"

It was.

"Tell him I want his apples and if he asks 'how much?', I'll cut his balls off."

The translation that followed saw the apples pass to the SC as a gesture of peace and friendship between the great Captain Something-or-Other and the Roman Army.

"Right, that's it. Tell Captain Fantastic to either move out of the kingdom or report into Brigetio first of every month. Anything in-between or outside will be bad. For him."

With that, the parley party walked back to the Forward Century. The SC tossed fruit to each of them. He took a noisy bite himself. "These are good fucking apples."

The barricade was disassembled – for free – and everyone fucked off as instructed. The local Macromanni levy ran panicking for home when they learnt the bronze-armoured sellswords had abandoned the great patriotic endeavour. Once the carts were hauled off the track the Mercs climbed up on to the bank, just off the road which the SC adjudged was, while not being ideal, acceptable. As the Roman column of Silver Force marched forward, Legionaries from each Century shouted up to the bank that the freebooters were all wankers and pig defilers but, gentlemen of fortune to a man, the gentlemen of fortune took it all smiling and waving, happy to be out of the sun, paid not to fight the Roman Army and considering future commercial opportunities from Brigetio Fort.

The Auxilia eventually rode back in from the flanks and reported a great victory against the enemy in the forest, several thousand strong, apparently. The SC told them to piss off and screen. Off the cavalry galloped in a mood.

An hour later, the second stoppage to Silver Force occurred as the enemy levy reappeared, running back towards the Romans, still in panic…

The SC sighed.

"What is it now, surely they can't be thinking of having another pop at us?"

Except on closer inspection the NCO could see all the enemy's weapons had been discarded, except for the more agricultural utility items, and a delegation of Macromanni elders came forward to protest that, *'They had run away, which the Roman's wanted, so why were they being murdered by the horse soldiers?'*

The SC rolled his eyes and took all the Macromanni prisoner 'for their own protection'. One of his Optios from Persia made a knowing, questioning glance to his boss as the bindings went on.

'A Numidian caravan…I've only seen one and it was horrible…'

The SC slapped the NCO's helmet down heavily and grimaced in annoyance at his cavalry standing off ahead, like annoyed, sulking cats.

That was it for excitement and now here they were, first into the meadow. The SC had finished his current apple and was demanding a panicked, fumbling, Legionary tell him where the boy's pugio knife was – it was under the SC's boot – when a picket shouted warning.

"Incoming troops southwest!"

The sentry pointing out the direction with an upraised spear.

SC moved his foot – the young Legionary looked shocked and aggrieved – picked up the knife and threw it into the ground an inch from the lad's cock.

"Don't be a twat."

Then the NCO made off to the picket, eyes following the pointing spear's direction. It was obviously a Roman column, from Gold Route, but Army was

Army and the three cohorts were stood-to in battle formation as a flood of coded flag signals went off to the approaching force and were returned.

Half an hour later Felix rocked up, beaming.

"Salve, Senior Centurion."

"Salve, First Spear."

Someone who wasn't beaming was Prince Herminaz, leaking blood from a bandaged thigh with an entourage of now just eight men, one on a litter who was obviously going to kark it given the colourful location of his bowels.

"Well done, SC, made it here first. Can't say I'm surprised. Have fun?"

"Usual bollocks. Boys did well, though."

"Good. Got some prisoners I see…Right. Well…that'll come in handy… later I suppose."

The SC sniffed an acknowledgement without making eye contact with his superior, instead looking at the prince.

"How's his Highness? Looking a bit glum, is it?"

Felix turned back to Prince Herminaz, exclaiming, "The great Prince Herminaz fought like a lion, a battle worthy of a saga. Proving he is a true friend of Rome, showing loyalty in blood."

The Prince Herminaz gave Felix a dark look but couldn't keep it up and slumped onto a camp chair one of his surviving retinue had just unfolded.

"Selflessly volunteered to single-handedly lead the vanguard against the enemies of Rome, thus proving his worth?"

"That's the sort of thing, SC."

"How many of them were there?"

"Maybe just shy of four hundred."

"Very selfless of him."

"We helped a bit at the end."

"Lose any men?"

"Nah. Cuts and bruises. You?"

"Bollocks to that. Want an apple?"

"Thanks. Nice apple, where did you get it?"

"Long shit story. So, the prince now, he's only got, what, less than ten men now?"

First Spear made a vague circling gesture with his apple.

"Yeeees. I think you might be right."

"Great opportunity you gave him to – you know – to prove himself a loyal ally of Rome."

"I thought so. Sometimes, though, you know – cultural differences. Had to explain it a bit, point out what a good thing this could be for him."

"We're all about bringing the benefits of civilisation to the barbarian horde, aren't we, First Spear?"

"We certainly are, Senior Centurion. Now, speaking of barbarian hordes…"

"Where are the other couple of thousand enemy warriors we expected this side of the river? Just what I was wondering, FS. I imagine they've either gone home, which would be the sensible thing, or, almost just as sensible, concentrated all their proper troops on Bronze Route with its big proper road, isolated from us."

"Probably the latter, though, isn't it, SC?"

"Reckon so. Do we go and get Alba?"

"Not yet. Let's stick to the plan and, to be honest, we kind of knew this situation was likely. First Cohort Centurion has got the Gunwagons and we took his officers for him."

"Right you are, FS. Where's the other one, by the way? An officer? You're missing one, aren't you? The very quiet young gentleman?"

"Oh, yes. Well, he is dead."

"Glorious solo charge into a melee of barbarians…?"

"Pulled off his horse and hacked into pieces, got it in one, Senior Centurion."

"That going to be a problem?"

"I don't think so. Fourth son, Grandfather was the last senator. Thick as shit and he died like a hero. Brings the family military honour for the future, probably a win all round."

"Mum will be sad."

"Yeah, but then that's what mums are like. We gathered the bits up and got them into a bag. Right, shall we get a brew on?"

Neither Alba or, more importantly, any of the Bronze Force foot scouts had found a single white marker stick on the hostile northern bank. Moving west from the pontoon bridgehead at night's end, letting Felix's Gold Force pass by first, not a waystick could be seen. Luckily the large, widening main road of Bronze Route was easy to spot for the force's right turn north up into the high hills. Even so, the scouts reported the complete absence of whitewashed direction markers as 'worrying'. It was a whole hour's march, just as the sun began to truly lift, before Bronze detachment found a different sort of road sign.

Alba had borrowed Exfil guides for the march, securing the services of the grizzled lead scout of the boatmen. A hundred paces ahead of the column Werewulf had risen out of a bush making arm signals, silhouetted in the first light.

"Column halt, no signal, pass it back," Alba ordered. No horn blaring: instead the Cornicifer relayed the 'hold' command back by word through the centuries, gun teams and veteran triarii – also borrowed from the river team.

"Escort, on me."

Sixteen Legionaries fell out of the Lead Century and formed up around Centurion Alba. As they walked forward so did the old river scout, maintaining the hundred pace distance between his trackers and the following escort party.

Round the next bend of the bright, limestone track Werewulf had stopped and as the escort approached, faint golden light revealed a grizzly scene: seven heads on poles, or more accurately, lances. First Century Centurion Alba held the escort back and walked up alongside the scout, looking up at the heads, one still dripping.

"Can we use a torch, Lead Scout?"

"I know who they are."

"I reckon I do as well. Best tell me, though."

"No white sticks on the path, Centurion. That's who they are."

"No. No white sticks. For Immunes, they weren't a bad bunch of blokes – no offence, Werewulf."

The old scout spat. "They were as good Infiltrators as I've ever seen. Only seven scalps up there though, no team Skipper."

Alba thought about the Infiltration officer for a second; he'd liked the Skipper but right now none of that mattered.

"They're watching us, I take it?"

Neither the old scout nor Alba looked into the forest shadows at their flanks, gazes instead fixed upwards.

"At least twenty, couple of riders, the rest dismounted. They won't do anything, I reckon. Just enjoying the show."

"Well, at least we now know this is the right direction," the Centurion commented drily, eliciting a slight sideways glance from the wolfskin-clad scout.

Alba turned back to the escort, all wide white staring eyes, and crouched perceptibly lower than they should be behind curved shields.

'Fuck,' thought Bronze Force's leader.

The veteran scout got in first. "That's it, boys, take a good look. It's what happens sometimes, just part of what we do. Look hard, won't be the last time you see this stuff."

The escort shuffled a little, Alba was of a different school from the likes of Werewulf and the SC so had the party turn away to watch the treeline.

"Lead Scout: let us get our brothers down. Lay them to the side of the road, we'll come back and make it right."

The two lifers worked heads off lances. It was bad work, not for recently gifted Scarfs, not first time out at night at any rate. Seven Roman heads were soon piled carefully behind a mossy granite outcrop. The rock was easily identifiable if they made it back and would be out of sight of the marching column as it came forward.

Placing the last head down in the grasses Werewulf looked at the face of Two. They'd stuffed something into the man's mouth. The veteran grunted and Alba straightened up, giving him a stare *'Don't say a word to anyone.'*

The escort party fell back to the column at double time, past the cocky red-haired Legion/First Cohort Signifier at the front, and back into their Century. Alba had sworn the escort to silence but, soldiers being gossips, ordered his forward eighty men fall out and move back to the rear under the watchful eye of First Century's Centurion following behind. With First C nestled securely between two veteran triarii blocks, the Optios then moved the Second Century of the First Cohort to the vanguard with the Third shuffling up behind it.

"Ignorance is bliss, eh, Centurion?" Werewulf remarked to Alba, as he watched First Century jog to the rear.

"Dunno about that, but it might stop an outbreak of the heebie-jeebies. Right, let's make some noise to scare the shades away."

Orders were given, the Lead Cohort's Formation Cornicifer rang out the advance notes that were then picked up along the column by his bandmates. Red held his orange banner aloft and strode forward. Finishing their command blasts, two horn players flanked the standard-bearer, slotting inside the four 'Eagle Guards' and blared out the new Legion song.

The summer dawn now seemed to rise quicker through the trees than before and the Legionaries tramped forward belting out the alternative, filthy, marching libretto to the river people's/Senior Centurion's score. Only the First Century mumbled within themselves fearfully from near the back, glancing worriedly around at the treeline. Their Line Centurion and Optio had, however, been put on their mettle by Alba and the NCOs got the men looking forward and singing with enforced vocal enthusiasm. Vine staff and staves poking or thwacking away at anything seeming to lack appropriate moral fibre.

The fishmonger's laughing daughter said to Uncle, 'You randy old sod,
That's clearly a minnow not an oceangoing cod.'
He looked around and slipped...a squid upon the hood,
'How's that?' he cry,
'Well we can try,'
And the tentacles felt good...

The column passed the granite rock unremarked. First Century Centurion getting right into his eighty, up against the faces of the men: "Just look left, go on I fucking dare you!"

The tramping and singing continued on for twenty verses, including the unspeakable chorus, then, just as Bronze Route finished...

"Nine months later she had an octopus for a bairn,
Her dad did a mental and said to her 'you'll learn...
Bab looks just like my brother, you dirty little whore,
But it's a hefty size so a baby we'll ignore.'
Pa ripped it from the swaddling, slapped babe upon the counter,
Took out his hatchet Chopped it up,
Sold calamari priced up at a 'family discount...er'."

...First Centurion Alba saw Werewulf and his scouts signalling ahead, from below a rise in the road. He lifted a hand in a fist, waiting for his desire to be clocked by the command Cornicifers before shouting, "Halt!"

As the blasts sounded and the column shuffled to a stop, Alba detached a new 'sixteen' escort from the front and walked up towards the scouts.

Making the road's rise, Alba stood with the old tracker peering over the other side. The appearance of a Centurion over the brow of the hill, crested horsehair plume and all, elicited a wall of noise from the reverse slope.

"Right. Well now, there's a lot of them."

"There sure are, Centurion. Up for it as well, by the looks of things."

The shallow down-slope road opened up in front of the observation party. Despite the recent heat the marsh to the right looked in fine fettle, ready to sink anything that put a foot into it.

Every other bit of visible ground, the road ahead and the opening plain to the left, was packed with a variety of hostile troops.

"Just for fun, what have we got here then, scout, as if for an idiot?"

A few stones and arrows began to fall about them and the escort stepped in to protect the Bronze Commander, shields up. Alba ignored the tinkling and clumps of small projectiles, surveying what was sure to become a battle ground.

Werewulf acted the friendly tour guide as instructed. "Easily four thousand souls I'd say. Lots of levies, that goes without saying. Then we've got a big chunk of Macromanni regulars on the road in front. Shields, armour and proper weapons."

"Probably sent here by the old king to help us clear his southern kingdom from the bandit incursions that have been plaguing the area?"

"If you say so, Centurion. You can go down and ask the King's son whose over there leading things, he's the one with the silver helmet screaming at people. Then we've got some nasty-looking mercenaries over on the left behind the levies: look handy, possibly Thessalians. Various Germanic peoples dotted about, and that big swathe of tartan foot soldiers curving around, linking the road to their right flank, are your actual Dacian regulars. Veterans, by the looks of it. Met them before. Know their business."

"Very good, Lead Scout. You didn't remark on the sea of cavalry behind the 'Possible Thessalians'."

"Well, it's a massive amount of cavalry, armed to the teeth, First Century. Five squadrons of Roxolani horsewomen, heavy armoured cavalry I don't recognise, Macromanni lancers, then anyone else who's got a pony and a long sharp stick. It's a good spot they've picked."

"It is. We can't deploy. Let us have a think," Alba decided.

As he began to model various scenarios, all of which saw Bronze Force inevitably bottled up or massacred, he noticed the smell of onion. Eyes watering, the NCO looked about, or more accurately under, him.

"Hello, Guns. Come for a look-see?"

The tiny dark man, who had wormed his way into the escort unasked, was peering through a shield gap under the Centurion's right elbow. Deciding he needed a better view, the gunner walked out of the cordon towards the marsh end of the road, oblivious to the dirt being kicked up by projectiles around a pair of colourful, non-standard issue, pointed orange boots.

"You two, go with him," Werewulf instructed, and a pair of Legionary escorts ran out from the small tortoise. The shieldmen tried to provide some cover for the little gunner who didn't make the task easy, moving about, crouching down, lying down and laboriously doing something with a complicated wooden triangle with sliding corners. A hard rain pattering down all the while.

"He's at least wearing some armour today," Werewulf noted, as he and Alba waited for their gunner to die. Chainmail had been forced over Guns although the red beanie hat had remained the little man's only form of head protection.

At the conclusion of adjusting the triangle, both with and without a bronze pendulum, Guns ambled back into the cordon and his thick moustache described a wide grin up at the First Century Centurion. They then all shuffled back off the shallow rise, to much booing, and once out of line of sight the gunner 'borrowed' Centurion Alba's vine staff – everyone was too startled to say anything – and, obliviously, sketched out an idea in the dirt.

Today would be the high point of young marshling Ock's whole life. What an interesting day it'd been already! The night before all of her family had swam-quiet to invisibly watch the strange men moving about in their waters. These strangers knew the reed-way of fish breathing (much later Ock would recognise them as prophets) and were preying on the local Groundlings at the Firm-edge. Mum decided it was best to leave the fish-men alone, they were only hunting Walkers so it would seem, so the marsh tribe quietly floated back off home to the raftings and got some sleep.

Cage-wise the morning was great! The little girl had five baskets full of eels and crayfish already – so that sorted Mum – and then, just as she was about to swim home, little Ock had come across THIS. With enough food gathered, she wasn't going to miss THIS for the world. Whatever THIS was.

The little fisher girl half lay, half stood in the water, watching from the marsh on her float raft. THIS was definitely a fight, Ock decided, a big one though. Like when Mum's boyfriend had a punch up with one of the cousins. The boyfriend was also a cousin but distant and it was hard to avoid such couplings, living in the confines of a marsh. Like that type of fight, she thought, but much, much bigger.

In front of Ock, on the Firmway leading towards the great smoke, were 'lots'. All Grounders: centaurs, women she wasn't related to, and men, everyone carrying so much metal.

There were twoscore of them in Ock's raft-hamlet, sometimes they met with the other Marshlings on religious days to bang drums and keep the Deep King out in the river. Festive days like that was 'many'. On market days, they would go into the three big smoking places to the north, where there were many, many people.

But what was in front of Ock was definitely 'lots', much more than 'many, many'. She pulled a crayfish out of a submerged basket, cracked its shell, took some sweet herbs from a pouch and snacked on the living flesh, settling in to see what was to happen. It was definitely a beast the Firm People were fighting, that was the threat. The girl could hear it from the forest, a singing – definitely singing – huge creature invisible behind the treeline that the whole world had gathered together to keep it out of the flat-firm.

Ock chewed and craned up, tipping back her reed-woven sun hat for the best view. The noise from the Lots was huge, the Grounders were obviously trying to scare the creature away. All chanting and shouting in the strange tongue of the hard lands.

"When will the beast appear, Maisie?" little Ock asked her doll of folded grass and twine stuffed into a sodden green smock with pockets. Maisie the doll offered her thoughts to the girl. A shot of fear ran down Ock's spine.

"Yes Maisie, you're right, it MUST be the Deep King."

The doll went on. *'Finally, the great god has hauled itself out of the great, blue, tongue to feed on the unworthy.'* Maisie confirmed.

Ock looked around uncertainly at the brown-black waters around her knees, imagination running. Then the girl clutched her talisman remembering the Marshlings were pious people, not like the Grounders, and doll Maisie told Ock that *'Had not sick Uncle Jig been offered in the sunken cage to his Highness at last solstice?'*

Something was happening.

"Wow!" and "Wow!" again.

Groundlings were suddenly thrown up in the air or began falling over. Ock watched a person cartwheel high up, a leg coming off, and crash back down again. People were flying everywhere and the Groundlings shouted and screamed, they even let go of the expensive metal sheets, each plate enough for a…'a lot' of hooks and wire to be fashioned…all just thrown away. The jumping about and flying went on for ages and never got boring, no sign of the beast, though.

'It did hid in the forest!' Maisie said, and sure enough the Groundlings shouted towards the trees, demanding the creature show itself. But, Ock knew, the River King was too canny for that and was probing forward with its great, invisible barbels. *'As thick as a man's leg'* – as Uncle Roi would drunkenly describe them, he who claimed to have seen the great harvester of souls on two actual occasions having wandered away far towards the blue tongue in his youth.

Ock could believe Uncle Roi now, though, each huge invisible whisker swept men and women high up into the blue sky towards Sister Sun.

Finally, a great prince – he must be a prince because he had an amazing metal hat that glistened like scales – came forward and waved at his Lots. Many, many of the Groundlings ran up the Firmway into the forest. Ock couldn't see anything but a big crashing and bashing and screaming and shouting sounded out. The commotion was like the time her mum's boyfriend had snuck into the store cage, taking a whole skin of marsh-plum water before steeling village shaman's tambourine, flail and a drum – but much louder. Uncle Roi had had to pike-tie and sink boyfriend into the marsh until he sobered up.

The noise suddenly stopped, the girl waited and waited until Maisie decided, *'No one's coming out of the trees, princess Ock!'*

Ock was a princess, she knew that. Ock spent a lot of time in the marsh on her own.

Then Groundlings began leaping into the air again screaming and shouting. Grounders were horrible to the Marshlings, especially when the family traded at the smoke, and Ock now firmly rooted for the River King yeeting the bullies up towards the sky-marsh above. "Although the prince is nice." She admitted to Maisie.

The silver-hatted prince did look nice, all silver and gold with a clean orange tunic. He was brave as well, Ock thought, out front again urging more of his cousins into the forest's maw. Those didn't come back either, or the next lot, or

435

the ones after that. Each time the sylphy monarch in the trees got even madder and so he made men jump into the air all the time now.

Ock took a fresh crustacean out and salted it as she saw actual, real, girl centaurs run up the path. They ran forward on their four legs, an even greater commotion came from the forest – shouting, screaming, whining – and then the horse women came back out of the trees, but less than the many that had gone in.

The prince and all of the Lots then blared out tinny horns and started walking away towards the big smoke. They tramped and trotted back from the forest, Ock was disappointed for a moment that it would all end, but the Grounders then stopped and turned back towards the woods. For a time, there was no jumping about, the clever prince had moved his people away from the whiskers. Silence, then a rumble…

"He is coming out, Maisie! They've let it out of the forest! Oh no!"

The little girl pulled her hat down over her eyes and thought invisible thoughts. *"I am a weed, a stone, a little minnow…Please don't see me,"* but she just couldn't help herself from peering out and ignored the first rule of being invisible: *'You must never look, girl!'*

The monster blared from the trees and a rhythmic low grumble got louder and louder.

"Scared…" Maisie squeaked from inside the girl's damp smock. The King was just as her uncle described: dark, reddy-brown skin and great silver plates overlapping each other. A great river god emerged from the forest and unfurled itself, flopping slowly out across the Firm, atop its dorsal back rose great spikes. Ock could see faces and legs of sacrifices inside its scales, unworthy persons the river leviathan had taken into his dark soul over the 'lots' of people-before-time.

The Groundlings screamed defiance, but it was nothing to the low keening blares of King Catfish's voice. Then, all of a sudden, the monster jumped forward and ate them all up into his belly.

Felix made a mock grimace of censure as Centurion Alba and Bronze Force walked up to the broken-down farmhouse on the assembly plain, sun halfway down as it was.

"You're a bit late, First Cohort."

"Better late than never, First Spear. Bet he beat you, though."

"You can bet your bollocks I did," confirmed the SC to the dishevelled Alba, chucking him the last of the apples: he'd save two out of superstition.

"Thanks, Senior Centurion. You two look very clean," remarked the Bronze Commander, armour ripped open in two places, bandage on his left hand, blood and bits of jelly smeared into every surface, rivet and segment groove.

First Spear Felix grimaced.

"Don't rub it in, Alba. Left all the fun for you. What are your casualties?"

Alba took a proffered tablet from an Optio and read off the wax marks: sixty-three dead, one hundred and twenty-nine wounded.

It was a lot.

"Them?" SC asked.

"I didn't stop for hands, but easily a few thousand lying about back there. Half of that aren't getting up again."

Felix nodded in approval. "Well done, Centurion Alba. How were the men?"

"Fought like veterans, First Spear. When it was going badly, they didn't run away; when it went well, they didn't run away with themselves. Truth be told, we wouldn't have made it here without the Gunwagons, Mars himself – I tell you now!"

"More like Apollo, Centurion Alba, but then I'm not a priest. That scruffy little artillery bastard proved his salt then?"

"Well SC, you can call him that to his face but I wouldn't say anything except 'Sir' to him at a distance of over fifteen paces."

"We've got to move, First Cohort. Full report later, but in a nutshell…?"

"Right, FS. So – they bottled us up at the forest exit, wood line ended on slight ridge so we couldn't deploy. Guns put the Exfil scouts in a tree and brought the wagons up behind the decline about thirty paces back, he was very precise about it. Exfil Triarii on the road, had them all lying down, Second Century of my Cohort behind, Third and Fourth in the trees as a stop."

The Senior Centurion frowned at a detail. "Where's your First Century in all this, then, Centurion?"

"That's another story I'll come to in a moment, SC. The Master Gunner was able to provide fire support without line of sight, skimming over the ridge decline at full depression – had the back wheels chocked – dropping the ordnance down into the packed enemy, Exfil scouts adjusting fire from up an elm. That went on for a bit, enemy then woke up and sent troops at us, swapped triarii and Second Century about, depending on how many legs was coming. Once we repelled an attack, our forward troops got back on their bellies and the Gunwagons laid into the enemy some more. Luckily, as we were running low on bolts, their prince – Macromanni King's actual son, apparently – got a bit tired of being shot to pieces and moved back out of range. We came over the ridge, deployed into the clear area and had an old-fashioned fight."

Alba stretched out his arms towards his men collapsed and bloodied in the great meadow.

"We won. Signifier gets a bump, I reckon. See that silver helmet on the top of First Cohort's standard? Macromanni King's first son, Werewulf assures us. All or nothing charge for our banner pole, must have thought it was an Eagle and got excited. Our Red took his horse's legs out with one end of the banner pole then throttled their general to death with the stave."

"Not bad for a carter."

"Not bad at all, SC. Then they all mostly made off north and east. Roxolani irregular didn't leave though, tracked us all the way until just half an hour ago, firing those bloody great big arrows. Guns has managed to get one of their bows and seems fascinated by it, hardly a peep out of him."

Felix smiled at this, but needed to ask, "Your First Century of First Cohort?"

Alba relayed the tale.

The SC wasn't sure he approved of the First Cohort Centurion's course of action. Chopped comrades' heads, mouths stuffed with their own cocks – he'd have left them on the poles and made sure each Legionary had really looked as they marched by.

Felix grimaced, "Well, that's a pity. I liked their Skipper."

A finger bent to the sun in secret prayer.

The SC made sure not to roll his eyes.

"Wasn't there though, not up on a pole, FS. No sign of him."

First Spear crossed his arms and gave this information a few seconds' thought.

"Well, nothing we can do but keep an eye out. Daylight's burning and we…"

He pointed straight out towards the large middle village to the north, around which swarmed lines and dots - straggling levies - making their way back to the 'safety' of home, "…have some shopping to do. Half an hour."

The SC and First Century Centurion Alba acknowledged the command.

At first, neither Mum or her boyfriend or Uncle Roi believed her and asked where all the crayfish had gone "You greedy little piglet!" (the hamlet had an actual pig that ate fish). Then little Ock produced a great, immense square of metal with swirling patterns and a few inset jewels. She told the story again and at the conclusion, gingerly, the little community set out on half-floats dragging carry-rafts.

The girl took them to the place where the King had fed and, as befits his followers, they piled the crumbs from His table on to the little vessels. Great, great riches of leather, cloth, so many metals and horseflesh all hauled back, then further trips made. Messengers were sent across the land of In-betweens and the Marshling tribes swarmed to take unbelievable bounty from the Firmland. Little Ock became a high priestess, the Marshlings' first, with a gold woven diadem of jewels that never tarnished, and she lived to be a Many and a Lot years.

Chapter Forty-Five

Approach to Brigetio Fort
A summer squall
Danube border

"Birdies!" the Emperor's Nephew shouted over a sudden downpour, pointing up at the sky ahead.

Legate Scaurianus and the other mounted members of the forward party saw that, despite the rain, a black mass of kites, crows and ravens whirled ahead in a lazy vortex.

"Optio Ruben: thoughts?"

"Brigetio Fort should be just around the next bend, Sir."

"Under all that carrion?"

"Yes, Sir."

"I don't think we need a madman with a wooden frame to tell us that's not a good omen."

"No, Sir."

"Right. Escorts dismount and stand ready. Who wants to go for a look?"

All the lictors dismounted and formed an escort guard ahead of the lead horses.

"Anything wrong up there? I believe we have stopped even though it's a bit wet, but then I'm not a military man!" Aulus Pallo Scipio's distinct tone shouted out from the caravan behind. Scaurianus looked back from his horse and saw the civil servant had crawled through the driver's hatch and now stood up on the running board next to the teamsters, white tunic rapidly dampening.

"Could be, could be, Scipio. Can we borrow some of your Assyrians?"

He could, and four black-robed figures moved up into the treeline and disappeared forward, slipping into a familiar wood above the riverbank road to reconnoitre. The military component of the caravan waited with stoic patience, the civilian element less so.

"Right, I'm bored and getting soaked," and the awful whirring sound of two wheels started up.

"No, madam, please don…" Scaurianus attempted.

A Gaulish Auxilia patrol had just finished their first good breakfast in a month and set out contently east from the Brigetio Fort gates, looking for something new to complain about or kill. Sleepy from the fatty milk provided by the newly-procured dairy herd, the twelve-strong squadron only managed to scatter off the southern Danube shore path just in time.

"Get off the bloody road, boys!"

Before the dozen Gauls had time to throw anything sharp or curse, a colourful gilded chariot passed through them as quick as dysentery.

At Brigetio Fort, the Senior Centurion was up on the gatehouse shouting at something when he caught the noise on the air: spinning wheels and wet mud.

"That's a fucking chariot!" and many semi-suppressed memories from his Army childhood stirred all at once – in a bad way.

"Stand to! You down there, stand to!"

Legionaries who were spending the morning clearing up the mess from the temporary camp built by the river folk (now vacated, the owners going back to their life traditional life of stabbing each other at a traditional proximity), ran about grabbing items of war. With an appreciation for rapidity learnt from their recent blooding, wobbly clumps of shield wall quickly appeared.

"What the fuck is that?" the SC growled as a vehicle appeared on the bank track to the east, below the observation hill.

An Optio instantly supplied an explanation. "It is a gilt Egyptian two-team hybrid wardriver driven by…"

"That bloody woman!"

"…Lady Sobe Lassalia of Trading House Sadiki."

The vehicle slalomed deftly around two thickets of defensible men and turned hard in front of the gate, mud spraying up into a halt.

"Well, hello there, my big, fine-crested friend! You are alive, good on yer!"

The SC looked down from the rampart scowling in realisation that he hated the driver of the chariot more than chariots themselves, which were right up there on the list above almost everything else to be found in the known world the NCO had encountered to date.

At that moment, number eight on the list of things to be despised rode in breathlessly from the east road, raising javelins for a 'shutting the stable door after' strike at the chariot.

"Halt those Gaulish idiots, Optio."

The Optio ran out on to the signal plank and did some shouting at the Auxilia horse.

She, the driver of the chariot, seemed unfazed and oblivious.

"Hold that pretty, this rig's worth more than your whole twenty-five-year contract so be careful."

She stepped down from the footboard and gave the reins to a Legionary who, without a second thought, stepped his shield and fell out of formation to do so.

"You missed me, Centurion Maximus?"

"I missed our fu...supplies. Didn't bring them with you, then?"

"I like you, you're funny. No, I didn't, but I did bring your commanding officer, back down the road getting wet. He's a bit worried about you what with all those corpse pickers up there."

She then glanced over the river to where the carrion-eaters wheeled thickly at the ridge. "We've also got the Emperor's Nephew in tow and all sorts of exciting people with us for a visit. Now, you going to invite me in for a glass of wine or leave me out here watching this dress get all...clingy?" A wolf whistle from the east tower in appreciation. Sobe smiled and winked, she still had it.

The SC wiped still greasy hands on the balustrade, for a moment moving the parts around in his head.

"Gate guard, open up and escort the...visitor...inside. Send the pickets back down the road and see if they can find a Roman General anywhere. Get the FS up here. Find some officers as well. A senior officer is approaching."

Chief Armourer Galba was sat in a folding chair under the Armoury awning, fiddling with a maimed plate segment. He looked up as a familiar, cloaked figure jogged towards him through the summer downpour.

"I thought you had deserted, Optio Ruben."

"I thought I might have as well, Chief Armourer Centurion. Turns out I didn't though."

"Well, that is good to hear. Nice holiday? Any idea what's been going on?"

"Not really, Boss. You?"

"Absolutely none, but we're not all dead. See you brought people with you."

Galba rose, looking at a shower – not the rain itself but an Army acknowledged collective term for any group of officers and senior NCOs – on the parade ground getting soaked, greeting guests. He raised a questioning eyebrow to Ruben.

"Legion Legate, the Emperor's actual nephew, the supply woman who runs Sadiki, a civil servant, some assassins and the bloke who burnt this fort down."

"A cake would have been fine. We've been a bit short on cake around here, Supply Liaison."

"Sorry Boss, it's a long…"

Galba clasped his Optio's hand, "…story about a load of the usual old Army bollocks. Let us go get a drink and I'll show you the new Armoury."

"Don't want to go and meet the Big Boss?"

"Anyone asked me to? Then I want a drink, Ruben, and we can piece all recent events together, if not for the record, then for at least half a laugh."

An hour later, a sodden Military Legate Scaurianus took a boat across the Danube and stood high up on the ridge opposite the Fort, looking down at the dark gorge's new floor below.

The keening of carrion feeders and patter of light rain the only noise. His old comrade from the mountains, First Spear Felix, stood next to him waiting. Even Scipio, the third member of the party, didn't say a word.

"A Numidian caravan, then?"

"Y'Sir. No carts, see. Had to transport the stores back somehow."

"Right."

"Didn't have the men for prisoners after, so…seemed like the only practical course of…"

Legate Scaurianus half listened, surveying the huge carpet of dead lying in the valley below.

"Scipio?" Legate Scaurianus asked quietly.

The Scipio made a little shrug "Well, this isn't actually Roman territory so, not sure its any of our responsibility. Perhaps it was some sort of…plague perhaps? Water born miasma so close to the river…"

Scaurianus wiped the rain from his brow as he surveyed three village-worths of twisted, dead Macromanni men woman and children all dumped in a rocky ingress, all bled out to white. Looking about he saw a great smudge of brown gore that had not quite been washed away from a ledge above this charnel house.

Not difficult to work at what had gone on. Walk over the pontoon, all nice and calm, drop supplies in the fort, friendly legionary tells you time to go home. Got to go by a special route though, the Roman offers to show the way. Relieved, back over the strange bridge, up the hill a bit... probably been brought up to that ledge in threes and fours. When would you work it out, when did the truth of going home reveal itself? Straight away? On the bridge? Waiting a bit while the ledge around the corner was busy?

But the Legate was a practical man, "Plague it is, then."

The feast was a great success, outside trestles under shade awnings, the rain having cleared up two days before and all was well with the world. Stores and, consequently, bellies were full. The senior officer had finally arrived and not arrested anyone for treason. Scaurianus first made a short speech introducing himself – *'an ex-foocking--Consul!'* whispered Legionaries to each other proudly – glossed over the 'legate/general' bit and toasted the XXXth and their first great victory over the enemies of Rome.

All simple and straightforward, as opposed to the very carefully worded letters he'd sent by express to the Senate, the King of the Macromanni and Governors of both Pannonias. Less 'great victory' and more ambushed while transporting stores then assisting the allies of Rome in 'di da di da di – definitely not an illegal war – de dum de da'. He'd also made First Cohort give the prince's head back to the Macromanni King via diplomatic courier but let them keep the helm.

Scipio meanwhile broke the habit of a lifetime and decided to be overtly useful, smoothing over relations with Prince Herminaz and his tiny army. In fairness to Scipio, his actions were more to do with *'he'd had an idea'* following recent rumblings on the Rhine border and, possibly, wasn't sat next to the huge German noble with the weeping leg out of selfless altruism. In fact, the leg had to be sorted, an Assyrian medico was put on the job with various poultices and unguents.

Some bad reciprocating speeches from the XXXth's three remaining officers were made, then everyone got eating and drinking. The haul of stores carried back to the Fort by the rope-hobbled captives were much, much more than Felix had anticipated, as he explained to Scaurianus sat next to him.

"Reckon supplies had been flooding in for months, ready for a major reinforcement and a big push south. Another week and the north shore would have been swarming with new troops."

"Lucky you led a light scouting mission then, wasn't it, First Spear?"

Felix eyed his commander carefully, but the man just continued eating a marrow stuffed with white goats' cheese and moved on.

"Good cheese, by the way. From upriver, you say? One thing, Felix: I haven't met the CP yet."

"We don't have one, Sir, only man never to arrive."

The Legate pulled a face and turned to the guest of honour to his left who was doing something dangerous with a long knife and a snail until a lictor stepped in and took over the operation for the best interests of the Imperial family.

"My lord, I am led to understand you were crucial to arranging the muster of departments for our new Legion. My congratulations to you, a fine job and we are assembled."

"Um, yes. Amazing, isn't it? Believe me, I'm as surprised as the next man."

Cornelius Ulpia Mako had a de-housed snail popped into his mouth by one of his enormous Praetorian killers.

Scaurianus was the next man and internally concurred with the observation before following up with a supplementary question:

"One item, Sir – are we still expecting a Camp Praefectus at some stage?"

Hedgehog froze, thinking, if not fast, then at least at an amble.

"Erm…"

He looked about and pointed uncertainly. "The…erm…Senior Centurion there?"

"That's the Senior Centurion, my lord."

"Ahhhh. So, a Camp Prae…it's different then?"

The Legate waved a hand, having now solved the mystery of the missing CP and disliked wasting time or the torture of small animals. "Ah, no, I see now that you are right. Forgive me."

"Am I?"

"Yes, my lord. Please, have another snail."

The Lady Lassalia seated on the other side of the Hedgehog shouted encouragingly, "Of course you're right, you're the Emperor's Nephew," eliciting an approving grunt from Mako's lictor behind the camp chair.

"It would be almost impious to believe otherwise," put in the Scipio mischievously from next to Lassalia, leaning forward on the long trestle 'high table'. That was a bit much, Scaurianus thought – the Emperor wasn't a god…yet – so turned back to Felix.

"We need a Camp Praefectus, you want it?"

The First Spear shook his head.

"Like his lordship said…" and the Centurion pointed to the SC.

"That's your best pick. Plus, I know your views on…'Things'."

Funny 'Things' in the night, secret signs…

"'Things', right. The SC's not, then?"

"No, Sir."

"Humour me as per 'Things'. Didn't want him or didn't want to, as far as you know?"

"I think it is a mutual understanding, Sir. He's not what you would call a convivial joiner. Great horn player, though."

Scaurianus regarded Felix for a moment reflecting on 'Things'. In all other respects, the FS was a grownup but…everyone has their tics.

"He'll be your superior. Can that work?"

"The SC's a nasty lump of hate-filled gristle who can find fault in everything. Personally, I can't stand him. It'll work perfectly. Bump First Century Centurion Alba up to Senior Centurion, all be good."

Scaurianus indicated the SC and everyone in the bump should be brought to him 'after presents'.

The Legate had decided to do the presentation ceremony at the end of the feast as it would get at least one meal under the belt with the Legion itself. Now they'd had their tea it was time for medals.

Felix rapped his vine staff on a waiting attendant's rig three times for attention. "Stand for the Legate!"

Thousands stood.

A midsized chest was opened in front of Scaurianus' Primary Lictor. Next to it sat a wax tablet with Felix's recommendations annotated. One by one the commended were called up to the loud cheering of all, especially tentmates.

The standard-bearer Red: "Citation for particular bravery and destruction of the enemies of Rome". Twenty others received the same.

'Guns', stuffed into a cleaned tunic, and the Extraction Tribune received "Citation for innovation and skill in craft allowing the destruction of the enemies of Rome".

All four officers were awarded, one posthumously: "Citation for initiative and leadership in the field allowing for the efficient destruction of the enemies of Rome."

The SC received his medal with a grunt, Alba his with a broad grin. Not on the list (because he'd written it) First Spear Felix, however, was given a prominent award, also '...for initiative in the field and command', by his 'old friend' the new Legate. This was on the Scipio's advice, "Because if the Senate don't like what they hear then the trip to a 'displeasure rowing bench' should be a representative, group day out."

"Not up for anything, Chief Armourer?" Optio Ruben asked, sitting next to his boss on the Immunes trestles.

"Bollocks to that, Ruben," Galba replied, eating a chicken. Not relaying the frank conversation he'd had with the First Spear resulting in his name being smeared off of the awards tablet. Instead, Cadet Bullo was beaming at his bit of be-ribboned, beaten bronze for '...services in engineering and skill resulting in the destruc…" Cadet-sharpener Briscos also had an award but was holding it up to the light in a calloused hand staring through the medal distantly as it swung before his eyes.

Once the awards were done there was general cheering followed by the surprising, except for those that knew her, sound of a woman's voice as the tall Alexandrian-Egyptian stood up.

"Now some of you know me…"

Big shout back, a few whistles and a threatening growl from the direction of the Senior NCOs trestle where the SC sat, "…and I've come with presents for you all!"

Huge bronze-studded chests with the Sadiki Osiris and palm icon were carried before Sobe by Legionaries happily impressed for the task. One by one the Lady Lassalia flung open the heavy lids.

"Now, I asked Optio Ruben what you might all like and as you've been good boys…first of all, you: Copper Top with the pole, come over here."

Red sprang up and bounded over, yellow-ribboned medal temporarily tied around his neck before being affixed to his rig the next morning. "Look what I've got, finest desert pussy cat…"

From the chest, Lassalia pulled out a package wrapped in protective hessian and carefully unfolded it: a perfect cheetah's pelt already stitched with an inlay of red cloth and the head bound to a metal scalp cap. The Legion Signifier took it, beaming, turned to Scaurianus who gave a nod, and then Red placed the mantle upon his head. The canines (smoothed by a Sadiki artificer) bit down on the ex-carter's head, ginger curls spilling out, and the spotted cloak hung down to his arse – it must have been one big cat.

Lesser pelts were brought out and presented to the Cohort Signifiers, Red was given the job due to his new rank as Leading Standard-bearer and that Sobe really couldn't be bothered.

Lady Lassalia meanwhile revealed bales of fine, dyed red cloth, all for the Legate.

"You're going to have to replace those orange drapes at some point."

Gold thread also emerged and then a complicated and previously unseen Iberian stamp press for Galba (who accepted it gratefully) was hauled over on a trolley.

"Nice to meet you at last, Armourer. We can talk about those little rude notes later!"

Various ornate Egyptian knives and trinkets were distributed about the Legionaries who looked upon them as the greatest treasures ever viewed by man, each one assuredly having been plundered from the triangle-tomb of a long-dead Pharoh (not knocked off a dozen a day at the Alexandrian-Sadiki prefab shop for tourists). Each bit of tat was definitely 'lucky', the men decided.

"Now, we have a special present for my old friend. Senior Centurion, would you come up here…"

Much cheering.

With an evil look, the SC got up and walked to the top table, eyes threatening murder.

"This is for you."

A long sandalwood box was proffered to him, which he placed on the table and opened. He looked at the contents and blinked, then carefully picked up the object and showed the men who cheered some more. It was a beautiful brass tuba, with the horn wrought into a Persian manticore's head.

"Like it?"

"Yes. Know this, though, I despise…"

"I'm sure you do, but now you can make up a little song about me."

One last box, rosewood and smaller than the great chests, but with the Legion's designation etched into the plaque alongside the Osiris and palm. "First Spear Felix, I believe this should be given to you as president of the Centurions Mess."

Felix stood up, grinning, and joined the Lady Lassalia who indicated he should open it quickly in the manner of someone who probably has better things to do, like drink.

The First Spear opened the chest, grin now ear to ear, and lifted out one piece from the new canteen – a silver-encased glass cup, the metal worked into a scene of the great river Danube with fish leaping while tiny, enamelled Legionaries marched. 'XXX' was inscribed around the rim with space for later inscriptions and honours. Felix held it up to the men.

"Our first silverware, boys! Now we are a Legion!"

"Not quite, we aren't," whispered the civil servant to the Military Legate.

While presents had been happening, Scipio had slipped up the bench's pecking order next to Scaurianus.

"When do you think, Scipio?"

"My black-clad friends say in three days. The special cargo has already left Vindabona. Lassalia confirms the schedule."

"And it contains 'luxury goods'…?"

"Definitely it 'does contain'."

It was evening, after the feast, and Brigetio Fort was in a 'festive' mood, with two brawls and a light stabbing filling the XXXth's little glasshouse up like a small but reliable spring. Legate Scaurianus sat in the western administration block, in conference with the Scipio, Lady Lassalia and, also summoned, Centurion Chief Armourer Galba. While Galba's reputation for technical efficiency marked all the right 'useful person' boxes for the ex-Consul 'plebeian road builder' the Chief Armourers presence was also due to Army protocol. One of the top order Centurions needing to be present for senior promotions, and Felix wasn't about. Scaurianus knew why Felix wasn't about but, annoying as it was if you wanted a Roman Legion to run right, those evenings when certain 'Things' happened with, seemingly, random individuals disappearing were not to be fussed over.

Alba, however, had had it made plain to him, by Felix, that disappearing off to the supplementary ice store wasn't in his stars for the evening. Orders were orders.

Outside the office, standing at attention in the summer evening and fully rigged to a man, the SC, Alba, another Centurion, a senior Optio, a junior Optio and the full chain that would all fill out the 'bump' waited. Scipio and Lassalia were just present for the first appointment of Camp Praefectus, however.

Legate Scaurianus signalled for the Senior Centurion to be brought in. Galba got up and requested the SC's presence, who marched through the door fully polished and ready to make the best impression on his new Legate, which in the SC's view was that: no one better fuck about with the running of his sections, no matter who they were. In a perfect world, you would only ever have one formal meeting with the new senior officer – on his or your arrival. Quite what Alba and the other men were all doing milling about outside, the SC had no idea, though. And it annoyed him.

The Legate looked over the SC standing at fierce attention and could 'read' all the Centurion was trying to convey before a word was said.

'Yes,' thought Scaurianus, *'Felix was right about this one. No point praising the NCO's role in recent events, I wasn't there, and this is one who'd only see positivity as weakness.'*

"Senior Centurion, you stand before me on this day of…"

A lictor-scribe read out the date from behind a strung up old bedsheet.

"…and from this day you are to immediately undertake and be confirmed in the role of Camp Praefectus of the un-augurated Legion of the XXXth. I so declare under the gods as Legate Decimus Terentius Scaurianus, Commander in situ of the XXXth. Do you accept as a freeborn citizen of Rome?"

An actual pause.

Lady Lassalia took a sip of wine.

"I've never seen you surprised before, big man. I'm enjoying the moment."

"Perhaps he was hoping the generalship was still open…"

"Shut up, Scipio. Centurion, if you could please answer me."

Everything in the Senior Centurions brain revolted.

'I've only been an SC for five minutes. The world was unfair and unjust where nothing good ever happened. A full CP???'

"Well?"

The Senior – now potentially CP, it would seem – pulled himself together.

"I accept humbly under the gods as a free citizen of Rome and contracted to the Legions of Rome. Long live the Empire, long live the Emperor, long may glory be brought to the XXXth."

"Good. Congratulations, Camp Praefectus. Now, there's a job that needs doing and doing well. In three days' time a special cargo is moving down the, now secure, river from Vindabona. We need to be ready for it."

"Very good, Sir. What is the cargo, if I might ask?"

Scaurianus told him, and the freezing stab of terror reassured the new CP that the world was indeed unfailingly terrifying, shit and awful.

"May I be dismissed immediately, Sir?"

"You may."

"Not staying for a celebratory drink, Camp Praefectus?"

"No, Lady, but I will…" the CP's teeth ground but he knew the truth of it "…need your help."

Evening festivities ended right there for the men of the XXXth as the freshly minted Camp Praefectus marched out of the admin-laundry, screaming for his team of Optios and setting about drunken Legionaries with his vine staff. By halfway across the parade ground, he'd issued twenty orders and three 'requests' to the Lady Lassalia who followed in his wake – she enjoyed the novelty of being in another's wake.

The men of the XXXth spent the next two days slaving naked or in loincloths. Every item of their clothing, including spares, washed in great laundry vats relocated to an outside tent camp. Rigs were polished, repolished and set to one side of each dormitory, only the guard rotation being allowed to touch their weapons and armour. The village to the south made a killing from breaking down and sacking up lime dust from the quarry. A couple of workers supplied by the headman set to mixing huge vats of whitewash which, as soon as thickened, was applied to every part of the fort by naked Legionaries with spreading chemical burns and eyes streaming from the fumes.

The parade group was raked, the dirt pathways between buildings were weeded and raked, whitewashed stones placed everywhere. All ground-based vegetation got pulled up, some trees outside the fort the CP thought were particularly un-Roman chopped down, the bakers and kitchen staff re-cleaned their tools and were only given permission to produce cold cuts so as not to dirty any of the gleaming coppers.

The new CP and Galba had a frank discussion regarding tidiness as the Armoury was repairing the damage done to kit during the last engagement, with the Legate finally interjecting that the presence of actual work being done would not demean the Legion. A single change in tone occurred in amongst all the shouting as the Camp Praefectus sat down with Guns and his handler to plead – actually pleading – that the artillery man try and affect some sort of uniform for just one day.

The luckless and least competent Seventh Cohort were set to the worst job. Under guard by the Eighth Cohort, they crossed the river to build huge pyres in the gorge that burnt day and night, corpses feeding the flames, bright with human fat. Even the carrion-eaters couldn't stand it and buggered off. On the evening of the second day, men rotated to be washed in the Danube using lavender soap from a recently arrived special wagon.

"Chum, it's all I could get at short notice, and the boys will smell lovely. And it'll keep the Scorpions out!" Lassalia explained to the fuming CP.

Once washed, the entire Legion slept outside under artillery tarpaulins so as not to contaminate their beds, clothes or dormitories. The barracks were also unliveable-in for more than five minutes due to the thick paint fumes that three coats of 'Army White', liberally applied, will produce. Briegtio's walls were now half a thumbnail thicker than they had been a year ago.

On the morning of the cargo's scheduled arrival day six-thousand-odd men took one more dip in the river, sun dried standing up, ate some hardtack naked then, under strict supervision, were fully clothed, armoured and armed. Stood to, the new Camp Praefectus made at least two inspections of men and Brigetio Fort itself, an army of polishers, painters, weeders, rakers and cleaners in tow. To alleviate the almost inevitable fainting the men were fallen out and allowed to stand in designated shaded areas by the walls. Optios and rake-men ready to minimise any damage to the geometric curving sweeps every piece of ground was now covered in.

Finally, just after noon triangle, a signal went up from the high tower: "Vessels approaching, signals received. Codes confirmed. 'Eagle', I say again 'Eagle'."

"Subtle," remarked the Scipio from outside the old laundry.

Legate Scaurianus stood up from his camp chair under the command awning, fully adorned in armour, and made a nervous look to Scipio who smiled warmly back, crisp white toga shining like the Fort itself which now looked bright as a pearl from all angles.

The Legate then gave a nod over to the Camp Praefectus stationed by the entrance to 'his' parade ground (he would eventually have to relinquish control of the area to SC Alba, but only after this day). Legionaries carefully filed along a complicated series of raised duckboards, the ten Line cohorts shuffled to their positions on the square. Once assembled the boards came up and any imperfections were quickly raked over as the Legion stood at full attention.

Scaurianus mounted a horse and with Mako, Scipio and the three senior officers of the Legion, carefully circumvented the parade area to the gate house – gleaming white wood- nodding for the newly rehung doors to be opened before trotting out to the quay. Even the quay had been whitewashed. When the young Exfil Tribune pointed out it was now too slippery to use and might cause a major treasonous accident, during the expected disembarkation, rope mats had been quickly woven and nailed to the decking.

Seven large barges floated in from upriver – normal conveyances, no ivory oarlocks or gilt thwarts – and were docked by the ever-efficient Shore Master, with the Exfil Tribune standing at attention in 'nominal command'.

Once the craft were tied up, fourteen railed gangplanks dropped smoothly down in unison, immediately secured by the shore crew who then rapidly stepped back as fifty massive Praetorian Guard crashed out of the lead vessel, forming a tight cordon on the bank road around Scaurianus' receiving party. Legate Scaurianus thought he saw a nod between the Hedgehog's lictors and a giant of a Praetorian Centurion.

Civil servants then came out of the boat. Wax, papyrus and stylus' ready to record every moment then…the luxury cargo emerged.

"Nephew!"

"Ah, ahaha ah, Uncle Emperor!"

The Fort's greeting party dismounted as the Emperor of the civilised world bounded down the gangplank smiling happily. He was dressed in cured-leather armour, nothing fancy. It was still top-of-the-line gear with indented Imperial motifs, but no enamel or gold plate. He was being a soldier's soldier this afternoon, the key members of the receiving line noted, making sure to adjust the tone for the day accordingly.

All close-cut hair, flat face and long-limbed, the Emperor jumped ashore, clasping arms.

"It is good to see you, sister's-son."

"I am glad of that, really…a bit of a novelty, eh, Uncle? Ahahah!"

"Hush, hush. You have done a remarkable job here, funny little Cornelius. Hasn't he, old friend Scaurianus?" the Emperor said to the Legate with a wink.

"He has indeed, my Lord."

"As you all have, as you all have! Scipio, if this little project of ours continues in this manner we shall have to call you 'Scipio Danubus'!"

The aristocrat laughed with full, unfeigned warmth. "Very good, my lord."

'*No pithy rejoinder for once, eh Scipio?*' Scaurianus thought.

"Now, who's going to introduce me to my Legion!"

Through the fort's gate the party went, Praetorians seamlessly redeploying in step as the Roman Emperor made his way up to the parade ground dais. A thunder of left feet rumbled up from the earth,   Marcus Ulpius Traianus Nerva beamed in appreciation at the dazzling spectacle of the XXXth brought to attention (the Cohorts having been put to ease at the barges arrival specifically so the CP could smartly bring them back to attention for effect).

"My goodness, Scaurianus, who is the Camp Praefectus?"

Scaurianus indicated the CP stood at rigid attention just below the raised platform.

"Camp Praefectus!" the Emperor called down. "I'm used to the world smelling of paint but the men and this fort practically hurt my eyes."

"Sorry, Sir."

"Haha! Well done that man."

"Sir."

"So, Legate…?"

The ex-Consul stepped forward. "Men of the XXXth Legion: greet your Emperor!"

"OOH! OOH! OOH!"

"Men of the XXXth, all Legions of Rome may greet their Emperor – but only you may also greet him as…General!"

Silence as the mind of the average Legionary tried to work through this riddle.

The Emperor took a step forward, touching Scaurianus' arm.

"Thank you, Legate."

Then in a louder voice,

"Brave men of the XXXth Legion, you have been formed, formed by my nephew, formed up by a noble Consul, formed by the very gods to one purpose. YOU are to be MY Legion. I am to be your General. I name the XXXth Legion as 'Ulpia' after my very name, and proud I am to do so. As, already, valiant proven fighters on both water and land, your sign shall be the Capricorn."

'Weren't the Vth a Capricorn, Scipio?'

'I doubt they'll object given the circumstances, Scauri.'

Now the men of the XXXth got it.

"OOH! OOH! OOH! OOH! OOH…!"

The cheering did not stop, and after a minute the CP made to turn in censure but caught Felix's eye, stood at attention just behind him, who gave the smallest shake of the head.

The noise went on until the Emperor raised his hand for silence, which occurred instantly.

"You are now about to be formally inaugurated as a Legion although, I hear, you started without me…"

Hands spread wide, and a pantomime raise of the eyebrow to Scaurianus who stood stock still in response – big laugh.

"Now, after the religious obeisance…"

A trio of Tier One Imperial Priests had also disembarked from the convoy with huge sky-frames and a spectacular-looking white bull on a leash.

"…I look forward to getting to know you all and to have a tour around this fine example of a Roman fort of the front line. Then we shall be about the business of paying our friends in Dacia a little visit, if you're not tired of hammering them already, of course!"

Shouts, cheering and screams from the XXXth summed up a heartfelt declaration that, no, they had not had enough of killing Dacians or any of their allies. The Emperor Trajan Smiled, everyone smiled.

'This is how it starts then,' muttered Galba. Felix next to him winked back.

Later, after the inspection of the men, the tour, observing drill, thanking people, meeting the stunned headman from the southern village, listening politely to some huge German's rambling and having an entertaining chat with a most useful woman, the Emperor Trajan sat alone with Aulus Pallo Scipio. He was reading, Scipio was 'admiring' the spectacular Imperial campaign tent- complete with marble statue of Alexander- erected beside the admin building. 'I don't want to get in the way, CP, so you just put me wherever.'

Trajan finished the document in front of him.

"My goodness Scipio, this is very grave news indeed. Untrustworthy allies, penetration on to Roman soil, raids, attacks, Dacian gold everywhere, in everything evil points towards our great state. Reluctantly, I believe we must once again defend the freedoms of Rome and its people."

"A saddening but necessary duty, I believe, mi'lord."

"The little enterprise you set up here last year, your Combined Intelligence unit. It has borne great fruit, I commend you, Scipio. Detailed, comprehensive recording of all the inequities prosecuted against us is exactly the sort of thing our senate needs to know about. At dawn, we shall send a copy straight to the Capitol and, I think, a few to the Tribunes of the Plebs in order to apprise the mo…our citizens of these flagrant actions by bad neighbours."

"Very transparent, Sir. If the document is to be read out in the forum, might I take the liberty of producing Tribune copies with just the salient points?"

"The best bits? Yes, yes, I like that idea. Don't want to confuse the people. Perhaps even a one-pager for the Senate, do yer think?"

Scipio chuckled.

"Indeed, very good, Sir."

"Just one thing, Aulus – I can call you that, can't I?"

"It would be the greatest of honours to me."

"Thank you, I feel we are so close, you and I. So just between two men, this report…do you remember when we had that chat, a year or two ago, about all the things that might need to happen in order to mobilise for Dacia?"

Scipio remained perfectly poised.

"I'm not sure…"

"Yes, yes, you do. It was very useful, and you, Aulus, went away and actually wrote up what a perfect Senate missive might look like. It was really very good, full of horror and presumption. In fact, I have it with me in the file lattice behind me."

"You do, Sir?"

"I do, Aulus, read it on the voyage down here. Now, the thing is, that hypothetical Senate report and this 'new' one I have in my hand, produced by the new and extremely costly spies of yours – they are identical."

And the Scipio laughed warmly.

"I'm afraid, Sir, they are not. I must correct you there."

The Emperor Trajan turned behind him and pulled out a papyrus from a file cube.

"My goodness, my memory goes, but let's have a look, then…"

Scipio uncrossed his legs smoothly.

"I can save you some time, Sir. You see there is one vital difference between the documents. This report in front of you has been signed by the head of our Special Operations Intelligence Group, the organisation especially set up to provide an independent view of the border. As you have correctly pointed out the report is backed up, or so I am told, by a thousand interviews, scout reports, bribes and all sorts of intercepted this-and-that. All with receipts. The thing is, it would have taken ages to read through it all and as you said to me before I left Rome, quite wisely I thought: 'Time was a friend to Alexander but an enemy to all others.'"

Trajan looked half amused at the Scipio.

"Has…this Head of the Special Operations Group…actually read it, the document?"

Scipio's hand remained comfortably clasped as he re-crossed his legs. "I imagine so, he signed it after all."

"Well, that is true. Can we get him in though, just to clarify a few things? Just for my peace of mind."

"Alas no, Sir. As with so many of our Intelligence heroes the leader of our Special Operations Group perished not a few days ago in the line of duty. Just having signed this report, in fact."

"I am sorry to hear that. What happened?"

"Well, I had our official author take me over the river on a little factfinding tour of hostile territory. There we happened to bump into the new Camp Praefectus, very professional and by-the-book type, who was burning…some sort of waste I think it was. So, we got chatting and there was one of those awful embarrassing coincidences where someone let slip that someone else had set fire to a Roman Army fort on purpose and not only any old Army fort but this very one we sit in! You wouldn't know to look at it, would you, Sir? Very tidy, the Roman Army, I've noticed that about them."

Trajan crumpled his brow, listening carefully.

"Anyway, there was a bit of an awkward pause, regretfully the Camp Centurion thingy is a bit of a stickler and there are needful processes to be pursued around such things as military arson. Nothing a simple civil servant like myself could do for even such a useful, trusty intelligence expert in the face of the Army, so regretfully…matters went through the proper channels. Quite fast-flowing channels at that, the Centurion had the poor man bound hands and feet then chucked him on one of the bonfires with the other…waste."

The Emperor of the known world banged the table.

"Aulus! That's not playing properly. You're supposed to say something like 'met an unfortunate acci…' Oh, sod it, never mind. Neat. You're always so neat, you Scipii, everything tied up in a bow. Too efficient by half."

"Shall I have a banishment wardrobe run up, Sir?"

The Emperor started to reread the report smiling happily again.

"No, not yet, because this is really rather good stuff. Do you think the Dacians really have elephants?"

"I imagine we'll find out, My Lord."

Many, many miles to the east, way past the new bridge manned by the IVth Legio there was another Emperor, who was not smiling. King Decebalus regarded the wooden cage from his throne thoughtfully.

"Let him out."

The two horsewomen of his allies, who'd brought this gift, bridled but with a wave of the finger blue-tartaned royal bodyguards moved forward and cut the straps of the – well, it was more like a hamper than a cage. The guards leant in and pulled the stinking captive to his feet.

Dacian monarch regarded the man held up in front of him. Even covered in welts, wounds and filth he looked like every other Roman soldier the King had ever seen. Yes, some were different colours but they all looked the same, he thought with a sigh. How did Rome just churn them out?

"Get him cleaned up, bandaged and fed."

Then, in perfect Latin: "You and I, Roman, are going to have a little chat later."

And as the Skipper was dragged off to be bathed and dressed, he wondered if that chat would involve hot irons. It didn't, however. Instead, King Decebalus would sit on a balcony asking the Tribune all sorts of questions about the Immunes' life in-between gazing south west over the landscape, waiting.

The days of harassment by proxy had ended, the stratagem of continued cost and annoyance failed. Now, it was only a matter of time before full war started, Emperor to Emperor.

* * *